THE NIGHTINGALE AFFAIR

ALSO BY TIM MASON

The Darwin Affair

THE
Nightingale
Affair

a novel

TIM MASON

ALGONQUIN BOOKS
OF CHAPEL HILL
2023

Published by
ALGONQUIN BOOKS OF CHAPEL HILL
Post Office Box 2225
Chapel Hill, North Carolina 27515-2225

an imprint of WORKMAN PUBLISHING CO., INC.
a subsidiary of HACHETTE BOOK GROUP, INC.
1290 Avenue of the Americas,
New York, NY 10104

Printed in the United States of America.
Design by Steve Godwin.

This is a work of fiction. While, as in all fiction, the literary perceptions and insights are
based on experience, all names, characters, places, and incidents either are products of the
author's imagination or are used ficticiously.

The publisher is not responsible for websites (or their content) that are not
owned by the publisher.

Library of Congress Cataloging-in-Publication Data

Names: Mason, Timothy, [date]– author.
Title: The nightingale affair : a novel / Tim Mason.
Description: First Edition. | Chapel Hill, North Carolina : Algonquin Books of
Chapel Hill, 2023. | Summary: "Inspector Charles Field hunts a serial killer
targeting Florence Nightingale's nurses in Crimea and women in London"
— Provided by publisher.
Identifiers: LCCN 2022057989 | ISBN 9781643750392 (hardcover) |
ISBN 9781643755106 (ebook)
Subjects: LCGFT: Novels. | Detective and mystery fiction.
Classification: LCC PS3563.A799 N54 2023 | DDC 813/.54—dc23/eng/20221208
LC record available at https://lccn.loc.gov/2022057989

10 9 8 7 6 5 4 3 2 1

First Edition

For Mel and Angela Marvin

Her family was extremely well-to-do, and connected by marriage with a spreading circle of other well-to-do families. There was a large country house in Derbyshire; there was another in the New Forest; there were Mayfair rooms for the London season and all its finest parties; there were tours on the Continent with even more than the usual number of Italian operas. . . . Brought up among such advantages, it was only natural to suppose that Florence would show a proper appreciation of them by doing her duty in that state of life unto which it had pleased God to call her—in other words, by marrying, after a fitting number of dances and dinner-parties, an eligible gentleman, and living happily ever afterwards.

—Lytton Strachey, *Eminent Victorians*

I consider it presumption in anyone to pretend to decide what women are or are not, can or cannot be, by natural constitution. They have always hitherto been kept, as far as regards spontaneous development, in so unnatural a state, that their nature cannot but have been greatly distorted and disguised.

—John Stuart Mill, *The Subjection of Women*

How very little can be done under the spirit of fear.

—Florence Nightingale

PART ONE

ROME, 1851

I n his youth he had been wealthy and acclaimed. His name was known throughout the Continent, his devotees queuing for hours to hear him sing. He was a sought-after society guest; heads of state sent their compliments. Unlike many of his kind, Massimo Ignazio Flammia moved with precision and grace. The chest that held his magnificent lungs was broad and manly, and his face—when he was young—had been that of an angel. He was articulate and well spoken, conversant in five languages. Women flocked to him, well-born ladies, titled ladies. Despite his condition, or perhaps because of it, he had been able to bring those he selected for clandestine trysts to unparalleled heights of ecstasy.

All that was long over.

True, at the invitation of the pope himself (Gregory XVI), Massimo had joined and was still a member of the Sistine Chapel Choir, but the pay was insulting, the repertoire stultifying, and the small boys annoying. Invitations diminished, dwindled, and finally stopped altogether. Women, titled or otherwise, no longer pursued him. He walked the streets of Rome unrecognized.

He missed the recognition bitterly, but he did not miss the women. He had turned against them.

It all had happened so gradually he hadn't realized his danger. Even before his era, female singers had been allowed to perform on stages here and there, of course, but according to Massimo, these were *loose women, obviously.*

Then there were more and more of them. It was hard to believe, but eventually they became more popular than Massimo and his kind! In a matter of years they had taken his roles, every one of them, despite the undeniable inferiority of their voices. All that he had achieved, all that he had given up, and all that had been taken from him, including his testes, had been for naught.

Mother said it was our path to riches and fame, and she was proven right, never mind my tears at the time. She was a wizard with needle and thread, was Mother.

No, women were not his friends. There were two of them now, English girls, already seated when he entered his box at the Teatro Argentina. They looked and quickly looked away as he folded his frame onto the petite gilt chair and set his bag at his feet. A new work from Verdi had opened here the week before, after its premiere in Venice. Now, Massimo would see it for the third time. Teresa Brambilla was singing, and it gave Massimo pleasure to sneer. The story of the opera, in his opinion, was vulgar. So was the leading lady, who played a character called Gilda, daughter of the Duke's corrupt court jester, Rigoletto. The Duke, too, was corrupt. As were the noblemen. Everyone here, in fact, was corrupt or, in Gilda's case, imbecilic.

Oh, yes, we're to believe she never leaves the house except to go to church. Ha! Brambilla looks like a whore after a busy night.

The music, though, was irresistible to him. It was, after all, the great Verdi. Massimo adjusted his fine silk cloak about his shoulders and took his embroidery from its bag. The women in the box looked again. Massimo stared them into blushing submission. He was not about to allow any nonsense from the likes of *them* to mar his little pleasures. The gaslights dimmed, the overture began, and the great red drape rose majestically.

It was during Gilda's first-act aria that everything went wrong. He became aware that the English girls were scowling, one of them snapping her fingers at him. Others around him were hissing! Had he been singing without realizing it? Had he committed the aria to memory, was he making a scene?

Oh dear, I suppose I was. A simple melody, really, "Caro nome." Well, at least now it should be clear to all whose is the superior voice!

A uniformed porter appeared and addressed the angry young Englishwomen. *"Perdonino signore, il teatro chiede venia per il disturbo."* The man gestured and two other porters materialized at Massimo's side. They were telling him in whispers that he must leave. It was a nightmare, it couldn't be happening. They were actually touching him, lifting him up and propelling him to the exit! An outrage! The great Massimo Flammia, ejected!

He strode at a great pace, unseeing, through the dark streets, his rage uncooled by the chill, damp air, a forgotten man spurned by the world. He knew from experience he should calm himself; he knew his weaknesses and knew he could not afford to make another mistake. His superiors had overlooked his fits of rage for the last time, they had told him so. He stopped in his tracks, set down his embroidery bag, and took deep breaths. He was trembling; tears stood in his eyes. There, across the piazza, beyond the elephant and the obelisk, was the Basilica di Santa Maria sopra Minerva. He reslung his bag over his shoulder and crossed the square. He would pray to the Holy Mother, he would implore her to purge him of his thoughts.

The cold, dank darkness of the empty church was a comfort. He hurried to the nearest shrine, lit by a half-dozen guttering candles. He dropped to his knees and looked up into the Virgin's face imploringly, but her eyes were not gentle, they were fierce; they belonged not to Santa Maria but to one of the young Englishwomen at the opera house, the finger-snapper: judgmental, unforgiving, full of scorn. He hid his face and began to sing.

Caro nome che il mio cor festi primo palpitar,
Le delizie dell'amor . . .

The broom hit him between his shoulder blades and he fell forward. "You can't come in here and sing!" He rolled over and found an elderly nun staring down at him, shaking her broom in his face. No! He would not touch her, he would be strong, he would not defile this holy place, not with the Holy Mother watching him with implacable eyes. But then, somehow, the nun was on the floor and he was standing outside on the basilica steps, clutching his bag to his chest and panting.

The girl crossing the piazza was perhaps twenty years old. She had the bored slouch of a veteran, whatever her age. She was dark, with tightly curled black locks peeking out from a shapeless bonnet. Her cloak was threadbare. She glanced up at the man on the church steps and distractedly opened the left side of her garment to offer a glimpse of her well-shaped bodice and then pulled it tight again as she passed.

"Stop," he said. "How much?"

"Depends."

He steered her through the streets at a brisk pace in the general direction of the river, talking to her about embroidery.

A pair of schoolboys discovered the body in the Tiber the next morning. Details of the crime were published in the late editions that afternoon. Certain officials at the Vatican noted them with dismay. They did not report their suspicions to the authorities; they merely dismissed Massimo quietly and sent him packing.

Suddenly homeless and without an income, the castrato eventually left Rome, on foot most likely. It is thought that he spent some months at Rimini, mending sailcloth for fishing vessels. There was a rumor of him at Marseille. Eventually, though, he disappeared from record altogether.

1

LONDON, MAY 5, 1867

It was a service flat in a handsome building opposite Regents Park. The leaseholder was a wealthy merchant named Vining, but he rarely was to be seen there. Flat 4 at No. 8 Hanover Terrace, however, had a reputation, and Inspector Charles Field had parked himself nearby more than once to observe the comings and goings of certain highly placed men and women. This was Field's least favored sort of work for hire, now that he was no longer with the Metropolitan Police and did not in fact merit the title of "inspector." Still, he had mouths to feed and his retirement years to bear in mind. In this instance, Field had been engaged by a member of Parliament who harbored misgivings concerning his much younger wife. Field already knew the member's suspicions to be fully justified. In the space of three weeks he had observed Mrs. Hythe-Cooper, fair-haired, compact, and comely, enter the building three times. On the first occasion Field had quietly entered after her and watched as she climbed the steps to Flat 4. Then, and each time thereafter, she was followed five or ten minutes later by a valise-toting gentleman, perhaps forty years of age, with a neatly trimmed blond mustache and rosy cheeks. This person, the detective subsequently discovered, also sat in the House of Commons but on the opposite side to Mr. Hythe-Cooper.

Jeremy Sims was a Whig who represented the citizens of Tewkesbury. The cuckolded Tory was the Honorable William Hythe-Cooper, a former military man who now stood for Reigate. The three previous illicit visits Field had observed each lasted fifty-five minutes, almost to the minute. First Sims would leave. Then Mrs. Hythe-Cooper would emerge with not a hair out of place. She would bestow a brief, vague smile upon the world at large if it was fine, or put up an umbrella if it was not, and walk briskly round the corner and up Hanover Gate. The Honorable's townhouse was not far, which, Field thought, must have been convenient for her. After today, the inspector would make his report to the husband and await his further instructions.

Here she comes now, bless her, fresh as a day in May.

The young woman climbed the steps, produced a key, and disappeared within. Field consulted his pocket watch. If Sims arrived on schedule, the inspector would have the better part of an hour to read the several newspapers with which he'd armed himself.

THE FLAT WAS musty as always, perhaps because it was used only now and then. The apartment's windows did not face Regents Park but rather a courtyard behind the building, a small but prettily planted oval of spring blossoms and budding shrubs. Still, she thought, it would have been more pleasant and less . . . illicit, somehow, had it looked out on the park. All was quiet, but Susan Hythe-Cooper, as soon as she'd taken off her hat and laid it on the settee, felt she might not be alone.

"Hallo? Jeremy?"

There was no response.

"Is someone there?" she said.

She waited a moment for a reply that did not come. Then she shook off her hesitation. She had grown up a hardy country girl at a rural estate, the daughter of the master of hounds. She had hunted and ridden with the best and was not easily frightened. Susan pulled off her gloves and continued down a short passage to the bedroom.

"Oh!"

"I know what you've been doing," he said.

INSPECTOR FIELD OPENED the *Illustrated Police News*, always interested in the activities of his former colleagues. Today, though, apart from a burglary at Russell Square and the suicide of a vicar's wife, there was nothing of interest. Field unfolded *The Times*. The front page concerned itself almost exclusively with the Reform Act currently being debated vociferously in Parliament. The Whigs had proposed legislation that would grant the right to vote to a modestly greater number of British males, voting previously having been the sole prerogative of landowners and the wealthy. Even this measured proposal had aroused great consternation. To give the vote to the common man, said the Tories—and a considerable number of Liberals—would be to invite chaos. Mob rule. An end to civilization itself. This, in fact, was the opinion of *The Times*. On the other side of the argument was the *Evening Standard*, which had been running a controversial weekly column, written anonymously, that laid out arguments in favor of a vast expansion of enfranchisement. Field's wife, Jane, was an avid reader of the feature, titled Notes from Our Future. The *Evening Standard* backed the Reform League, a sizable body of citizens who had the audacity to claim a voice in the institutions that ruled their lives. The league intended to stage a rally in Hyde Park at this time tomorrow. The home secretary had forbidden them to do so.

Thereby ensuring chaos instead of just a bit of noise, thought Field, *and my boy, Tom, will be on the front lines with the mounted police.*

The inspector glanced up in time to see Jeremy Sims climbing the steps at No. 8, valise in hand and a spring to his step. Now that the MP had arrived, Field anticipated a leisurely read and was glad of the bright, dry day. He folded shut *The Times* and opened yesterday's *Evening Standard*. Its crime section mentioned the Russell Square burglary and covered two assaults upon women, one within the bonds of matrimony and one without. The Notes from Our Future column concerning the current debate in Parliament cited an incident wherein a female in Chelsea accidentally had been allowed to cast a ballot in the previous year's pollings. The woman had been arrested, of course, but *the world as we knew it had not come to an end*. Field thought this was a weak argument. Was the writer saying there should be *no* restrictions as to who may or may not vote? Female as well as male?

Field folded the *Standard* and just barely caught sight of Jeremy Sims fairly flying from the building opposite only minutes after his arrival, his cheeks no longer rosy but ashen. The inspector stood and watched him dodge a carriage and enter Regents Park at a brisk pace. Field hurried across the road, fiddled with his ring of passkeys, and climbed the steps to Flat 4.

The door was ajar. A short passage led to a modest sitting room. Field entered it cautiously. Two ornate chairs flanked an unlit fire. There was a settee, on which rested a fashionable lady's hat. An ormolu clock ticked loudly on the mantel, and to either side of the clock, portraits of a gentleman and lady, forebears of no one knew whom, stared dismally into the pendant dust motes. The door off this room led Field along a short corridor to the bedchamber. Mrs. Hythe-Cooper lay fully clothed on the bed. Her eyes were open and staring, a thin, livid bruise round her throat. Field hurried to her side and touched her still-warm neck and wrist. There was no pulse. The woman's lips were parted, as if in surprise. The track about her neck made Field think of other victims he'd examined who had been dispatched by a silk garrote or something of that nature. The bruise's dull red color accentuated the whiteness of her skin and her youth.

Not yet thirty years of age, at a guess.

There was a small kid glove on the floor at the foot of the bed, and another hung off the side of a chair in the corner. A small mirror on the wall near the chair was splintered. On the floor beneath it lay an ornamental ashtray. Field looked again at the body of the young woman and her clothing. Very little disarray there.

A struggle, but not much of one.

Could Jeremy Sims have strangled his lover in the few minutes he'd spent with her? Certainly. But why? He'd looked cheerful enough on his arrival, just as he had on the three previous occasions Field had observed him. More likely, Sims had discovered the body and fled. If that were the case, the killer must be close by still.

The bedchamber held a large wardrobe and a single closed door. Field flung open the wardrobe. It was empty. The door revealed a small dressing room, a wooden commode, and a porcelain basin. The inspector retraced his steps from the bedchamber along the passage to a tiny pantry and a servant's entrance. He found the door there unlocked. He opened it, revealing a landing that led to a set of service stairs. Field descended them quietly to a passage below the street at the basement level. It was deserted.

He climbed the steps again and returned to the bedroom. Under the bed he found a single page of what seemed to be parliamentary minutes, which he pocketed. Except for Mrs. Hythe-Cooper, the flat was unoccupied. As he passed her again, something caught his eye. He leaned down for a closer look. Carefully, he put thumb and forefinger into her mouth and came out with a square of embroidered fabric, decorated with an ornate red blossom. Field stood erect, taking a deep breath. He hesitated for a moment, uncertain. He reinserted the patch of cloth into Mrs. Hythe-Cooper's mouth. Then he took it out again and pocketed it.

He hurried out of the flat and quietly mounted the front stairs, looking into unlit corners from one landing to the next, up three flights to the top, but he found nothing and no one. Then he padded down again.

A charwoman with a bucket on the steps made way for him and watched him leave the building. She glanced up the staircase apprehensively, then started to climb. Field was already in Regents Park when he faintly heard her staccato screams. By then, of course, Jeremy Sims was nowhere to be seen.

Field stood stock-still in the vernal world and tried to gather his thoughts. A nanny pushed a pram. Dogs barked and birds scolded. Field realized he was shaken to the core. He reluctantly had to admit to himself that this was not the first time he'd found an ornamental rose in the vicinity of a dead woman's mouth. Twelve years earlier, in the Crimea, he had hunted down the man responsible, cornered him, and watched as he died by suicide.

He took the cloth square from his pocket and examined it.

Yes, there's no mistaking it.

Field took a seat on the nearby bench and stared at No. 8 Hanover Terrace. He'd got the right man, hadn't he, all those years ago?

There was always the doubt, admit it, right from the start.

Field cast back his mind to September of 1855.

When I got the message, my first thought, summoned to the personal home of the secretary of state at war, was What have I done now? *But when the servant showed me in, Sir Sidney Herbert treated me gracious, called for tea and served it himself when it came.*

A problem, *he said,* has arisen in the Crimea, as if we didn't have enough already.

A problem? Putting it lightly, Sir Sidney. Here we were, arm in arm with the French of all people, fighting the Russians who wanted to snatch a chunk of Turkey from the Turks, this Crimea everyone was on about. But according to The Times, *the army had made a bollocks of it all, with no proper care for our sick and wounded soldiers, who were dying in terrible numbers.*

It seems, Inspector Field, *said Sir Sidney,* that women are being harassed out there. Miss Nightingale's crew. Frightened. Even threatened.

Then he showed me the letter. It was from Miss Florence Nightingale herself, the rich young society lady who'd gathered up thirty-eight nurses months earlier and sailed out to the rescue of our fighting men. I confess it was a bit of a thrill to hold these words, from Nightingale herself, writ in her own hand. The gist was clear enough: the medical men and the military brass had no time for Nightingale or her women. Since their arrival the men had, how had she put it? Erected a very palisade of resistance to our efforts. *Evidently this wasn't news, it had been going on from the beginning. Now, though, someone seemed to be stalking the nurses if they left the Barrack Hospital for any reason, especially from dusk to dark.* A bogeyman, *she wrote,* perhaps trying to scare us out of the Crimea. *She couldn't go to the head doctors or the British ambassador in residence, explained Nightingale. To do so would be seen as proof positive that women had no business in the male worlds of war and medicine.* Could you not send out someone who would be *our* ambassador? *she asked of Sir Sidney.* To scout out the mischief-maker, if indeed he existed? *It was signed* Ever truly yours, F.N. *with a postscript:* Send two thousand knives, forks, and spoons immediately. The soldiers at Balaclava are forced to tear their meat like animals!

Well, that was bad enough. But now, according to Sir Sidney, he'd had a dispatch via electric telegraph. A woman had been killed. Murdered. Not one of Nightingale's crew but British nonetheless, and she was wearing the cape of a Nightingale nurse. What's more, the dead woman's mouth had been covered over by a bit of sailcloth embroidered with a red rose. It was stitched there, closing her mouth.

Good God.

We agreed this was dreadful. Bizarre and cruel. But back then I fancied myself a rising star with the Metropolitan Police. I had a full roster of cases I was pursuing in London, I couldn't just up and leave. When I said that, the weather changed. Sir Sidney set down his cup.

According to Commissioner Mayne, it's not only *cases* you pursue, Mr. Field, but a rather too full roster of young women and, whether you have the time or funds for it, horses at the track.

It was like he'd struck me.

Do you deny it?

I couldn't speak. He went on to praise my work as a detective, but I barely heard him. My face felt on fire. Then he put the knife in and twisted it.

For God's sake, man, you're not particularly young anymore, you know. What are you doing with your life? The valiant women out there in the Crimea, nursing our soldiers, enduring hardships we can barely imagine, are in need of a protector. Are you him?

It took time, but finally I looked him full in the eye and said I would endeavor to be so. See that you do, Mr. Field, *he said.*

I had one final question.

Sir, what will be my title, my official function?

A British subject has been murdered, *said Sir Sidney.* You're a policeman. It's simple enough, really.

And that was that. I went out one man and came back another.

NOW, TWELVE YEARS later, Charles Field sat on a bench at the edge of Regents Park staring at No. 8 Hanover Terrace. Mrs. Hythe-Cooper lay within, her death as yet unreported, unmourned by anyone but himself. Field frankly hesitated to go directly to his old friend, Sam Llewellyn, to report the murder in Flat 4. In the time since Charles Field had been encouraged to leave the Metropolitan, his former subordinate had risen from constable to sergeant, and then, just recently, had achieved the rank of detective inspector. All this time, Sam and Charles had remained the closest of friends. But now, what to do? The bit of embroidery pointed not to Jeremy Sims, MP, but in another direction altogether and was itself an impossibility: what he had found and dealt with in the Crimea was singular, as was the deranged murderer, and it all had ended with the man's death. Or so he fervently wanted to believe.

Once again, he took the patch from his pocket and stared at it.

Why did I take the bloody thing?

If it was someone else operating today, someone with knowledge of the madman's crimes, an imitator, had Inspector Field deliberately been placed in the position of being first on the scene? If so, by whom and why? Who knew about his current assignment? His client, certainly, but was there anyone else? Of course, someone might have observed him here on the three previous occasions when he'd been watching the address at Hanover Terrace. Field glanced about. Because of the fine spring weather, the park was more populated today than it had been recently. Two schoolboys passed, in earnest conversation. A bearded man took a seat on the bench opposite and shook open his newspaper. A shopgirl on a nearby bench carefully unwrapped a sandwich. A man in his thirties hurried by, consulting his pocket watch but then pausing to look at Field before walking on. Field was used to such observations, ever since Charles Dickens had made a famous man of him.

There were other reasons for Field's hesitation. His client, the Honorable Hythe-Cooper, might not wish the private detective to report his wife's murder to the police, involved as it seemed to be in an affair and, worse yet, a liaison with an MP of the opposing party. He might not even pay the detective's fee. Field hated thinking in this politic, cautious way; it offended his policeman's heart, just as it hurt his human heart to walk away from the poor woman in Flat 4. She had been young and full of life this morning. She did not deserve this cruel ending. She did not deserve to be left alone, abandoned, Field felt, as he abandoned her, making his way out of the park, heading for home.

The bearded man on the bench opposite watched him leave. Then he closed his paper, stood, and stretched, lifting first one knee as high as it would go and then the other. He extended his arms and rotated his torso this way and that, this way and that. The afternoon, he felt, had played out well. Earlier in his life he may have acted on caprice, but the years had taught him discipline and restraint. On the one hand, he now was an agent in a noble cause. On the other, this was a long-awaited reckoning, and he would savor every moment.

He took up his tall hat from the bench and placed it firmly on his head. He flung a red silk scarf about his neck and began to walk. There was ahead of him still the business of the evening.

2

Belinda Field, a petite seventeen-year-old with curly black hair and finely chiseled features, met her adoptive father at the door of his Bow Street home, breathless with news. "Mr. Field, you'll never guess!"

"I'm sure I won't."

Belinda was as voluble today as when she'd been taken in by Charles and Jane Field. The years she'd spent with them had taken off some of her rough edges. She was now clean and tidy. She could read and write. She no longer stole, although she came and went oftener than her adoptive parents liked; she had been a child of the streets, after all, and London was her territory. *It's not proper for a young lady, it's not right, it's not safe!* These arguments availed little. Currently Jane was instructing Belinda in the basics of nursing, and the girl hoped to begin soon her formal training.

"Who do you think sent Mrs. Field a note?" she said.

"Truly, Belinda, I haven't a clue."

Jane Field, née Rolly, appeared on the kitchen stairs, holding a letter. "Miss Nightingale, my dear! She wants me to come work for her again, after all this time!"

Field was startled by the name, since it had been on his mind all afternoon.

"Does she now? What for?"

"Just to help with her correspondence," said Jane, "and other odds and ends, she says. She wants to see you, too, after she's explained my duties and introduced me to the household staff. May I send round that we'll come?"

"Of course, of course," he said. "When is this to be?"

"Tomorrow!"

"Do *you* wish it, Jane?"

"I think it's quite an honor to be asked. She sees almost no one, you know, and she never goes out—she's an invalid, poor dear."

Field searched his wife's face. She evidently was not thinking of the terror she herself had experienced as one of Nightingale's nurses in the Crimea.

"Well, then," said Field, "of course we'll call on her. Is Tom about?"

"He's in his room," said Belinda, "and has been ever since he came home from the stables. He's impossible these days, he's *that* full of himself!"

"Tom's uneasy about tomorrow," said Jane.

"He has every reason to be so," said Field. "Belinda, give me back my hat, if you please. I've just now remembered I told Sam Llewellyn I'd stop by at the end of the day."

"You'll be home for supper?"

"Mrs. Field, I wouldn't miss it for the world," he said as he hurried out.

Tom Ginty's room was on the second floor at the back of the house. On his bed lay the uniform he'd be wearing tomorrow, virtually his first active-duty day with the Metropolitan Mounted Police. Tom himself was shirtless, staring into the mirror above a porcelain basin on the nightstand. He frowned at his reflection. Tom had been a butcher's apprentice seven years earlier. Then a homicidal maniac had snatched him from

Smithfield Market and tried to make a killer of him. Inspector Field eventually tracked the boy down and, with Sam Llewellyn's help, plucked Tom and his de facto sister, Belinda, from the burning house in which their abductor perished. Together the policemen had carried the children through the snowy night to safety and healing. The Fields had adopted Belinda and, after Tom's mother died, raised them both as their own.

The freckles of Tom's face had faded somewhat since he was a butcher's boy, and the face itself was thinner, but his hair was still a vibrant ginger. At twenty years of age, he was a slender young man with handsome features, except for his left ear. His captor all those years ago, Decimus Cobb, had bit most of it off. His fine new uniform would not hide that from the world; on the contrary, the signature top hats worn by the Metropolitan's Mounted Branch called attention to it, at least to Tom's way of thinking. And that slight disfigurement was nearly all Tom could see of himself.

He turned from the mirror angrily, dropped to the floor, and did one hundred press-ups.

DETECTIVE INSPECTOR SAM Llewellyn found it hard to think of Charles Field as anything other than his superior. Field long ago had plucked him from a crop of young recruits and taught him how to be if not a *good* policeman, then at least an *effective* one. Llewellyn owed his career to the man. Therefore, whenever they got together Sam usually arranged for them to meet in the Eagle and Child rather than in Sam's small office at headquarters. Llewellyn felt uncomfortable sitting behind a desk from his former boss. He preferred standing before it at attention.

Today, however, they did meet in Sam's office and did sit across from each other. If Sam looked unsurprised that Charles had dropped by, and more than usually watchful, Charles didn't seem to notice.

"How is Rebecca?" said Field.

"My wife is in the pink, thank you, Charles."

"And young Josiah?"

"Thriving," said Llewellyn.

"Glad to hear it. So, what do you reckon's the matter with the Honorable Walpole? Shutting the park to the demonstrators tomorrow simply begs for an ugly row."

"I don't think it's the home secretary behind it, really." Llewellyn lowered his voice, even though the office door was shut. "I believe it's Commissioner Mayne. He despises the Reform League for what they done to him at last year's rally." Commissioner Richard Mayne was the head of the Metropolitan Police, Llewellyn's superior officer, and Field's frequent sparring partner when he'd been on the force.

The ex-policeman shook his head. "So merely because he caught a rotten potato or two a full year ago, Mayne is determined to crack skulls come Friday."

"I hope it only comes to that," said Llewellyn. "The mounted police will be armed, you know."

"It's a damn shame. Our boy, Tom, will be in the thick of it, his first day on duty."

"I'll keep an eye on Tom, Charles, have no fear of that."

"So," said Field nonchalantly, "what else is new, Sam?"

The younger man regarded the older for a moment. "We had a nasty murder this very day, Charles. Off Regents Park."

"Sorry to hear it. Details?"

"The victim was a woman, a lady."

"Dreadful," said Field. "Cause of death?"

"Strangulation. The lady in question was the wife of a prominent MP."

"Shocking. Suspects?"

"As a matter of fact, Mr. Field, I'm glad you asked. I'm in need of advice."

"If I'm able, Sam, you know I'll help in any way I can."

Llewellyn stood and opened his office door. "If you'd step across the way, I'd like you to see something." He led Field to a door along the corridor and opened it. He gestured and said, "After you, sir."

An old woman was seated at a bare table drinking a cup of tea, with a constable standing behind her. She set down her cup abruptly, staring at Field.

"Is this the man you described to me, Mrs. Tupper?" Llewellyn asked. She nodded tremulously. "The man on the staircase who ran from the building?"

"Yes," she said in a small voice.

"Oh, for God's sake," said Field, "the charwoman!"

"Big man?" said Llewellyn. "Clean-shaved, barrel-chested, runs as quiet as a cat?"

"Yes," said the woman, "that's him precisely."

Field beamed. "I *thought* I knew you from somewhere, my dear!" To Llewellyn, he said, "Barrel-chested?"

The old woman also looked to Llewellyn, alarmed.

"But, darling," continued Field, "there's no need to quake so. I didn't commit this crime, I merely discovered the body!"

Llewellyn said, "You neglected to mention it, Mr. Field."

"I was getting to it!"

"Oh, yes, I'm sure. *Anything you can do to help*, that's *you*, Mr. Field."

"Come, Sam . . ."

"I seen him before today, Officer," said the charwoman. "He's often skulking about out there, staring at our front door."

"I'm a private detective, ma'am, I'm just doing my job."

"That's as may be," said Llewellyn.

"Oh rubbish, Sam!" said Field.

Llewellyn turned back to the woman. "I'll question him closely, Mrs. Tupper, but I have reason to believe he's only another witness, like you. But unlike you, he did *not* come forward with his information."

"Sam . . ."

"He used to be a well-thought-of policeman, Mrs. Tupper—can you believe it? I thank you, ma'am, for your assistance today. Constable O'Brien here will put you in a hackney cab."

The constable led the woman from the room, and Llewellyn turned to Field.

"Why should I ever trust you, Charles?"

"I'm afraid there's more, Sam," said Field.

"More?"

Field regarded his protégé and close friend. "Shall we step across to the Eagle?"

It was primarily a policeman's pub, the Eagle and Child. As they entered, some of the constables looked up from their drinks and nodded at the detective, their former superior, while others broke off their conversations and moved away. Even after he was sacked, Field was known to claim he was still a member of the force, when it suited his purposes. This was a source of deep displeasure to the higher-up officers, but it amused many in the ranks, who remembered fondly their days working for *good old Inspector Bucket*, as he was widely known. So it was over a pint that Field told Llewellyn about his client, Hythe-Cooper, and his own surveillance of Mrs. Hythe-Cooper and Jeremy Sims.

Llewellyn whistled. "I was just on my way to break the news to Mr. Hythe-Cooper."

"How did you identify the victim?"

"From papers in her reticule, letters and such. Now I'll have to get hold of Jeremy Sims right quick. On the surface of it, he's our man."

"Was she interfered with?"

"Coroner says no."

"Of course," said Field, "Sims was only in the flat for a minute or two. Still, that would be time enough to put a length of silk round her neck and twist it."

Llewellyn regarded his former superior closely. "You said there was more, Charles."

Field took a pull of his pint. "The fact of the matter is, Sam, I found something in the poor young woman's mouth."

"You what?"

Field took the embroidered rose from his pocket. "This."

"Bloody hell!"

"Shh, Sam, not so loud."

Llewellyn lowered his voice. "You removed evidence? From the woman's mouth? Why in God's name did you do that?"

"I dunno, to tell the truth. But look at it proper, Sam."

Llewellyn took the square of fabric from him, examined it, and looked up at Field.

"The Crimea?"

"Too right," said Field. "Sam, did you ever tell anyone about my time out there?"

"That was Josiah Kilvert's show, not mine."

"Did Kilvert talk about it?"

"I should say so. It's where you found him, at that hospital out there, when he was a lowly soldier. Very proud of it, he was, being taken under your wing."

"Did he share with you details about the case we handled back then?"

"No, sir. Josiah was a good Baptist and a modest man. To the day he died, he would never speak to me, nor no one, about such things as that, what that man did to the women he hurt. No, Charles, it was you who told me all about it. You once gave me quite an earful after a few whiskies. Is this it? The embroidered rose?"

"Seems like." Field stared at his beer. "And now, out of the blue, Miss Florence Nightingale wants to see me and Mrs. Field tomorrow. And I am left to demonstrate, to my own satisfaction, that the dead do *not* in fact walk the earth." He pulled his watch from his pocket. "Must run."

"Not so fast, Inspector. Give it!"

Field seemed surprised to find the red rose had returned to his hand. He dropped it on the bar beside Llewellyn's elbow. "Sorry."

"And, Charles," said Sam, as Field made for the door, "no more of your little japes with me, all right? Charles?"

Perhaps Field didn't hear his longtime friend, because all he said over his shoulder was, "Do look after Tom if you can!"

3

Less than an hour later, Sam Llewellyn stood among the throng in the Central Lobby of the Palace of Westminster, hat in hand, waiting. The gallery was packed with constituents speaking with their representatives, or attempting to do so, and with MPs talking to, or shouting at, one another. The voices of dozens of men in the octagonal stone chamber created an echoing din. From the intricately tiled floor beneath Sam's feet, to the glittering array of mosaics in the huge vault above, the impact was impressive and dizzying.

Finally, a warden came through the crowd, followed by an imposing, florid man in his sixties.

"Is this him?" said the florid man.

The warden nodded assent and withdrew.

"Well?"

"How do you do, sir? I am Detective Inspector Llewellyn of the Metropolitan."

"Good for you. I'm a busy man."

"I wonder, Mr. Hythe-Cooper, if there might be somewhere more private where we could talk?"

"No, there mightn't. What's this all about, Constable?"

"It's detective inspector, actually."

"And . . . ?"

Llewellyn hesitated. Dislike was setting in, but Inspector Field had long ago warned him against it. *Clouds your vision, Sam. It does mine, anyway.*

"I'm very sorry to say that your wife perished today."

"What? My wife *what?*"

"She was murdered, Mr. Hythe-Cooper."

"For God's sake, keep your voice down!" The MP stared at Llewellyn. "Susan? Dead?"

"I am very sorry, sir."

Hythe-Cooper looked to the vault high above and shook his head. He returned his gaze to Llewellyn, the MP's face even more flushed than it had been.

"Who did it? Was it that snake, Jeremy Sims?"

"Why would you suggest Mr. Jeremy Sims might have done such a thing?"

Hythe-Cooper looked about, then leaned close to the policeman. "Who knows? Lover's quarrel?"

"That's how it stood between them, sir?"

"You heard me! Why are you standing here, wasting my time? Go and apprehend the damned rogue!"

Llewellyn had already been informed by Jeremy Sims' wife that her husband had departed that day for Tewkesbury "to consult with his constituency." Police there had been notified by telegram to be on the lookout for the MP and to detain him if he turned up. But now Llewellyn put on his most impassive policeman's face. "The Metropolitan are proceeding with their inquiries, sir, in their own fashion."

"Incompetent fools." The MP turned away in disgust.

"Sir, a moment, please." Hythe-Cooper turned back reluctantly. "You are able to account for your whereabouts this morning, I imagine?"

The member for Reigate was silent for a moment. "How dare you?"

Llewellyn smiled sympathetically. "You will be asked, you know. At the inquest? Especially given the state of your marriage."

"Never."

"The proceeding should be held in the next couple of days, after the coroner has made his report, and we will require your testimony there."

"In public, you mean? I refuse, absolutely!"

"I'm afraid, sir, that is not an option open to you." Llewellyn shrugged. "Jealousy, of course, is one of the very oldest of motives."

The florid man looked as though he might strike the policeman.

"What did you say your name was, Constable?"

"Detective Inspector Llewellyn. That's two ells twice, if you'd care to write it down."

"Commissioner Mayne will hear of this," said Hythe-Cooper.

"Indeed. I intend to tell him straightaway."

The Honorable turned to leave, but Llewellyn raised his voice. "Mr. Hythe-Cooper, did you do service in the Crimean War at all, sir?"

He stopped and turned back to the policeman. "'Course I did. Eleventh Hussars. Whyever do you ask?"

Llewellyn stared steadily at the MP for a long moment, employing a technique taught him years earlier by Inspector Field. Then he said, "What, sir, would you wish the coroner to do with the remains of your loved one when he's finished his work?"

The man's face was now brick red. "She wasn't my loved one, she was my god damned *wife*!"

4

The gas lamps were being lit in the West End and up and down the Strand. At the end of the working day, citizens caught omnibuses for home, or bustled from pub to pub, while others hurried from restaurants to theaters.

In an alley round the corner from the Strand, William Hythe-Cooper, MP, stood in a shadowed niche, waiting. Here there was no bustle; the passage was used only by those who had business nearby, and these were few. Finally, a set of footfalls preceded the appearance of a dark-bearded man of middle years, with swept-back black hair and a bright red silk scarf slung raffishly about his neck. Hythe-Cooper let him pass, just, and then used the scarf as a handle, grabbing it and slinging the man against the brick wall.

"What the bloody hell have you gone and done!" hissed Hythe-Cooper. "Coop! For God's sake!"

"It's not *Coop!*" said Hythe-Cooper, looking about him. "It's not anything anymore. You don't know *me*, I don't know *you* and never did! *Shit*, Jack! Who told you to do *that*? Not me! Not anyone, am I right? No one paid you to kill her, no one told you to, no one asked!"

"Let me go!"

"This was all you, acting on your own!"

Looking about again, the MP released the man.

"Be honest," said the man called Jack, breathing heavily and straightening his scarf. "Secretly, you were pleased. Go on, admit it."

Hythe-Cooper shook his head. "I thought you were done with that sort of thing, years ago."

"Henry II said to his men, speaking of Thomas Beckett, 'Will no one rid me of this turbulent priest?'"

"Oh, stuff it!"

"You said as much to me, speaking of your wife."

"Never! I never did!"

Jack touched his neck gingerly. "So *that's* what it feels like," he said, and grinned slyly at Hythe-Cooper.

"Dear God, you're strange. You were a fool and a madman back in the Crimean, and you still are. Just keep clear of me from now on, d'you hear? And no more of those damned anti-suffrage meetings, I'm done with them and you!"

Jack's grin vanished. "I don't think you are, actually, Coop. After today, you're in *my* power, not the other way round."

"I'll get you," said Hythe-Cooper. "I'll find a way."

"Oh, what times we used to have, remember? I do. I do. Now, you mustn't make me late for work."

He strode off, his scarf flapping behind and Hythe-Cooper staring after him.

5

The next morning, Charles and Jane Field sat waiting in the reception foyer of a fashionable Mayfair townhouse. An ornate tray on the entry table opposite them bristled with calling cards: many persons came to call, but few were admitted. From the floor above came an angry female voice. It rose, broke off, and rose again.

"For an invalid, she makes quite a noise," said Field.

"Hush, Mr. Field! She is very ill."

The ex-policeman nodded thoughtfully. "Her lungs ain't affected, apparently."

"Mr. Field!"

"Sorry, my dear."

"You remember how upset Miss Nightingale becomes. They're forever throwing obstacles in her path."

"I don't remember her shouting at Scutari," said Field, "when she had every reason to do so. She was often angry but never proclaimed the fact."

"Out there, she was fighting mortal enemies. She had to watch her every step. The chancellor up there is an old friend."

"Good God, I hope she don't consider *me* an old friend, or I'm in for it."

Jane touched her husband's arm, and he looked up to see the chancellor of the exchequer, Benjamin Disraeli, descending the stairs, hat in hand and flushed of face. Disraeli glanced at the couple. "Is that Mr. Field?"

Field rose and bowed.

"She awaits you, sir," said Disraeli. "Having first warmed her hands in *my* entrails, she is now ready for *yours*. Best of luck, old boy!" Popping on his tall hat at a rakish angle, the chancellor continued down the next flight of steps to the street below.

"Don't make me go up there alone," said Field to his wife.

"But she *wants* to see you alone, Mr. Field—she told me. Go on, you knew her of old, and she's not grown horns since then."

Field rose and mounted the stairs to Nightingale's bedchamber. The door was open. She was at her desk, writing, when he entered.

"Good morning, Mr. Field," Nightingale said, briefly glancing up, her steel pen continuing to scratch across the paper. After a moment she put it down, turned to Field, and looked at him appraisingly. "You have aged. So, as you plainly may see, have I."

Field felt a surge of affection for the valiant nursing pioneer who, because of her labors and self-sacrifice, had become one of the most loved women in the world. Upon her return from the Crimean War, she had turned herself into a virtual recluse at age thirty-six. She rarely left her home, but she was now more influential than ever, lobbying for a revolution in military and medical procedure, pushing, pulling, and sometimes tormenting heads of state from her chaste Mayfair bedroom. Today, she was a fine-boned woman of forty-six, dressed simply but expensively in gray, her brown hair parted strictly down the middle, a white lace shawl about her shoulders.

"Your dear wife will be a great help to me, I know," said Nightingale, "as she was all those years ago. Thank you for allowing her to return to my service."

Field bowed. "Miss Nightingale, I rejoice to see you again."

"Do you?" she said. "I wonder."

"Indeed I do, miss!"

"Mr. Disraeli and I have cordial relations and the occasional significant disagreement. I thought a rumor of the latter might have drifted down and disturbed you below." Suddenly she was smiling impishly.

Field nodded. "Just a whisper, miss."

"The chancellor does not suffer from excessive humility, and I thought he might benefit from a little correction."

"I confess to having felt some trepidation, in case you had the same in store for me."

"It's too early to tell, isn't it. Do take a seat, old friend. Your wife has been telling me of your doings and about the young people whom you've taken in and raised."

"We had no children of our own, and then, by some miracle or other, we did," said Field, taking the nearest chair, which, he found, was still slightly warm from the chancellor's backside. "Our Belinda is growing to be a lovely young woman and is destined for your school, we hope."

"I look forward to meeting her."

"Our Tom is the light of our lives, when he's not tempting me to throttle him. He has been accepted into the Metropolitan Police, I'm proud to say—Mounted Branch. He's been training for months, and today, as a matter of fact, is his first day on full duty."

"He'll be busy, then. Isn't there to be a great demonstration in Hyde Park?"

"Yes, miss. The mounted police will be at the front line of whatever ensues with the Reform League fellows."

"The Reform Act is what brought Mr. Disraeli here today, as it happens. Everyone wants one to weigh in on this side or the other. It was John Stuart Mill yesterday, urging me to speak out publicly—in favor of women! As if I was opposed to them! I declined Mr. Thomas Carlyle's request for an audience, as that exalted philosopher definitely *is* opposed to women, but Mr. Gladstone came last week—yes, sir, the prime minister himself. No one was to know he'd been. I almost expected him to wear a false mustache over his real one and was quite disappointed when he didn't!"

Field laughed with Nightingale. But surely she hadn't summoned him here to discuss the issues of the day?

"I, too, was childless," said Nightingale. "When I went out to the Crimea, I acquired thousands of them—fine young British lads. A great many of them died. Hundreds and hundreds. They died despite my best efforts, killed not by war but by the incompetence and indifference of the army and the doctors. We are called upon by God to forgive. Perhaps God will one day grant me the ability to do so."

Field nodded. "I was there, miss. I saw."

She rose stiffly, steadied herself on the back of her chair, and paced the length of the room and back. "I understand you are no longer a policeman, Mr. Field," she said. "You left the Metropolitan?"

"I wasn't given the option."

"I had heard that, of course, from others. But you continue to employ your investigative skills nevertheless."

"In a private capacity."

"You are engaged from time to time by Mr. Charles Dickens, I believe."

Field did not respond.

"I know this," continued Nightingale, "because Mr. Dickens told me so."

"Ah."

"Now it is I who wish to employ your services." She sat again and seemed to consider how best to proceed. "You understand that my health is not sound."

"It grieves me, Miss Nightingale. I hope and trust you soon will regain your strength and reenter the wide world."

She laughed and shook her head. "I don't know that I *want* the wide world, sir. I had seen enough of it by the time I was thirty-five to know that it was not all it's made out to be. And to correct you, Mr. Field, I may have lost my health, but I haven't lost my *strength*. I have a duty to this world, and to my God. Mankind must *make* heaven before we can *go* to heaven, as the phrase has it." She grew serious. "You and your wife, I believe, are very nearly the only persons who know that ill health is not the sole reason I keep to my rooms."

Field regarded her somberly. "We discussed this long ago, miss. What I said then I will say again: the man you so rightly feared is gone. I myself witnessed his demise."

"Yes, you were always quite confident on that point."

"Miss Nightingale, am I not to believe my own eyes?"

She smiled, not warmly. "But just think how often it happens that we mistake one thing for another."

Field shook his head in frustration. "It's up to you, miss, of course, to believe me or not. But I simply pray you might free yourself from this—forgive me—self-imposed bondage."

"My fears are groundless and typically feminine."

"I did not say that . . ."

Nightingale's voice rose by degrees. "I live in a self-imposed *bondage*, frightened by the chimera of a woman's overwrought imagination. Thank you for illuminating my errors, Mr. Field."

She stood, giving Field no choice but to do the same. "You are unfair, miss, as it seems to me."

"*What do I care if I am?*" Under her breath, she said, "I should have thought, Mr. Field, for the sake of your own wife . . ."

"For the sake of my wife, Miss Nightingale, I beg you to refrain from communicating these fears."

"Do you take me for a brute, sir? That is why I confided them to *you*, not her."

Field took a deep breath. He regarded the woman before him. He towered above her, in height and bulk, but the face staring up at him was fierce and determined.

"Forgive me, miss. I can understand your fear."

"Fear is not what I'm feeling, sir. It's anger. As you say, twelve years ago *you were there, you saw*. And now, it has begun again."

"What makes you say so, Miss Nightingale?"

She pulled a piece of fabric from a pocket in the folds of her dress, and Field's heart sank.

"He's back," she said.

The inspector looked from the embroidered red blossom to Nightingale's face. He realized that *wishing* there were no connection between the young Mrs. Hythe-Cooper and the famous nurse would not work.

"How did you come by it?"

"It was found in a classroom at St. Thomas by one of our nursing students."

Field nodded. "Was it directed to any particular student?"

"Not that I am aware, sir."

"And no young woman was harmed?"

Nightingale shook her head. "You have seen this pattern before, Mr. Field. You know with what horror it was associated."

Field nodded. "I'll look into it, miss."

"There is an attitude of laissez-faire with which the male of the species is strangely content."

"Whatever that is, Miss Nightingale, I shall endeavor to avoid it."

"Send your wife up to me now, please." She sat again at her desk and took up her pen with finality.

Field hesitated. "Excuse me, Miss Nightingale, but this will remain our secret, will it not? Mrs. Field don't need to know of it, do she?"

Nightingale looked up at him, her face suddenly compassionate. "Of course not, Charles."

She resumed writing, and Field descended the stairs.

Jane was standing anxiously at the bottom, alongside a housekeeper who also had heard the raised voice of her mistress. Field smiled and said, "She wants you, Jane."

"What was the matter?"

"Nothing at all, my dear. Miss N. and I had a lovely reunion, which included a very temporary misunderstanding."

The housekeeper, an ample older woman, sniffed skeptically.

"Mrs. Digby, this is my husband, Mr. Field."

The housekeeper, frowning, made the slightest of curtsies.

"Enchanted," said Field.

"It will be all right, Mrs. Digby," said Jane. "I'll go up and look after her."

Digby nodded and, with another dark look at Field, descended the stairs to the kitchen below.

"Do go to her," said Field. "She understandably prefers your company to mine."

Jane searched her husband's eyes, but they told her nothing. "I am now thinking, sir, she only took me on again in order to get to you."

"Nonsense, my dear." He kissed her cheek. "I'm going to step round the corner to see if I can spot our Tom keeping Hyde Park safe from the common man. I'll see you at the end of the day."

As he descended the steps to the street below, Field realized he still clutched the embroidered linen square. He stuffed it into a pocket, put his hand in the air, and hailed a hackney carriage.

"St. Thomas' Hospital, driver!" he shouted. "Surrey Gardens!"

6

For 650 years an institution calling itself St. Thomas' Hospital had existed in Southwark, a short distance below London Bridge. It had many incarnations, but in 1860 Florence Nightingale added to them by founding in its precincts a school for nursing. Soon, though, the construction of the Charing Cross railway forced the ancient hospital and the newly established school to take up temporary residence on the grounds of the Surrey Pleasure Gardens while permanent facilities were built for them at Lambeth.

Charles Field's coach took him through the wooded gardens and around the pond to the old music hall, where he alighted. One still could see signs of the fire that had ended the entertainments there. Now, white-cowled nurses wheeled patients, well wrapped up, onto the grass to benefit from the fresh May air. Detective Field entered the building and soon found himself hurrying to keep pace with the matron as she was finishing her rounds of the wards, trailed by five young nursing students.

"Miss Nightingale did not inform me that anyone was coming to see us, Inspector Field," said Mrs. Wardroper, a woman in her fifties with a sturdy build and a no-nonsense demeanor.

"Nevertheless, as Isaiah said to the Lord God, 'Here am I.'"

The woman stopped abruptly, causing her entourage of trainees to stumble to a stop as well. She gave Field a critical scrutiny and then sped on. "We are nearly done here, sir, and can talk in my office," she said over her shoulder, "but everything is in order, as far as I am able to tell. Our operation is moving as smoothly as it can do, given our transient circumstances."

"I am delighted to hear it, ma'am."

Mrs. Wardroper paused at the bed of a rotund middle-aged man and cast a baleful eye on the young freckle-faced trainee who attended him. "Sister Prudence, have you turned your patient this morning?"

"Turned *and* bathed him, Matron, and this one ain't heavy, oh no, not him!"

"Sister!"

"Sorry, Matron," said Prudence with a little curtsy.

"Go on," said the fat man in the bed, "she's an angel. I didn't cry out once, and me with my gouty toes. Reminds me of me own mother, she does, but better looking by far!"

"Prudence," said the matron, "follow along with us now, and keep your observations to yourself."

"Yes, ma'am, sorry, ma'am."

As she left the patient's bedside, Sister Prudence shrieked and slapped the man's hand. "Cheeky!"

The matron's face reddened. She took the girl by the elbow and propelled her forcibly away from the bed.

"For shame, Sister Prudence!"

"I did not invite that man to touch me as he did!"

"Be still! You have given the entire ward a demonstration of the behavior that has long plagued our reputation as nurses, a reputation we are only now beginning to overcome. What is a nurse but a drunkard and a trollop? That's what gentlefolk say of nurses. Fortunately for us, one high-born lady gave up her place in society to show what a fine, even noble, profession ours can be. Do you have the slightest idea what Miss Nightingale endured so that you could be where you are today? *Do you care?*"

Sister Prudence's lips quivered, and a tear ran down her freckled face. Inspector Field dropped his head and coughed quietly. The matron turned on him.

"This is not for your ears, actually, Inspector."

"My ears can take most anything, Matron. I'm sure the girl didn't mean no harm."

"But harm us she does, sir, when she misbehaves! We here are watched, our every move is scrutinized. There are many who are eager for us to fail."

"Madam, I understand. My own wife is a nurse. She was at Scutari and Balaclava with Miss Nightingale."

The matron stared. "Dear Lord, you're Jane Rolly's husband."

"She has borne my unworthy name these twelve blessed years."

Dropping her voice, she said, "How is she? Better, I hope?"

"Fully recovered, I should say. Never better, and that's saying something."

"Stop a moment. That means you're *Charles* Field, the famous inspector Bucket!" The matron crossed her arms triumphantly, as if daring the man to deny it.

Field forced a smile. "So people have said, Matron."

The notion that Charles Dickens had modeled Detective Bucket of *Bleak House* after Inspector Field simply would not die, it seemed. The nurse trainees studied the detective with renewed interest.

"Well, then," said the matron, in motion again, "let's to my office." She pushed through a double set of swinging doors into a corridor, followed by her students and Field. "You girls, off to class now."

"One moment, please, Matron," said Field.

"Yes?"

"May I ask whether any of you does embroidery?"

"What an odd question!" said the matron.

"Anyone?"

Five of the six trainees tentatively raised their hands. "I expect we all do a bit of embroidery," said the matron, "when we have the time."

"I don't," said Prudence, tucking a stray shock of reddish hair back under her cowl.

Field produced the square of linen fabric, embroidered with the rose. "Did one of you send this along to Miss Nightingale?"

The young women shook their heads, but the matron's cheeks reddened.

"Mrs. Wardroper?"

The woman took the fabric from the inspector and examined it. "Why do you ask, Mr. Field?" she said.

"Well, as long as your young ladies are all well and thriving," said Field, "it's of no consequence."

The matron surveyed her trainees. "Where's Alice?" she said suddenly.

Sister Prudence looked down, a blush rising to her freckled face.

"Prudence?" said Wardroper.

"I'm sorry, Matron, but I don't know. She was slow getting up this morning." Prudence turned to Field. "We share a room, you see. So I expected she'd be a bit late, but then she never appeared."

"And you never said a word?" said Mrs. Wardroper.

Sister Prudence pulled out a handkerchief and blew her nose. "I didn't like to peach on her, did I. But I did tell Alice she shouldn't be so free with her acquaintance."

"*What* acquaintance?"

"She has a beau. A hospital visitor, I believe. Chatted Alice up when she was doin' her rounds. A gentleman. She sometimes goes off to see him."

"Worse and worse!" said the matron.

"Matron, would you be so kind," said Field, "as to look in on this Alice?"

"Of course," she said. "Sister Prudence, you go off with the others now."

"One moment, Prudence," said Field. "Did the beau have a name?"

The girl's brow furrowed. "Did she once call him Arthur? She keeps herself close, does Alice. But she did say she shared a relation with him. An auntie, I think she said. Maybe his name was Tuttle?"

Field registered surprise. "Arthur Tuttle, the actor, or some other Arthur Tuttle?"

"I don't know, I'm sure," said Prudence. "Don't even know for sure if it was Arthur."

"All right," said the matron. "Off you all go!"

The young women hurried along the corridor. When they were out of earshot, Mrs. Wardroper turned to Field.

"Those of us in the nursing community have heard the stories that came from the Crimea all those years ago, Mr. Field." She held up the square. "Is this from that era?"

"I honestly don't know, ma'am."

"God help us," she said under her breath. "Wait here, sir."

The matron hurried to the staircase. She was surprised as she reached the top floor to find the inspector climbing silently only two paces behind her. He put a finger to his lips and winked.

"I understand these precincts are for the young women only," he said, "and I shall hold them inviolate, ma'am."

The woman snorted. "Poor Jane Rolly." She turned and listened at the closed door. She opened it abruptly and went in, Field following right after. Two narrow, neatly made-up beds were side by side, but the room held no nurse trainees. The matron opened the door of a wardrobe. One side had female clothing on hangers; the other side was empty. Wardroper stooped and slid open a drawer at the bottom.

"Her traveling valise is gone, as well as her clothing." She stood and said, "I'm afraid we've seen the last of Alice Wheeler."

"Do you often lose students to suitors?" said Field.

"Certainly not, sir. At least, we struggle against it. The smallest hint of scandal would be ruinous to this school."

"Well, I thank you for your help, ma'am."

"Do please greet your wife from me."

"I shall."

He descended the stairs thoughtfully. What was the connection between the school and the bit of fabric Miss Nightingale had put in his hand this morning? Perhaps she was mistaken about it having been found at the school. But where *had* it come from?

He found a hackney cab and settled in for the ride home. *Now, I wonder how our Tom got on with the big demonstration in the park today?*

7

Tom Ginty was keeping his fine bay at a restive standstill with pressure from his knees and heels. He and a dozen other mounted policemen were stationed just inside Hyde Park's Cumberland Gate, backed up by dozens of London constables, while other groups of horsemen and foot constables from the Metropolitan Police, more than fifteen hundred of them, guarded each of the park's nearly twenty entrances. There was to be no repetition of last year's debacle, when members of the Reform League, forbidden the park, had pulled down the railings and surged in, pelting the police with fruit and rampaging, off and on, for three days.

The orders barked at Tom and his fellow horsemen by Sergeant Butts this morning had been clear: they were to rush the demonstrators if they advanced, and at his signal they would fire on them. None of it felt real to Tom. His horse, Sallie, she was real. This fine May morning was real, as was his new uniform and, hard as it was to believe, his new position in the world. But Englishmen firing on Englishmen?

Never.

Tom furtively stole another glimpse of himself, glancing down at his uniform. A scarlet waistcoat peeked from beneath his powder-blue jacket. His handsome dark blue trousers hugged his thighs, and his tall leather boots were black and gleaming. A sword hung from his left hip and a pistol from the right. His gear pleased him greatly.

Sergeant Butts' shrill voice rang out. "File . . . *'shun!*" Tom and his mates snapped to attention. "Twos wheel . . . *right!*" Two by two, Tom and the other horsemen turned their horses to face the wrought-iron doors of the Marble Arch. These were slowly pulled open, and a trio of mounted officers rode in. Tom recognized Commissioner Sir Richard Mayne in the lead. An officer who seemed to be Mayne's aide-de-camp rode beside him, and not far behind, looking somewhat uncomfortable on horseback, came Detective Inspector Sam Llewellyn.

This trio rode past the line of mounted police, and as they did so, Llewellyn, with a perfectly serious demeanor, turned to Tom and winked elaborately. Inwardly, Tom swelled with pride, but as Llewellyn moved off, he suddenly frowned, staring back at Tom's right boot. Tom anxiously glanced down.

Horseshit!

A sizable clump of the stuff clung to the heel of his otherwise shiny right boot! Acquired back at the stables, no doubt, just before he'd mounted Sallie. How could he have missed it? What if Sergeant Butts should see it? Or Commissioner Mayne himself! The commissioner, in fact, was addressing the unit of mounted police, but Tom could not focus on what he was saying.

" . . . our people, stationed throughout London, have reported groups of men approaching the park from every borough," Mayne was saying. "You must ready yourselves for them. This time we'll give the ruffians and drunkards something by which to remember us!"

Tom took his right boot out of the stirrup and gave it a little shake.

The dirt remained where it was, but Sallie started forward and Tom frantically yanked the reins to pull her back. The two horses flanking him reacted, one stepping nervously forward and the other sidestepping, their riders struggling to control them. The ripple spread from horse to horse, up and down the entire line, until finally the commissioner stopped talking and stared.

"Troops . . . *re-form!*" screamed Sergeant Butts. Commissioner Mayne was talking angrily to his aide and pointing in Tom's direction, but then—as it later seemed to Tom—everything stopped, all motion ceased, and the only thing that existed was the growing sound of men, singing. All eyes turned to the streets leading to the park: where minutes earlier there had been no one, there now appeared a mass of humanity, singing as they marched.

> May just and righteous laws
> Uphold the public cause,
> And bless our isle . . .

Orderly and inexorably, rank on rank, they came by the thousands up broad Park Lane. And now, marching up the Edgeware Road and spilling into Bayswater Road, were thousands more, all of them singing "God Save the Queen."

> Not in this land alone,
> But be God's mercies known
> From shore to shore:
> Lord make the nations see
> That men should brothers be,
> And form one family
> The whole world o'er.

Commissioner Mayne led the senior officers off to one side and signaled Sergeant Butts. Butts snapped to attention and barked: "Unit . . .

advance!" Tom and the other mounted horsemen moved forward toward the gate. "Unit . . . *halt!*"

The front line of the demonstrators surged up to the Marble Arch and stopped, and behind them, thousands shuffled to a standstill. To Tom's eye, they did not look like ruffians or drunkards. Their voices rang out.

God save the Queen!
Send her victorious,
Happy and glorious,
Long to reign over us,
God save the Queen!

The anthem finished, and an eerie silence fell. One heard birdsong, and church bells telling the hour. Tom found himself staring into the eyes of one of the demonstrators in the front line, a lad his own age, about twenty feet distant. The young man seemed to be staring back. *Wait.* Tom knew him. He had been one of the other apprentices at Smithfield Market, hadn't he? Yes, surely—*Jim, was it?*

Commissioner Mayne gently spurred his horse and moved majestically to the grand gate. His powerful voice rang out, tinged with a refined Irish lilt.

"You are hereby commanded to disperse!"

Given the size of the massed crowd, it remained remarkably quiet.

"Leave these precincts immediately, and go to your homes or suffer the consequences!"

Mayne looked out into a sea of faces and waited. A moment later, he turned his horse and rode back into the park. "Sergeant!" he shouted. "Begin!"

"*Draw weapons!*" cried Butts.

Tom glanced quickly at his mates. Up and down the line, they were pulling their Beaumont-Adams revolvers from their holsters. Back at the barracks they all had loaded their guns with shot and black powder; this model did not need to be cocked, the guns were ready to fire. Tom, too, drew his own weapon and held it vertically by the side of his head.

Yes, it is Jim, that's him.

The young man in the front line seemed to have recognized Tom as well. He pushed his cap back and nodded tentatively.

"Take aim!"

Tom glanced about him. Were they really about to fire on their fellow countrymen? The world as he knew it was ending. Tom slowly lowered his arm and extended his revolver toward the crowd. His hand shook. Jim's face bounced about the top of his sights.

"Ready!"

Abruptly, Tom raised the gun again.

Sergeant Butts' voice pitched even higher. *"Ready!"*

My first day, thought Tom, *and my last.*

"Ginty, take aim!"

Tom continued to hold the revolver upright, his hand shaking. He could not help it; tears sprang from his eyes, completing, as Tom saw it, his utter disgrace.

"Ginty!"

There was a clatter of hooves. A horseman was galloping along Park Lane toward the Marble Arch, shouting and waving an arm. His coat was blue; he was one of the Metropolitan's own.

"Commissioner!"

The horseman rode hard past the rows of demonstrators, shouting as he came.

"Commissioner Mayne!"

The commissioner said something to Sergeant Butts who, after a quick back-and-forth, screamed at his men. *"Weapons up!"*

Mayne rode forward, through the Marble Arch, followed by his aide and Sam Llewellyn. The horseman reined in his horse and came to a clattering halt. He spoke rapidly; the commissioner seemed to react with disbelief, then anger. The young policeman pulled a folded paper from his tunic and passed it to his superior. Mayne opened it and read. He looked briefly to the heavens, shaking his head.

From the gathered multitude came a growing murmur. Mayne looked out at the crowd.

"Is there a leader amongst you?" he shouted. One tall, slender man stepped forward, taking off his hat. "Listen you, whoever you are," the commissioner's voice trembling with scorn and rage, "I shall hold you responsible. Any breach of order and decorum, and you will be taken into custody and dealt with mercilessly." The tall man looked confused. He spoke briefly to Mayne, his question inaudible. The commissioner shouted his reply.

"Home secretary has lifted the interdiction, *the god damned park is yours!*"

With that, Mayne spurred his horse hard, and rode off. A murmur began, growing to a roar as the word spread among the thousands until it was deafening. The mounted policemen holstered their guns and drew aside as the tall man, waving his hat as a banner, led the way into Hyde Park. Amid all the confusion of tramping men and roaring cheers, Tom was startled by one voice speaking directly into his ear.

"You're done, Ginty," snarled Sergeant Butts. "Finished!"

THERE WAS A discreet rap at his office door. Disraeli glanced up and said, "Come!"

The chancellor's private secretary put his head in. "Message from your wife, sir."

"Do come in, Monty. What does Mrs. Disraeli have to say?"

"It seems she's been watching the activities in the park from your home, sir. She reports that the police have moved back, and the demonstrators in general seem to be thoroughly enjoying themselves."

Disraeli laughed. "Mary Anne is wonderful. She may not be able to remember which came first, the Greeks or the Romans, but her heart is as big as the world. Don't tell anyone, but she sympathizes with the Reform League, frankly."

Monty smiled and crossed to his employer's desk, handing him an envelope.

"She also sent this along, sir. Said it had been delivered by messenger."

"Right," said Disraeli. "Listen, you run along home now, I'm going to pack it in early myself."

The private secretary bowed and left, and Disraeli sliced open the envelope. He pulled out a single folded page, from which fell a square of brightly decorated fabric. Confused, he opened the note and found a short message written in a bold hand.

Do you think weel let a filthy Jew betray the nation?

8

Inspector Field found his family in the kitchen, silent, their eyes on him as he descended the steps. Belinda stood at the range. Jane Field sat at the table, and Tom, still wearing his uniform but without the jacket, sat beside her, holding her hand. Jane looked up at her husband with red-rimmed eyes and smiled wanly. "Hello, Mr. Field," she said.

"My dear," said Field. "Tom."

"Hello, sir," said Tom, somberly.

Field attempted a smile. "Does someone want to tell me who died?"

Tom and Belinda exchanged glances, and Jane said, "Did you not see our Tom in the park, Mr. Field?"

Field hesitated for a moment, then said, "I did, indeed. You looked grand in uniform, son, I was very proud."

"Oh dear," said Belinda under her breath.

"What's that you said?" said Field.

"Tom has been sacked, Mr. Field," said Jane.

"Sacked?"

Belinda whispered, "But it's not that."

"*Sacked?*" said Field. He hung his hat on the stand near the kitchen door. "You had better not be sacked!"

"I am, though, sir."

"Dear God, months of bloody training thrown away! On your first day? I don't bloody believe it!"

Tom stood abruptly and climbed the steps to the foyer.

"Tom!" said Field.

They heard the street door open and slam shut.

There followed a silence, during which Field avoided the eyes of the two women. "Belinda," he said, "put the kettle on, would you?"

Jane said, "I don't believe you did go to the park, Mr. Field." She toyed with a bit of fabric on the table.

"I'm sorry, my dear, but all of this has got me a little confused, frankly."

"You *must* be confused," said Jane, looking up at him, "if you thought you'd gone to the park when in fact you hadn't."

The inspector sat beside his wife. "I apologize, my dear. Miss Nightingale asked me to look into a little matter, and it took up my afternoon."

"Did the little matter look anything like this?"

Jane turned over the cloth in her hand yet again and looked up into her husband's eyes. There on the table lay the square of embroidered fabric.

Field, aghast, patted his own pockets.

"Sister Wardroper sent it by messenger," said Jane. "You left it behind at St. Thomas, it seems."

"Bloody hell."

"Language, sir!" She tapped the red rose with a finger. "You told us he was dead!"

"He *is* dead, my dear," said Field to his wife. "You must believe me."

"How can I? How can I believe the things you say?"

"Who's dead?" said Belinda.

Field spoke gently to his wife. "Today is not yesterday, nor is it twelve years ago. Today is today, and we will get to the bottom of this and all will be well."

Jane shook her head. "That is what you said back then, and all was *not* well, was it, Charles." She looked up at Belinda. "Men are forever telling women that all will be well, they'll handle everything, but it's not true. It's not true!"

"Please," said Belinda, "what are you two talking about?"

"You know I was with Miss Nightingale in the war," said Jane. "Well, the world is bigger than you can imagine, and far more dangerous. I was like you, knowing nothing of the world, traveling I knew not where, sailing by faith alone, believing that this woman who had handpicked each of us nurses would get us through. Miss Nightingale was out there on deck with all of us when finally we sailed into the harbor, Scutari on one side before us and, in the distance, the domes and spires of all Constantinople. We were taken aback by the splendor—I was, anyway. It did not look a bit like London. One of the sisters said to Miss N., 'Oh, do let us be quick to our work!' And she said, 'The strongest of us will be wanted at the washtub!'"

"And that was true, wasn't it, my dear?" said Field.

"There would have *been* no washtubs had not Miss Nightingale bought them herself at Marseille with her own funds! *And* soap *and* sundries." Jane stood. "The stench from the drains was everywhere. The sick and wounded men were sprawled about anyhow, in their own filth and gore, hundreds of them, the dead with the living. There was no welcome; the doctors despised us. The officers and orderlies smirked and leered.

There were rats by the hundreds, and biting fleas. And there was worse, far worse, waiting for us."

"My dear, it was all a long time ago."

Field attempted to draw his wife into his arms, but just then the kettle began to shriek and Jane started at the sound.

"Please," she said.

She broke free from his embrace and fled the room. Belinda looked at Field, stricken. She turned off the flame beneath the kettle.

"If you'd gone to the park, Father, you'd know they ordered Tom to fire on the crowd, but he wouldn't do it, and a good thing, too, or there'd been a massacre, but that's how he lost his position with the Mounted Branch."

"Oh, dear God," said Field.

There was a pounding at the door.

The inspector rose to answer it and Belinda followed him. Sam Llewellyn stood there, solemn, along with an abashed-looking Tom.

"I found this one sprinting up the road at a terrific rate," said Llewellyn.

"Tom," said Field, "I just now heard from Belinda that—"

Tom interrupted him. "Mr. Llewellyn has got me back in the Metropolitan."

"Did he now? Well done, Sam!"

"I went straight to the home secretary," said Llewellyn, "explained what happened, and Walpole reinstated Tom on the spot."

"Splendid!"

"And then he resigned from the government."

"Walpole's gone?"

"It was his last official act, getting Tom his position back."

"Well, sorry about all that, Mr. Walpole, but this calls for a celebration!"

"Not yet, Charles. You need to come along with us."

"Where to?"

"The Nightingale School, St. Thomas' Hospital."

Field recognized the gravity with which Llewellyn spoke and had a good idea what it must mean. He turned back to Belinda. "See to your mother, will you, my dear?"

She nodded.

"And Belinda?" said Tom.

"Yes?"

"Bolt the door."

9

Jack loosened his red silk scarf. It was growing hot in the assembly room. By day it was a Baptist chapel, but once a week it was rented to the Anti-Suffrage Society. There was a large crowd tonight, perhaps three dozen men and several women, and a mixture of classes, from the upper to the artisan and even a bit lower. One strange man sat near the front, his chair set at a distance from the others, with a black veil to his top hat, obscuring his face.

The society had heard from Thomas Carlyle, the fiery Scottish writer and historian, who likened liberalization of voting laws to a leap in the dark, to *shooting Niagara*. He begged the crowd to purchase a copy of the *Evening Standard* next week in order to read the *filth* promoted by the anonymous author of its weekly column, endorsing *votes for whomever!* They needed to realize their danger.

Jack's breathing quickened. He sat forward and looked about the room. People were shaking their heads in disgust.

Carlyle was followed by the Earl of Carnarvon, Henry ("Twitters") Herbert, the secretary of state for colonial affairs. He argued against any expansion of voting rights, and parsed the word *aristocracy* for his audience: Greek, for "rule by the finest." Both speakers were received warmly by all; it seemed it wasn't only members of the upper classes who resisted liberalization of the laws. Many who occupied society's lower rungs felt voting would be *best left to their betters*.

Now the final speaker, Robert Gascoyne-Cecil, tall but stooped, with a thick black beard, seemed to be wrapping up his speech.

Jack felt a blossoming of pride. *They say a Gascoyne-Cecil has stood in Parliament continuously since the days of Henry VIII.*

"We feel there can be no doubt that the so-called Conservative Disraeli has played us false. He promised that it would never be the fate of this country to live under a democracy. Gentlemen and ladies, he lied. His scheme to enlarge enfranchisement will swell the voting rolls by a far greater number than he claims. And, of course, the prime minister is completely in Disraeli's hands. Derby is the dog and Disraeli the tail that wags him!"

There were cries from the crowd.

Shame! Down with 'em both! Shame!

"I am convinced that the Jew's bill, if passed, would trigger a deluge."

"A swarmery!" shouted Carlyle.

"Indeed," said Gascoyne-Cecil, "to use Mr. Carlyle's felicitous term, *a swarmery*—the rabble rising to the top and the blind leading the sightless!"

Never! For shame!

To his own surprise, Jack suddenly stood and addressed the crowd.

"Let us not forget Mr. John Stuart Mill, who wants *females* to be voting, as well, God help us!"

Laughter and jeers from the crowd, both the men and the women.

"Nor is he the only one!"

There was renewed applause. Jack acknowledged it with a bow and noticed as he did so that the man in the veil had turned round to look. The man raised the black tulle that hung from his top hat, revealing a cadaverously white face and sunken eyes that stared at him. The veil fell again, and Jack sat.

Gascoyne-Cecil continued. "Benjamin Disraeli has long had it planned, this calamitous course. It is incumbent upon us to stop it in its tracks, and we shall use all means at our disposal to do so!"

Oh, will you, my lord? thought Jack. *Will you use* all *means?*

He looked about with secret disdain. He was playing as great or greater a role than any of them, even my lords and ladies. He was tempted to stand up again and say, *I have done more in a day to advance our cause and hinder theirs than any of you,* but to do so of course would be ruinous. He must remain quiet, unsung. His journals would be released upon his death (*long hence, if it please God*) and then it would be for historians to proclaim his worth. He sensed the meeting was about to break up. He was determined, at any rate, to introduce himself to the principal speakers. They made his old "friend" Hythe-Cooper, who had been so rude to him, look insignificant.

"As the weeks draw nearer to the vote at the beginning of August," said Gascoyne-Cecil, "we shall plan strategies with members of the cabinet to prevent this fatal course of action. My motto is a simple one. It's certain that whatever happens will be for the worse, so it is in our best interest that as little happen as possible!"

Laughter and applause. With a nod to the others at the front, the great men stood. The meeting was over.

Now!

He shouldered his way forward through the crowd, everyone talking at once and making for the door. But now there was someone tugging at him, a woman.

"Oh!" he said. "It's you. Leave off, will you!"

"A man came round, askin' about that rose you give me, I thought you should know."

"Mrs. Digby, let me go!"

"But he was a detective!"

"Go back to Nightingale's kitchen, Mrs. Digby, where you belong!"

"I don't know wot it's about, but I don't want no trouble!"

Jack shook her off violently. Cecil and Carnarvon were speaking together, and very nearly out of the room.

"My lords!" said Jack, hurrying toward them. The two men glanced at him briefly, then continued their conversation. "Pardon, my lords, if I might have a word, just to applaud your efforts and to say that you are not alone in this cause?"

This time they looked at him askance. Gascoyne-Cecil turned back to the Earl of Carnarvon and said, "My brother not long ago had one of his constituents approach him *in a hotel lobby*!"

The Earl shook his head and clucked.

"I told my brother it's a shame we don't carry powdered insecticide for such unwelcome pests."

And they were gone. He stood, trembling with humiliation and rage. "Sir?"

He wheeled round and found the veiled man staring, presumably, at him.

"Pay them no mind." The voice was hoarse, whispery, barely audible; it was a voice that rarely was used. "Full of themselves, known 'em all my life. I don't much like to see a man cut dead like that, goes against the grain. D'you mind not looking at me quite so directly? Seabury's the name. Don't often have people round, but you might come dine tonight if you like. What's your name?"

"Jack," he said cautiously.

"My carriage is just outside, Jack, it drives right into my home. It's quite nice, you never have to see a soul."

Jack nodded, and the two men left, a red-faced Mrs. Digby staring after them.

Thus did Jack meet Henry Neville, the eccentric 4th Duke of Seabury. At the House of Lords, Seabury was known as the Invisible Peer, traveling to and from the Houses of Parliament veiled and, when seated without his hat and veil, always at the far end of a back bench. In the Peers' Dining Room, he sat at a remote corner table, facing the wall. Eventually Seabury did appear to achieve invisibility; other peers, knowing his aversion to being seen or spoken to, obliged him. He came and went unnoticed. People simply forgot he was there.

10

Field, Llewellyn, and Tom were met at the hospital entrance by Matron Wardroper, in nightdress and cloak. She led them across a long expanse of lawn to a filigreed wooden enclosure at the edge of the pond. The structure held two young women. The one who could not stop sobbing was the healthy one. The other, lying on an ornately carved bench overlooking the water, was silent. Her bonnet was off, her long brown hair undone; her lips were parted and her eyes closed.

Llewellyn looked to Field, who gave him a slight shake of the head.

"Is this the missing Alice, Matron?" said Field.

She nodded.

"You shut her eyes for her, I imagine? Kind of you, ma'am."

The young woman's sobs continued.

"Tom, this is Sister Prudence," said Field. "Take her inside and find a cup of tea for her."

Prudence seemed to see Field for the first time. She put a hand to her mouth and her sobs came to a hiccoughing stop. Tom offered an arm to her, and she suffered him to lead her across the grounds.

"Matron," said Field, "this is Detective Inspector Sam Llewellyn, who will be handling this matter. I'm just an observer."

"Ma'am," said Llewellyn, and she nodded.

"This gazebo," she said, "is not on hospital property, actually. Could we say that none of this has anything to do with the Nightingale School for Nursing?" She looked hopelessly from one man to the other. They said nothing, and the senior nurse shook her head.

"I must sound heartless to you," said Wardroper. "But as I grieve for this poor girl, I grieve for my school. They'll shut us down for this. There are those who have been waiting for any excuse to do so. They despise our work. It's women getting above themselves, they say, and in the same breath they say it debases womanhood."

She sat down next to the body, and stroked Sister Alice's cheek.

"Poor child."

"Matron," said Llewellyn, "who was it found her?"

"Prudence. When Alice didn't appear at supper, or after, Prudence says she went out looking for her and found her here, just as you see her. 'Why did you look *here* for her?' I asked her, and she said it was where Sister Alice sometimes went to meet her beau."

"Who might have been Arthur Tuttle, according to Prudence," said Field to Llewellyn, "but she wasn't certain."

"Arthur Tuttle, the actor?"

"She didn't know if she'd got the name right," said Field.

"Matron," said Llewellyn, "I hesitate to ask this of you, but before we arrived, did you have a chance to ascertain . . . ?"

"The poor girl was strangled, sir. She also may have been assaulted. Her underclothing was disarrayed."

Mrs. Wardroper put her face in her hands and began to sob. The men remained silent.

"I'm sorry," she said, choking back her tears. She blew her nose. "Forgive me."

"Have you sent word to her family?" Llewellyn asked gently.

"I shall try. She came to us from Birmingham, I believe. I don't know that she had much in the way of family."

"Well, according to Prudence," said Field, "she had a relation in common with the man she was seeing, an auntie."

"I don't know anything about that," said the matron. "This morning was the first I heard of it."

"The girl's family name?" asked Llewellyn.

"Wheeler." She looked at the men imploringly. "Do you think it was this man, this Tuttle person, who did this to her?"

Field shook his head. "No way of knowing at this point, ma'am."

"Matron, go in now," said Llewellyn. "Have a cup of tea yourself. I'll be along in a moment to ask one or two further questions of you and the girl who found Miss Wheeler."

The woman finally stood, pulled her cloak tighter, and crossed the grounds to the hospital. When she was out of earshot, Llewellyn said, "Charles, you seem to be acquainted with these people—what is going on?"

"I was with them this morning after my interview with Miss Nightingale, who, by the way, has received an unwelcome red rose herself."

"Has she now?" said Llewellyn.

"She said it was found here at the school, but no one here seems to know of it. How it came into Nightingale's hands I don't know."

Field sat beside the body. He pointed to the livid line round the neck and looked up at Llewellyn. "Silk did this. Same as Hythe-Cooper." Turning back to the corpse he said, "Forgive me, child," and leaned in close to the face and the partially open mouth. He gently parted the lips and peered in. "Nothing." His eyes ran along the girl's body, stopping at one of her hands. He examined the fingers. "See this, Sam? A little thimble-shaped callus on the middle finger. My sister used to get this, sewing."

"Perhaps she was a seamstress or factory girl back in Birmingham," said Llewellyn.

"Perhaps." Field patted the pockets of her coat, put a hand in one and came out with a fold of thin paper. He opened it to reveal the fine lines of a pattern.

"Good Lord," said Llewellyn.

"Here's how you create a rose with needle and thread, Sam." Field passed the pattern to him.

"Was this child *making* the wretched things for someone?"

Field stood and surveyed the gazebo. A half-moon alternately lit and hid the scene as scudding clouds moved across its face. Something glinted up at him from the pond, just below. Field stepped down off the platform and stood at the water's edge.

"What's this?"

He crouched, reached for a half-submerged shape, and came up with a large dripping handbag. He set it in the gazebo and climbed up after it. "Sister Alice's traveling valise, I'll wager, missing from her wardrobe this morning."

Llewellyn knelt and gingerly opened the valise, revealing a tangle of underclothes, a sponge bag, and a worn leather case that turned out to hold embroidery needles. At the very bottom was a single square of fabric, an unfinished rose.

Field stepped back into the gazebo. "My sister used to be paid ha'penny per dozen for her decorated handkerchiefs," he said. "Hour after hour, from first light until the last candle was put out. I wonder how much Alice Wheeler's lover paid her? Did he reward her with promises? 'Come, run away with me, my dear!' Makes me angry, Sam."

"Two murders in two days, and now we see they're clearly connected. The coroner's men will soon be arriving, Charles, and my colleagues. I let you have a look-in because of what we were discussing earlier, but now you must make yourself scarce."

"Right."

"I'll talk to the girl now. Prudence, you called her?"

Field nodded. "You'll let me interview Tuttle?"

"What? I never said that!"

"But you *will*, am I right?"

"I am no longer your acolyte, Mr. Field."

"I've no uniform, see? I can chat with Tuttle without him knowing I'm questioning him."

Llewellyn finally nodded. "All right, Charles. You might as well. I've got Jeremy Sims to interview first thing tomorrow morning."

"Do you now?"

"Turns out he wasn't off visiting the voter, like his wife said. He was cowering in his library, but conscience got the best of him, according to Mr. Sims, and he came down to the station."

"To confess?" said Field.

"Not to murder but to just as bad, at least in his wife's eyes: clandestine meetings with the late Mrs. Hythe-Cooper. He claims they were 'discussing policy.'"

"Is that what they're calling it these days? I must inform Mrs. Field."

"I'm letting Sims and his conscience stew together overnight, along with Sims' wife, of course."

"That should be uncomfortable," said Field. "I wonder if he was also having policy discussions with the late Alice Wheeler."

"Aye."

"Of course, Sims is possible. He shows up at Hanover Terrace, commits the crime, and runs away. Runs *here*, perhaps, to close the books on his outstanding accounts. And the roses? He's a nutter, got a thing for 'em, it's nothing to do with the Crimea. Who knows? Trouble is, I'd taken a shine to Jeremy Sims, Sam, as I'd observed him, going about his pleasures. Eager, cheerful. Never hangdog, never guilty-looking."

"You always used to warn me against taking a fancy to a suspect," said Llewellyn.

"Yes, but now I'm old and given to weaknesses, as you see."

Llewellyn smiled. He missed working with his old boss.

"If it comes to that," said Llewellyn, "my suspect of choice would be Hythe-Cooper himself. Jealous husband hires you to investigate his wife, knowing it will lead you to Jeremy Sims. Hythe-Cooper is waiting for his wife at the flat. He dispatches her and walks out the door when you're not looking and makes his rival look guilty as sin."

Field nodded. "You've got something there. I was reading the papers in the park, I didn't expect to see my couple emerge for nearly an hour. I certainly wasn't on the lookout for anyone else. Oh! Did I tell you, Sam, the service entrance to the flat was unlocked?"

"No, you didn't, Charles, as it happens," said Llewellyn.

"Oh, don't be sour. But again, the rose, the rose, stuck in her mouth?"

Llewellyn shrugged. "Well, Hythe-Cooper did serve in the Crimean."

"How'd you know that?" said Field.

"Oh!" said Llewellyn. *"Didn't I tell you?"*

"Samuel!"

"I asked him, didn't I. Mr. Hythe-Cooper might have known all about the embroidered roses."

"Well, I never run into him out there, far as I recall," said Field. "I suppose there's no keeping the roses quiet?"

"Keep 'em from the press? Not bloody likely." Llewellyn pulled his watch from its pocket. "The theaters will be letting out within the hour, Charles. You might catch Mr. Arthur Tuttle before he toddles on home."

"Thanks, Sam. I'm off."

TOM GINTY SAT opposite Sister Prudence at a table in the hospital refectory, both of them silent, motionless, their tea untouched. Tom kept his eyes averted from the girl. Finally, he said, "She was your friend?"

"No."

There was a silence.

"You knew her, though?"

"We shared a room, of course I knew her." Prudence blew her nose. "I keep thinking I could have made this not happen, I could have done things different with Alice, I could have said, 'Stop a moment, Alice, stop and think.'"

Tom nodded, looking off, but said nothing.

"She didn't like me much," said Prudence. "I don't think she wanted to be here. Alice didn't want to be a nurse, she wanted to find a husband."

"You think that's what she was up to tonight? Out looking for a husband?"

"Are you questioning me?"

"I'm with the Metropolitan Police, miss."

"You could have fooled me," said Prudence. "If you want to question a person, you need to talk to 'em, don't you? You can't be so quiet, you got to ask 'em questions. Am I mistaken?"

"I'm with the Mounted Branch."

"Where's your horse?"

There followed the longest silence yet. Finally, Prudence sighed and said, "If you're questioning a person properly, you can't keep your head turned away from them, pretending you're not there. You've got to look 'em in the eye."

Tom said nothing. He stared resolutely at the opaque windowpanes. Outside, it was now fully dark.

"Whatever happened to your ear?"

Tom darted a glance at the girl and looked away again.

"You needn't turn your head," she continued, "you needn't try to hide it, you *can't* hide it, for goodness' sake, it's *there*, just like it is. You look fine. Your other ear is quite nice."

Tom stood.

"I never saw a dead person before," said Prudence.

He looked directly at the young woman. "I did," he said. "More than one."

"Was it awful?"

"Yes." Tom steeled himself to say more, to try to explain himself, his strange history, and, not incidentally, his ear, but she spoke first.

"*Who did this?* Last night Alice was alive. She was in the bed next to mine, she went to sleep, I heard her breathing, and then I went to sleep. It's not right, it's not right."

"No, miss. It's not."

The young woman blew her nose again. Tom felt himself at a loss. Why had he come? Why had he thought he wanted to be a policeman in the first place? He'd had enough of cruelty and murder when he was a boy.

"Will you find the man who did this and stop him?" said Prudence with sudden urgency.

That's why.

Without waiting for a reply, she said, "What's your name?"

"Ginty, miss."

"No. Please. Your other one."

"Tom."

"Thank you. Call me Pru, won't you? I didn't mean to chide you, Tom. It's just I'm so awfully frightened."

At that moment the matron entered, and a few minutes later Inspector Llewellyn came into the refectory. He begged young Prudence's pardon but said he needed to ask her and the matron a few questions. Tom listened intently but said no more that night.

11

The carriage made its way from Westminster to the part of London known as the City. The Duke of Seabury said not a word, nor did he raise his veil, but sat at the farthest reach of the cushioned interior from his baffled guest. Finally, the carriage paused at No. 2 Cloak Lane. It would be understandable to think the street had been named for the garment, located as it was near the Guild of Merchant Taylors. In actuality, the name was derived from the Latin word *cloaca*, meaning "sewer," for beneath it ran the buried Walbrook River and the sewage it sometimes carried.

A liveried servant appeared, swung open a gate, and the horses proceeded into a courtyard. The man in livery put down the steps and opened the carriage door without ever looking at his master. Likewise, the elderly butler who held open the townhouse door kept his eyes averted, although this man did give Jack a slight bow after first looking at him in confusion. The foyer was candlelit, and the air was filled with the aroma of roasting chicken.

"I generally sup alone," said the Duke. "D'you like chicken? I keep a few hens on the hob round the clock should I ever find myself peckish."

The old butler held out his arms, and Jack realized the man was waiting to take his hat and scarf. He gave him his hat but not his red silk scarf.

"We'll be two tonight, Thorne," said Seabury, lifting his veil.

Thorne took his master's hat and veil and placed it on the long narrow table that bordered the foyer, alongside a half-dozen other hats just like it.

"Well, Jack, when you're not fully engaged with the suffrage question, what occupies your time?"

"Shakespeare, sir," said Jack. "I'm a descendant."

"What? Lord, d'you hear that, Thorne? Oh, he's gone off to fetch our supper. Never mind, come along with me. You must tell me more!"

In the dining room they found the butler hurriedly setting a second place at the long table, then bowing and retiring. The Duke directed Jack to one seat and took the opposite for himself.

"Do you go often to the theater?" said Jack.

"Alas, not since I was a lad, when I was sometimes taken by my mama."

"Pity. I'm an actor, by trade."

"A celebrity! And a descendant of the Bard, you say?"

Jack shrugged and nodded. "Through no virtue of my own, sir."

"Ha! I studied him, of course, and used to know a deal of his verse by heart, but now?" He shook his head.

Jack studied his host for a moment and then took a chance. "There is a tide in the affairs of men," he orated, "which, taken at the flood, leads on to fortune!"

The Duke applauded. "Bravo, sir, bravo!"

Dinner was served by the elderly Thorne.

"I don't keep many servants, Jack. Poor old Thorne here is the only one admitted to the *inner sanctum*. He was a young man here in my papa's day, weren't you, Thorne?"

"Indeed, my lord," replied the butler.

"The rest of the staff I house in the old winery. Having people about puts me on edge, d'you know what I mean?"

Jack nodded.

Why me, he wondered. Did the Duke fancy him? If so, Jack would nip that in the bud. During the meal, Jack did his best to resist looking directly at Seabury, keeping his eyes on his plate the rest of the time.

"You're quite right, of course," said Seabury, "when you say it's the women's vote that's lying in wait. There's the real danger."

"Indeed, sir."

The two of them were like-minded! Perhaps it was as simple as that. Here was a Duke offering him his friendship! Eccentric, but wasn't that just the way with great men?

"Did you know, Jack, that Victoria, until she was eighteen years of age, was not allowed to go up or down a flight of stairs without someone holding her hand? Because, of course, she had a good chance of becoming Queen, and her mama feared she might fall. So there she was, on mother's orders, always accompanied by governess or nanny, always held by the hand, always watched. The day she was crowned, Victoria—who was a cousin of mine at some remove, I forget which—had her mother shipped out of Buckingham Palace posthaste."

"I did not know that, sir," said Jack.

"You see, I'm trying to explain myself, and doing it badly. Trying to explain why I've invited you here when I've invited so very few."

Jack stared, then remembered he was not supposed to stare.

"Although no one ever held *my* hand," said Seabury, "I *was* a sickly child, and while the former Duke, my papa, didn't care much one way or the other about me—nor did Mama, really—because of my health, the staff were ordered never to let me out of their sight. *Not ever.* So I took to hiding from them. Again and again. Sometimes for days. I imagine Victoria wished she could do the same, now and then. My own parents were never the wiser, but staff were often frantic." He turned to the butler who stood at the sideboard. "D'you remember, Thorne?"

Thorne cleared his throat. "Oh, yes, my lord, you led my parents a merry chase."

"I suppose I'm hiding from them still." The Duke sighed. "One friend I had. Only one. A gardener. He found me repeatedly, but he didn't turn me over to the others. He brought me food instead. Little lunches, bread and cheese, which we shared. Until someone else would find me. Eventually they realized the gardener was helping me, so he was let go. Big black beard like yours, Jack, and a bit of a Yorkshire accent, like yours. In fact, he looked so like you, I thought of you as an echo of my past. D'you remember him, Thorne?"

Thorne looked down at Jack Hall with his hooded eyes, and then looked away.

"I do indeed, my lord."

When they'd finished the pudding, Seabury rose.

"Do you like tunnels, Jack?"

Jack managed a noncommittal smile.

"It's all tunnels here. Within the house there are passages put in by me and known only to me. And beneath the house, well, it's *all* tunnels. I can get from here to the river, and up again almost to St. Paul's without anyone the wiser. A brewery used to be on this side, and a winery on the other, and I bought 'em both for their belowground chambers, y'see? My workmen dig in the dead of night and tip the dirt into the streams that run beneath London. They find all manner of Roman bric-a-brac—it's great fun."

Not knowing what to say, Jack said nothing.

"They're doing their best to ruin my fun, of course, the aldermen and the fools in the Commons. They've got this man, Bazalgette, digging up all London to put in a bloody great sewer. I've got a case at law against him and his diggers and the aldermen and the lot! They're infringing upon my liberty, and I don't mean to stand for it! Let me show you something."

The Duke led him past somber portraits, presumably likenesses of his ancestors, to the rear of the dining room. There was hung a painting that featured a profusion of blossoms. It was the only work in the room that did *not* feature an ancestor. When Seabury touched the single robin nestled among the flowers, that section of wall swung open. He looked at Jack gleefully.

"Not the only secret door in the house, I'll have you know. It's such fun!"

He led Jack down a short flight of steps. At the bottom, Seabury turned a knob on the wall and, with a whoosh and a series of pops, gas lamps ignited and revealed a row of doors set along one wall, beyond which lay a vast unlit chamber.

"Yonder's where they kept the vats of beer, Jack. These little rooms here were the brewery offices, I imagine, but now look—they're door-ways, passages!"

Each cubicle bore a sign.

BREAD STREET

SHOE STREET

THREADNEEDLE STREET

WATER LANE

"I'll take you through some of them sometime, if you like," said the Duke. "You go along unseen by anyone, and then you emerge above-ground from some nondescript door and no one pays you the least bit of attention!"

A grin creased Seabury's cadaverous face, revealing an uneven row of yellowed teeth.

"Remarkable, sir," said Jack.

"Well, young man, it's an old man's folly, but it gives one something to do. All this is strictly between us, you understand."

"Oh, yes, sir—it goes without saying."

Seabury looked at Jack speculatively. "In that case, I'll show you something truly remarkable. Follow me." The old man led Jack a short distance beyond the lit area. "Mind how you go."

There was a sound of moving water somewhere nearby and then a *pop!* and another light flared up. The door bore no sign. The Duke opened it with a key. There before them was a young man straddling a bull, holding up its head with one hand and plunging a knife into its neck with the other. The light glinted warmly off the white marble with which the figure had been sculpted eighteen hundred years earlier. The men beheld it in the silence it seemed to command.

Finally, the Duke said, "The great god Mithras. My workmen came upon it. See there? A brass seat with hints remaining here and there of gilding. For a priest or leader to sit on and meditate upon the god."

Jack nodded mutely.

"Well," said Seabury, "the night is getting on and it's time you must be going. I do hope you'll come again!"

12

The play featured at the Adelphi was *Go to Putney*, a farce whose title was taken from a colloquial euphemism for "go to hell (on a pig)." Inspector Field witnessed the last half of the last act. As soon as the curtain fell, he made straight for the Lamb and Flag across the road and ordered a double whiskey before the place began to fill with other theatergoers.

He devoted his attention to the door and soon was rewarded by the sight of the full black beard and pomaded, swept-back hair of the veteran actor for whom he'd left a note at the stage door, Mr. Arthur Tuttle. Field gave him a quick appraisal. Had this been Alice Wheeler's lover and killer? Tuttle stopped just inside the door, surveying the crowd while a man with him took his cape and hat. Now Field stared at the actor pointedly, and when he was sure he had Tuttle's attention, he raised both his glass and his eyebrows by way of invitation.

The actor condescended to bestow a wry smile in Field's direction as he approached.

"Bravo, sir," said Field. "What will you have?"

"Gin. Kind of you. You enjoyed our little piece of nonsense?"

"If you mean did I enjoy the observations of the sea captain in the play, I did, sir, I did. Naval man myself. Retired. Field's the name."

Tuttle sighed and shook his head. "It's not *Lear*, but I feel I *was* able to squeeze a drop of nectar from the embryo playwright's unripe fruit."

Good Lord.

"I witnessed your *Lear* a couple years back, Mr. Tuttle," said Field honestly. "Top-notch."

Tuttle brightened visibly. "You thought so?"

"What does it matter what I thought, sir? I'm nobody. But the critics? Unanimous."

The actor allowed himself a self-deprecating smile. "Well, so they were. I see that what's-his-name—*Percy*—has found us a table." He nodded in the direction of the person who'd taken Tuttle's cape and hat and who now stood waiting. "My regular man required the night off, but so far, with this *Percy*, I've nothing to complain of. Would you care to sit, Mr. Field?"

"Honored. Let me settle up." Field dug in his pocket for coins, laying a couple out on the bar, along with a square of embroidered fabric. Tuttle looked from the bar to Field's face, his demeanor changing.

"What's that you've got there?"

"What, this?" said Field, and slid the bit of fabric across to the actor. "Not sure where I picked it up. Pretty little thing. After you, sir." Field took his glass and Tuttle's and waited for the actor to lead the way.

Tuttle stared at the red rose, then clapped it to his heart. "Sound trumpets!" he said with sudden passion.

Heads turned throughout the pub.

"Let our bloody colors wave! And either victory, or else the grave!"

Field stared.

"I was younger then, of course," said Tuttle in a more normal voice, crossing to the table. His man pulled back a chair and the actor sat. "Played all the Henrys. Makes one pine for the Wars of the Roses. This is *Percy*, Mr. Field, my substitute dresser. Percy, meet Mr. Field."

Percy, a pimple-cheeked young man with ginger hair, made a bow.

The actor's stentorian voice rose again. "Once more unto the breach, dear friends; once more! Or close the wall up with our English dead!"

Again, heads in the tavern turned toward Tuttle. There was a smattering of applause; whether it was sincere or ironic was hard to tell.

Field stood suddenly. "Hark!" he declaimed, "the shrill trumpet sounds, to horse, away, My soul's in arms, and eager for the fray!"

Now it was Tuttle's turn to stare. Field sat again and said, "I long ago wished to go on the stage, sir."

"You should have done so, Mr. Field!" declared Tuttle.

"'What fates impose, that men must needs abide,' sir."

"True enough." Tuttle turned to his dresser. "Percy, fetch us more drinks. And do have whatever you will for yourself, Percy."

"Very kind, sir," murmured the young man, and he slipped off to the bar.

"My usual man is another case like yours, Mr. Field. He had high hopes, aimed at theatrical stardom, and became instead a lowly dresser. It's not for everyone, of course, the actor's life."

"My little red rose put you in mind of Shakespeare?"

"Of course, sir. House of bloody Lancaster, the Bard's playground. I went right through the lot. Now?" Tuttle's face fell. "I'm the cantankerous old sea captain in a work of no merit whatsoever. Sad times, Field. Very." He downed his gin.

Did the embroidery have no effect on the man except to remind him of past glories and present mediocrity? The dresser returned, managing to carry a fresh gin for Tuttle, a whiskey for the inspector, and a half-pint of cider for himself.

"In sad times, Mr. Tuttle," said Field, "I turn to family for comfort. Do you not?"

"Family?" He threw his arms wide to embrace the occupants of the Lamb and Flag and, by extension, the universe. *"This* is my family! *You* are my family! The yearning faces looking to the lit-up stage for inspiration and consolation—*they* are family to me, sir!"

Dear God.

"And among the yearning faces in the dark," said Field, "are there no closer loved ones? No Mrs. Tuttle, no little Tuttles, no grand-Tuttles to comfort you, to carry on the family heritage?"

"I have led the life of a vagabond, Mr. Field, from one engagement to the next. You imagine my existence to be bathed in adulation and glory. Well, ofttimes it is. But behind all that are the one-night engagements, the cheap inns, the bad food. I have known love. Indeed, *passion.* But always on the fly, sir, always."

There isn't enough whiskey in the West End to get me through this.

"What about young Alice Wheeler, then, ducks?" said Field. "Does your pretty little niece not count at all in terms of family?"

The actor and the dresser stared at Field.

"Niece?"

"The young woman you asked to embroider that red rose for you, Mr. Tuttle— *that* niece."

Tuttle realized he was still holding the square of fabric. He tossed it across the table to Field.

"I have no niece, sir."

"Well," said Field, "you certainly don't have a niece named Alice any longer, on account of her being newly dead."

"Alice?"

"Was she your niece or your lover or both?"

The actor shook his head and turned to his dresser. "It's happened again, Jack. Oh, sorry, *Percy.* Fetch my things." Percy nodded and went to the hat rack in the corner.

"What's that, then?" said Field. "What's happened?"

"Did you know, sir, the word 'fan' is short for 'fanatic'? Every now and again a person will pose as a fan and turn out to be a complete lunatic." He stood. "I don't know how I should have a niece, given that neither of my parents had siblings."

As the dresser draped the actor's cloak over his shoulders, Tuttle downed his gin.

"I bid you good night, Mr. Field."

He swept out of the pub, followed by Percy, who drank his cider as he went.

Prudence herself said she was unsure of the name of Alice Wheeler's lover, thought Field. *And for this I went to* Putney!

13

W hile Jane Field and Belinda sat up in the kitchen waiting for Mr. Field and Tom to return, Jane tried to
explain to her daughter why the appearance of an
embroidered rose earlier in the day had so unnerved her. Belinda and Tom
knew about her service with Florence Nightingale during the Crimean
War; it was one of Jane's proudest stories. But now she finally told her
daughter about the man who had stalked and killed women at Scutari—
women who wore the identifying uniform of the Nightingale nurse.

Belinda watched her mother carefully. "There's more, isn't there," she
said.

"He attacked me as well, Belinda."

The normally effusive young woman spoke quietly. "Yes? Go on,
please."

"I thought it was a fly that landed on my throat, we had plenty of
flies at Balaclava. But it wasn't a fly. I fought him off, and he ran away

like the coward he was. Never forget, Belinda: one must fight. A man who attacks a woman is obviously a coward, it stands to reason, don't it."

"What happened to him?"

"He killed himself," said Jane. "We think."

Belinda gave her mother a sharp glance. "You *think*?"

Just then a key turned in the street door, the two women stood, and the inspector came down the steps into the kitchen.

"You're very late," said Jane. "Where's Tom?"

"He stayed on with Llewellyn for a bit."

"Stayed on where? Why?"

Field looked from his wife to his daughter. "Sit down, please, both of you."

He sat with them and quietly told them about the murdered women, the rose-patterned embroidery found on one yesterday, and the sewing pattern on the other, killed just today. Belinda stared straight ahead, taking it in, but Jane shut her eyes as she listened.

"I am sorry to bring such news into this house," Field said when he'd finished.

Jane opened her eyes and wiped the tears from them.

"It's for *them* I'm sorry. He's back, then?"

Field glanced from his wife to his daughter.

"I told Belinda about Scutari, Charles, she knows. Are you saying he's back, after all these years?"

"I don't see how he can be."

"It's someone else?"

"Yes, unless the dead rise again."

"Maybe, Charles, he didn't die."

"He did, though," said Field. "And now we've got someone *else* who wants to boast of his deeds by attaching this signature. What's he after? What's the point of it?"

"Same as it was all those years ago, I expect," said Jane. "To menace women. To keep us down. It would have worked, too, if it wasn't for Miss Nightingale's being so stubborn."

Again, a key turned in the street door, and moments later, Tom, looking somber, came down the steps into the kitchen.

"You all right, Tom?" said Belinda, and he nodded.

Jane got to her feet and moved to the range. "I've cakes in the pantry," she said, lighting the flame beneath the kettle.

"A grand idea, Mrs. Field," said the inspector, and Jane went off to fetch them. In a lowered voice Field said, "What did Llewellyn get out of the girl?"

Tom bristled; there was something about the tone. "What did he get out of the girl?" said Tom. "You mean Sister Prudence?"

"Yes, yes, who do you think I mean?"

Tom took a deep breath. His surrogate father had often rubbed him the wrong way throughout Tom's adolescence and did still. Logically or not, Tom sometimes even resented the fact that the man had saved his life.

Never allowed to tell him to sod off, am I.

"Tom?" said Field.

"Detective Inspector Llewellyn asked Sister Prudence to tell him about Sister Alice's beau."

"And?"

"Pru said she only saw the man briefly, once when he showed up on the wards and once more, at a distance, when she saw Alice meet him in the gazebo. Maybe forty-five years old, maybe fifty, maybe more. Hair combed back, black or graying. Full beard."

"That would be about right for Arthur Tuttle," said Field, "with whom I just now spent a delightful half hour. It would also describe a thousand or so other men in London. *Pru*, is it?"

Tom's face flushed, and Belinda looked from one man to the other, feeling the tension between them.

"She *asked* us to call her that—Mr. Llewellyn and me, both!"

"Did she now," said Field, raising his eyebrows. "A very wise man once said, 'Never take a fancy to a witness.'"

"She's scared, sir."

"That wise man was *me*, son."

"Oh, *do* sod off, Mr. Field!"

"Now just one minute!" The inspector rose, and Belinda jumped up as well, looking anxiously between the two men. Just then Jane emerged from the pantry bearing a platter of cakes and stopped, taking in the scene.

"Charles?" Jane said. "Tom? Belinda?" All three of them knew that crisp tone of voice from past experience. "Sit down, please."

They did so. Jane filled the teapot with bubbling hot water and put the platter on the table. No one moved.

"*Well, go on!*" said Jane.

Belinda grabbed a cake, and then so did the men. The four of them ate the sweets, but silently. Finally, Field cleared his throat and spoke.

"Tom, what you did today, refusing to fire on the crowd—well, I'm proud of you."

But Tom was staring at his adoptive sister. There was a twitch happening about her eyes, and a slight jerk to her head, tics she'd had when Tom first knew her, when she was a young girl and they both were captives of a madman. Now it reappeared only rarely, when she was particularly upset.

"Belinda?" he said, "are you all right, then?"

She nodded and managed a smile. "The trouble is, Tom, sometimes the past comes back. Ask Mother."

Jane reached across the table and squeezed Belinda's hand.

"It's gone bedtime for all of us," she said. "Shall we go up together, Belinda?"

The young woman nodded.

"You're safe with us now," said Field. "I promise."

"Are you saying 'all will be well'?" The inspector looked suddenly stricken. "Sorry, Father, I couldn't help myself."

She gave him and Tom a peck on the cheek, then climbed the steps with Jane.

"Tom?" said Field. "How about you? You all right?"

The young man shrugged. "Disobeyed orders, didn't I. They're not like to forget it, the brass."

"It'll come right, son."

Tom smiled and shook his head. "Doubt it. Good night, sir." He started out and then turned back. "It's just this. We all act like Belinda's the same as any other girl. She's not, not after what she went through, living with that man, that Decimus Cobb." It was one of the few times in the seven years since his imprisonment with Cobb that Tom had spoken the name. "Me neither, matter o' fact. I'm not *normal*, but with me you can see how not normal I am." He pointed to his disfigured ear and attempted a laugh.

"Tom . . ." said Field.

"Everybody can see it. That's just the way it is, ain't it. But with Belinda, it don't show. She lived with what I lived with and saw what I saw. You can't say to her 'act like a lady, act like a normal person,' because she's not one. We have to be careful for her."

Field nodded and Tom climbed the stairs.

WELL INTO THE night Charles Field lay awake beside his sleeping wife. The nightmare into which he'd been thrust twelve years earlier had also brought into his life his greatest joy, his own dear Jane. Now, for his wife, the nightmare had returned. For Miss Nightingale herself, the nightmare had returned.

But the girl lying back there in the gazebo won't ever wake from hers. Nor will Susan Hythe-Cooper. Someone's on a tear and no one's safe, no women certainly. It's the Beast of the Crimean all over again.

He confessed to his crimes! They were his final words before dying!

Field slept fitfully. Miss Nightingale's words sounded again and again in his ears.

Just think how often it happens that we mistake one thing for another.

PART TWO

SCUTARI, TURKEY, 1854

H is journey out to the Ottoman Empire had turned out to be long and uncomfortable but filled with interest. It seemed *everyone* was on their way to Turkey these days, with the great armies of Europe uniting to repel the Russian invasion of the Crimean Peninsula. It all was so exciting. And once he arrived, the air of Scutari itself, stinking of decay and death, held something of the exotic for him with every breath. It moved him to seek out adventure.

His sort.

From one tavern to the next, he gauged the possibilities. There were girls for sale everywhere, that would be no problem. But that was no different from back home, and he was here searching for a brand-new stage on which to perform. Finally, in the seediest of the bars he visited, a broken-down wood-framed structure nearly tilting into the harbor, he'd found his miracle, an old Italian. The man actually had begged to be heard!

"Mi benedica padre, perche ho peccato . . ."

"I don't speak Italian, old man, if that's your lingo."

And the old man switched to English!

"Father, forgive me, for I have sinned . . ."

He stopped the Italian again. "No concern of mine, old man. D'you mind standing off a bit, you *do* reek, you know."

But the Italian was desperate to speak.

No one listened to him *ever*, he said. And he had something to confess.

It was so hard to make people understand his anguish. He had given up on the priests. Whenever he started to tell them about his vision, how the Holy Mother finally had found him at Marseille and demanded of him a reckoning for his past sins, standing before him wrapped in blue flame, burning him with her eyes, the priests would cut him off. He was dismissed as a madman. When in desperation he approached the Marseille police with the confession insisted upon by the Holy Mother, they had laughed at him and sent him packing.

But *this* man seemed different. Sympathetic, understanding. Respectful. He wanted to know every detail of his story. It took the older man nearly an hour to explain his past and the crimes he had committed. He had repented years ago, because *the Holy Mother demanded it.*

"Yes, quite. You sewed *what* over their mouths?"

The Italian had hesitated.

"Tell me," said the man.

And then, shamefacedly, Massimo produced from his worn coat a coarse square of sailcloth onto which a red blossom was embroidered.

"You don't do this anymore, Massimo? I mean, with the women and all?"

"Never! Not for many years!"

"Why not?"

"Because is wrong! Because I am ashame!"

"I should think so." The newcomer drew the brightly colored rose to him and regarded it closely. "I imagine this was your signature back then, so to speak."

"*Cosa?*"

The man looked off, as if in thought. "If someone found this where it oughtn't to be, they'd think of you, wouldn't they."

"I do not understand," said Massimo.

"How much d'you want for it?"

For the first time, the Italian looked at the newcomer as if he regretted confessing to this particular man. There was something *off* about him.

"How much would you want for, say, five of these?"

The man signaled the waiter, summoning more drink, and laid a row of coins on the table.

And for the old man—and for the newcomer—that was that.

14

LATE SEPTEMBER 1855

For Inspector Field, the journey to Scutari was a blur.

His travel difficulties began in London, as he made fare-wells to certain young women, none of whom was aware of the others' existence. One of them, a young widow, suggested that Mr. Field might be liable for a breach of promise action.

"My dear," Field had said, "I never could have aspired to your hand in marriage, you know that. You belong to a higher station in life by far and deserve a better man than I." He blushed as he said it, the words of the war secretary sounding in his ears. "Forgive me if I've worshipped at the altar of your beauty, unworthy as I am to have done so."

"Do get out."

Soon, though, he shut up his small flat and was off. Field had never before crossed the Channel, and his first passage was far from smooth.

On the French side, a series of carriages carried him on spotty roads to Paris, his back and bottom suffering with every jolt. Paris itself got Field's attention as he passed through it, but soon he was heading south toward Marseille, changing carriages and horses at every stage. He shared the conveyances with French men and women who, to his mind, had a great deal to say to one another, at great speed, *and not a word intelligible.*

Even on the Continent, Field was known as the inspiration for Charles Dickens' Inspector Bucket, and when he reached Marseille, a local policeman met his coach.

"Inspector Field, I am Pierre Jean-Louis Hyacinth Manuel of the Police Nationale," he said, offering his hand, "but friends and family, and even some of my enemies, call me Hyacinth. I hope you will do the same and come dine with me."

Field shook the man's hand and accepted the invitation gratefully. He was travel-weary and faced the long sea journey to the Ottoman Empire in the morning. "Hyacinth? Truly?"

"Yes, indeed."

"I never before heard of a bloke named for a blossom, but travel expands one's horizons, I'm told."

"Inspector," said the Frenchman, "before it was a blossom, it was a boy! A Greek boy who came to a bad end, but let us not think about that."

The two policemen, about the same age, enjoyed a lively conversation over dinner, talking shop for the most part, about malefactors they'd pursued, apprehended, or missed. As to the present mission, Hyacinth was surprised to learn, first, that Field had been dispatched such a distance to investigate a single murder and, second, that he'd been sent by none other than the British secretary of state at war Sidney Herbert.

"*Oh, mon Dieu!* You poor sod, sir!" said the Frenchman. "Is that the right word, Charles? I mean, one policeman to another?"

"It's precisely the right word, my friend. Either I get lucky, or I shouldn't bother to return, that's pretty much the message I took away with me."

Hyacinth whistled. "Perhaps it's not an ordinary killing, then?"

When Field told him about the fabric covering the victim's mouth, the Frenchman became grave. "I don't like it, Inspector Field. It suggests to me *la rituelle, le fétiche.*"

"I'm guessing those words are other ways of saying 'you poor sod.'"

"Indeed. This is perhaps a habit for your killer."

"Meaning, he's like to do it again," said Field.

"Or has done so already."

The waiter came and cleared away the dishes. To lighten the mood, perhaps, Hyacinth mentioned his wife and two children with pride and seemed to expect Field to reciprocate, but the inspector did not. The awkwardness passed, though, when dessert and brandies arrived at the table.

"If I ever am able to be of assistance, Charles," said Hyacinth at the end of the evening, "I do hope you will call on me."

"And you me, sir!"

The inspector set out across the Mediterranean for the Ottoman Empire the next morning. The late September sea was rough, but the steamship made good time, even so, coming into the Scutari harbor on the morning of the fifth of October. Instantly, Field was swept into a swiftly moving stream of men and beasts, alien tongues, sights, sounds, and odors. Turkish, French, Sardinian, and British soldiers swarmed the crowded harbor, coming and going. Field had no trouble spotting the Barrack Hospital: it stood on the promontory above the bay, a massive square structure with a high tower at each corner. The policeman hoisted his satchel and made his way up the hill.

Ragged children ran alongside him, begging for coins or bread. *Mister, Mister!*

Men pulled and prodded wild-eyed horses up the muddy road to the town above, while in the ditches feral dogs chewed furtively at the rotting corpses of mules and other nameless creatures.

Mister!

The stench was staggering.

And somewhere in all this stinking mess is a man who sewed a rose onto a woman.

15

Field hadn't enjoyed an abundance of sleep on his sea voyage. His legs were wobbly beneath him, and his traveling bag grew heavier with every step along the building's long facade.

Where'd they put the bloody door?

The Barrack Hospital was so named because it once had been the principal barracks of the Ottoman armies, and the structure was enormous. The inspector finally came to an arched entrance from which emerged a pair of gentlemen wearing blood-flecked white frock coats. Field stopped them, asking where he might find Miss Florence Nightingale.

The two of them looked him up and down. "Reporter, are you?" said one.

The inspector was about to introduce himself when he thought better of it. "That's right," he said.

"If I had any say in the matter, you fellows would be locked up for the duration."

"Or shot as traitors," said the other.

The pair walked on.

Already popular, and I only just got here!

Field picked up his satchel and marched into the hospital, where he soon found a porter.

"Detective Inspector Field of the Metropolitan Police, London, here to see the hospital director, Dr. Hall."

"Yes, sir," replied the porter. "If you'd follow me, sir."

As they walked, they passed wards in which Field glimpsed uniformed women moving among rows of beds. The porter led him to one of the corner staircases, and they began to climb. At the top floor, along a broad corridor, was a row of open windows with a view of the sea. Field paused for a moment to inhale the fresh breezes. Four floors below, the grass was dotted with crosses. Clearly, it was a cemetery.

"Inspector?"

Field turned from the window to find the porter gone. In his place stood a clean-shaven, fair-haired young man with a prominent brow and high hairline. He had a quiet, deferential manner, and the hint of a Yorkshire accent.

"I'm John Stanhope, sir," he said. "Dr. Hall will see you now." He took Field's satchel from him, opened the door, and gestured him in.

A vast expanse of Persian carpet lay before him. At its far end stood a middle-aged man of erect military bearing, his hands clasped behind his back. His hair was black except for a dab of white at the widow's peak, dabs in the mutton-chop side whiskers, and another brushstroke of white down his chin.

"Inspector Field," barked the man with the military bearing, "John Hall. Will you take tea or something stronger?"

"Thank you, Dr. Hall," said Field. "Something stronger, if you please."

Hall's thin lips relaxed marginally, and he clapped twice. "Hanif!"

A servant wearing Indian garb bowed at a sideboard and took the stopper from a crystal decanter. He poured two whiskies and placed them on a silver platter. Meanwhile, neither Hall nor Field had moved. Stanhope had taken himself to a far corner and stood, apparently ready to be of service but otherwise humbly content to be ignored.

There's a half acre of carpet between me and Dr. Hall, is this how we're to meet, standing at attention and shouting at each down the length of the bloody room?

The silver platter floated toward him, and Field took his drink. Then the servant journeyed slowly to Hall with his. Field fought an impulse to laugh.

"They yanked me out of the Punjab," said Dr. Hall with a nod toward the servant, "and put me in charge of this show."

Field said, "Makes a change, I imagine," for want of anything better to say.

"Miss the grub. The climate. Cheers, sir," said Hall.

"In your eye, Doctor," said Field.

The two men drank. An awkward silence followed. Field turned to the servant at the sideboard.

"And you, Hanif? D'you miss the grub?"

Hanif's eyes widened in surprise.

"The climate?"

But Hanif was not to be drawn, his face becoming a stone mask.

"So," said Dr. Hall, "you've come all the way from London."

Field shrugged and said, "So it would seem, sir."

"You've become quite famous, you know, thanks to Mr. Dickens."

"You mustn't believe all you hear, Doctor."

"Where have they put you?"

"I have a place booked in town," said Field, "but I've not seen it. I came to you straight off my ship."

"Well, that's no good." Dr. Hall suddenly was in motion, voyaging across the room, approaching Field and offering a handshake. "You must be done in. We've plenty of space here in the hospital—let us offer you lodging, for tonight or for however long you might wish."

"That's a kind offer, sir. I must say, I am weary, and I'll take you up on it."

"Certainly, certainly. Do sit."

Field sank so deeply into a sofa that his knees rose almost to his eye level. The whiskey was of the highest quality, and when Hanif quickly appeared at his side and offered a refill, he accepted. The inspector felt himself relax a bit into his plush surroundings. Dr. Hall remained standing.

"May I ask," he said, "how you managed to secure a room in town? The place has been full up since the war began, and the prices are staggering. Stop, don't tell me. Sidney Herbert laid it on for you."

Field smiled and shrugged.

"It's all a bit peculiar, you know, Field," said Hall. "In the midst of deadly conflict, Secretary of State at War Sir Sidney himself dispatches a London policeman to investigate the death of a prostitute?"

"I hadn't heard she was a prostitute."

"Or camp follower, however you want to put it. The second victim was just a worker, a housekeeper, I believe."

"*Second* victim?"

"Found her about a week ago," said Hall. "Oh, of course, you would have still been en route."

"This victim," said Field, "was she similarly defaced? The patch of cloth over the mouth, the rose?"

"Just like the first, yes."

"Well, whatever these women might have been," said Field, "they were cruelly used, and I need to know by who. Have the local police any thoughts?"

"They posit the obvious. The murders had to have been the work of a lunatic, they say, and we agree. Some mad-eyed Turk."

There was a gentle rap at the door, and a young man with a full mustache and a head of thick, wavy brown hair stepped in.

"Oh! Sorry. Shall I . . . ?"

Dr. Hall sighed audibly. "No, Mr. Cox, do come in. Inspector Field, meet Nigel Cox, assistant to the ambassador."

"I hardly see the man, of course," said Cox, "tucked away on his lovely yacht, moored safely offshore!" The young man barked twice, a mirthless laugh. "Wait, now—Inspector Charles Field? Of the Metropolitan?"

"That's right."

Cox started to move toward Field, then stopped. "I am pleased to meet you, sir. I've read about you at length."

"Indeed?"

"Mysterious, ain't it, the red rose attached to the mouths of the women? I assume that's why you're here, the murders and all."

"Mr. Cox!" said Hall. "To what do we owe the pleasure, if I may ask?"

"Oh! Sorry. Yes. It's just, they've had word below, sir, and they're expecting a shipload of sick and wounded from Balaclava within the next hour."

"Thank you, Mr. Cox, that will be all. I'll be sure to tell the ambassador that you long for his company."

"Oh, now—no need for that!"

"Goodbye, Cox," said Hall.

Nigel Cox's face darkened. He bowed and left.

Field looked quizzically at Hall.

"Someone's *nephew*, I believe," said the doctor with distaste.

From his place in the corner, John Stanhope murmured, "He is highly strung."

"Well, gentlemen," said Field, "all this is disturbing, indeed, and I see my work is cut out for me. I'll want to speak with you and the other doctors and interview the Turkish police, but tonight I must introduce myself to Miss Nightingale and then take myself to bed."

"Ah, Miss Nightingale," said Hall. "A generous, well-meaning woman, indeed."

"She's working out to everyone's satisfaction?"

Dr. Hall hesitated, then said, "As I say, her intentions are good. But we are medical doctors. We are also army men. We know our jobs, we've been at them a long, long time. Sometimes the offer of assistance actually can cause more trouble than it's worth."

Field nodded cautiously.

"Still, for a young woman of wealth and high status to leave all that and put herself in such company, well . . . she's got pluck. Stanhope will show you where you can bunk down for the night."

It took Field two attempts before he could extricate himself from the plush sofa. He'd only had two drinks. Hadn't he?

"From the look of you," said Hall, "I'd put off meeting the Nightingale woman until morning."

"Perhaps you're right, sir."

"I speak now as a physician."

As Field followed John Stanhope along the corridors of the Barrack Hospital, he thought of the main case he'd been pursuing when called away on this mission: a doctor, a killer with multiple victims, one after another, operating in Staffordshire. If that was the sort of thing he was dealing with here, it was urgent the individual be stopped. Some appetites were unquenchable.

Stanhope stopped before a door and turned a key, which he then handed to Field. The young man struck a match and lit a lamp on a bedside table. As the light rose, a spacious, elegantly appointed bedroom became visible.

"Nice digs," said Field. "Now, where might I find Miss Nightingale?"

"But I thought . . ."

"A courtesy call, Mr. Stanhope. It's only proper."

16

———

There were fully a dozen people, almost all female, rushing in and out of Nightingale's tower headquarters when Charles Field first saw her. He knew it had to be Nightingale; she was the calm eye of a whirling storm, standing at her desk, answering questions and asking them, issuing orders, and occasionally making entries in a ledger as she stood. Her voice was quiet but had a reedy strength that cut through the seeming chaos about her.

Nightingale glanced in his direction. "May I be of assistance?" she said.

The activity in the room slowed to a stop and all eyes turned to him.

"Miss Nightingale?" he said.

"Yes?"

"Sir Sidney Herbert sent me."

"Oh, of course! How do you do, Mr. Field? Welcome! I must tell you, we are expecting momentarily the arrival of casualties. They're still coming in from the battle that took Sevastopol, you see, and the skirmishing that continues in its aftermath. We'll need everyone to lend a hand, the number of sick and wounded is likely to be very great. D'you think you're up to it? A shame, after your long journey, but it can't be helped, I'm afraid. Still, you look fit enough, so there's that."

Field nodded uncertainly.

She's serious? Yes, I do believe she is!

Nightingale crossed the room and briefly shook his hand.

"Oh dear," she said. "You've been drinking."

"Dr. Hall gave me a drink, yes," said Field, "when I introduced myself."

She waited, as if for him to continue, so he did.

"I may have had a second," he said, feeling like a schoolboy.

"Of course. How jolly. Are you quite certain you're able to assist us?"

Field was by no means sure of this, but he nodded. Nightingale turned to one of the younger women in the room. "Mrs. Rolly, kindly lead our new arrival down to the refectory and feed the poor man something substantial before he faints."

In the days and weeks that followed, Field would come to know Nightingale's breathless speed. He would also come to know Jane Rolly.

THE INJURED AND sick just kept coming, the soldiers borne up from the quay, stretcher after stretcher. They were met by Miss Nightingale and her women for preliminary evaluation and treatment at the Barrack Hospital's portico and then carried by orderlies inside, into the already crowded wards.

As Nightingale moved from one patient to the next, a slender man in the uniform of the naval brigade would say a few words in her ear, as if making introductions. Field observed the pair with interest. Currently the uniformed man and Nightingale stood above a young soldier whose face glistened with sweat; the slings about his right arm and torso were filthy and had come loose. He had soiled himself, and he stank.

"This is Jenkins, Miss Nightingale," said Ordinary Seaman Josiah Kilvert, "a ladderman just like I was."

The boy seemed to recognize Nightingale's name. "Please, miss, don't look at me," he whispered. "I'm not fit to be seen."

"Nonsense, Mr. Jenkins, we'll put you to rights. You're in hospital now." And then she smiled.

The boy wept. Nightingale drew a cloth from her apron and dabbed the sweat from his brow.

"You're an angel, just like I heard," said the boy.

"No, son, I'm just a person." She turned to the slender man. "Shears, please, Mr. Kilvert."

Kilvert produced a pair, and Nightingale cut the slings from the boy's neck and shoulders. When they were off, Field was shocked to see the young man's shirt seemed to be alive and moving. He leaned close to Kilvert's ear. "What, in God's name, is that?"

"Vermin, sir. This lad's been shipboard for days, crossing the Black Sea. They took Sevastopol this time, but my lot didn't. Not four months ago, that was me lyin' there, covered in lice and stinking." He tilted his head in Nightingale's direction and said, "She took care of that."

"Mr. Kilvert was born under a lucky star," said Nightingale as she cut off the young man's shirt. "Instead of shattering his scapula as it was like to do, the Russian bullet that struck him bounced off it and exited his trapezius."

"Fully half my mates never made it across the four hundred yards to the Russian fortification, sir," said Kilvert.

To her patient, Nightingale said, "We'll get you cleaned up and into a proper bed, Mr. Jenkins, and you'll feel a deal better."

"I can take over here with the rest of it, Miss Nightingale," said Jane Rolly, who stood ready with a basin of soapy water.

Charles Field looked at her in wonder. *If that young thing can do work like this with a cheerful demeanor, then so bloody well can I.*

"If you'll let me have the shears, miss," he said, "I'm game."

"Right, then," said Nightingale, passing the scissors to Field and going on with Kilvert to the next pallet.

"Have a care, sir," said Jane. "This man is in pain."

"You'll let me know if I go wrong, won't you, son?" Field said to his new patient.

Jenkins managed a nod.

"You see, Mrs. Rolly, I'm gentler than I look."

Which must have been true, because after he'd been stripped, cleaned, and covered by a blanket, young Jenkins was asleep with a smile on his face as the orderlies bore him into the wards. Another nurse put the soiled clothing into a basket and carried it off to be added to a growing bonfire, which lit the night behind the hospital.

Jane led the way to the next patient, and Field followed after.

"How does your husband feel about you being out here," said the inspector, "doing such work?"

"Oh, I'm not married, sir."

"I thought Miss Nightingale called you missus?"

"All us nurses are called missus, married or not. It's supposed to keep us safe from the officers and doctors, but it don't really work. Miss Nightingale's society friends back in London designed this outfit we're forced to wear for the same reason." Jane indicated the gray dress and cap she and the other nurses were wearing. "It's all to repel men!"

Another of the sisters, a stout, ginger-haired Irishwoman named Clara, laughed and said, "I told Miss Nightingale that I could handle most any hardship and bear most any burden, but if it hadn't been for her, I could not endure this cap!"

"Let's not forget the sash!" The two women laughed. The nurses all wore a diagonal sash with SCUTARI HOSPITAL in bright red letters.

"Where are the doctors?" said Field.

"Well might you ask, sir," said Jane.

Clara said, "The wounded men are generally the lucky ones, sir. The doctors will happily set a broken leg or take off a gangrenous foot, and they're quite good at it. Those men might even survive. But most of this lot, they're simply sick. Dysentery and the like. Cholera. The doctors don't want nothing to do with 'em because there's nothin' they *can* do with 'em, and they're much likelier to die."

"Also," said Jane, "the doctors wouldn't want to catch nothin' themselves, would they." She lowered her voice. "They despise us, Mr. Field. The doctors, the military officers. Even the orderlies! This is their world, you see, and women don't belong in it. You should have seen this place when we first got here, there aren't words to describe it. The filth, the stench. The death. Along comes Miss Nightingale and starts to improve things straightaway. Then the reporter for *The Times* sends off dispatches to London, telling how Miss Florence was turning the hospital round, her and a pack of women. The brass? Well, I never felt such hatred."

"Mrs. Rolly!" Nightingale was two patients ahead of them. "Come along!"

"On my way, Miss Nightingale!" Turning to Field, Jane whispered, "I fear for her, sir, I truly do. That's why you're here, isn't it? After those poor women were killed, I fear for us all."

"Surely you don't imagine it was a doctor or a military person responsible for the attacks?"

The young woman stared at him steadily.

"Mrs. Rolly," said Nightingale again, "I need you!"

"Coming, miss!"

17

Inspector Field had intended to find a quiet moment first thing the next morning when he and Miss Nightingale might sit down together for a private talk but found when he awoke that it was nearly ten. He hurried to make himself presentable. There was water already in the porcelain basin in the room, and he wondered if a servant had filled it before Field retired in the early hours of the morning. Then he saw there was a straight razor unfolded next to the basin. He picked it up and set it down again. It was not his own. It struck him suddenly that he had slept in another man's bed and then indeed noticed a small cameo of a young lady on the bedside table, which he hadn't seen before.

He decided to go unshaven until later in the day. As he left the room, an orderly carrying an armful of linens was passing.

"I say, young man," said Field, "do you know when the usual occupant of this chamber is returning?"

"Not anytime soon, sir," said the orderly, Cockney by his accent.

"He's left all his things, you see."

"Shouldn't wonder. Dr. Talbot expired, sir." The young man pointed a finger to his head and pulled the trigger.

"Really?" said Field.

"Bang, sir!"

"When was this?"

"Dunno, three or so weeks ago?"

"Well, what of his effects?" said Field.

"What of 'em? All yours, if you like."

When the orderly started to hurry on, Field called out to him. "Young man, if you would, kindly give me fresh water in the basin and a cake of shaving soap, if you have it."

"O' course, sir," said the orderly, rolling his eyes. "Just think of this as the Turkish Savoy, sir." And the young man disappeared down the hall.

After several inquiries, the inspector found Florence Nightingale on the hospital's lowest floor, below ground level in what appeared to be a laundry, with a row of red-faced women scrubbing linens in soapy tubs. Nightingale herself stood before a pair of large copper boilers, the first of which had a young man's legs protruding from beneath it.

"Any joy, Mr. Robinson?" said Nightingale.

Field heard a sharp knock, and then Robert Robinson, an Irishman sixteen or seventeen years of age, scuttled from under the copper, a spanner in one hand and rubbing his forehead with the other.

"Yes, miss, I'm happy to say," he said. "Should be just a matter of minutes, miss."

"Well done, Robert. Oh, here's Inspector Field of the Metropolitan Police. Say hallo to Inspector Field, Robert."

"Hallo, sir!"

"Among many other things, Mr. Robinson now escorts our nurses when they leave the Barrack Hospital for any reason after dark. For that matter, he does the same for me, protecting my safety and my virtue and looking out for the muddy bits."

The young man grinned, blushed, and scratched his head of thick black hair.

Field nodded. "How do you do, Mr. Robinson?"

"I'm well, sir."

"When you do your escorting, do you ever see this person who's rumored to be following the nurses?" The inspector glanced at Nightingale. "This bogeyman?"

"Hard to say, sir."

"Why should it be hard? You see him or you don't, it seems to me."

Robinson looked at his boots.

Nightingale said, "Inspector, it may be difficult for you to understand, as it was for me, when I first came out. But what might seem clear-cut and unmistakable in the world we come from is less so here."

Field stared at her. "I'm afraid I don't follow, miss."

"I'm not surprised. Give it time."

Nightingale gingerly patted the great copper boiler. "There was nothing like this here when we arrived. I can't imagine how the army thought the hospital was going to clean its linens without hot water, can you?"

Field shook his head.

"Fortunately, we were able to purchase these in Constantinople."

A woman at work at a nearby washtub looked up at them and said, "All at Miss Nightingale's expense, sir. She won't tell you that, but it's true."

"Good morning, Mrs. Stamm," said Nightingale. "Is your little boy feeling better?"

"He's feeling well enough to run me ragged, miss."

"Happy to hear it!"

Nightingale started to move on along a corridor leading out of the laundry.

"Miss," said Field, "I wonder if I might beg a few minutes in private with you, when you can sit down with me and share what you know of these murders and this stalking of nurses?"

"I shall be happy to share what little I know, sir, but it will have to be in motion and rather less private than you might have wished, for this is a very busy place."

"Of course," said Field. "I'll be quick. The first victim, Miss Nightingale, did you know her?"

"I did not, sir. What an ugly word, 'victim.' Latin for something awful, I imagine. As I understand it, Mrs. Dumphries was a war widow, her husband having been killed in the battle of Inkerman soon after she arrived here to join him. Tragic. No children, I believe, so there's that."

"When did you learn of the murder?"

"It was the morning after the crime was committed. Evidently there had been some debate the night before whether to inform me or not, the subject being unfit for the ears of a lady. Eventually, though, because Mrs. Dumphries was wearing clothing that signified she might be one of my nurses, they deigned to tell me."

"So they brought you along to identify the body?"

"No, indeed, Inspector! Once again, they felt it would be an improper sight for these delicate eyes, which see death in such numbers on a daily basis. Incomprehensible."

"Who is 'they' in this instance?" said Field.

"I believe it was Mr. Stanhope, Dr. Hall's aide. Or perhaps it was one of the ambassador's men, Nigel something. Cox, I believe. Never mind, those two act only on orders from Dr. Hall, or my lord the ambassador. Soon enough it was determined the woman was *not* one of mine, although she wore the cloak and sash of our nurses."

"Is the uniform widely available, then?" said Field.

"I shouldn't think so, they were made expressly for our crew." She turned and led him along a short connecting passage that brought them into a large room where the air was thick with the aromas of beef, mutton, and roasting fowl. On one side was a large open hearth with chickens on spits, and pots of various sizes suspended at varying distances from the flames. On the room's other side were four black ranges, each with men and boys tending pots and fry pans.

A figure presiding over one of these caught Field's eye. It was a man with a large floppy red cloth cap perched at a raffish angle, a purple cape about his shoulders, and a bright yellow apron, stained here and there with splatterings from fry pan and saucepot. He had a modest blond beard edging his chin, and he smiled and hummed as he worked.

"Come along, Inspector," said Nightingale.

They approached the colorfully dressed man.

"Monsieur Soyer?" said Nightingale. Soyer glanced up at her and beamed.

"Ah, mon cher rossignol, bonjour!"

"I'd like to introduce to you Inspector Field, from London. Inspector, this is Monsieur Alexis Soyer."

"How do you do, sir," said Soyer, setting down a ladle and shaking Field's hand.

"Pleased to meet you, Mr. Soyer."

"You may not be aware, Mr. Field," said Nightingale, "but Soyer here is the most famous French chef working in England, fought over by one aristocrat after another and paid vast sums for his services."

"Please, mademoiselle . . ."

"But it's true, sir! Just you drop his name at the Reform Club, Inspector, and see if they don't offer you a membership on the spot. But this man gave up all those commissions and all that income to sail out here with his assistant and lend his expertise for the sake of our sick and wounded soldiers—imagine that!"

The chef shrugged. "One could not be unmoved, if one read *The Times*. There was much to do here, sir."

"When he arrived," said Nightingale, "he found the army cooks routinely boiled meats all day—mutton only, by the way—and when their shift was finished and the mutton distributed, they poured out all the liquid onto the grounds behind the hospital."

"I could not believe it," said the Frenchman.

"He wept," said Nightingale. "This big man standing before you actually shed tears. And then he only *just* was prevented from throttling the nearest cook!"

Soyer appealed to Field. "But sir, what would *you* do? All that flavor, all that goodness, to cast it away! You understand my feelings, I'm sure."

"Certainly," said Field.

"Where is your assistant, Monsieur Soyer?" said Nightingale.

From another range, a slender young Black man, stirring another pot, looked up and said with an accent that suggested a London background, "Right here, miss."

"Inspector Field, meet Mr. Taylor."

"How do you do?" said Field, trying not to display his surprise to see a man of his color in this context.

Mr. Taylor smiled, as if to acknowledge Field's private thoughts. "Call me T.G., sir," he said, and then he winked, adding to the inspector's confusion. "Welcome to Scutari."

"If you'll forgive me asking," said Field, "where are you from, Mr. Taylor?"

"Croydon, sir. You're forgiven."

"It was Mr. Taylor, in fact," said Nightingale, "who identified the body of that poor woman. Wasn't it? Or was it you, Monsieur Soyer?"

The two men glanced at each other and hesitated.

"We both were in the vicinity, mademoiselle," said Soyer. *"C'était tragique."*

"You identified the body?" said Field. "By that, you mean to say you knew the woman?"

"Non," said Soyer. "I knew merely that she was not a Nightingale nurse, never mind her attire."

"I knew her," said T.G. "Mrs. Dumphries. Saw her about, now and then. An awful business."

"Well," said Nightingale, "Inspector Field is here to investigate the crime."

Taylor's attention went back to his pot, and Nightingale started to move off, but Field hesitated.

"I'll want to speak with both of you later," said Field, "about the night of the murder and the, um . . . unique features of the crime."

Nightingale stopped and turned back to Field.

"Mr. Field," she said, "do please assure me that you're not mincing words because of *my* presence?" Her demeanor was suddenly stony. "Because *a lady* is present?"

"Well," said Field, "I didn't like to go into detail, miss."

"On my account. I see. You didn't like to mention the detail I've been *waiting impatiently for you to bring up*. The mutilation of that poor woman, her mouth covered over by *this*!"

Nightingale reached into a pocket in her apron and produced a square of embroidered fabric, stained by dry blood.

"I asked for it, you see," continued Nightingale. "When they'd done their cursory examination, and before they lowered that young woman into a nameless grave, I pestered them until they gave it to me. I'm told the other woman they just recently found had a similar device cruelly attached. Of her, I know nothing, I don't know that our paths ever crossed, but I imagine the authorities disposed of her in a similar, anonymous fashion because of her lowly status as a worker and a female."

Nightingale put the cloth square into Field's hand.

"Mr. Field, please do me the honor of *not* being like all the others."

"Forgive me, miss, if I misspoke."

Alexis Soyer and T. G. Taylor looked on; indeed, the entire kitchen staff was watching the exchange between their beloved leader and this London policeman. After a moment Nightingale gave him a brief smile, relieving the tension in the room. Nodding toward the patch, she said, "Isn't this what you in your world would call a clue?"

"It is, miss," said the inspector.

"It's the Lancaster rose, I imagine," she said. "The Wars of the Roses and all that. Of course, it may have no significance at all other than to represent some person's cruel depravity. What do you think, Mr. Field?"

"At this point, I have no idea."

She nodded. "It's an old English word, 'clue.' It long ago meant 'a ball of thread.' It's said you can use one to find your way out of a labyrinth if you're clever."

She turned on her heel and left him staring after her.

18

Inspector Field found from one day to the next that the military doctors of the Barrack Hospital were almost universally unavailable for interviews. They were fully engaged in the wards. They were visiting patients or operating on them. The doctors were taking their noon meal or dining together in the evening. And in their postprandial hours, John Stanhope explained apologetically, military protocol took effect, an invisible portcullis descended over the upper reaches of the hospital, and the outsider was excluded.

We'll see about that, boyo.

But whether the protocol was intended to thwart his work or not, Field discovered it to be remarkably effective in doing so.

He decided to seek out an old ally, but it took him several days to find him.

Clouds of slowly drifting smoke rendered barely visible the figure seated alone at a table in the far corner of the crowded tavern. He was tilted back in his chair, his head resting against the wall, a cigar in one hand and the other extended rigidly to the table where it clutched a glass. The features of William Howard Russell, correspondent for *The Times* of London, came into focus as Inspector Field drew nearer to him. Below the brim of a crushed hat was a creased brow and a broad stubbly face, mustached and glowering.

"Charlie Field," the man rumbled with an Irish brogue, "sure I thought you'd be in prison by now."

"They'll never take me alive, Willie."

Russell's laugh was a snort. "On the run then, as I thought. There can be no other reason for you to turn up in this pest hole."

"May I join you?"

"May you? Wait—let me first check my dance card." He glanced about him briefly. "Yes, by a miracle I do seem to be free." Russell extended a hand to shake Field's.

"Just back from the front, are you?" said Field.

"The front? What's that? My readers want me to declare the war over now that Sevastopol has fallen, but it falls to me to explain the front's merely shifted. Seriously, Charlie, what in the name of God are you doing out here?"

Field pulled out a chair and sat, looking about at the crowd. "You know, I never before even crossed the Channel."

"Bloody strange choice for your first holiday," said Russell, raising a hand to beckon the barman. "Young man! *Garçon!* A glass for the gentleman!"

"You're getting famous back home, you know, Willie," said Field, "second only to the Nightingale woman."

"I do know, Charlie. That's why I'm sticking *The Times* for a steep rise in pay. The Queen dotes on me, I'm told." The journalist belched and lit a new cigar from the stub of his old one.

A waiter materialized, put a greasy glass on the table, and moved off, seeming to vanish in the murk. Russell filled the glass from the brandy bottle on the table and Field peered about. There were men of all types and several nations standing at the bar and seated at tables scattered here and there. The variety of garb alone was dizzying to him. Beneath the odors of tobacco smoke, dark coffee, yeasty beer, and men's bodies lay a dank stink from the many spittoons.

"Quite a show, ain't it," said Russell. "That table there, with the bottles of red? Sardinians." Five young soldiers in blue were crowded around a too-small table, conversing energetically. "It's Italian, only different, the language they're shouting, but it don't matter 'cause they all talk at once and nobody listens anyway."

Russell nodded in the direction of three uniformed men at the bar speaking with a mustached, white-hatted man in a long blue cloak and billowy orange pantaloons. "The French don't generally favor this place because of their natural superiority, you understand. But you still get a few in here, generally looking to buy a girl. Those Frenchies are negotiating prices with a local purveyor of scrubbers, I imagine. The pimp is having a small cup of what they call coffee out here, although that's not what you or I would call it. Alcohol is forbidden the Muslims, Charlie, but in a port town like this, it represents a good portion of the revenues, so we infidels are free to drink ourselves to oblivion."

"Cheers," said Field, raising his glass and then eyeing its contents doubtfully.

Russell nodded in the direction of a table of glum-looking, grizzled men. "Merchant seamen. Back and forth they go, across the Black Sea and up from the Med. I've been watching that one there, with his face pressed to the table and his eyes shut. I'm not sure he's working on his beauty sleep, I've begun to think the bloke's dead. His mates haven't noticed, or don't care." Russell's laugh became a coughing fit. When he recovered he said, "So what are you about, Detective Inspector Field? There's a story here."

"Perhaps, but it ain't for you, Willie. I need a bit of help."

Russell reached for the bottle and topped himself up. "You're paying, then, I imagine."

"How do you get on with the fellow in charge of the hospital here, Dr. Hall?" said Field.

"Dr. John Hall, in his heart of hearts, wants me dead. But to my face he's all smiles. Same with the lot of 'em. The common soldiers salute me, if no one's looking, but the doctors and the young officers despise me. I'm peaching on 'em, that's how they look on my articles. Of course, none of 'em are used to it, having reporter chappies at the front hanging the military's dirty drawers out before the public. It's a brand-new thing, and guess what? They don't like it!"

Field sniffed the contents of his glass and then moved it away from him. "What do you make of Miss Nightingale?" he asked.

"Quite mad, but then many saints were, I'm told. She's leagues above me. It's well known that God talks to her, but the Lord and I haven't been on speaking terms since I was an altar boy, and that's some time ago now."

"And the brass?" continued Field. "How do they get on with Nightingale?"

"They hate her worse than they hate me. She makes 'em look bad, see? With help from me, of course."

Field leaned across the little table toward the newsman. "It's the strangest thing, Willie: I've been searching *The Times* for your story about the British woman murdered here about three weeks back, found with her mouth sewn shut."

Field observed Russell's demeanor shift from a truculent geniality to a guarded watchfulness.

"Never wrote one."

"Why not?"

"I'm here covering the war, not local crimes."

"You heard about the murder, then?" said Field.

"I may have done. For that matter, how'd you hear of it?"

"Did you know the woman?"

"No!"

"How do you know you didn't know her, Willie?"

The reporter took off his misshapen hat and ran his fingers through his greasy hair. "You mean to say you came out here to investigate a single murder?"

"Since then, there's been another," said Field.

"First I've heard of it. But there's a war on, if you hadn't noticed— we're surrounded by corpses, we've got bodies by the thousand!"

"How did you know you didn't know the first woman?" Field said again.

Russell glanced uneasily from group to group in the smoke-filled tavern. "Saw the body, didn't I."

The inspector raised his eyebrows. "Do tell." Field took the bottle and refilled Russell's glass. "Go on, I'm all ears."

The reporter tossed back his drink. "I was in the next room."

"You *what*?" said Field.

"It's a small community, Inspector Field, you'll find that for yourself before long. The British keep to themselves, for the most part. Now, it happens that when war was declared, a sweet old thing from Luton came out here and opened a little inn. A few rooms, an almost decent bed, an almost decent breakfast. Or you can have your room by the hour. Or the half hour if you're pressed for time, Mrs. Dinkins is very understanding. On the night in question my own pleasures were interrupted by screams coming from the next room over."

"You mean the woman was being murdered, then and there?"

"Oh, no, Charlie—these were the screams of the man she was with. Seems he dozed off after having a go and woke to find his lady dead beside him, with a rose tacked over her mouth." Russell replenished his glass and drank again.

"So she was a prostitute?"

"No, Charlie. Soldier's widow. Mrs. Dumphries was of these female fools who come out here to be with her soldier, and when her soldier gets himself blown up in battle, she's stranded. Penniless. They have to get in the game or they'd starve. There's a whole tribe of these women squatting in a stinking hole by the Barrack Hospital, babies and all. Miss

Nightingale's taken to giving them honest work, some of them, if they're sober enough. Who do you suppose is washing Her Majesty's hospital linen?"

"This isn't quite the story I was told," said the inspector.

"Mother Dinkins must have sent someone running to the Barrack Hospital, because in minutes Dr. Hall's man was on the scene, and Nigel Cox, the ambassador's aide. I imagine they started inventing the official story there and then."

An older man, hollow-eyed and gaunt, was making his way through the tavern, going from table to table. He approached Field and Russell, his hands outstretched imploringly.

"Mi benedica padre, perche ho peccato."

"Yes, yes," said Russell, "we've heard it all before." To Field, Russell said, "An Italian, they call him the Mendicant. He sings for drink money. Big operatic voice, if you can believe it. When the mood takes him, he goes about confessing his sins."

"Mi benedica . . ."

Sounding very like the Irishman he was, Russell, attempting a foreign tongue, said, *"Da quanto tempo non ti confessi,* old chap?"

The man replied, *"Da una ora."*

Russell burst into laughter and waved the man away. "This lost soul has let a whole hour go by without making his confession. Shocking, really."

The waiter with the dirty apron appeared and roughly took the man by the arm. The Mendicant seemed transformed by the touch.

"How dare you, man!" he said in very passable English.

"Out, out, out!" said the waiter, propelling him to the tavern's door as the onlookers laughed.

Field turned back to Russell. "This Mrs. Dumphries," he said, "she was wearing the uniform of a Nightingale nurse?"

"I can't imagine any woman wearing it voluntarily. You've seen it I imagine."

Field nodded.

"But yes," continued Russell, "the sash with the bright red 'Scutari Hospital' was wrapped tightly round her neck. It was what strangled her."

"Good God."

"What's interesting is, whoever did it didn't wake the man lying right there next to the woman, even as a bit of cloth was stitched to her lip. That poor bugger, waking up to a corpse, was out of his mind with terror. He was shaking, sobbing, crouched on the floor, still in his smalls."

"I'll need to talk to him," said Field.

"Well, that'll be difficult, Charlie, on account of him the next day blowing his brains out."

"Who was he, do you know?"

"Man named Talbot," said Russell. "A doctor. 'Physician, heal thyself.' Well, not this time."

Field felt a tingle of gooseflesh along his arms. The razor, the cameo. Field had slept in the man's bed.

Russell pulled Field's untasted glass of brandy toward himself, regarded it thoughtfully, and drank it off. "You have to understand, old friend, they're primitive out here. Brutal. Above all, superstitious. If you spend any time here, you catch it, too. Even the sane ones start talking about the Beast of the Crimean."

"The what?"

"Stalks the streets, say some, cloaked in black, with luminous red eyes. Flies through the night like a bat, say others. Or else it's a vapor that moves silently like a fog, invading you, taking you over. It's sheerest lunacy, Charlie. Ask any whore. She'll tell you all about it."

19

The long, low wooden structure that hugged an outside wall of the Barrack Hospital had been erected by the Turkish army years earlier as a stable to serve its cavalry. The horses were long gone and the stable abandoned. Nurse Jane Rolly, who had volunteered to be Field's escort, paused with him before a door that hung from rusted hinges. "You must watch where you step, Inspector. It's quite possible here and there to go through the floor."

She pulled the door as far as it would creak open, offered him her arm, and led him into a dark void, although outside it was bright day. As Field's eyes adjusted to the low light, sounds came to his ears of babies crying, a rooster crowing, and women talking, scolding, laughing, and weeping. Here and there he saw a flicker of candlelight. He smelled an exhalation of gin before he realized that a woman was standing directly before him, looking up into his face.

"Is this 'im?" she said. "The big London detective, come to save us from the beast?"

"There, there, Nellie," said Jane, "you needn't crowd him so, give the man some room."

"Who's crowdin' who, Sister, with your arm in 'is? I can tell which way the wind blows!"

"All right, Nellie, that's enough!" Jane disengaged her arm awkwardly. "This is Inspector Field of the Metropolitan Police."

"Look everyone!" cried Nellie. "The peelers 'ave arrived!"

"Nellie," said the inspector, "I've come all this way just to talk to you! Tell me about the beast."

The woman's head wobbled a bit and turned lazily round, as if checking surroundings. She looked back at Field.

"Strangest thing, Officer. He's always there, but when you look? Nothin'! You 'aven't got sommat to drink about you, sir? I'm that parched."

Another woman appeared at her side and took her by the arm. "Come along, Nellie." Then, "We're not all like this, sir," she said to Field.

Nellie shook off the woman's hand angrily. "Like *wot*, Fiona? Like someone 'oo traveled to earth's end to be with 'er man when country called? Like someone 'oo broke 'er 'eart out 'ere and was left with nothin', no man, no nothin', 'cause they marched 'im off to Inkerman and never marched 'im back? Is *that* wot you mean, Fiona?"

"There, there, Nellie," said Fiona.

"You ain't the only one, Nellie!" cried another voice.

"That's just it," said Nellie, "I ain't!"

A crowd of women was gathering around them, watching and listening.

To Field, Nellie said, "The officers don't care tuppence for the men, sir, much less do they care 'bout us. The officers, they treat the men like dirt. Skint rations and uniforms in tatters. 'March off now,' they say.

'Bayonets at the ready,' they say. 'Mind you stay well ahead of us!' And when 'alf of 'em are cut down, the brass run back to their officer's clubs, and their servants bring 'em tea and biscuits!"

From some of the other women came denials.

"At Alma and Inkerman, the officers fell with the men, Nellie!" cried one.

"My man wrote me before he died, they brought the letter to me," said another. "Sir George Cathcart led them on valiantly, he wrote, till the Russians cut him down."

"And Lieutenant Dowling!"

"And Major Wynne of the Sixty-Eighth!"

But Nellie by now had given way to tears. "What in God's name is Inkerman, anyway?"

Jane spoke up. "We're so sorry, Nellie, I'm sure."

One woman said, "Most of us is grateful, Sister. Miss Nightingale hires me regular to do the washing."

Another said, "Me, too."

"She's an angel, is Miss Nightingale."

"Who else besides Nellie here," said Field, "got the sense they were being followed, or watched, or maybe threatened?"

"It's hard to say, Inspector," said Fiona. "Is it real, or is it just because of the rumors that you feel ready to jump out of your skin half the time?"

"I never felt nothin'," said another.

"Load o' rubbish," said a third.

"Oh, it ain't rubbish." A woman with an infant in her arms approached. "At the bazaar, at the end of the day, you can pick up scraps of food for near nothin', the stuff they're not goin' to put out the next day. I had my basket full and was hurryin' back here 'cause it was gettin' dark. Didn't hear a sound, but the thing come up from behind and hissed in my ear, nearly stopped me heart. I spun about and couldn't see no face, just a black cloak and a hood. '*Get out*,' it says, clear as clear."

"Is that so?" said Field.

There was nodding and a murmur of assent from a number of the women.

"Well," said Jane Rolly, "my ghoul didn't speak, but I certainly felt someone following me on at least two occasions as I made my way to town and back. Nighttime, this was. Footfalls behind me, and when I'd stop to look, they'd stop, too."

"But you saw no one?" said Field.

"It was dark, and there were doorways and alleys a man could duck into. You can ask the other nurses. There's more than a few of us knew we were being stalked."

"And you and the other nurses were wearing the Nightingale uniform?"

"Oh, yes, sir," said Jane, "we don't stir without it."

Field turned to the woman holding the baby and said, "But *you* weren't wearing this costume?"

"No, sir. Well, I might have borrowed one of their caps I found in the laundry room because there was a chill that night, but no, I wasn't wearin' no uniform."

"I see," said Field. "This is your child?"

"Oh, no, sir. I'm just lookin' after her. Her mother died of the fever a couple of weeks back, so we mind this babe by turns, a few of us."

"Well." Field paused. "You women are to be commended."

"Commended by who?" said a young voice from a farther part of the dark stables.

Field decided to plunge on. "Do any of you have you an idea how Mary Dumphries might have come to be wearing this uniform?"

There was a silence, the women looking at each other. The voice from the back said, "Desperation?"

"Who said that?" said Field. "Come up here where I can see you, if you please."

Picking her way between unseen obstacles, a diminutive girl who looked to Field's eye to be not more than seventeen years of age walked toward him. Her black hair was cut in a fringe, and her eyes were a piercing violet. She obviously took care with her attire and appearance, despite her surroundings.

"By the end," she said, "Mary's clothes were in tatters, she might 'a' picked up anything to keep out the cold. She weren't particular about that, nor what she did for pennies."

"What d'you mean?"

"Twice the pay for same amount o' work, way I look at it."

Someone snickered.

"What's that mean?" said Field.

"That'll be enough, Rose," said Fiona. "Mary was an unfortunate woman, now let's leave it there!"

Field said, "I understand that she prostituted herself, is that right?"

This question prompted averted glances and shuffling feet. An infant began to cry, to which a dog somewhere replied by barking. Field decided to take a different tack.

"Tell me, Rose," he said, "did you lose your husband out here, too?"

She shook her head. "I'm not married, sir. It was my sister I come out here with, but she died on the ship before we ever got here."

"I'm so sorry," said Field.

"Never got to see her Dennis, did she. And then he was gone, too."

Rose looked at Field beneath her neatly cut fringe, her intensely violet eyes boring into him with something between anger and hopelessness.

"As to Mary Dumphries," she said, "what choice had she? Her, with her little boy to feed and clothe? Way I look at it, she didn't have no other way."

"She had a child, Rose?" said Jane Rolly. "This woman had a *child*?"

"Oh, yes, Sister. Proud of him, she was."

"Where's Mary's little boy?" said Fiona, turning to the gathered women. "Who's minding him today, then?"

"Mrs. Stamm," said Rose. "She took him and her own boy out walking."

"How old is Mary's child?" said Jane.

"Four," said Rose. "Misses his mum. We had to tell him she went up to heaven."

She drew a fist across her eyes and then looked Field directly in his. "Sir, if you're here lookin' into her death, here's this. I seen Mary that night, before she went out. Yes, she had got a nurse's cape about her, it was a chill night and wraps is hard to come by. But they said it was a nurse's sash she was strangled by, but she never was wearing such a thing. Why would she? I know the nurses here have got to wear 'em, beggin' your pardon, Mrs. Rolly, but anyone else would look a fool, walkin' about with red letters sayin' 'Scutari Hospital,' wouldn't they? Someone brought it on purpose to do for Mary. Hateful, I call it."

20

The police station at Scutari was a two-story stone structure with barred windows. Field introduced himself to one of the men at the front desk and produced his card, asking if he might speak with the ranking officer. The desk sergeant rose, walked stiffly to a nearby door, and rapped gently. He disappeared inside and a few moments later returned, followed by a thickset man of middle years wearing a tight-fitting green uniform and a bright red fez. His jet-black mustache was immaculately trimmed, waxed, and curled up at the ends. The man was looking between Field's card and Field himself.

"Detective Inspector Charles Field of the Metropolitan Police, London?"

"That's right."

He checked the card again and looked up, shaking his head as if in disbelief.

"Sir, allow me to introduce myself. I am Superintendent Second Class Saleem Tulman of the Scutari Constabulary." Tulman looked keenly into Field's eyes, stepped forward, and thrust out his hand. "May I?"

"Of course," said Field, shaking the man's hand, "by all means. How do you do, Superintendent?"

"It is an honor."

Bewildered, Field said, "The honor's all mine, sir."

"I want you to know, sir, it is in the original that I have read Mr. Charles Dickens. All of it, every word. More than once. It is an unexpected honor, indeed, to meet Inspector Bucket, sir."

"Well," said Field, "I hardly know what to say. I myself have never met this Inspector Bucket, so in a way I envy you."

Superintendent Tulman stared for a moment and then burst into laughter.

"Of course! That is *just* what Mr. Bucket would say! Very good, sir, very good, indeed!"

Tulman gestured, wide-armed and beaming, to the men at the desk and another policeman who stood at attention by the door, seeming to invite his underlings to share in his joy. The baffled men did their best to reciprocate with smiles and nods. Field felt the need to bring the introductions to a close.

"I've come to you about serious matters, Superintendent Tulman."

Tulman's face fell immediately. "Of course! The women, the British women. Come with me."

He led the inspector into his office and begged him to have a seat. "So," said Tulman, "we are dealing with two murders that we know of. Mary Dumphries, killed at the bawdy house. And Helena Swain, another British. She worked as a maid at the Barrack Hospital."

"They tell me at the hospital," said Field, "that Scutari police believe the murders were the work of a lunatic."

"Odd," said Tulman, taking a seat behind his desk. "*I* am the Scutari police, sir, and I am quite certain I did not confide my opinions to anyone at the hospital. Why should I? The officers and doctors would not pay attention, they being British, and me, a lowly Turk." Tulman stared steadily at Field, a sharp glint to his eye.

"That's how it stands with the British, is it?" said Field.

"Oh, sir, the French as well look down on the peoples they have come to save. Never mind. You will understand me, sir. I am a policeman, I have a job to do, whatever the officials may think of me."

"I think I do understand, Officer Tulman. My own superior officer often lets me know how far beneath him I rank in the grand scheme."

Tulman cocked his head and shrugged, as if to acknowledge the universality of such behavior. "Certainly there is lunacy involved here," he said, "the crime is bizarre! But when the British say 'lunatic,' they mean 'not British.'"

Field smiled. He was beginning to like the effusive Saleem Tulman.

"May I ask," said Field, "if you had a chance on the night of the Mary Dumphries murder to interview the doctor who was with her? The man who later blew his brains out?"

"Dr. Talbot? Of course I spoke with him! I believed at first he was the killer! Once I got him to stop his wailing, I asked him many questions! To which he gave evasive answers! But then, Inspector Field, I was told by the ambassador's man that Dr. Talbot could not be detained overnight by authorities of the Ottoman Empire. They whisked him away! 'Will I be able to continue my interrogation tomorrow?' said I. 'Of course!' said they. But in the morning, at the hospital, they said, 'Alas, the doctor has made off with himself!'"

"You said you believed Talbot was the killer *at first*. But no more?"

"Even that very night, sir, I reached a different opinion. To begin with, I thought his fear and trembling came of horror at what he had done, never mind his claims that he was asleep when the woman was strangled." Tulman leaned toward Field and spoke in a confidential tone. "You and I know, sir, that strangling is a noisy, thrashing sort of business."

Field nodded. "Sounds like a lie, don't it, sleeping through all that."

"Indeed, sir. But as I spoke with him further, I came to suspect something more than evasion was going on. The doctor's fear was not born of remorse or apprehension of punishment for the crime of murder. No, this man was in immediate terror, in terror of his own life. This I believe."

"He feared someone?"

Tulman shrugged.

"Do you mean, Superintendent, you doubt Talbot died by suicide?"

The man sighed. "I do not know, Mr. Field. Perhaps Dr. Talbot was after all guilty of this crime and decided that he preferred his own way out to that of the hangman's. But maybe, after being snatched away from my authority by his countrymen, he encountered the person he feared so greatly, and this person stopped his mouth forever."

The superintendent stood and moved to a wooden cabinet of wide drawers. Suddenly he turned back to Field and said, "That rude Frenchman from the hospital, he too came to me that night and interfered with my investigation!"

"How so?"

"He came to take away the young Black man!"

"I don't understand," said Field.

"I found him, the Black—Mr. Taylor, so called—I found him just outside Mrs. Dinkins' bawdy house that night. Was he leaving the scene of the crime? I seized him and questioned him then and there. Made him look upon the body, which was an unlovely sight, sir. Someone must have sent word to the Barrack because the Frenchman showed up in a French temper. He promised to raise the devil with both the English and French officials. You understand, Inspector, we Turks have little power over our benevolent allies. I had no choice but to give him back the Black man, never mind he might be the guilty man, never mind he might have gone back to the hospital and dispatched Dr. Talbot and called it suicide. Here we have two British women cruelly killed, and they tie my hands with their interference!"

Tulman turned back to the cabinet, muttering angrily. He selected a drawer, pulled it out, and from it took two large brown envelopes. He carried them to his desk, sat and opened them. Inside one was the sash Field had seen the nurses wearing at the hospital, with the hospital's name in bright red letters. Tulman laid it out on his desk and put next to it the contents of the other envelope: a long red silk scarf and a square of fabric.

"The breath is stopped by the hospital sash in the one instance," said Tulman. "Pinned to the mouth by a single stitch was the pentagram Miss Nightingale later insisted on possessing."

"Pentagram?" said Field. "I took it for a blossom."

Tulman shrugged. "I see a five-point star, sir, dressed as a rose. It is an ancient symbol. For some, the badge of Lucifer. But you fellows wore it when you invaded my country on your way to the Holy Land."

"*We fellows?*" Field hesitated. "Oh! D'you mean during the Crusades? Before my time, actually."

Tulman gave him a look which seemed to suggest Field's point was irrelevant. Then he returned his attention to the square of fabric. "The other woman was dispatched by this red scarf. To the mouth of this woman was attached this *other* red patch. Why?

It's a pity I let Nightingale's man take the first pentagram, because there was a very interesting difference between the two."

"But she turned it over to me, Superintendent," said Field. He fished in his pockets and came out with the embroidered piece of cloth the nurse had called a clue.

Tulman beamed. "But this is splendid! So like Inspector Bucket! May I?" Tulman laid the two patches side by side. "You see the differences, of course."

"Of course," Field said, picking up each one, feeling them, and examining them front and back. "The one Miss Nightingale gave me, the one that was attached to the body of Mary Dumphries, is made of a coarse linen, and the pattern is sewn onto it."

"The fabric is sailcloth, sir."

"The other," said Field, "from the more recent murder, is a cheap, thin cloth, and the image is stamped on or dyed, not sewn."

"Correct on all counts but one, sir," said Tulman. He held up the bit of dyed fabric. "This was found on the most recent *discovery*, not necessarily the most recent murder. The body of the poor housekeeper on whom this was sewn was thrown in with those of deceased British soldiers at the hospital cemetery. It was found last week when workers went to dig fresh graves and discovered a hand sticking up out of the earth, as though begging for help."

"Is that so?" said Field.

"It is so. Her identification papers, required by law, were on her and quite legible. Helena Swain. British. My coroner guesses her life was ended around the same time as Mary Dumphries was killed."

Field looked at the two squares of cloth again. "Like, and not like."

"Indeed," said Tulman.

"This one is crude," said Field. "Dyed, ready to wear. While the other is handmade, and you might say it's almost elegant."

"At first, I gave it no thought," said Tulman, "but it has been growing on my mind. Does the difference say anything to you, Inspector Field?"

Field hesitated, looking from one patch to the other.

"The woman was not buried deep," said Field.

"Not deep like the soldiers."

"So: hastily buried, in the dead of night most likely. Perhaps our chap who's got a thing for roses hadn't one of his pretty ones at hand, and he had to make do by cutting up a decorated handcloth or napkin." Field shook his head. "But if you're in a hurry, why bother with the bloody roses at all? I can't make it out. There's another answer here, I think, but I'm too thick to see it."

Tulman frowned. "This, of *Inspector Bucket*, I refuse to accept!"

•••

BEFORE RETURNING TO the Barrack Hospital, Field decided to give up the rooms in town the Foreign Office had rented for him. With occasional guidance from townspeople, Field made his way through Scutari to the central market, a crowded, bustling place where vendors shouted and tugged at Field as he passed. When he came upon a textile stall, he paused. Red silk scarves similar to the one he'd just seen at the police station hung by the dozen on wooden pegs. At another stall nearby he found robes decorated with geometric patterns and pentagrams galore. But he saw nothing he would call a rose.

The landlord, when Field found him, was not pleased.

"You will pay me the rent in full, sir! And the damages!"

"Damages?" said the inspector.

"Follow me," said the landlord.

At the top of the stairs the man indignantly directed Field's attention to a door whose lock had been broken. "When you failed to appear, vandals came."

"Well, that's hardly my lookout, now is it?" said Field.

The man threw open the door, revealing a modest sitting-room, and beyond that, a bedroom. On one wall of this room was a crudely painted stick figure, female and obscene, and a few words written in English.

Your next, Britisher Pig!

"I see," said Field. If anti-British feelings of native Turks could be harbored even by the Dickens-loving Superintendent Tulman, they must be widespread. "I imagine I'm the pig in question. I shall do my best to see that you are fully reimbursed by the Foreign Office, sir."

A chill wind made its way up the steep road from the harbor as Charles Field climbed it, deep in thought. As he reached the plateau above, he saw men laboring with shovels in the broad field that lay between the hospital and the cliffs that towered over the sea. The turf beneath Field's feet grew spongy, and here and there gave way. He realized he'd found the vast, ill-defined precincts of the British military cemetery at Scutari.

God knows how many British lads lie here.

To honor the men, and pay respects to the late unremembered Helena Swain, Field took off his hat and bowed his head. A thought interrupted his prayer and he looked up.

Pray God there's not more women hid beneath my feet.

21

Early the next morning, as Field went in search of Dr. John Hall to complain about his lack of access to the medical staff, he heard a loud cry and then a sobbing, pleading voice coming from the ground-floor ward. He hurried along the corridor. Turning into the ward he saw Florence Nightingale standing at a patient's bed, holding his hand, but he was not the source of the piteous cries. Both soldier and Nightingale stared silently at a neighboring bed, and Field realized that all the patients in all the beds along this side of the ward were intent on the same thing. The sobbing rose and fell.

It came from a young man lying not far away. He was surrounded by men in white frock coats. Dr. Hall held a saw in one hand; at his side was a small table laden with surgical instruments. Other men encircled the bed, John Stanhope among them. The orderly at the foot of the bed held a towel and a bucket. Nightingale disengaged from her patient and quickly moved along the rows.

"Her Majesty's army calls upon you to be a *man*, soldier!" Hall was saying. "That foot has to go. Your dancing days will be over, but you'll *live*. Now stop the damn blubbering at once!" Hall nodded to the orderly who stood at the head of the bed. That man pinched shut the patient's nose with one hand, and when the soldier's mouth dropped open to breathe, inserted a leather bit into it.

Nightingale returned, pulling a rolling screen, which she placed before the bed of the impending amputation, thereby hiding the scene from all the other patients on that side of the ward. Field saw Dr. Hall watching her movements in silence. Then the doctor seemed to notice the inspector's presence for the first time.

"Inspector! Come for a drink at the end of the day!"

Like we're on a bleeding rugby pitch! thought Field.

Dr. Hall turned his attention back to the screen, gestured irritably, and Stanhope moved to the screen and wheeled it away. Field felt his face flush. He glanced at Nightingale. She again was holding Jenkins' hand, but her expression was impassive.

"Ready, then," said Hall.

Stanhope and an orderly opposite him gripped the soldier's thighs. The orderly at his head pressed down his shoulders, and the man with the bucket moved closer. When the doctor began to saw, the bit flew out of the soldier's mouth, and his scream hit Field like a blow to the sternum.

IN THE LATE afternoon Inspector Field made his way to the top floor of the hospital, where the vast red carpet awaited him. There were perhaps ten men in Dr. Hall's parlor, and Hanif was serving drinks. Field imagined most of the men were other physicians. There were also two uniformed army officers, one a young man with pink cheeks and ginger hair who was in conversation with Dr. Hall, the other a stout man in his forties who was talking to John Stanhope. There was a palpable air of relief among the medical men, finished with another grim day on the wards. The air was thick with tobacco smoke.

"Inspector," barked Dr. Hall, "come meet one of our success stories, Major Spencer-Churchill."

The smooth-cheeked young man, no more than twenty-five years old, grinned and raised his glass.

"Cheers, Inspector! Spot of fever, took a breather from the war, but fit as fit now. Champing at the bit to get back at it, really. Chase the Russian bear back into his den."

"Happy to hear you're on the mend, Major Spencer-Churchill."

"Do call me Spence, everyone does." The young man pointed to the other officer. "And that's old Coop, of the Hussars."

The stout man nodded coolly, and Field inclined his head. He realized that Stanhope now stood before him, offering him a glass of whiskey.

"Much obliged."

Stanhope smiled. "Sir."

"Remember me, Mr. Field, sir? Nigel Cox, aide to the ambassador?" Cox slurred his words just a bit. Dr. Hall looked askance at him and then looked away.

"Vividly, Mr. Cox," said Field.

One of the doctors, still in his bloodstained smock, approached Field, drink in hand. "Name's Menzies, Inspector. Surgeon."

The accent was Scottish. Field inclined his head. "How do you do?"

"D'you have a *suspect*? Do you anticipate an *arrest*?"

"Not today, Doctor."

"In that case, don't you think, for the safety of these women, you'd better advise the Nightingale woman to take her nurses and return to England before one of *them* falls victim to this madman?"

"I don't believe it's my place to do such a thing, sir," said Field, "seeing as they were dispatched by the war secretary. Besides, they're needed here, ain't they?"

"I think we physicians know what we're about, without some debutante barging in, trailing a ragtag of women of questionable repute."

Questionable repute? You lot have been drinking before I got here, that's sure.

Dr. Hall spoke up, mimicking a woman's voice, Nightingale's presumably. "'Do you employ anesthetic in your surgery, Dr. Hall?' I do *not*! I'd much rather hear a soldier bawl out lustily than sink silently into the grave!"

"Hear, hear!" said a couple of the other men.

Menzies said, "I think we are all agreed, Mr. Field, that you have no business at Scutari and that it's only someone's damned impertinence that got you here!"

There was a moment's stunned silence in the room.

"Hang on a bit, old man," said Spencer-Churchill with a little laugh. To Field, he said, "My family's quite keen on Miss Nightingale, my father knows her father, sort of thing. So: no harm done, none intended?"

"None, indeed," said Field.

"What Dr. Menzies may have meant, Inspector," said Dr. Hall, "is that we are curious to know what is your mission here, precisely?"

The words of the war secretary came back to Field. "A British subject has been murdered, and I'm a British policeman. Simple enough, really."

Dr. Hall persisted. "War secretaries don't generally send constables halfway round the world every time a woman of easy virtue gets her just desserts, believe it or not!"

Easy virtue. Just desserts. Inspector Field knew from experience that his own temper was not always his friend, so he did his best to damp it down. He smiled apologetically and said, "I do what I'm told and go where I'm sent, the decisions aren't my own."

"It's obvious," said Menzies, "it was the Nightingale woman who sent for you."

Field smiled ruefully and shook his head. "You know, this is the first time since I arrived that I've been face-to-face with most of you. If I were a suspicious man, I'd wonder why."

The men stared.

"Fortunately," said Field, "that's not my nature. I know each of you gentlemen will be most eager to assist my inquiries into the violent deaths of two British women. If any one of you has information that might be helpful, please know that you can come to me individually, and in strict confidence, of course. I won't tell a soul."

Dr. Hall said, "You must be joking."

But Field continued as though he hadn't heard. "And this, I'm sure, will be of interest to you. One of the victims, Mary Dumphries by name, a war widow, left behind a child who is now an orphan, and so finds his little self in straitened circumstances. I imagine my friend, Mr. Russell of *The Times*, will convey your tender regard in this light to his many readers back home, including Her Majesty the Queen. She especially will be happy to know that you've each contributed personally to a fund for the little boy and for the other British children who are half-starving in the stables below."

The stout officer set down his drink and walked ostentatiously out of the room.

"I say, Coop! Wait for me!" cried Spencer-Churchill. Quickly turning to Field, he said, "Capital idea, Inspector! Here's a half crown to get it going."

"Thank you, Major!"

The young man dropped the coin into Field's hand and hurried out after the other officer.

Field looked around expectantly at the others. "Anyone else? Later perhaps? I know you'll want to be generous. Cheers!"

Almost instantly Field ceased to be the center of attention. Backs were turned on him, more drinks were poured, and conversation became ever louder. The inspector was about to take a quiet leave of the gathering when he heard a soft, accented voice just behind him.

"I do miss the *grub*, sir." Field turned to see Hanif close by, looking anywhere but at him. "I do miss the climate. I miss my wife, very much." Hanif turned his eyes to the inspector. "I miss the company of decent men."

The servant moved off. Field headed for the door, but Stanhope intercepted him.

"Inspector, will you continue to be stopping with us, or are you moving into your rooms in town?"

"I would just as soon stay on here, if you'll have me."

"By all means, sir!"

Once out of the tobacco smoke and the din of drinking men, Field went to one of the open windows along the corridor. The night air was cold but fresh, and he breathed deeply of it. He *hadn't* hidden his anger, and he knew it. It was a fault he'd given way to all his life.

Temper gets the best of me, and what good does it do?

Lights flickered here and there on the harbor. From far below came the faint sound of someone singing. Field leaned out over the sill but couldn't see the source.

I'm blowed if it ain't opera. Way out here.

It *was* opera, if he had known. Gilda's first-act aria from Verdi's *Rigoletto*.

22

In the morning, a knock at the inspector's door revealed Sister Clara, there to tell him that Miss Nightingale wished to speak with him. Field thanked her and then hastened to dress and ready himself. More than halfway through his shave, he realized blood was dripping from his chin into the porcelain bowl on the nightstand. Rarely did he nick himself. Field held out the razor, the better to look at it, then dropped it on the nightstand. It was the late Dr. Talbot's. He'd been using his own razor for days, how could Talbot's have reappeared on the nightstand?

But there his own razor was, on the opposite side of the porcelain basin. Had he not stowed the other one in the wardrobe? Perhaps he'd only meant to.

He toweled his face dry and attached a sliver of sticking plaster to his chin. As he was on his way out of the room, something else caught his eye. It was the cameo of the young woman, there on the bedside table, just as he'd found it after his first night. But he'd taken the cameo and put it on a shelf of the wardrobe, he knew it. All right—someone was playing unwelcome jokes on him.

Field found Nightingale in her tower office, alone for a change, standing before an open window overlooking the sea, holding a letter but not reading it. She turned and gave him a smile that quickly vanished.

"Oh dear, you've been injured," she said.

Field stared, then realized she was talking about his sticking plaster and was not being serious.

"I'm expected to survive, miss."

She folded the single page letter and inserted it into its envelope.

"I was just thinking about the Aegean, Inspector Field. Come look."

Field joined her at the window.

"The Sea of Marmara, just there, gives into the Aegean," she said. "Azure *here*, the color of slate *there*. But just now I was wondering for how many centuries has the blood of men run into it? During how many wars have its tides washed against these shores? Somewhere out there ancient Troy is supposed to lie, more or less. From Troy to Gallipoli, and how many other battles in between? Now, here we are again. Please have a seat, sir."

Field took a chair before the nurse's desk, but Nightingale remained standing.

"Your presence on the floor yesterday was not helpful." She held up a hand to stop him speaking. "It was no fault of yours. You came upon us by chance, I imagine, and there's no reason you should realize how delicate is the chemistry of the male, being one yourself."

"But, miss—"

Nightingale spoke over him. "Dr. Hall was quite right, of course; the soldier's foot needed to come off. The doctor saved the man's life, and he did it rather well. But when the doctor saw you there, he saw you as a male *witness*, and he was reminded of my presence, and of another ancient war, the one waged eternally, ad nauseam, of men against women. It was a small comfort I tried to give the other patients, a *minute* comfort, but in that context, for that doctor, it was too much."

"But what did *I* have to do with it, Miss Nightingale?"

"Your face, for just an instant, showed your disapproval of Dr. Hall's actions."

"But I *did* disapprove. You tried to spare the others the sight of one of their mates being cut up, and he prevented it."

"I saw your disapproval," said Nightingale, "and I saw Dr. Hall see it. That was all it took to reignite his personal war."

"Well, then, I begin to understand the reception I got at the doctor's drink-up at the end of the day. I'm afraid I made things rather worse for you at that gathering as well."

"I was afraid of that." She held up a hand again. "No. No need to apologize, sir, that's not what I'm seeking. I'm trying to convey what it takes for a woman to accomplish anything whatsoever in a man's world so that you might better understand our situation."

She circled her desk and sat.

"The hospital you see today, with all its faults and dangers, is positively idyllic when compared to what we found here when we arrived. Back then, the mortality rate for the British soldier was staggering. One could argue that the battlefield was hardly more dangerous for the soldier than was this hospital; he was almost as likely to die here. There were few provisions, no linens, no bandages. Very little soap. The food was execrable, and the drains and cesspit beneath this great structure were overflowing. The whole place stank, and it was running with rats. To get from that state of things to this took massive effort. Not by pushing, because there is no pushing the male if one intends to move him. No. One needs to be persistent and never, ever show signs either of weakness or overt resistance."

Field nodded. "The doctors think, because I have not arrested a suspect in the few days I've been here, I should pack all you up and ship you off home."

Nightingale nodded. "For our own good, I imagine."

"Doubtless."

"Do you know who might have killed these women, Miss Nightingale?"

"No! Certainly not."

"Do you have suspicions?"

She hesitated.

"No, not even suspicions, Inspector. But I do have sick and wounded soldiers, and I must be seeing to them now."

Field rose, bowed, and left, glancing back at Nightingale who was staring back at him. What he missed as he left the room was seeing her take up an envelope. She reopened it. On a single sheet of paper had been drawn a crude stick figure. Female. Oversized breasts and pudendum. A savage *X* slashed over the oversized lips. It was violent and obscene. The handwriting was sound, but the spelling made her think of a rude, unlettered boy.

Your next!

Nightingale stared at it for a moment more and then tore it in half twice. It wasn't the first time she'd had a message from this anonymous correspondent.

23

The two men sat at their usual table in the darkest corner of the small tavern at the very edge of the harbor, the older man staring at the empty glass the other had put before him.

"Tell me again."

"Mi benedica, perche ho peccato . . ."

"No, no, no, not that. Just answer my question. In English, old man. What kind of stitch did you use?"

The Mendicant shook his head. *"Non é importante."*

Months earlier, when the man first had heard Massimo Flammia's confession, he seemed to take pity on him, buying him drink and food and listening to him with what he'd taken for sympathy. But slowly Massimo began to fear *he was giving the man ideas*. Perhaps it was not sympathy he aroused in the man, but impure excitement? By then, though, he'd come to rely on the money the man gave him, and the drink, and the listening, even if it was tainted. So great was Massimo's loneliness, he would have told his story to the devil himself, if only he would listen.

"What stitch?" said the man again. "In English!"

"It is simple. Running stitch. To be quick. But I repent long ago."

"Yes, yes, we know all that. But *why*?"

"Because is wrong!"

"No, man. Why did you *do it* in the first place?"

The Mendicant put his head in his hands and muttered.

"I can't hear you!"

The man lifted his head and stared hopelessly at the glass before him. "To close the mouth," he said.

"Exactly! Now, you have something for me?"

Massimo glanced about and then took a flat, worn leather folder from within his threadbare coat. He laid it on the table, and the other man opened it, just a bit, offering a glimpse of embroidered roses.

Suddenly the empty glass was full. The Mendicant picked it up and drank while the other reached into his coin purse and put down two coins on the table, one at a time.

24

Florence Nightingale was telling a story.

Inspector Field had been with the nurses of Scutari for two weeks, and until tonight all he'd ever seen Nightingale do was work, from dawn until late at night. Much of her administrative work involved doing subtle battle with the openly hostile doctors, and a Sphinx-like requisitions clerk who seemed to be sitting on a small warehouse of desperately needed supplies but refused to release them—or even locate them—until a baffling number of forms had been submitted and approved by persons who occupied obscure offices in far-off Whitehall. Meanwhile, the tally of the British dead grew from day to day. But Jane Rolly affirmed what Nightingale had told Field: the numbers were far down from their early days at the Barrack Hospital, when new burial pits were dug with numbing regularity.

The rest of the day Nightingale received patients or attended those already hospitalized. She supervised a nursing staff composed of a variety of women, among whom were a number of rivalries. There were the Irish Catholic sisters, and the Anglican sisters, who looked on the Irish with arch suspicion. Because Nightingale treated both groups equally, the Anglicans decided Florence must be a secret Catholic, and—again according to Jane Rolly—spread rumors to that effect, rumors that reached all the way to London. The working-class nurses like Jane were looked down on almost universally, but it was plain to see that they, and the dedicated Irishwomen, were Nightingale's favorites. It was with the women of Florence Nightingale's own class that she clashed most.

For the most part, though, Field observed Nightingale marshaling her nurses to the care of the British soldier. And when the long day ended, and most others slept, she made the rounds alone, or accompanied by one or another of her devotees, often young Mr. Taylor (T.G.) or Ordinary Seaman Josiah Kilvert. Twice in those early days she gave Field leave to accompany her. From bed to bed, from ward to ward, the nurse walked miles in the night, offering a word, a smile, or a cooling moist cloth to a feverish brow. She often sat beside the sickest of them, writing down their final messages to loved ones back home, taking charge of the soldiers' few remaining coins, and promising to send them on. Sometimes she simply rubbed the cold, hurting feet of the dying, offering comfort until it was no longer needed.

For the first time in British military history, the common British soldier was being cared for with compassion, as a human being. Even the great Wellington had called the common soldier, the men who had helped him defeat Napoleon, *scum of the earth, enlisted for rum.* The soldiers of the Crimean War knew that Miss Nightingale was different, and they revered her for it.

But tonight she had ended her labors earlier than usual. A small group found themselves by invitation in Nightingale's quarters. Her aunt, Mai Smith, had opened a bottle of wine, and Miss Nightingale was telling a story.

"It happened this past summer," she said, "when I went across the Black Sea to Balaclava."

"And very nearly didn't come back," said Mai.

Jane Rolly piped up, addressing Field. "When she was desperately sick with fever, Dr. Hall deliberately sent out the wrong boat for her, trying to ship her back to England!"

"I don't remember much of the fever," said Nightingale, "but I do remember that Dr. Hall's plan was foiled, and so here I am."

"It still makes my blood churn!" said Jane.

"Yes, but do let it churn in silence, Mrs. Rolly, you're ruining my story."

"Sorry, miss."

Field smiled, and then saw Jane glance at him, blushing. He erased the smile from his face.

"At some point out there," said Nightingale, "I think *before* the fever came upon me, I was housed in a mean little hut with a nun to whom I had not been introduced. I soon realized we occupied this hut with a rat. A great big one. 'There's a rat,' I said to the nun, 'do you see him?' In response, she smiled at me, beatifically. I got out of the bed we were sharing and grabbed a broom. 'I mean to get him,' I said. Another smile from the nun—radiant but now tinged also with concern."

"Oh, I know!" said Sister Clara. "It must have been Sister Angelica, who's stone-cold deaf!"

Nightingale pointed at Clara. "High marks to you, but I had no idea at the time. I soon realized she was confused, and then terrified by yours truly, but I hadn't yet put it together that she could neither hear nor speak. Still, there was the rat. Gripping my weapon, I was crafty, I was clever, but so was the *rat*. Shall we call him Dr. Rat?"

Everyone laughed.

"Whack! But Dr. Rat was no longer there, he was *here*. Whack! Whack, whack! The rat's eyes burned red with hatred. Speaking of eyes, Sister Angelica's by now were wide with horror—she had no idea what I was doing. She saw no rat, she saw only the madwoman with whom she was sharing a bed, hurtling about the hut with a broom!"

This time Nightingale herself laughed with all the others.

"Finally, my weapon found its mark. In only four, or possibly fourteen or forty-two blows, the rat was dead. I'm not proud to say that I did a victory dance, then and there, but I did. When I looked for applause from Sister Angelica, I saw that she had pulled the blanket over her head, so I just flung Dr. Rat out the door and joined the sister in bed, triumphant."

There was laughter and applause from the small group, but then Mai Smith nudged her niece. "Flo, there's someone here."

All eyes turned to the door, where John Stanhope stood.

"I'm so sorry to interrupt, but I need to speak with Inspector Field." Field rose.

"Shall we step away from the ladies?" said Stanhope.

Nightingale stood. "If you please, sir, do share what you've come to say with all of us, won't you?"

"Are you sure, Miss Nightingale?" said Field.

"When I am unsure of a thing, Inspector, I shall let you know. Stanhope?"

The young man cleared his throat. "There's been another attack."

"One of mine?" said Nightingale.

"No, miss," said Stanhope.

"Fatal?"

"Yes, miss."

Nightingale closed her eyes for a moment, then opened them and said, "Take me to her."

Stanhope looked to Field, as if in appeal, but Field was unforthcoming. Stanhope turned back to the nurse.

"I am afraid, miss, that I have my orders and you are forbidden the crime scene."

"Me, specifically? Orders from Dr. Hall?" said Nightingale.

"No, miss," said Stanhope, "the order came from the superintendent second class of the Scutari Constabulary, miss."

"Then bring me to the superintendent *first* class, sir!"

"The interdiction applies not just to you, miss. The Turkish police want no women there."

Inspector Field stepped between them. "Miss Nightingale, if you'll allow me, I shall look after this poor woman as best I can."

"All right, as I seem to have no choice."

"Mr. Kilvert?" said Field. "Would you be kind enough to accompany me?"

To Nightingale, Kilvert said, "May I, miss?"

"Of course," she said.

The two men moved to the door.

"One moment, Stanhope," said Nightingale. "This woman, this victim, was she, too, wearing the uniform of my nurses?"

"Just the cape, miss."

25

The buggy carried them down from the hospital into town along a dark cobble-stoned road, lined with one- and two-story structures of plaster or wood, many of the second floors jettying out over the first. Nigel Cox managed the reins, and John Stanhope sat next to him, while Field and Kilvert occupied the bench just behind them. They came to a stop outside a house, which Field realized was not far from the tavern where he'd met William Howard Russell. Indeed, it was possible to hear a faint din coming from the tavern just up the street. Two Turkish policemen were stationed outside, their lanterns lighting the dirty yellow plaster facade of the building. Lantern light from within moved jerkily from window to window.

"*Selam*," Stanhope said to the policemen at the door as he got out of the buggy, and they touched their caps to him.

"Help you down, sir?" said Cox.

Field looked to Kilvert and back. "Are you talking to me?" he said, and Cox nodded. "I think I can just about manage it, young man."

Superintendent Tulman emerged from the house. "You were quick, Mr. Stanhope," he said. "Inspector Field, I would rejoice to see you again, but for the circumstance, alas."

Angry male voices erupted from within the house. Tulman turned and shouted in Turkish, and the voices fell silent. Tulman turned back to Field, who approached and shook hands with him.

"A tragedy, sir. A horror. Another woman, her breath stopped." Tulman opened a leather satchel worn at his side and produced a red silk scarf. "By this. And covering her mouth, the red pentagram. The rose, if you will. Why?"

"Where is the victim, Superintendent Tulman?"

"Just inside, sir."

Field attempted to look over Tulman's shoulder, but Tulman held up one hand.

"Perhaps," he said, "she came along the road, fearful of someone following her. It is an unsavory locale, after all. In a panic, she stepped in here to hide from him."

"Perhaps."

"And perhaps not," said the Turkish policeman. "Perhaps this woman was a *guest* in this house, and that was her undoing?"

"I have no idea, sir. May I see the body?"

"I have one idea, at least. I have near at hand a person we may wish to question regarding this bizarre crime. And the strangest thing of all, Inspector Field? This person has been calling for *you*, sir. This past hour. By name, again and again."

"*What?*"

Tulman barked into the house again, and after a few moments two policemen came along the corridor and stood in the door with *Times*' correspondent Russell between them.

Russell, in his shirtsleeves with his braces hanging down, said, "What took you so damned long, Charlie?"

"*Charlie*," said Tulman. "This man calls you *Charlie*. You do not deny that you know this man?"

"Of course I don't deny it!" said Field. To Russell, he said, "What in God's name is this, Willie?"

"You tell me. This is where I live, I rent the rooms just up the steps. I was sound asleep, I woke to a hue and cry below, and then these fellows came pounding at my door. They say another woman's been killed, and I assume she's what I just passed, off the hall, covered by a sheet."

Tulman laid a hand confidentially on Field's shoulder. "The extraordinary thing is, Inspector," he said, "this Mr. Russell of *The Times* of London was also present the last time we found a woman in such a state, dead with a flower on her mouth. Then, too, he was newly risen from bed!"

Field nodded, looking at Russell. "That, Officer Tulman, would get *my* attention as well."

"Oh, come, Charlie!" said the journalist.

"May I see the body now?" said Field.

But there was a stir going on by the buggy. "Clear off!" shouted Nigel Cox. "Go away, why don't you?"

Field turned to see a sunken-cheeked man peering at the house. After a moment he recognized him as the beggar from his evening with Russell at the tavern. It already seemed a lifetime ago.

"Ah," said Tulman, "the Mendicant. Mr. Cox, you must understand, this man is a witness, he found the body, he notified the police!"

The man said, "*Grazie*," and then gave Cox a scornful, triumphant look.

"All right, Superintendent," said Field, "let's have a look. Kilvert, you remain where you are for now." Tulman motioned the policemen at the door who escorted the reporter back along a short corridor, and Field and Tulman followed. The covered form was in a vestibule just off the hall leading to the stairs. Solemnly, Tulman lifted the sheet.

The piercing violet eyes were open and staring, the fringe of black hair hardly mussed. The distinctive cape of a Nightingale nurse hung loosely from her shoulders.

"Oh, dear God," said Field.

"You knew this woman?" said Tulman.

"Yes, I knew her. Briefly." Field crouched by the body. He touched her hand, and then her neck. "Interfered with?"

"Possibly," said Tulman. "The police doctor will determine."

Field stood and turned to Russell. "Is there a side to you I'd not been aware of, Willie?"

"Charlie! For God's sake, no!"

"Something you keep from the world, with all your far-flung travels? If I journeyed to other locales from which you've reported, would I find a record of young women, decorated and dead?"

"Of course not, Charlie! What's wrong with you?"

"When did you retire for the night?" said Field.

"Hours ago, it must be. I was traveling back here much of the night before. There's a war just over the way, remember? I'm covering it."

Field spun round, strode down the hall and out the door to where the Italian man still stood, looking in. The inspector pointed back to the house and said, "Did you *find* the girl? Or did you squeeze the life out of her?"

"He can't understand you," said Cox.

"But I *can*, signore, I can speak very well," said the beggar, glaring at Cox and Stanhope, "as you know!" Turning to Field, he said, "I *found* her. From the road I saw her boots, they don't move, so I go straight to the police."

Field took a survey of the man before him. He likely wasn't much more than fifty-five years old, but the years had not been kind to him. His swept-back greasy hair was gray, tinged with yellow. Of medium height, he had a cadaverous face, but his torso was broad, and he stood more or less upright.

Field turned to Kilvert. "Come with me, Josiah. I need you to witness."

Kilvert followed Field back into the house. The two men stood above the body and Field nodded to Tulman, who again lifted the cloth from the young woman's face. Kilvert gasped. "Inspector, she works in the hospital laundry!"

"Indeed."

"God have mercy," whispered Kilvert, staring.

To Tulman, the inspector said, "I met this child a few days ago. British. Living with the other abandoned British women and children in the old barracks stables."

Field glanced at Russell. He turned to look at Stanhope and Cox, standing just outside, peering in. "Officer Tulman," he said quietly, "were those two present when the previous victim was found?"

"Stanhope and Cox? Soon after, yes."

"And the man you call the Mendicant?"

"Not to my knowledge, no, although he lurks about here and there and turns up like the bad British penny."

"And the Frenchman who cooks for the hospital, Mr. Soyer, and his assistant, the young Black man—all of them were there that night? Not to mention Dr. Talbot. Remarkable."

Officer Tulman shrugged. "As you say."

Field looked down at the body again, lying helplessly on the floor, with a thin stripe of red round her neck and an embroidered, five-pointed flower over her mouth.

"Her name was Rose," said Field.

Tulman nodded. "Here, Inspector, is one other thing you might consider. Perhaps, sir, she was not killed here, where you see her, but elsewhere."

Field looked up. "Why do you say that?"

"It's an old house, the entry is dirty and marked by many feet, so it is hard to say. But there are scuffs on the backs of this poor woman's heels." Tulman pointed to marks on the floor of the hall leading to the vestibule. "I see here, and here, marks that perhaps were made by the backs of this poor young woman's boots. Was she dragged in here?"

Field nodded. "As you say, it would be difficult to be certain. But from the feel of her, she's been dead hours and could have been moved here."

The Turkish officer turned to the journalist. "Mr. Russell, my men have found no needle, no thread in your quarters, and I will not instantly take you in for further discussions. Not yet. But have a care. My people will be watching you."

"And I'll be watching *you*, sir!" said Russell. "And waiting for an apology from *you*, Inspector Field!"

"Willie?" said Field. "Be still." He turned to the Turkish policeman. "What will happen to this girl now, Officer Tulman? Miss Nightingale will want to know."

"*Miss Nightingale should not be here in the Ottoman Empire!*" said Tulman with sudden heat. "Nor any of these women. War is for the man, not the woman." Tulman looked down at the body. "I have read the Dickens. I know you people think differently to us. But I believe this child would not be here, in this condition, if Miss Nightingale had stayed away."

He looked up at Field. "My people will take good care of this Rose, and I shall treat her as I would my daughter. You may tell Miss Nightingale that, sir."

In minutes, Field and Kilvert were seated again on the rear bench of the buggy as Cox and Stanhope started them on their return to the Barrack Hospital. Field glanced back and saw Tulman and the other Turkish policemen watching them go, as well as the *Times* journalist. The Italian beggar had vanished.

A chill fog was rolling in off the harbor. Field glanced over at Josiah Kilvert, who had pulled his coat close about him, seeming to huddle into himself. Why had he invited this innocent to accompany him, to witness this violation of young life? Field thought back to his own baiting of the British doctors, threatening them with the stories William Howard Russell might write for *The Times*, soliciting funds for those living in squalor beneath the hospital. They would realize Russell gave Field the means to communicate with the public and, in a sense, with the Queen herself. Did someone kill this young woman, this Rose, and move her body to the newsman's lodgings in order to make Russell a suspect and destroy his standing as a reporter?

Field leaned forward. "Mr. Cox, drive us to the old stables, if you please."

"What, now?" said Cox.

"Yes, now."

Stanhope turned around to face Field. "I don't think that would be wise, sir, at this time of night. The women will be sleeping, and those that are not will be in their cups most likely."

"Nevertheless."

So Cox drove them down around the side of the hospital and stopped the carriage before the old stables.

"Your lantern, please, Mr. Cox," said Field.

Cox took the lantern at his feet and handed it back. Field turned the wick up and saw apprehension in Cox's face.

"Don't worry, Mr. Cox," said Field, "I won't break it."

Field watched Cox for another moment, then stepped down from the buggy and moved to the lopsided door. He held the lantern up to his own face and knocked.

"It's Detective Inspector Field," he said loudly, "can someone please come and speak with me?"

A dog within began to bark and then another.

"Coming, Inspector!" said someone from within.

There were nearby sounds of a bar being thrown, and a hook unhooked. The door opened a crack, and Field moved the light closer to his face. The door opened further.

"It's Mrs. Stamm, sir, how may I help?" She looked beyond Field to the men waiting in the cart. "Oh dear, is it trouble?"

"I'm wondering, Mrs. Stamm, when Rose left the premises."

"Rose Lambert?" said Mrs. Stamm. "She's here, as far as I know." She turned to speak to someone within. "Isn't Rose here?"

"No," said a voice, "she went out this afternoon."

"At what time?" said Field. "Does anyone know where she might have been going?"

Now there was a gabble of anxious voices within.

"Dear God," said Mrs. Stamm, "don't tell me something bad has happened to that child?"

"I'm afraid so, Mrs. Stamm."

The woman put her face in her hands. A moment later she brushed away tears and turned angrily to the others. "We have to keep track of each other, for God's sake! We must!"

"Who saw her leave?" said Field. "When did she go?"

A woman Field recognized as Nellie appeared at the door. "This afternoon, like I said." Nellie peered out at the other men. "It were soon after that man come callin'."

Field turned toward the cart. "Which man, Nellie?"

Nellie pointed.

Nigel Cox spoke up. "I came to see for myself what you told us about, Inspector. I never even knew this place had people in it. I thought, if it's all true, I should make a contribution to the widows and children, see?"

"Today, this was?"

"Yes, sir."

"You took a few days to think it over before you made your way down here."

"I suppose I did," said Cox.

"Did you talk to anyone in particular, Mr. Cox?" said Field.

"Yes, it was a young woman. Striking eyes."

"Did this young woman with the striking eyes *leave with you*, Cox?"

"No, sir! I told her you were raising a fund and thanked her for talking to me. I left her standing at this door and walked back to my rooms."

Word was spreading throughout the stables, and women began to cry, some holding each other while they sobbed.

"I'm very sorry to bring this terrible news to you, ladies," said Field.

"Just two more questions and I'll leave you for tonight. Nellie, did Rose tell you where she was going or who she was going to see?"

"Nah. I just thought she was going to market."

"Was she wearing a Nightingale cape?"

"Oh, no, sir! Them things is bad luck."

Field took this in.

In that case both the cape and the bad luck found her. The killer dressed her in it, didn't he, the bastard, just as he brought a hospital sash to do for Mrs. Dumphries.

26

They had managed a casket somehow, on Miss Nightingale's orders, and dug a proper grave. The procession moved solemnly down the hillside to a spot overlooking the sea. The pallbearers were Charles Field and Seaman Josiah Kilvert at the front; the chef, Alexis Soyer, and his helper, T. G. Taylor, at the back. The war widows who lived in the stables followed and then the nurses of the Barrack Hospital who could be spared from duty came after them. Florence Nightingale and Mai Smith brought up the rear. A cold wind whipped the women's skirts about their legs.

It was apparent, as the men lowered the casket into the earth, that it weighed very little. Rose had been petite.

There were brief remembrances of Rose Lambert, and Mary Dumphries, who had not been offered the dignity of a funeral. Mary's four-year-old son, his hand held by Jane Rolly, began to cry. Jane hoisted him up into her arms, and the two of them wept together. One of the nurses who had known the murdered housekeeper, Helena Swain, spoke about the woman's hard life and hopes for the future. Mai Smith read *from dust thou art, unto dust shalt thou return* and then led them, reciting the Lord's Prayer.

The scene was observed from the top of the hill by a trio of men, their topcoat collars turned up against the cold.

"I shall have to spend the rest of my life repairing the damage that woman has done my reputation," said Dr. John Hall.

"Nightingale is a passing fancy, sir," said John Stanhope, "nothing more."

"Damned petticoat tyrant," muttered Hall.

"Perhaps," said Stanhope, "this latest corpse will prompt the war secretary to recall the nurses."

"As you may recall, Mr. Stanhope," said Hall, "the first murder prompted Sidney Herbert to send out the London policeman you see below. I shouldn't be surprised if Sir Sidney now sent out a squadron!"

A sound of singing came to the men's ears, a hymn, faint under the gusts of wind. It began to rain.

Hall hunched his shoulders and buried his hands in the pockets of his coat. "Lot of fuss to make over a woman of low repute," he said.

"They do say the war is winding down," ventured Nigel Cox, and the other two turned to stare at him. "It's just something one hears." He looked as though he wished he'd kept his peace.

"And when the war does wind down?" said Hall. "What's your next posting to be, Mr. Cox?" He turned and started walking toward the Barrack Hospital. "Doubt it'll be with the ambassador, who seems to be looking for a new man." Glancing back at Cox, he said, "It's just something one hears."

27

Inspector Field was happy to accept Alexis Soyer's invitation to join him in his quarters after the funeral, especially since it was Field who had suggested it to the Frenchman in the first place. After the two of them had shaken the wet from their coats and were standing backsides to the fire with glasses of cognac in hand, Field said, "I don't mind telling you, Mr. Soyer, the death of this girl Rose has hit me hard."

"Indeed, sir."

"In my line of work," continued Field, "I see death often. Goes with the position, don't it. Never pretty, violent death. But you come to take it in stride, you get used to it. For the police detective, 'death hath lost its sting,' you might say. But this child struck me special. I had no more than a few minutes acquaintance with Rose, but that was enough to tell me she was out of the ordinary."

Soyer nodded somberly.

"Did you know her at all?" said Field.

The chef shook his head.

"But you did know the other woman, Mrs. Dumphries."

Soyer started to speak, but Field cut him off. "No, I beg your pardon. That was Mr. T. G. Taylor who knew her, and you who didn't."

"That's right."

The inspector sipped his cognac. "Very good, this."

"It should be," said Soyer. He held his glass up to the lamplight and swirled the contents.

"But you *did* know Mary Dumphries well enough to know she wasn't a Nightingale nurse—have I got that right?"

The chef's shrug could signify assent, dissent, or indifference. *I'm supposed to take my pick, I guess*, thought Field.

"You saw the body, did you, that night?" said the inspector.

"The policeman, the Turk, brought me to see, yes. Dreadful."

"This was because you and Mr. T. G. Taylor were, what was it you said? 'In the vicinity' when Mrs. Dumphries was found dead. What does that mean?"

"My English is not so good, Inspector. 'Vicinity' I thought means 'close by'?"

"Oh, it does indeed, sir, your English is top-notch. So that's what you said, and now I'm asking, What d'you mean by it?"

The chef raised his shoulders again, as if to say, *Who can tell what anything means?* and then turned to warm his front side. Field followed suit.

"Just so I'm perfectly clear in my understanding," said the inspector, "you and Mr. Taylor were *where* exactly that night?"

Soyer sighed, staring at the fire. "Always it is," he said finally, "the human looks for *la nourriture*, the food one needs to feed the body, the soul."

The inspector gave Soyer a wry grin. "So, to translate, the two of you stepped out for a bite to eat, is that it?"

The shoulders again and a tilt of the head.

"You could say, sir."

"What did you have?" said Field, somewhat abruptly.

For the first time, Soyer's glance darted to Field's eyes and then away.

"I was speaking spiritually, Inspector."

"What did you have spiritually, then?"

There was a pop among the glowing logs on the fire and a small collapse. Soyer set his glass on the mantel, took an iron, and crouched to straighten the pile.

"Why do you ask this?" he said, without looking up at Field.

"I might want to step out myself, Mr. Soyer, one of these nights. Sample what the locality might have to offer."

Soyer stood again.

"So what did you have, you and T.G.?" said Field. "Spiritually or otherwise?"

"Goat, I imagine. They have little else round here." Soyer sipped his cognac.

"The two of you, you and T.G., strolled about Scutari in search of a meal, found an inn, and dined together on goat, is that about right?"

Soyer picked up the poker and knelt again by the fire but this time without any obvious reason to do so.

"Mr. Soyer?"

"My wife, Emma, died twelve years ago," said the Frenchman.

"Very sorry to hear it."

"Did you know, Mr. Field, that she was an acclaimed artist?"

"I did not, sir."

"The youngest ever to have a painting chosen for the Great Exhibition, the very youngest."

"You must have been proud of her, Mr. Soyer."

The man stood. "I want to think she would be proud of me, out here, doing this work with Miss Nightingale, caring for our soldiers when the army would not."

Field nodded. "I imagine she would have been right here at your side, helping you."

Soyer's brow furrowed. "Perhaps, perhaps not. You understand, she was an artist, she had no understanding of a kitchen whatsoever."

"Ah."

"When she died, there was such a hole in my life, Mr. Field, I thought it never would be filled. But after years and years, one requires *la nourriture*, even so, among those of us who remain. The living. One searches for it."

The two men stood in silence for some time, the crackling of the fire the only sound.

At last Field said gently, "Sir, is Mr. T. G. Taylor what you found?"

"He is a fine man, Inspector. Emma would approve, I know she would."

Field nodded. Soyer offered him a cigarette, which he declined.

"So you and T.G. did *not* in fact dine together that night?" said the inspector.

"We did." He lit his cigarette. "But he is a young man and cannot always be at one's side, you comprehend?"

Field nodded, although he didn't.

"We parted for the night, it is understandable. But not long after, word comes here that my dear friend is taken by that fool of a Turk policeman. T.G. was only passing by that house, but the fool Turk has seized him and dragged him up to see the dead woman! I sped to his side, I let the Turk know how stupid he is!"

Something in the fire whistled and cracked, and the dwindling logs collapsed again.

"You're certain T.G. didn't step into this house," said Field, "where a young man can find a woman for the night?"

Soyer seemed surprised to find his glass empty. He went to the sideboard and poured himself another.

"I put up a monument to honor my wife, sir, in the Kensal Green. When I go, I will be laid beside her." He held up the bottle, offering it. "Mr. Field?"

"Mr. Soyer, you're certain Mr. Taylor was not already in Mrs. Dinkins' inn, with a woman?"

The chef stoppered the bottle. He looked Field in the eye and said, "Certain? No. But of the gentility and goodness of this man, of that I am completely certain, Mr. Field."

28

F ield found T. G. Taylor supervising the crew in the vast Barrack kitchen and asked if he could have a word.

"I'm all yours, Inspector!" said T.G. Turning to a lad minding a spit in one of the hearths, he said, "Oi, Ahmed! Is it your actual intent to set that bird alight?"

The fourteen-year-old kitchen boy ran a hand through his thick black hair. "Sorry, Mr. Taylor."

In a low tone, T.G. said, "Turkish lad, Mr. Field. Lost his father to the war and his mother to the fever. Turned up at our door."

"I see," said Field. "Perhaps, Mr. Taylor, we can find a quiet place in which to talk."

"We can do anything we set our minds to, Inspector, but not that, not just now. Monsieur Soyer and I were a full two hours away from the kitchen this morning, and he's still not back, as you see, but it was a lovely service, sir, and no regrets on that account."

"Surely you can spare a few minutes more?" said Field.

"Surely you can speak to me right here while I work, sir! It's a bit insensitive of Monsieur Soyer to quote Napoleon to an Englishman, but he never tires of telling me that *une armée marche sur le ventre*."

"You speak the lingo?"

"Ahmed, I won't warn you again!" T.G. turned back to Field. "My mam was the souvenir my papa brought back from Martinique to Croydon before he set off for unknown shores, never to be seen again, so it's my mother tongue, you might say, *le français*. And it's true: an army does march on its belly."

"It's about you and Mr. Soyer I want to speak," said Field. "It's a conversation you might not wish young Ahmed, or anyone else, to overhear, sir."

T.G. looked at Field for a long moment and then took off his apron. "Bloody flics are all the same."

The Barrack Hospital was an enormous structure, and T.G.'s quarters were on an upper floor, at the far, deserted end of the female nurses' wing. T.G. flung open the door and motioned Field to enter.

It was a monk-like cell. There was a narrow iron bedframe, the bedclothes made up with military precision. On one wall hung a crucifix and a small mirror. On the bedside table, Field noticed, was a book with a piece of fabric stuck in to hold a place. Beside it was a miniature portrait of a middle-aged Black woman wearing a white turban bound by a jeweled brooch.

"Here you have it, Inspector," said T.G., "this is where I plot my murders."

"Is it, now," said Field.

"This is why you want to have a word, is it not? You're not otherwise interested in me, say, for conversation or friendship, I assume."

Field picked up the book by T.G.'s bed.

"Dickens' *Barnaby Rudge*, Inspector. You're Mr. Dickens' bosom friend, as I understand it."

"Not always. Haven't read this one."

"I have, sir. This is my second go. It's all about how quickly a few men can turn into a mob. Pick a group to single out for hatred—Roman Catholics in this case, but most any group will do—and before you know it you've got innocent folk hanging by lampposts and all London aflame. That's *Barnaby Rudge*, sir. You should read it one day, you might benefit by it."

"I prefer to read men, and right now it's you who's on my list. How did you and Mr. Soyer meet?"

"Picked me up on the street, didn't he. Somewhere in the West End, forget just where."

"How long ago?"

"Donkey's," said Taylor.

"You're quite the wag, aren't you, T.G.," said Field. "You must have been the toast of all Croydon."

"The place has never recovered from my departure, I'm told. Traveled in style ever since. The best hotels, the finest restaurants. Alexis taught me everything I know."

Field nodded. "Right, so now you're going to open your heart to me and teach me what *I* need to know, that's what you're going to do, Mr. T.G."

"Sooner die, sir."

Field flushed.

"We can arrange that, too."

"All alike, every single one of you."

"Were you with a woman at Mrs. Dinkins' inn the night Mary Dumphries was strangled? For that matter, were you with Mrs. Dumphries?"

There was a knock at the door and a female voice. "Mr. Taylor?"

After a moment's hesitation, T.G. opened the door, revealing Jane Rolly.

"I'm afraid you're needed in the kitchen," she said.

"Pardon me," said Field, "but I need him right here, and that's where he's going to remain for now."

She looked between the two men.

"Oh, for goodness' sake, Mr. Field," said Jane, "are you *interrogating* Mr. Taylor? About these dreadful crimes?"

"This is a police matter, Jane. Now please allow me to proceed with my investigation."

She shook her head. "It's *Mrs. Rolly*, if you please. When Mr. Soyer and this man arrived to save our very lives, sir, the chef thought he'd left his pocketbook on the train and sent T.G. back to fetch it. Turned out Soyer hadn't left it anywhere, he had the pocketbook with him the whole time, but T.G. never returned. So Mr. Soyer went in search of him and found him behind bars, locked up in the jail. Why? Because the police didn't like his black skin, that's why."

She turned to T.G. "Do come, sir. Mr. Soyer's arrived in the kitchen, and not to put too fine a point upon it, he's drunk."

Jane shot a dark look at Field and left them alone.

"Inspector," said T.G., "I was *not* with a woman that night, women not being in my line, if you take my meaning. I was quite alone, taking the air, but Monsieur Soyer can be a jealous man from time to time. He don't always believe it when I tell him I care for him. It's a failing, but then which of us is without sin? Am I free to go?"

Field finally nodded, and T.G. left him there, still holding the copy of *Barnaby Rudge*. He opened it to the fabric place-marker. It had been stitched very simply, quite possibly by a mother's hand: *Theo. Gabriel Taylor*. Field set down the book and hurried out of the room.

"Mr. Taylor!" he called, down the long corridor. T.G. stopped and turned, and Field hurried toward him.

"In the only conversation I had with the young woman we buried this morning, she used a phrase I didn't understand."

"Yeah?"

"She was talking about Mary Dumphries. She said something like 'twice the pay for same amount of work.'"

"I'm surprised at your ignorance, man of the world like you," said T.G.

"It's something you've heard of?"

"Certainly. It's something I've *done*, come to that." The young man turned his back on Field and kept walking. Over his shoulder he said, "It's when a whore takes on two blokes at once, sir."

29

Mrs. Dinkins of the Dinkins Inn was barely five feet tall. Perhaps sixty-five years old. She was a study in gray, with streaky gray hair beneath a gray bonnet, a gray knit shawl about her shoulders and a full, dark gray skirt. The papery skin of her face was a lighter shade of the same color. She wore an inexplicable string of pearls round her neck and a quizzical expression as she looked up at Inspector Field, who stood, hat in hand, at her door.

"I am afraid, sir, we no longer have rooms to let here," she said.

"I've not come about a room, Mrs. Dinkins."

"Have we met? So many have come and gone, I can't always keep track."

"I'm Detective Inspector Field, ma'am. May I come in?"

"Well, of course you may! Much too cold to stand about, with that wind straight off the harbor. Goes right to the bone, it does."

She bundled him into the two-story house and shut the door.

"I didn't quite catch the name, sir," she said.

"I'm with the Metropolitan Police, London, Mrs. Dinkins. Inspector Field, Detective Division."

"Oh! You've come about that poor girl. And all the way from London, too! Come this way, then, and I'll put on the kettle."

Field followed the woman into a small kitchen. She offered him a chair while she filled the kettle.

"It's along of that girl that I stopped letting my rooms, as a matter of fact," said Mrs. Dinkins. "It was all too much for me, at my age. And they do say the war will soon be over, and that of course will ruin me, so I've got my eye on a little house at Newbiggin-by-the-Sea. Have you ever been?"

"To Newbiggin?" said Field. "I don't believe so."

"Oh, it's lovely. We've no milk, I'm afraid, but I do have sugar, my men always want their sugar!"

She struck a phosphorus match, and a blue flame leapt up from a gas ring with a loud retort. She took a tea canister from a shelf and pried it open.

"What brings you to Scutari, Mr. Field?" said Mrs. Dinkins.

"Why, the death of that young woman we were just talking about— Mary Dumphries. I'm here investigating her murder."

"Murdered, was she? Shocking."

Is she shamming? Or genuinely addled?

The kettle began to whistle and went on whistling while the woman carefully tipped two spoonfuls of leaves into the brown teapot on the table. Finally, she lifted the kettle off the flame and poured steaming water into the pot. She sat down opposite Field, having neglected to turn off the gas ring.

"My sister moved to Newbiggin-by-the-Sea, was it two . . . *no*, three years ago."

The inspector hesitated, then rose and turned the knob to extinguish the flame. Dinkins didn't seem to notice, and he sat again.

"She says there are ever so many girls there in need of work, and young men in need of girls, so there you go!"

"You're a madam, then?" said Field.

"I'm a widow, Mr. Field. I lost Mr. Dinkins in the Railway Bubble."

Right, she's off her nut, or she's posing.

In a sharper tone, Field said, "Do I understand you to say you run houses of prostitution, Mrs. Dinkins?"

But now her attention was on the cups of tea she was pouring.

"Sugar?"

Without waiting for an answer, she put two large spoonfuls of sugar into each cup, stirred them, and pushed one across the table to Field. She smiled at him and took a cautious sip from her own cup.

"Do you keep a register of your guests, Mrs. Dinkins?"

"I do, of course."

"May I see it?"

She smiled again and pointed to a large book on a shelf by the kitchen door. Field rose, took the book, and set it on the table. He found the last entry and paged back from there.

"You only recently stopped letting rooms, it seems," said Field. "You managed to overcome your distress about Mary Dumphries' murder until just a few days ago?"

"Oh, yes. I had a letter from my sister at Newbiggin, on the Tuesday I think it was, urging me to close up shop and join her there."

Field found the date he was looking for and ran a finger down the page.

"Do you know your clients personally, Mrs. Dinkins?"

"Some of them," she said.

"I see Mr. Russell was here on the night of the murder."

"Oh, he's a regular. Writes for *The Times* and smokes cigars, but he's a gentleman, even so."

Field read the next name on the list.

"James Talbot?"

"Poor Mr. Talbot," said the woman. "He died, you know. Blew his brains out, they say. So of course I had to give it all up, it was just too much for an old lady like me."

Field turned the page over and back again. "Only those two men, that whole night?"

"No, John Hall was here, too, with Mr. Talbot. His name should be in there, too."

Could it be?

"Dr. John Hall?" he said.

"Oh, he's a physician? I didn't know. But he and his friend were inseparable, they shared everything."

"His friend?"

"I told you—Mr. Talbot! The man who killed himself. Would you like a biscuit?"

Field shook his head. "These two men, Talbot and Hall, shared everything, you say. Even women?"

The little woman seemed to be shocked.

"Please, Mr. Field," she said. "I have only British gentlemen here. I don't ask them what they do, or with whom. I rent them a clean room and offer them a nice breakfast, if they like."

It was almost too easy. A mysterious stranger didn't have to enter the room quietly and kill the prostitute while her client slept—the killer was there all along, another one of her clients. It was a threesome that went wrong. And Hall's inseparable friend, James Talbot, had witnessed the crime and committed suicide the next day. Or had he, too, been killed? Could it be that Dr. John Hall, the head of the army's entire medical team in the Crimea, was the killer?

"What about Black men, Mrs. Dinkins?" said Field. "Did you ever have a Black man as a guest?"

"A Negro?" she said. "Not as a rule, but let me think. Yes, I think there was a Negro here the night of the murder, but briefly, as I recall. So many come and go."

"Forgive me, Mrs. Dinkins, but just to be sure: *John Hall* was here the night Mary Dumphries was strangled?"

"He was."

The inspector didn't know what to think. As a witness, this woman seemed anything but reliable. But two men *who shared everything* struck him as a credible story. *Twice the pay for same amount of work.*

"Would you be so kind, ma'am, as to take me to the room in question?" said Field.

In a few minutes they were upstairs, and Mrs. Dinkins was opening a door that gave off a narrow corridor. The room was good-sized, and the bed, neatly made up, was capacious.

"This was where they found that poor girl," she said, "*and* Mr. Talbot, so dreadfully upset."

"And Dr. Hall? He was here, too?"

"Who?"

Field took a breath to hide his impatience. "John Hall, Talbot's friend."

"Oh, no," said Dinkins, "he wasn't here. He must have gone by then."

"Man of about sixty years, this John Hall? Dark hair and beard with little tufts of white?"

Dinkins stared at him. "Why, no, I shouldn't think so. He struck me as a younger man, Mr. Field. But then, so many come and go, it's hard to keep track. I sent a runner to Miss Nightingale's hospital when I saw that sash round the woman's neck, and a couple of young men from up there came soon after. Mr. Talbot was carrying on something awful, and Mr. Russell was standing there, half-dressed. I didn't know where to look!"

Field went to the window and tried to raise it.

"It don't budge, sir, I've tried and tried."

"Where did Mr. Russell stay?" said Field.

"Mr. Russell's room is opposite. He always asks for it." Mrs. Dinkins crossed the corridor and opened that door. It was a smaller room, but it offered a glimpse of harbor through its window. "Before long, the police were here, and other folks coming and going, and lots of shouting and carrying on, and it was all too much for me."

Field had her open a third room to him. "No one in here the night of the murder?"

"No, business has fallen off terribly."

"There's another room down there I see, at the end of the hall," said Field.

"Yes, our smallest. The poor beggarman hid in there. He don't like the police and they don't like him."

Her remark took Field up short. "Beggarman?"

"An old Italian. I sometimes let him sleep here for a few pennies. The room's too small to let properly in good conscience. His mind is off, you see. Still, he's got nice enough manners, and I give him a cup of tea when he shows up, or fry him an egg, and where's the harm in that?"

"I suppose it remains to be seen, Mrs. Dinkins," said Field uncertainly.

If this is Miss Nightingale's ball of thread, thought the inspector, *it's not leading me out of a maze but deeper in.*

30

They were gathered at Inspector Field's request in Florence Nightingale's tower headquarters, everyone crowded together, perched wherever they could: nurses, two of the women who lodged in the stables, the various men and boys who had become members of Barrack Hospital entourage by intent or accident, plus Mai Smith, and of course Mrs. Smith's niece, Miss Nightingale herself. She stood at her desk as usual, and seemed, as usual, preoccupied with other matters while Field spoke.

"From now on," said Field, "none of you women will venture out alone. You'll go in twos or threes, or not at all."

Field watched Nightingale disappear behind an ornamental screen and return with a valise, which she planted on her desk and seemed to be examining. "Miss Nightingale?" he said.

"Yes?"

"Might your nurses forgo their capes and caps and sashes when leaving the hospital?"

"I'm afraid not, Inspector," she said. "Dr. Hall won't have it, for some reason. I asked him after the first incident, but he was adamant. Perhaps he feels the costume keeps us in our place." She consulted a list on the desk before her, picked up a pencil, and made a tick.

"I'll have a word with Dr. Hall," said Field.

Nightingale glanced up at Field and said, "If you must. But do remember what I told you: Never push the male. Only sidle alongside and encourage him to think it was his idea in the first place."

Field felt the eyes of the women in the room on him and wondered, in a way that was unfamiliar, just how they regarded him. Was he simply another male who had to be handled with care, lest he bruise? He shook off the thought.

"Right, then. You women living in the stables? There's to be no borrowing of nurse's uniforms, not so much as a button, is that understood?"

"Yes, sir," said Fiona.

"*All* of you women, whenever possible, grab an available male to accompany you if you venture out. And please, this is most important, you nurses must keep an eye on your uniforms. If you have extras, keep them close, let no one borrow or nick them!"

Just then Alexis Soyer entered the room bearing a large tray, followed by T.G. Taylor carrying another.

"For my dear friends," Soyer announced dramatically, "a treat from the ovens!"

There were exclamations of delight as an irresistibly sweet aroma wafted through the room. After them came the young kitchen boy, Ahmed, with a platter on which small plates were piled high. Field was dismayed.

"This is a serious ʒathering, Mr. Soyer," he said. "Can't your treats wait?"

"Wait? *Wait?*" Soyer struck a pose, one hand to his brow. "*Les clafoutis* wait for no man!"

There was laughter and applause from the gathering, and Nightingale said, "I'm sorry, Inspector Field, but this is our chef's signature dish. You'll understand as soon as you've had a bite. Give the inspector a slice straightaway, please!"

"Flo," said Mai Smith, "this is actually a very serious matter."

"Yes, of course, you're right." To the room, she said, "Everyone?"

Soyer was cutting pieces of the custard dessert. T.G. and the kitchen boy were delivering them throughout the room.

"Steady on, Ahmed," said T.G., "we don't *fling* the puddings at the ladies, we *offer* them graciously."

"Yessir, sorry, sir."

"Don't be *sorry*, be *careful*!"

"Everyone! Please!" said Nightingale, in a louder voice. "The precautions that the inspector is describing are vitally important, especially now, during the time when I shall be away across the sea."

All heads turned to her.

"Flo?" said Mai.

"Miss Nightingale?" said the inspector.

"I've decided to return to the Crimea."

"Oh, no—absolutely not!" said Nightingale's aunt. "Not so soon!"

"My hoped-for inspection of the hospital at Balaclava was cut short in the summer by the fever that brought me down."

"The fever from which you still haven't fully recovered!"

"Mai," said Nightingale, "I've just received a note from an ally who shall remain nameless, telling me that the mortality numbers at Balaclava are climbing and approaching what they were when we arrived at *this* hospital. I have no choice."

Field cleared his throat. "Excuse me, miss, but with all these deaths rising up, what can *you* do about it but get sick yourself?"

Nurse Rolly turned on Field and said, "She can do there what she did right here, sir—fix it!"

It was the second time in a matter of days that Jane Rolly had expressed disapproval of Field, and he suddenly realized that her approval, or disapproval, meant more to him than he could explain, even to himself. Nightingale bestowed a compassionate smile on Field, one that he'd seen her offer the soldiers in her care who were least likely to survive the night.

"My dear inspector," she said, "we, all of us here in this room, and in this hospital, are at great risk of *getting sick*, as you put it. Every moment of every day. Even you, sir. Don't tell me you didn't realize this once you arrived. You could look about you and see disease and death at every hand. And yet you stayed, did you not? To do your job? So then, I am no more courageous, or foolish, than you."

Field bowed his head in acquiescence.

Extraordinary, he thought. *Never met a woman like her.*

Or had he? He glanced up at Jane Rolly. And Sister Clara. And all the other women who had come from Britain with Nightingale, not knowing what they'd find, and who, finding it worse than they possibly could have imagined, set about making it better.

T.G. put a small plate in Field's hands. "He mixes the black cherries and the red, Inspector," said the young man, "and adds a secret liqueur to make it all his own."

"Does he, now." Field ate a forkful and then looked up into T.G.'s eyes. "Good Lord."

"Told ya."

Between bites, Nightingale continued, speaking to the entire gathering. "My aunt, Mrs. Smith, will be in charge of the Barrack Hospital in my absence. Jane Rolly will accompany me, along with Sisters Louisa, Susan, and Novella. Sister Clara will be head nurse here, and you'll refer any questions or problems to her."

"Thank you, miss," said Clara.

"You'll need *me*, Miss Nightingale," said the young Irishman, Robert Robinson.

"Indeed, I shall, Robert."

"And me," said Kilvert.

"And you, sir."

"What about me, then, miss?" said T.G.

"You were a great help to me when I last crossed the sea, Mr. Taylor," said Nightingale. "Your abilities now will be needed more than ever in the kitchens, as the war seems to lighten, but winter approaches."

"I don't like to miss the chance of visiting Mother Seacole," said T.G.

"Nor do I, Miss Nightingale," said Alexis Soyer.

"I will be sure to convey your greetings to her."

Seacole was a Jamaican businesswoman and island healer who, offering her abilities to the troops, had appealed to the war secretary for the sort of help he'd given Nightingale. She'd been roundly turned down, but she went out to the Crimea anyway and put together an inn from scrap metal and wood. There she cared for recovering British soldiers, and she was now much loved by the troops. Nightingale, Soyer, and T.G. had invited her to dine with them when she was on her way to Balaclava, and they all had enjoyed one another's company.

Mai Smith shook her head. "Flo, never mind Mother Seacole. When your *own* mother hears of this, she will be furious."

"Fortunately, Mama is a long way away."

"All right, Miss Nightingale," said Field, "so be it. When do we leave?"

"Oh, but Inspector," she said, "you must stay here to protect these women!"

Field shook his head. "Whether it's a question of courage or foolishness, miss, I'm afraid I agree with the local policeman on one point at least. If you weren't here, I doubt any of these women would be in danger."

Nightingale took her time to consider this. Finally, she said, "The *Ottoway* leaves at six tomorrow morning. I shall be grateful of your company."

"What about me, miss?" said Peter, a twelve-year-old Russian boy who had wandered into the lives of the Barrack Hospital some months earlier from no one knew where.

"And me?" said William, a British boy of perhaps sixteen years who stood next to Peter, leaning on a walking stick because he had only one leg.

Field looked around the room at the others. No one laughed, no one smiled.

"I'm most grateful to you both," said Nightingale gravely, "and know that you would be a great help, but you will be needed more right here."

"Boys, remember what I taught you!" said Alexis Soyer.

William stood at attention and recited. "*Une armée marche sur le ventre!*"

"And Peter?" said Soyer.

"*Petit* à *petit, l'oiseau fait son nid,*" said the Russian boy.

Nightingale laughed again. "'Little by little, the bird builds its nest!' Indeed, Peter, it's true!"

Sister Clara folded the boy into her arms, and Robert Robinson clapped a hand on William's shoulder. To his utter shock, Field realized there were tears standing in his eyes.

It feels like family, this. Like none I ever knew, that's certain.

His interview with Dr. John Hall, conducted at the man's bedroom door later that night, was brief. When Inspector Field told Hall that he would be accompanying Miss Nightingale as she left for Balaclava in the morning, the doctor said, "First I've heard of it. Why in God's name is she going out to the Crimea? Mother Bridgeman has got things well in hand at Balaclava."

"Well, sir," said Field, "the way she put it, Miss Nightingale is superintendent of nursing on *that* side of the Black Sea as well as this."

Dr. Hall snorted.

Field then requested the Nightingale nurses be freed from the obligation to wear the Scutari Hospital uniform when moving about the town.

"*Denied.*"

Field thanked the doctor for the interview and turned to take his leave. But then he turned back.

"It's the queerest thing, Doctor. I suppose it's a common enough name, but I just this morning heard from the madam of the local British bawdy house that a John Hall was present the night of Mary Dumphries' murder. Strange, yes?" The doctor's face reddened. "Three in a bed, she said."

The bedroom door slammed shut in Field's face, and Mr. Stanhope showed Field out.

"Perhaps," said Stanhope quietly, "it was an impostor, this other John Hall? Good night, Mr. Field. God speed you on your journey!"

31

It was early morning, the day after the departure of the *Ottoway*. Dawn was just barely fingering the harbor. A cart, laden with burlap bags filled with potatoes, onions, and other root vegetables, stood waiting outside the two-story house, its horse, stamping and snorting, tethered to a lamppost.

Inside, Mrs. Dinkins welcomed her guest with more than her customary confusion.

"Why, Mr. Hall, you're very early! In any event, the Dinkins Inn is closed, it's finished, it is no more, Mr. Hall."

"I know, my dear. May I come in?"

"Well, it's all boxes and packing up in here, and I'm that fretful, sir, I'm run ragged by it all!"

Her visitor seemed unmoved by her ragged state but continued to smile fondly at her.

"All right, do come in," said Mrs. Dinkins, "if you wish."

Following her into the house, her guest took off his cap and loosened his scarf. Dinkins turned and looked more closely at him.

"Look how you're got up! And that's another thing. Why did you never tell me you were a doctor?"

"Who said I was a doctor?"

"The policeman from London did," said Dinkins.

"Did he now? What else did he say?"

"Oh, you know, he wanted to see the room where it happened and that sort of thing."

"You and the policeman had quite a conversation, then."

"Would you like a cup of tea?"

"I would, indeed, Mrs. Dinkins." She preceded him into the kitchen. "Did you tell him that I was here that night?"

"I did," she said, pumping water into the kettle. "You were, weren't you? So many come and go, it's hard for me to keep track."

"What did you tell the policeman about James Talbot?"

"Just what you told me to say, should anyone ask. Poor man blew his brains out." She lit the gas ring. "He did do, didn't he? I thought it strange at the time."

"People blow their brains out every day, Mrs. Dinkins."

She took two cups from a shelf and put them on the table alongside the teapot. She frowned.

"All the same, upset as he was, it still seemed strange."

"Mrs. Dinkins, I don't know that I can count on you."

"Sugar?"

"In fact, I'm sure I cannot."

"One or two?"

"Two, please."

She spooned sugar into both cups.

"Well, I've got enough to worry me, what with moving to Newbiggin-by-the-Sea and finding suitable premises and a brand-new clientele and all. It's hard at my time of life, I tell you. Ever since I lost Mr. Dinkins in the Railway Bubble I've had to look after myself. Always wondering, How am I to earn my bread? How am I to live?"

"Mrs. Dinkins, you really won't have to worry about any of that."

The kettle began to whistle, and the old woman turned back to the gas ring.

Outside, in less than a half hour, the horse was untied, and the heavy-laden cart made its way slowly up the hill, bound for the kitchens of the Barrack Hospital.

32

Days always began well before dawn in the kitchens of the hospital at Scutari. Alexis Soyer was long used to the hours demanded by his craft, from shopping the torch-lit predawn markets of Les Halles or Smithfield, to late-night meal preparations in the finest restaurants and clubs of Paris and London. Since T. G. Taylor had come into his life, however, Soyer sometimes allowed himself to sleep late. T.G. genuinely loved to be the first up and stirring, and Alexis genuinely loved letting him do so. This morning Soyer hadn't even heard his friend rise from the bed they shared once or twice a week.

Even now his T.G. would be lighting fires in the big hearth and in the gas ranges, and getting the boilers going. The kitchen boys would be stumbling after him, still half-asleep, performing their first tasks of the day. Deliveries from the town would be arriving at the kitchen's loading doors or would have been left just outside in the dead of night. Soyer smiled at the thought that the world of the cuisinier ran on its own time, whether it be at the Reform Club or an army hospital in a grubby little Turkish town.

It was a fine autumn morning. He threw off the covers and dressed quickly in the chill air of the bedroom. He would join T.G. for their morning hot chocolate and then begin the labors of the day. As soon as he entered the kitchen, Soyer was hit by the welcome smells and warmth of his domain. Already large pots of beef and mutton were starting to bubble.

"Ahmed," he said, "where is Mr. Taylor?"

The kitchen boy, sitting on a stool and warming his hands at the newly lit hearth, pointed to the big doors. "Taking in deliveries, sir."

"Then let us help him, shall we?" said Soyer. "I think you need waking up!"

"If you say so, sir."

"I do say so, young man, don't be cheeky."

"Sorry, sir."

The French chef threw open the doors, stepped out, and drew a deep breath of the fresh, salt-tinged air. He saw the sacks of bread that had been left out there in the night by the town's bakers and the bulging burlap bags from which seeped the blood from sheep and beef. And there was his T.G., dragging another bag off the back of a cart, grunting with the effort. He tugged again, savagely, and the burlap top split open.

At first Soyer thought it was a bird's nest somehow peeking out from the top of the bag. Twigs and sticks. He thought of the ortolan, a delicacy he'd had in his youth, songbirds boiled in Armagnac and served whole in their own nests. Then he realized it was not a nest. It was hair, gray hair above the wrinkled gray face of an elderly woman, eyes wide open, bulging, and a patch of bright red color where the mouth should have been. T.G. drew out a length of red silk from around the woman's neck.

"T.G.?" said Soyer, and the young man whirled about to see his mentor and his kitchen boy staring.

"No," he said. "No."

T.G. turned back to the bag and tried to pull the burlap up, to cover the hideous face.

Ahmed nudged the chef. "Mr. Soyer, sir?" he whispered.

Soyer and T.G. looked up to see two Turkish deliverymen approaching, pulling handcarts laden with sacks of flour. The Turks stopped, looked from the head of the elderly dead woman hanging off the back of the cart to the man with the red scarf in his hands. T.G. dropped the scarf and tugged once more at the burlap to hide the face.

The deliverymen left their carts where they were and ran.

T.G. cried, "Wait!" But of course they did not.

He turned back to the man and boy staring at him. To Alexis Soyer, T.G. had the hunted look of a cornered beast.

33

The *Ottoway* had crossed the Black Sea in only five days and nights, but then, at the Balaclava harbor, there was wind and a heavy swell. The harbormaster refused to allow the steamer into port, so the crew had lowered one of its own lifeboats to transfer Florence Nightingale, Jane Rolly, and Josiah Kilvert to shore.

"We could wait, miss," said Robert Robinson, who had turned a shade of green, "until we get a quieter sea."

"No, young man," said Nightingale, "I'm determined on this. You stay aboard with the inspector and the other nurses until the captain feels he can put safely into port. You'll be with us soon enough."

Kilvert would go first, stepping up into Field's laced hands, then lowering himself down into the little boat, joining the *Ottoway*'s first mate there.

Jane would be next.

"All right, Mrs. Rolly?" said Field.

"Only a few months ago Seaman Kilvert had such pain in his shoulder, it's a wonder to see him today," said Jane.

Her manner's not warm, thought Field, *but not cold. An improvement over recent days, anyway.*

"You lot take good care of your men."

She glanced up at him. "We do. All right, Mr. Field, here we go."

He cupped her in his arms, lifted her over the gunwale, and lowered her as delicately as he could toward the boat below. Kilvert reached up to receive her, and it was done. Miss Nightingale would be next, but suddenly the wind rose and the surge grew higher. Field, Nightingale, and Robert Robinson stood unsteadily on deck, clinging to the rail and looking down at the little boat rising and falling.

"This is madness," said Field.

Which evidently struck Nightingale funny, because she began to laugh.

"I'm serious!" said the inspector.

"I'm sorry, Mr. Field," said Nightingale. "It's just that I think you may be right!" She burst into laughter again and covered her mouth. "Sorry."

"Quite all right," said Field a bit gruffly.

"Mr. Field, I laugh when I'm nervous."

"Whatever you say, miss," said Field.

"Oh, don't be sour. You and I both know this is absurd, but we need to get on with it. You can manage my weight?"

"Of course."

"Right, then," said Nightingale.

Field watched the faces in the lifeboat rise up again.

"Up you go, miss," said Field. He stooped, scooped her up in his arms, and swiveled her out over the sea. At that moment the little lifeboat fell, while the deck on which Field stood shot up. He staggered, just managing to hold on to Nightingale.

"Good Lord," said Field. "Right. When it rises again, and we go down—"

"Now!" cried Nightingale, and he dropped her through the air and into the boat, the nurse landing with a shriek in a tangle of skirts and shawls. Field looked down anxiously. After a moment her distinctive laugh told him not only that she was nervous but also that she was well.

"Madness," he said.

Jane helped Nightingale to a seat and was straightening her clothing. Kilvert beamed up at Field and nodded. As the first mate began to row them away toward shore, Nightingale started to applaud the inspector, and Jane and Kilvert joined in.

"Huzzah, Inspector Field!" cried Nightingale. "Huzzah!"

At that moment Field felt his head grow cold and hot at the same time, sweat breaking out on his brow, and then to his horror he vomited violently over the *Ottoway*'s side. From the lifeboat came another burst of laughter, abruptly cut short and followed immediately after by a ragged trio singing "For He's a Jolly Good Fellow," growing fainter and fainter as the lifeboat moved through the chop toward shore.

It took the *Ottoway* another two days to come into harbor and offload its cargo and remaining passengers into the throng at the Balaclava port. Here, sick and wounded British soldiers were being carried onto ships that would take them back to the hospital at Scutari. Wounded French soldiers were carted off to French field hospitals. Merchant ships unloaded their goods from across the Black Sea and up from the Mediterranean, and fishing boats were bringing in the day's catches. Field was dazed by the crowds and still felt a bit queasy and unsteady on his feet.

Robert Robinson charged into the heaving chaos and impressed Field, as the boy managed to hire and organize a half-dozen men of several nationalities to carry the medical supplies from the ship to the British hospital.

But who's that fellow he just took on? thought Field.

"Robert!" he said.

"Yessir?"

"That man there! The older one—don't you recognize him?"

Robinson looked at the men who were carrying boxes down the gang-plank of the *Ottoway*.

"'Oh, him! 'Course I do, Inspector Field. That's Massimo, he does the odd job for us every now and then."

"The Italian beggar? How'd he cross the Black Sea then, does he walk on water?"

Robinson smiled. "He likely came on our ship, sir. He makes the crossing all the time, it's his livelihood, what little of it there is. He'll likely be on the next ship back by the end of day. But, sir, time presses, we must be off!"

"You trust him, this Massimo?" said Field.

"'Course not, sir! Now come, let's be off!"

Robinson took charge of the three other nurses who had made the journey, gathered them together with Field, and led the way. Suddenly, out of a sea of faces, the inspector saw another he thought he recognized: a young man, a thick brown mustache, glimpsed for just a moment, before disappearing into the seething mass.

Mr. Cox, the ambassador's aide, or I'm mistaken. And there's Superintendent what's-his-name! Tulman! Is this a mirror world, here on this side of the Black Sea?

But Officer Tulman vanished, too.

Robinson and the nurses were getting ahead of Field. He hurried to catch up with them, stumbled and caught himself.

This is what comes of days on a lurching ship, solid ground don't feel solid. Need some meat and a glass of beer, and I'll stop seeing things.

"Come *along*, Mr. Field!" cried Robinson.

34

The hospital at Balaclava was perched very near the edge of a cliff that plunged fifty feet down to the sea. The main building was a down-at-the-heels two-story affair, with a string of low huts leading away from it. When the war was at its height, these huts were filled with wounded and sick soldiers, but now the compound's population was much smaller. Across a plain dotted with army tents, a jagged range of hills rose, about two miles distant. Beyond those cliffs lay the city of Sevastopol, the goal of the past year's long siege and fiercely fought battles. As Field and the others approached the hospital, they heard a distant sound of artillery from farther inland, where the war had moved after Sevastopol's fall and the Russian evacuation of the city.

The first thing that struck Field as he walked into the main building was a peculiar odor, one that rode above the unpleasant smells to which he'd become accustomed at Scutari. Then he heard a familiar voice, low and measured, coming from a small office near the door. The frosted-glass door opened, and an elderly, dignified-looking nun emerged, followed by Florence Nightingale.

"But, Reverend Mother," Nightingale was saying, "I understand your concern for the souls of these poor men, and I applaud it. I share it. But their *bodies* need care as well . . ."

"How insulting you are, miss! Our labors make it obvious we do care!"

The nun and Nightingale turned a corner, and Field followed them into a crowded ward, with row after row of patients on cots. In there, the odor hit the inspector like a physical blow.

"Forgive me, Mother Bridgeman," said Nightingale. "I misspoke. But the physical wounds suffered by these men need frequent dressing, and their bed linens need to be washed from time to time, don't you agree?"

"Dr. John Hall has complete faith in me and the work my sisters are performing here."

Field saw Nightingale's cheeks redden.

"And by faith, one can move mountains, I firmly believe," she said, "but it takes two human hands and a tub of hot water to scrub a sheet."

There was a fearful cry of pain nearby. Field saw Jane Rolly bending over the bed of a young soldier. The man was breathless, sobbing, and Jane was speaking to him in low tones. She gently lifted one of his shoulders and put a soapy, wet cloth beneath, worked it rapidly back and forth and removed it, tossing the bloody cloth into a bucket at her feet, the soldier yelping piteously all the while.

"There, you see?" whispered the Reverend Mother angrily. "That poor man is in agony, and he'll soon die anyway, how can you have tortured him so? Have you no mercy?"

Jane quickly tore off a length of dry dressing, lifted the shoulder again, looped the cloth under and around, and tied it.

"Was it mercy," said Nightingale, "that allowed him to get to this state, Mother Bridgeman? For how long has he been allowed to lie there in his own waste? A week?"

The senior nun turned sharply and walked off, leaving Nightingale and Field to stare somberly at each other.

"Welcome to Balaclava, sir."

Field heard a faint voice and turned to see the soldier grasp one of Jane's arms.

A scratchy sound emerged from somewhere within him. "Thank you, Sister."

Jane slid a small pillow near the newly dressed wound, propping it up off the bed. "I'm afraid I'm not finished," she said.

"I know," whispered the young man.

Field approached Nightingale confidentially. "May I help her?"

She shook her head. "I'll assist. Bedsores require a practiced hand." Nightingale looked at Jane and her patient. "Mother Bridgeman is not a bad person, nor are the nuns under her—they're just overwhelmed, that's all. And Bridgeman is right. That poor boy, an amputee, will likely die soon. But Mrs. Rolly will keep him clean and well cared for until he does."

She started off to join Jane, but Field had one more question.

"Miss, forgive me, but what is the odor in here?"

She looked back at him.

"It is the rotting flesh of living British soldiers, Mr. Field." And she moved off to join Jane and her young patient.

THE MEN IN the Nightingale party stored the supplies they'd brought, and the Scutari nurses prepared a simple meal for them all. The Mother Bridgeman contingent snubbed the newcomers, looking after officers who were the patients housed in a couple of adjacent huts and otherwise keeping to themselves.

It was two nights later that Jane Rolly drew the overnight watch on the ward. At the end of the evening, she turned the lamps low and made a final round of the ward. A hoarse voice from the opposite end of the room called out to her.

"Miss. Please."

It was the patient with the severe bedsores she'd treated. Jane hurried to his bed. He was agitated, and his forehead glistened in the dim light.

"Someone's here," he whispered.

She took a cotton cloth from her apron and dabbed his brow.

"*I'm* here," she said.

The young man shivered and looked about furtively.

"Did you see him? Don't let him take me."

Jane had seen patients in such a state before. It often meant the end was near.

"I'm going to give you a little drink of port wine, young man, would you like that?" she said.

"Yes, please, miss."

Her patient's agitation slowly grew less, and he politely asked if he might have a little more. Jane laughed as she lifted the man's head and put the flask to his lips.

"There's money in my kit," he said, gesturing vaguely, "if you can find it. You must write down my mum's address and send it off to her."

"I've already written it down, dear, and sealed the envelope—remember? She must be so proud of her son!"

His eyes darted right and left. "Sneakin' about in here, it ain't right."

"There, there. There, there." Jane smoothed his hair and eventually he slept, as did most of the other men on the ward.

Jane turned down the remaining lamps, settled herself in a chair, and wrapped herself in a blanket. Eventually there were snores and whimpers. Once in a while someone would cry out in his sleep, or another would wake, moaning, and Jane would rouse herself to see if she could help, even if it was only to adjust bedclothes or a pillow or give a sip from the flask she carried. Then she would return to her chair and pull the blanket about her again.

She dozed. And woke. And dozed again.

She dreamt someone was speaking to her in a low voice. A distinctive accent. Scolding her. She'd done something very wrong. She should go now, hadn't she done enough damage already?

She opened her eyes and listened. Nothing.

"Who's there?" she said.

The ward was indistinct. She realized she'd been weeping in her sleep, and she brushed the tears from her eyes.

"Who is that? Who's there?"

There were snores. A moan, a whimper. The sounds of men sleeping. But someone nearby was *not* sleeping, she knew it. Someone was watching her, staring at her. Hating her.

She found the matches in a pocket of her apron and felt for the lamp she'd placed at her feet. Where was it? Surely it was here, on her right. But it wasn't, nor was it at her left side. She struck a match, once, twice, but when it burst into flame, the flame was all she saw, flaring up, the match burning her fingers. She dropped it.

Was it a low laugh she heard?

"Stop it!"

Something tickled her throat. She brushed at it, but it wasn't a fly, it was solid. It was silk. Warm breath on the back of her neck, and the silk grew taut.

"Missus Rolly?"

Blind terror seized her. She tried to get her fingers between the fabric and her throat, but it was no good, she could not draw breath. She threw her hands behind her head and tried to grab hold of ears, hair, flesh, anything, but she couldn't reach far enough. Bright spots appeared before her eyes, flashes, flaring and fading.

The voice at the back of her neck said, *Unclean!*

A sudden stinging pain pierced her upper lip. Desperate, she pushed her feet downward and thrust herself backward, the attacker stumbled, and the two humans fell back into a heap on top of each other. The silky fabric dropped away. Breath rushed into Jane's throat and she used it to scream.

The man pushed her off him and scrambled to his feet. Footsteps sped away into the darkness at the far end of the ward. Jane lay gasping where she'd fallen. A moment later a lantern beam fell into the room and approached, the light bobbing up and down with the man who carried the lantern.

"It's Inspector Field, Mrs. Rolly. Oh, dear God!"

Words tumbled from her as he helped her to her feet.

"He was . . ." She pointed to her neck. "He was . . . He talked to me in my head."

From the darkness, one of the men said, "There was someone here, sir, doing a mischief. He run off, just there."

"It's the beast," said another voice in the dark.

"Can a man do that?" said Jane. "Enter a person's head?"

"Hold still, my dear, for just a moment," said Field. He pulled the needle from her lip, and the dangling thread and the red rose. Jane caught a glimpse of it all, and then, for the first (and last) time in her life, she fainted dead away. Field caught her, just.

Others entered the ward.

"Kilvert!" said Field. "Is that you?"

"I'm here, sir," said Kilvert.

"Take care of Mrs. Rolly, will you?"

Mother Bridgeman appeared at the door. "What is going on?" she said.

"If you'd fetch smelling salts and some brandy, Sister, I'd be obliged," said Field.

Kilvert joined the inspector, who gently passed Jane, beginning to come to consciousness, to his arms. Field left his lamp with them and strode to the back of the ward. The patients, those that could, propped themselves up on their elbows to watch him go.

35

It was completely dark. With his hands Field found the half-open door that gave onto a landing crowded by buckets and foul-smelling mops. One staircase led up to the floor above, and another led down. These he descended and found at the bottom of the short flight a locked door. He tried the latch, but it was immovable.

Had the intruder jammed the lock behind him? Or had he sought to flee this way and found his escape blocked? Was the man here with him now, in this pitch-black vestibule?

"Go on, show yourself!" said Field.

Silence.

Wishing now that he'd kept his lantern, Field began to climb the other staircase. At the top he found another landing. He opened the door there to a roomful of mostly sleeping women. At the room's far end a couple of candles were lit, and three nuns were up and dressing, having been roused by the commotion in the ward below. They turned and saw Field's shadowy bulk in the distance. There was a shocked intake of breath, and Field realized he was the only intruder here.

The inspector retreated, hurried down the steps, and at the bottom tripped over one of the pails. He careened to the landing's other end, which is where he found another short flight of steps and a wide-open door at the bottom. Field ran out to the ground below, into the night, and stopped short suddenly.

What's that sound?

There was a booming sound, almost at his feet. And another. As his eyes adjusted, he realized he had run almost to the edge of the cliff, and it was the sea he heard, pounding the shore far below him.

Inspector Bucket meets an abrupt end, he thought, *or nearly*.

He stepped well back from the cliff's edge and turned in a circle, willing his eyes to pierce the darkness. The line of low huts stretched away into the distance. From somewhere on the hills above the hospital came a forlorn sound of bleating sheep. And always, the push and pull of the Black Sea.

Minutes had been lost. Whoever had found his way into the Balaclava Hospital had likely fled. It made no sense for Field to go off blindly into the night. He turned back, walking to the door from which he'd just emerged. Near the bottom step he found a shattered lantern lying on the ground.

Dropped it, didn't you, you cowardly bastard.

The inspector let it lie and decided to go round to the hospital's front entrance instead of this one, for fear of disturbing anything else the intruder might have inadvertently left behind. He walked to that door, climbed the short staircase, and went in. As he did so, a figure coming out of the little office ducked hastily back into it, shutting the door with a soft click.

Field froze. There was lamplight coming from the ward, and the soft sound of footsteps, most likely a nurse making the rounds. But the office was unlit; the frosted glass of the office door was dark. Whoever was in there had been taken by surprise and did not want to be known.

Right, then.

The inspector continued on into the hall, stopping directly before the office door.

"Mr. Field?" He turned and found Nightingale standing in the hall with a lamp.

"How is Mrs. Rolly?" said Field.

"She's in the nurses' hut, with Sister Novella looking after her," said Nightingale. "I gave her a sleeping draft, and I'm taking her watch."

"Was she assaulted?"

"There's a livid mark round her throat, so indeed she was assaulted, but otherwise, no. She was terrified, understandably so, but proud that she'd fought back. She kept saying 'I think I hurt him!' Mr. Kilvert has insisted on keeping watch outside the hut for the night."

"Good man," said Field. "And Mother Bridgeman and her sisters? Any trouble up there?"

"They've settled down. They seem to think it's we who brought this upset with us, and who knows but what they're right?"

"Well, let's hope the remainder of the night will be peaceful," said Field, and jerked an elbow backward, shattering the frosted-glass window of the office door.

Nightingale shrieked.

He spun round, flung open the door, and plunged into the dark office, emerging moments later with a well-dressed young man who was bent double, clutching his belly and gasping for breath. Shards of glass fell from his shoulders. Field threw him against the opposite wall, and Nightingale jumped back.

"Mr. Field, please!" said Nightingale.

"Now!" Field grabbed the man by his hair and lifted up his head.

"Oh, dear," said Nightingale. "Mr. Field, this is John Stanhope, whom you know. Dr. Hall's aide. Please do release him."

Indeed, it was Stanhope. He was still gasping for breath but trying to manage a smile. A trickle of blood ran down from his hairline on one side of his face.

Reluctantly Field opened the hand that gripped the man's hair.

"I don't understand," said Field.

"Clearly not," said Nightingale, "and why should you? I've not been forthcoming."

"You knew he was here?"

Stanhope looked up at Nightingale and she at him.

"I did not," said Nightingale. "My departure from Scutari was so sudden, I didn't have a chance to let him know my plans."

"But *I* let him know your plans!" said Field. "He brought me to Dr. Hall's door and he heard the whole thing, miss, about how you were leaving next day for Balaclava."

Stanhope still clutched his belly but attempted an upright posture. "I should have let you know I would be arriving, Miss Nightingale. I was just now coming to tell you that I'm staying in the medical officers' lodgings. I apologize."

"So what were you doing in that office, then?" said Field.

"I ducked in there to wait until the comings and goings out here had died down."

Field regarded him for a long moment.

"No, no, no, miss," he said, turning to Nightingale. "This is not good. Someone entered the ward this night, attacked one of your nurses with deadly violence, and then ran away when she raised a cry. And now I find this bloke, hiding in that office there. Furthermore, he ducks back in when he sees me coming! Miss Nightingale, this is *not good*."

Again, Stanhope and Nightingale looked at each other. Finally, she spoke quietly.

"Mr. Field, you need to know that John Stanhope has been my secret ally here in this dreadful struggle almost from my arrival."

"What's that mean?" said Field.

"It means that when John Stanhope, positioned as he is, learns of the latest attempt to thwart our work, whatever it may be, he quietly alerts me to it. It means when the food stores for me and my nurses were suddenly unavailable in the dreadfully cold February of '55, he let me know it wasn't a fluke, that there actually was a plan afoot to starve us out of the Crimea. That gave me time to find my way round the obstacle. His friendship means that when I was delirious with fever and had been carried aboard a ship, it was he who informed my friends that the ship was not bound for the hospital at Scutari, as they thought, but would carry me against my will back to England. Things like that."

"Let me guess," said Field. "It was him sent you the note saying you needed to look in at this hospital, and it was along of him that we took ship and sailed to Balaclava?"

"That's right, Mr. Field," said Nightingale.

"But no one must know, sir," said Stanhope.

A voice from the staircase startled the three of them. "Know *what*, Mr. Stanhope?" It was Bridgeman in her nightdress, staring down at them.

"Mother Superior," said Stanhope, "Dr. Hall wanted no one to know that I'd come to Balaclava to keep a watchful eye on the Nightingale party, for your sake and his, but as you may see, I've been discovered."

"I heard glass break," she said.

"I'm afraid so," said Stanhope. "I shut the office door with too much force. I'll have the window replaced first thing in the morning."

Bridgeman shook her head. "It's been a madhouse here since these people arrived." She turned and began climbing the stairs. "You may tell Dr. John Hall I said so."

The three at the bottom of the stairs looked at each other uneasily.

"None of that was true, Mr. Stanhope," said Nightingale.

"Lies come rather easily to your lips, Stanhope," said Field.

"I was a public schoolboy, sir. At Aylesworthy, one lied or one died."

"In future, Mr. Stanhope," said Nightingale, turning back to the ward, "kindly allow me to do my own talking. Good night, gentlemen."

"One moment, miss," said Field. "Please don't let anyone use the rear entrance to the ward before I've had a chance to search it in the light of day. I'm guessing the intruder dropped a lantern back there, and maybe other things as well, in his haste."

"Jane Rolly's lamp!" said Nightingale. "She kept on about her missing lantern as we put her to bed, the lantern she always kept sitting at her right-hand side, and how it wasn't there when she needed it. Find this man, Mr. Field, whoever he is. Stop him."

She returned to the ward.

"Inspector," said Stanhope, "I bid you good night. No hard feelings, I hope. I know I bear none toward you."

"Generous of you. Still, I learned something tonight."

"Well," said Stanhope, "the friendship between Miss Nightingale and myself had to come out sometime, I suppose."

"No, sir," said Field, "I wasn't thinking of that. I learned tonight that among the old Aylesworthians, one lied or one died. Good night, Mr. Stanhope."

Stanhope turned, pushed through the hospital's front door, and went off into the night, Field staring after him. He wished now he hadn't been so rough with the man; it made it hard to tell if it was *he* who'd put the scratches on Stanhope's face, or Jane Rolly.

36

When the inspector entered the hospital early the next morning, he found a Turkish workman replacing the frosted glass in the office door. In the ward, Nightingale and Jane were standing together at a bedside. The sheet had been pulled up and over the bed's occupant, and Field realized the deceased was the young amputee. Jane was speaking quietly to Nightingale.

"At various times through the evening he spoke to me of his mother. Hoping she'd think well of him. He was still in such pain, I wondered he could speak at all. But then I realized he was thinking *I* was his mother. He was saying goodbye to me and asking my blessing, and at the same time telling me his mum's postal address. I told him I did think well of him. I told him I was proud of him as ever a mother could be. Was that wrong, do you think?"

"No," said Nightingale.

"He tried to warn me. More than once he said, 'Someone's here, did you see him?' I thought it was just delirium."

Nightingale embraced Jane, and Field continued quietly on to the vestibule at the rear of the ward. There, beyond the buckets and mops, he heard voices from the bottom of the steps. He hurried down and found two men just outside. Kilvert was squared off against the Italian beggar, the so-called Mendicant, who held a broom.

"What's all this?" said Field.

"Inspector," said Kilvert, "I just now found this person a-sweepin' after Miss Nightingale put it about we weren't supposed to come near this door. I hope I stopped him before he done any harm."

"I do no harm!" said the man. "I think maybe the kind English give me a coin if I sweep, but no."

"You seem to turn up everywhere," said Field.

"Poor Massimo Flammia, nobody love him."

"I shouldn't think so, old chap. I see you've cleared away the broken lantern. What else have you swept up?"

"No thing!"

"What have you got in your pockets, then?"

Massimo looked bitterly at Field and shook his head.

"Turn them out!" said Field. "Kilvert, take the broom from him."

Kilvert did so. Reluctantly Massimo pulled out the threadbare linings of his pockets. Loose black tobacco fell to the ground, and a couple of coins, which Massimo stooped to retrieve.

"I sweep broke glass," he said. "That's all!"

"And last night?" said Field. "Where did you lay your pretty head? Or were you up and stirring hereabouts?"

The Italian shook his head bitterly. "Oh, yes, so polite, the English."

Field grabbed the man by his lapels and pulled his face close to his own.

"Did you enter this hospital last night? I'll know it if you lie."

Massimo shook his head. "No."

Field reached into his own jacket pocket and emerged with the embroidered rose found on Mary Dumphries. He held it before the Italian's eyes.

"Seen this before?"

Massimo winced. He looked into Field's eyes and said, "I think the devil sent you."

After a moment the inspector released him. The surge and crash of the sea below them sounded to Field's ears like accusation: he himself was to blame for not inspecting the area then and there, the night before. To Massimo, he said, "Oh, do go away."

For the inspector in the days following the abortive attack on Jane Rolly, the most notable change was in Jane's own demeanor. She seemed self-conscious of the swelling on her upper lip, ducking her head, turning her face. She flinched if Field came near her. She started at every noise. And in her eyes he saw only fear.

The Scutari nurses hadn't been in Balaclava a week when Nigel Cox appeared at the hospital with Stanhope in tow, and announced, somewhat grandly, that he was there representing the British ambassador and bore a gift for Miss Nightingale from Her Majesty the Queen. He made a little bow and smiled lopsidedly. Field guessed the young man had been drinking. Nevertheless, there was great excitement among the nurses and others who gathered round their leader as she opened the small parcel.

It was a brooch. "Designed by His Majesty Prince Albert," said Cox. "Himself."

"I am deeply touched by their Majesties' kindness, Mr. Cox," said Nightingale. "Please do let the ambassador know that."

"He'll be thrilled," said Cox.

Oh, yes, thought Field, *the man's drunk.*

Nightingale read aloud the inscription on the front. "Blessed Are the Merciful. Crimea." Turning the brooch over, she read silently.

"May we see it, miss?" said Kilvert, and she passed it to him. He read the backside to the others. "To Miss Florence Nightingale, as a mark of esteem and gratitude for her devotion toward the Queen's brave soldiers—from Victoria R. 1855."

There was applause all round, but Cox glared at Nightingale.

"He hates you, you know," he said. "The ambassador."

"Steady on, Nigel," said Stanhope.

"They all do. That's why they're throwing me out, they imagine I'm in your camp, but I'm not."

"Come along," said Stanhope, putting a hand on Cox's shoulder.

But Cox went on.

"I'm just trying to make my way in the world, and now I'm finished, they say, before I'd hardly begun! And somehow it's all your fault!"

"That's enough, Nigel!" said Stanhope.

"It's quite completely ugly," said Cox, "that thing the Prince made for you. You know it perfectly well, and when you're back with your own kind, you'll laugh about it, you'll show it about and laugh, you know you will!"

"I think it's quite lovely, Mr. Cox," said Nightingale. She held it up. "It represents love. Love for the soldiers here and respect for the women caring for them. Good day, sir."

Cox blundered out of the building.

"So sorry, miss," said Stanhope, following close after him. "The man's become a drunkard. You won't be bothered by him again, I've booked passage for both of us back to Scutari, leaving this evening." He glanced at the door. "That is, if I can keep him corralled between now and then. Farewell for now, Miss Nightingale."

The next morning there was a group of British soldiers, uniformed, scrubbed, and shining, waiting for the nurses outside the hospital. They presented Nightingale with a basket of blossoms plucked from nearby hillsides. Then an officer came leading a beautiful black horse up to the door of the hospital, declaring it hers to ride for as long as she might remain in the Crimea. Nightingale could not conceal her joy. She promptly arranged with her staff and Mother Bridgeman to be absent for a few hours from the Balaclava Hospital. She would take a select few of her people to view the fallen city of Sevastopol.

But one of those she selected, Jane Rolly, declined the invitation.

"Jane," said Nightingale, "it's because of you in particular I've come up with this scheme."

Jane looked up into her mentor's face for a moment, then dropped her eyes.

"I've been watching you, dear Jane. What befell you last week was bound to leave a mark. It's understandable. But we are healers, you and I. And we know about taking care of wounds and healing them. We bathe them with light and fresh air and good food and cheerful faces."

Jane looked up again, with anything but a cheerful face.

"Trust me?" said Nightingale.

Jane took a deep, shuddering breath and said, "Yes, miss."

NIGHTINGALE RODE THE horse at a walk for most of the four-mile journey, while Jane and Sister Novella walked beside her, and Field and Kilvert walked behind. On the broad field before the hills, Nightingale excused herself to the others and urged the beast forward to a trot, a canter, and a brief gallop, before returning to her people, her face shining.

Nightingale's remedy of fresh air and sunlight seemed to be working for Jane, and for Florence herself. The women chatted happily together, freed from the anxieties of the hospital. But as they approached the great cliffs which stood as a natural fortification before Sevastopol, Field realized that Kilvert was no longer walking at his side but was at some distance behind, standing and staring.

"Mr. Kilvert?" said Field. "Come along, then!" When Kilvert didn't move Field walked back to where he stood. "Josiah?"

Kilvert seemed to wake from a trance. The remains of a splintered, broken ladder lay a few yards from the path.

"Sorry, sir," he said. "I've been here before, you see. I was a ladderman.

It took us more than one year to cross these four hundred yards from our trenches. When I finally made it, just about there"—he pointed to a spot near the base of the cliff—"I got a bullet for my pains. Dead lucky, I was. For many of my mates, this was the last wretched bit of earth they ever saw."

Field nodded, and after a moment, Kilvert began to walk toward the ladies again. Field walked alongside in silence.

"You asked me to help you in your investigations, sir," said Kilvert finally, "and I've done nothing."

The inspector looked at the younger man with surprise. "You may have noticed, Mr. Kilvert, that I've done little more. Sometimes, *oftentimes*, it's like that, investigative work. You wait, and you keep your eyes open, or try. You hope for a light to shine and try not to sit on your thumbs. If you're lucky, a shaft of sun falls on something you've been staring at all along, and then when you make an arrest you look to others like a worker of miracles. But that's the last thing you are."

"Truth be told," said Kilvert, "I wanted to be a policeman myself."

"Did you now?"

"Since I was a boy. Don't know why. The policemen of Kidwelly were not impressive figures, by any means, and they were not often busy, except to manage the occasional tippler. But still I fancied myself, forgive me, sir, one day becoming a member of the Metropolitan Police of London Town. And now I know I never could be one."

"Whyever not?" said Field.

"Sir, I just now saw the Great Redan, as I did a little more than three months ago, and it stopped me dead in my tracks. How would that do, on the streets of London? A constable, froze by fear?"

"I have never known battle, Josiah, but I think it has to be a deal rougher than the streets of London, even on a bad night."

They continued up the steep slope and caught up with the others who had paused their ascent, waiting for them. Miss Nightingale, astride her beautiful black horse, looked as happy as they'd ever seen her. Before long, the party had reached a point from which they could see the city of Sevastopol, which lay in ruins after its long siege. Now that the Russians were gone, teams of men were laboring to repair and rebuild it.

On the ridge, Nightingale offered the horse to the other women to ride. Jane demurred, but Sister Novella, a dark-haired girl in her early twenties, was excited to try. There was much laughter as Nightingale tried and failed to get Novella up and seated in the sidesaddle, and applause when she succeeded.

"Don't you wish you could do this, Mr. Kilvert?" said Novella.

"You look like you were born to the saddle, Sister," he said. "I was not!"

Quietly the inspector said to Kilvert, "She fancies you, son."

"Got a girl back home in Kidwelly, sir, there's no one else for me."

"I'll tell you what, Josiah. When this is all over, you just ask your girl if she'd care to come with you to see me in London. If she says yes, we'll see about getting you a position with the Met."

Kilvert looked suddenly stricken.

"I don't think I made myself clear, Inspector Field. Are you a believer, sir?"

Field hesitated. "Not often," he said.

"Never mind that, sir. At the base of the Redan, last June, it was the beast I saw. He's not the Beast of the Crimean any more than he's the Beast of Kidwelly. There is only one beast." Kilvert broke off and glanced at Field. "You'll think I'm mad."

"No, I won't, son. I'm listening."

"Well, sir. The beast is not death. Death comes to us all. It can even be a gift. No, the beast is a force that wills not only the death of others but also the death of all things that live. His face is a horror, and his very breath is a torment. I do not care to meet up with him again. But thank you, anyway, sir, for the offer of a position."

37

The members of the Scutari contingent were taking their midday meal together the next day when the refectory door flew open and an ample woman of middle years strode in, carrying a heavy basket. She was dressed from bonnet to toe in bright red and yellow shawls and skirts.

"Miss Nightingale!" she cried.

"Mrs. Seacole," said Nightingale, rising from the table, "what a lovely surprise!"

Seacole beamed, put her basket on the table, and the two women hugged.

"I cannot stay, I'm run off my legs as it is, but when I heard you were here, I had to come!" Seacole's Jamaican accent was thick and luxuriant, her face a map of smile lines.

"Ladies?" said Nightingale. "Gentlemen?" There was a scraping of chairs as everyone stood. "I believe only a few of you have met Mrs. Mary Seacole, who founded the British Hotel at Balaclava, which is doing such good for our sick and wounded soldiers."

"Call me Mother Seacole, it's more comfortable, I think." She laughed. "'Founded' is a nice word, and 'hotel' is another, if we're talking about the pieces of scrap I hammered together to build it, but we do our best! So where is Monsieur Soyer? Where is Mr. T.G.?"

"Alas," said Nightingale, "we could not spare their services to the Scutari kitchens and had to leave them behind."

Seacole's face fell. "Oh, it is a damn shame, Miss Nightingale, I do enjoy them so." She retrieved a bottle from her basket. "Look what I brought for those good men, the champagne they require! Never mind, you can put this to good use, I'm sure."

Nightingale smiled doubtfully and shook her head. "Very kind of you, my dear, but we really couldn't."

"Oh, go *on*, miss. Also, I got pâté, real French pâté, just for you," she said, pulling other items from the basket, "and two cheeses. Do you know what a job I had finding them?"

"Well, it's very kind of you."

Seacole looked at the small assembly, all standing at attention. "God bless you, each one, doing God's work. Who is this big man?"

"Sorry," said Nightingale, "this is the famous detective inspector Charles Field of the Metropolitan Police."

Field inclined his head. "Pleased to meet you, Mrs. Seacole."

Her brow contracted. "You've come about the wickedness, then? You must have a care for these good people, sir. There's evil about."

She turned her attention to Jane Rolly. "I know this child from when I first passed through the Barrack Hospital. Jane, isn't it? A shadow has fallen on you. Come here, please."

Jane presented herself before the woman. Seacole searched her face and then engulfed her in an embrace. "'Be still and know that I am God'—this is what I say to my own self when I'm troubled, which is often." She kissed her on each cheek and then took a vial from a pocket in her voluminous layers of clothing.

"Two drops on your tongue before bed and again first thing in the morning, Jane. You'll promise me?"

Jane couldn't help but smile. "I promise, Mother Seacole."

Seacole's smile faded. "He has touched you, hasn't he, this creature?"

"I am the one who got away," said Jane. "The only one. He will go on hunting me, I'm sure of it."

Seacole sighed. She found another pocket close to her breast and pulled out a wooden peg, about four inches long, carved and painted at the top with a grinning white-toothed skull. "This little man will go with you and will frighten the bad man clean away!" She gave it to Jane and glanced at Field. "Between my little man and this great big one here, you will be all right. Now I must go!"

Seacole unloaded the cheeses and pâté from her basket onto the refectory table and then laughed again. "Look what I almost forgot! Your post!" She produced a bundle of letters, tied up with string. "They sent it on with me when they heard I was coming up here!"

This was good news indeed, and everyone crowded eagerly around the woman.

"Stop!" cried Seacole, feigning fear. "Help! Give me at least a running start!"

With another gust of laughter, she was gone, and they resumed their noon meal but now with a flurry of letter opening. Among the letters there were two directed to Florence Nightingale and one to Inspector Charles Field.

Field saw that his was an official dispatch, sent by Superintendent Second Class Saleem Tulman of the Scutari police. He opened it and read silently.

To my esteemed colleague, Detective Inspector Charles Field: I must with regret inform you of a new homicidal attack here and request your presence as soon as quite convenient to my honored friend. The

victim bore the insignia of the red pentagram (rose) over her lips.
She was a British woman of advanced years who was known to the
police as an innkeeper and panderer of disgraced young women. Two
witnesses saw the murderer with the victim, holding the red scarf that
ended her life. I have issued a warrant for the arrest of Mr. Theodore
G. Taylor, until recently in the employ of the Barrack Hospital but
now nowhere to be found.

Yours ever in admiration, etc. etc.,
Tulman

At the same time Nightingale was reading a letter addressed to her
from her aunt Mai.

Oh, Flo, there's been the most dreadful occurrence here and just
when things had been going a bit better. An old woman has been
murdered, presumably right here in the hospital kitchens, but
I don't for a minute believe it. T.G. was opening the morning
deliveries from the markets, and among the potato sacks was a
burlap bag that contained the body of the poor woman. That, at
least, is my interpretation, but others from town came upon him
and went running directly to the fool police superintendent. So far
we've managed to keep T.G. out of sight, but as we do so, others
become convinced of his guilt. (Poor Monsieur Soyer, you can only
imagine how he suffers!) Do come back soon, please, Flo. We need
you.

With love and a kiss,
Your poor Auntie

P.S. Can you for a moment believe that T.G. knows his way round
needle and thread? I cannot. Come soon!

Nightingale, stricken, looked up from the letter and found Field's eyes on her. In a brisk businesslike voice, she said, "I wonder if you might join me, Inspector, for a brief conversation."

"Of course, miss."

The others continued eating, reading their post, and chatting among themselves as the nurse and the detective rose. Nightingale picked up her other piece of mail and the two of them walked along the cliff above the sea. When Nightingale conveyed the message sent by her aunt, Field stopped in his tracks.

"They're *hiding* him? Are they mad?"

"I know for a certainty that T.G. is incapable of such wickedness," said Nightingale. "My aunt shares my opinion."

"What you and your aunt believe means nothing! Nothing!"

"Please, Inspector, contain yourself."

"But, miss, everyone will think he's done a bunk! It's practically an admission of guilt!"

Nightingale began to walk again. "According to Mrs. Rolly, you yourself had suspicions of T.G. Perhaps you do still. Does his skin color have something to do with that?"

"*It will do to a jury!*" said Field, "*I promise you!*"

"As I say, contain yourself and stop shouting like a . . . well, like a man!"

A burst of distant artillery rose suddenly, and the two of them looked toward the hills beyond the Great Redan. After another series of explosions, the noise was carried off to sea and was gone. They continued walking.

"At first, Miss Nightingale, I confess it, now you ask, the man being a Negro made me look at him closely. There were other factors, of course. But I came to realize that his dodging of questions about the killing of Mary Dumphries may have been for other reasons altogether."

The nurse waited for him to elaborate, but he did not.

"But what I said about juries still stands," he said. "A runaway Black man accused of murder would not do well in the dock."

"It is *not fair*."

"Perhaps not, but it's the way it is, miss." He hesitated, glancing at her. "I will need to question T.G. when I see him. I have been sent here for a reason, Miss Nightingale, and cannot declare a man innocent because he's been treated unfairly or because you and your aunt believe him to be innocent."

"Well, you disappoint me, sir."

"Miss Nightingale, please! One does not interrogate to incriminate only! Most often questioning leads to a person being *ruled out* as a suspect."

"I see."

"However," continued Field, "there is much about T.G. we don't know. He was . . ." The inspector searched for an acceptable word. "He was a person of the streets before Mr. Soyer took him on, I know that much."

Nightingale looked at him sharply.

"If he runs now," continued Field, "you and I will be plagued with the nagging question: Did T.G. have a side we never suspected? An ugly secret? That is, if he evades capture by Superintendent Tulman, which I think unlikely. Your aunt is wrong when she calls Tulman a fool. He's anything but."

Gulls wheeled and glided just above their heads, careening out over the sea and back again, crying, scolding, lamenting.

"I wonder, Mr. Field, if you can imagine what it is to live every moment of every day in the knowledge that you are considered *less than*. Substandard. Lacking."

She stopped and looked out toward the horizon.

"I was born to great wealth and privilege. But from the time I was a young girl, when I first realized that I forever would be *less than* and *lacking* because of my sex, the theme of my childhood became *not fair*. All

I ever wanted to do was to care for others. To tend the sick. My sister's injured dollies were bandaged. A village dog who limped was fitted with a splint until he was better, that sort of thing. As a child, I was allowed to play with such a dream. As an adult female of my class, all that would be forbidden and *was* forbidden me. By my parents. By society. And then God spoke to me.

"I don't say it lightly or boastfully. The voice was clear, distinct, and uncomfortable. I could go about crying 'not fair,' or I could go out into a world of need and *act*. Well, that got my attention.

"These dreadful crimes, Mr. Field, are aimed at women. And every crime of this nature is another mark against us nurses, as the world tallies it. Someone is not only satisfying a personal demon but trying to denigrate our work here as well, which is seen as an invasion of a male-only domain. This criminal, whoever he may be, is likely a madman. But he has many unknowing allies among sane, law-abiding, upstanding Christian males, Mr. Field. That is what we're up against. What T.G. is up against, as a Black man, is beyond my ability to grasp. If he is *wrongly* suspected of these crimes it is, well, *not fair* in the extreme. You have your work cut out for you, sir."

Field nodded. "I'll ask the Robinson boy to get us passage on the next steamer for Scutari, this evening, if possible."

"Oh, yes, do," she said with a sigh. "I'll leave it to you to break it to our nurses, and they'll need to be packed and ready to go. Thank you, Charles."

Nightingale continued back to her hut, pursued by the sound of the relentless, pounding sea. She pushed open the door and shut it behind her, feeling utterly spent. Suddenly she sensed she was not alone.

"Hallo?"

No response. She looked about the tiny quarters, into each corner. She willed herself to open the wardrobe. Shutting it again, she realized she still held, crushed in her hand, the second letter she'd received that day. She laid the envelope on the little table by her bed and flattened it

out. It had no address but only Nightingale's name writ in a big hand
on the front. She tore it open and took from it a sheet of paper on
which had been drawn the crude stick figure she'd seen before. Female.
Obscene.

Tick tock times up!

Nightingale stared at it for a moment and then tore it in two.

38

Ever since the morning the body of Mrs. Dinkins appeared at the hospital kitchens, Alexis Soyer, Mai Smith, and Sister Clara had been moving T.G. surreptitiously around the vast building, from one hiding spot to the next. Each day the trio shifted their fugitive, feeding him and endeavoring to keep up his (and Monsieur Soyer's) spirits, all the while formulating a plan to get him out of Turkey.

Superintendent Tulman appeared at frequent but unpredictable intervals. Sometimes he was accompanied by members of his police force; at other times he would show up alone. The daily work went on, and most of the hospital personnel (with the exception of the kitchen workers, who knew better) took it for granted that T.G. had fled, having been suspected of murder.

But the superintendent returned again and again. This morning Peter, the young Russian boy, had run into the kitchens.

"He's coming!" cried the boy. "Five minutes off!"

"Such a tiresome man, this Tulman," said T.G. from the corner where he'd been peeling potatoes, *because if I do nothing I'll go mad!*

"Come quickly, my dear boy," said Soyer. *"Nous te mettrons dans la cave."* Turning to the Russian boy, Soyer said, *"Merci,* Peter. Now fetch Mrs. Smith and Sister Clara. *Vite, vite!"*

Instantly the kitchen staff went into a well-rehearsed routine. By the time Tulman arrived, everyone was in place.

"Superintendent," said Mai Smith, "as I've said several times before, Mr. Taylor is no longer employed here. Check the ports, check the trains!"

"I thank you for your kind advice, madam," said Tulman, "but I have checked with all ports of entry and exit and am satisfied that Mr. T. G. Taylor has not left this country. Who knows? Perhaps he has not left this building."

Tulman walked portentously up and down the rows of kitchen help, who kept their heads down as they did their work: among them, young Ahmed turning the spit; one-legged William, propped on his crutch, stirring a pot; and Peter, who had climbed up onto a stool to wash a pot half his size.

Approaching Alexis Soyer, Superintendent Tulman said, "I recall well, sir, the first night I made your acquaintance. At Mrs. Dinkins' house, it was, she who is now so tragically no longer living. You shouted in the French language, and the English, because I asked questions of Mr. Taylor. You called me an idiot and took Mr. Taylor away." Tulman raised his eyebrows expressively.

"Forgive me if I was intemperate, sir," said Soyer, "but I knew my friend to be innocent of any crime."

Tulman nodded and regarded Soyer thoughtfully. "Your friend, your friend, your friend. What *sort* of friend, I wonder."

"A good, decent friend, sir."

Tulman smiled indulgently. "And yet, here we stand, very near to where Mr. Taylor was discovered with the lifeless old woman, a patch of colorful cloth tacked over her mouth, and the silk scarf that dispatched her in his hands. Perhaps the late Mrs. Dinkins had decided to tell the police finally all she knew of the night when the British woman was killed at her inn."

"So instead of going to the police," said Mai Smith, "this Mrs. Dinkins wandered up the hill and into the hospital kitchens to do so?"

Tulman shrugged. "I wish to see Mr. T.G.'s quarters."

"And you will be free to do so, I'm sure, the moment my niece returns and gives you permission to enter the floor where the nurses are housed."

"Each day you tell me this," said Tulman.

"We expect her any moment, Officer," said Sister Clara, "her *and* Inspector Field."

Tulman nodded and started to leave but then turned back. "Monsieur Soyer, please recall that the man who helps the murderer to escape the law is guilty also of murder. You ladies might do well to remember it, too. Good day!"

The officer turned on his heel and strode off, followed quietly a minute later by Peter.

Soyer moved to a small table and shifted it, revealing a trapdoor set in the kitchen floor. He lifted it and a moment later T.G. Taylor, blinking at the light, climbed up a short ladder and into the kitchen. He brushed straw from his shoulders and trousers and Soyer let down the door to the cold cellar.

"Took his bloody time, didn't he," said T.G., "while I'm squatting down there in the dark with the chilled beef I'm coming to resemble!" He attempted a smile, but it was fleeting. "Can't take much more of this, Alexis."

"Monsieur Soyer," said Mai Smith quietly, "it cannot go on. T.G. must go."

"No," moaned the Frenchman. "Please!"

"Alexis," said T.G., "be sensible."

"I shall go with you!"

"Oh, yes, and give away the game? Together we wouldn't make it half a mile. At least, *I* would not. There is a gap, you see, between you and me."

"Ahmed?" said Mai to the boy turning the spit.

"Yes, missus!" With a nod to the next young man down the line, he passed the roasting of fowls off to him.

"Ahmed will drive," said Mai to Soyer in a low voice, "and T.G. will be at the back. The disguises are waiting in the carriage. Ahmed will deliver T.G. to our friend at the harbor, who will take care of his passage to Rimini. Everything is in readiness, you see?"

Soyer did not respond.

"Ahmed," said Mai, "off you go! Mind you stop for no one!"

"Yes, missus," said Ahmed. Turning to T.G., he said, "We'll get you through, sir."

"There's a good lad," said T.G.

The boy ran out of the kitchen.

"I don't like this," said Soyer.

"Who knows, Alexis? We two may find each other again, far from here, after all this is over."

"Do you really think so?"

T.G. took his hand. "My mother used to say that even a bird with a long neck don't know the future."

Soyer managed a smile. "You'll find Monsieur Rozan at Rome, yes? You have the address, in the via del Corso?"

"Yes, yes."

"Monsieur Rozan is a good man, you'll shelter well with him and Madame Rozan until you're ready to continue on to London, whenever it may seem to be safe. Madame Rozan is an *excellent* cook."

"Well, then, I've naught to worry about, have I?"

Soyer embraced T.G., kissed him on each cheek, and turned away.

But just then Peter rushed back into the kitchens. "The superintendent's coming back and he's bringing the head doctor! Three minutes away!"

They looked from one to the other in dismay.

"Go!" said Mai. "Now!"

The Nightingale party made good time on their return. At the Scutari harbor it was young Robert Robinson who once again managed the transport for all of them and their luggage in a single large four-horse carriage. As they neared the hospital, they passed one of their own carriages going the other way with the kitchen boy Ahmed at the reins and a tarpaulin-covered cart at the back. Ahmed did not return their greetings but sped on.

"He'll be heading for the burial grounds, I'm afraid," said Nightingale, "the ones reserved for typhoid victims."

On this somber note, the party returned to the Barrack Hospital.

Inside, Dr. John Hall and Superintendent Tulman were squared off, facing Mrs. Mai Smith and Sister Clara on the ground-floor ward of the hospital, adjacent to one of the corner staircases. John Stanhope stood silently behind the men.

"The police want to search the Black man's room," said Dr. Hall. "Unless you're *hiding* the man, that seems a simple enough request, wouldn't you say?"

"Not without leave from Miss Nightingale, sir," said Mai.

"*This is not her hospital!* She does not own it, she does not rule it!"

"Certainly not, Doctor," said Mai, "but she is in charge of the nurses here, and of their quarters, and Mr. Taylor's room is on that floor."

"This is utter nonsense. I'll lead the way, Officer Tulman."

Mai and Sister Clara drew closer to each other, blocking the staircase.

"You must know, sirs," said Mai, "that should you invade the premises of our nurses without Miss Nightingale's leave, I shall send my protest via telegraph direct to the prime minister. He is a close family friend, and I'm sure he'll be most interested."

There was a moment's silence, the men glancing at each other, their faces flushed with anger.

"What's all this about my leave and messages to the prime minister?"

said Florence Nightingale, striding through the ward, followed by Inspector Field.

"Oh, Flo!" said Mai. "Here you are!"

"Of course I'm here. What is all this?"

"The superintendent wants to inspect Mr. Taylor's old room."

"And?"

"Well," said Mai, "it's about the old woman's murder, of course."

"I've heard of this terrible crime," said Nightingale, turning to the men. "I have complete faith in Mr. T. G. Taylor, but certainly you may search his room. I'm surprised you've not done so already, Superintendent Tulman, if I've got the name right. Oddly enough, in all this dreadful business, you and I have never actually met, owing to the delicacy of my sensibilities, I'm told."

Tulman bowed. "Miss Nightingale."

"Right, then," said Nightingale, glancing about the ward. "Mai, you've had losses?"

"Why yes, I'm sorry to say, Flo," said Mai, after a moment. "In fact, two more, only this morning. The typhoid's on the rise again."

Nightingale nodded.

"Gentlemen, let me lead the way. Inspector Field, if you would be so good, please participate in this search."

Field looked from Nightingale to her aunt. "No, miss, if it's all the same to you, I'll look about on this floor."

A flush came to Nightingale's face. "But it's *not* all the same to me."

Superintendent Tulman said, "Inspector, we have searched and re-searched this and other floors for days. I must insist you, as a representative of British law, join us now in Mr. Taylor's room."

Field and Nightingale stared at each other for another moment. "Of course," he said.

Mai Smith and Sister Clara stepped away from the staircase, and the others began to climb.

The search of T. G. Taylor's monk-like room was almost comical, the small chamber bristling with several large men and one small woman.

There was very little there to search. The bed was made up crisply. The wardrobe was empty. The eyes of the figure mounted on the crucifix were averted from the policemen and doctors.

As Tulman moved through the little room, Stanhope spoke quietly to Nightingale and Field.

"Nigel Cox has gone missing as well. We don't know where he is, but we've got people looking for him, on this side of the Black Sea and the other."

Tulman picked up the book on the bedside table.

"How can this be?" he said. "I have read all of the Dickens, Inspector Field, but I never before heard of this book, this . . . *Barnaby Rudge*."

"Nor had I, sir," said Field. "I'm told it's about unreasonable hatreds leading to innocent people bein' strung up from lampposts."

He realized that Nightingale was staring at him. Then he noticed the little framed portrait of the Black woman on the table was missing.

Took his mum with him, didn't he.

Field turned and left without another word.

AHMED ENCOUNTERED THE police roadblock within a quarter mile of the hospital. Turkish police surrounded the cart, eyeing the tarpaulin-covered form in the back. One of the policemen lifted a corner of the tarp, revealing a white sheet that plainly covered a pair of human feet. The conversation was in Turkish and was quickly over when Ahmed informed the men that these were hospital dead, bound for the typhoid burial pits.

The policeman dropped the tarp hastily and stepped back from the cart.

"Go! Go, go!"

INSPECTOR FIELD RAN out of the hospital and found Robert Robinson unloading the last of the luggage from the carriage.

"Robert!" shouted Field. "I need a ride!"

"Sir?"

ON A DESERTED side lane, the white-sheeted body at the rear of the cart rose up, cast off the sheet, and in a matter of minutes became a burqa-clad woman seated on the carriage's back bench. The cart at the rear of the carriage that had held the supposed body was detached and abandoned. With his passenger in place, Ahmed got the horses moving again, down the road that led to the harbor.

Finally, that woman, too, disappeared, and the carriage headed back, away from the quay and up toward the Barrack Hospital, young Ahmed filled with pride at his triumph. He was so pleased with himself he gave Inspector Field a cheerful wave as their carriages passed each other.

"Take us down to the docks, Robert, if you please," said the inspector.

Field arrived at the harbor in time to see a steamer just putting out from port, with T. G. Taylor standing on deck and gripping the aft rail. He stared down at Field without a hint of his characteristic good humor.

39

Weeks passed and the war drew down, although outlying flare-ups between the Russians and the allies were brutal and yielded more patients for the Barrack Hospital and burials for the military cemetery.

No new incidents of violence against British women occurred. A feeling grew that Mr. T. G. Taylor may indeed have been responsible for the stalking of women and the four murders. But then the discovery of a rambling suicide note in Nigel Cox's humble rooms at Scutari, which he had taken after losing his position with the ambassador, shifted suspicion to him because of its vitriolic tone regarding Nightingale and her nurses. The note, however, was not accompanied by a body, strangely enough, and offered no indication of where Mr. Cox might have taken himself to end his life.

The Italian known as the Mendicant also disappeared, no one knew where to, and there were those who pointed to him as the culprit. A local man was arrested for theft by Superintendent Tulman's men and subsequently found to have the remains of two women in his cellar—but no colorful cloth roses. There was renewed talk of the Beast of the Crimean. An air of disquiet hung over Scutari.

Alexis Soyer was no longer present to defend T.G. against innuendo or accusation. He was in Dublin, being honored for his lifesaving aid to the Irish poor during the Great Famine. And Charles Field himself was being pressured to leave Scutari and the war.

Perhaps, wrote Commissioner Mayne, his superior in London, *having failed to solve the war secretary's little mystery for him, you might redeem yourself by a more successful pursuit of Dr. Palmer, who oddly enough is not likely to stop killing merely because you've gone on holiday.*

Had the commissioner forgotten that it was he who had recommended Field for duty in the Crimea? The words *not fair* occurred to him and then reminded him of what Miss Nightingale had said.

The inspector was torn.

The message called to mind his earlier dogged investigation of the poisoning physician, Palmer. Field had developed a righteous hatred of the doctor and was determined to stop him. But he also was not overfond of Sir Richard Mayne and didn't appreciate any threats the commissioner might hurl in his direction. In addition, he had found an unexpected kinship here with these women and with the woman who led them. Although there had been no new attacks in recent weeks, he did not consider the women to be safe.

Then he got a telegram from Mayne.

Come at once. Palmer killed again. Repeat at once.

Inspector Field could not leave Scutari without making two principal farewells. As he hurriedly packed up the room he'd occupied in the hospital throughout his stay, throwing his personal effects into his traveling satchel, he rehearsed what he might say at each of them. He finally shut the bulging bag and took a last survey of the room.

That razor by the basin?

But he'd packed his razor. He looked into his valise, found his shaving case and opened it. Yes, his gear lay within. But he'd put Dr. Talbot's blade in the wardrobe at least twice in the previous months, along with the cameo of the young lady. Field opened the wardrobe. The cameo was there but no razor. No, that razor had reappeared yet again on the little stand that held the basin. Field glanced about the room. Was anything else out of place? His ride to the harbor would be waiting in a few minutes. He left the door key on the bedside table and on his way out ran into the Cockney orderly he'd met on his first morning.

"Young man, I'm leaving today, if you'd like to do up this room."

"Nothin' would give me greater pleasure, sir," said the orderly, "if it was any of my lookout, which it ain't."

Field continued on, choosing to ignore the sarcasm, but then stopped and turned back. "I say, Trinculo, who's been in there, then, doing up my room?"

"Dunno. Used to be Mrs. Swain did it, but she turned up dead and hasn't been replaced, has she."

"Helena Swain?"

"The very one, sir."

Field thoughtfully watched the orderly hurry off down the corridor, then turned and made his own way to Nightingale's rooms. He found her at her desk, writing by the light of a single candle. It was early afternoon, but a rainstorm had blown in off the harbor and cast the day in darkness.

"Please do have a seat, Mr. Field," she said, lighting another lamp. "Would you like me to send for tea?"

"No, thank you, miss," he said, taking a chair opposite her desk.

"Will you be happy to return to London?"

Her question was unexpected. His prepared speech vanished, and he realized he had no answer, or none he felt comfortable sharing.

Nightingale continued. "You'll be just in time for Christmas, won't you."

Christmas? What's that? No, if it comes to it, I'm not happy to return to my old life. What have I ever had back there compared to what I've found out here?

But what *that* was, exactly, he could not say, even to himself.

"Duty is duty, miss," he said. "I've been recalled. A man I've been pursuing for some time may soon find himself in a corner, if I'm sharp enough to put him there. Trouble is, his crimes seem to have inspired others to imitate them, so I'll need to make sure I've got the *right* poisoner in the corner, not one of the imitators."

Nightingale recoiled. *"Imitators?"*

"It happens, miss. Poisoning's currently the rage. Not long ago it was the garrote, although that seems to have reappeared here at Scutari, to our sorrow. I regret I wasn't able to do more and sorrier than I can say about that poor girl Rose, killed on my watch."

Nightingale nodded.

"Who did it, Mr. Field?"

Again, she'd taken him by surprise.

"Do you know?" she said. "Do you guess?"

"Well, Miss Nightingale, according to poor Mrs. Dinkins, there was someone who stayed at her inn and who passed himself off as John Hall. I thought it unlikely it was our doctor friend, and this name did not appear in the register on the night Mary Dumphries was killed. I should like to have identified whoever it was and had a talk with him. You know already the desire I had to speak with T. G. Taylor. Where is he, by the way?"

Nightingale smiled and said nothing.

"You're good, you are, miss," said Field, "if you'll forgive me. As to Mr. Nigel Cox, I never paid him much attention, and now I wish I had. In my experience of suicides, their last written words are often found quite handy to the corpse, but not always, by any means. For that matter, I regret I never asked someone who speaks the Italian language to hear the Mendicant's confession."

"Oh, old Massimo. His English is passable, but you might have asked *me*. I speak Italian."

"You do, miss?"

"My parents were inveterate travelers when they were younger," said Nightingale. "I was born in Italy, at the city of Florence. Hence, my name. Pity my poor sister, born in a Greek settlement outside of Naples called Parthenope. Yes, I do speak Italian." She smiled. "Massimo once told me he'd been a famous singer in his youth, but who knows what one could believe, coming from that addled soul."

"I must say, miss, I've never felt quite at ease with your *ally*, Mr. John Stanhope."

She nodded. "That much always was obvious. Some men just seem to have a natural antipathy for one another. Some women, too, I hasten to add. But Mr. Stanhope has been of such service to me, I do wish you would strike him from your list."

"A man may smile and smile and be a villain," said Field, and Nightingale laughed.

"You're always quoting Shakespeare at me, Charles!"

The inspector's face clouded. "Is it comical, miss?"

"No, Charles, not at all! It's just that you take me by surprise each time."

He looked off. "I suppose committing passages of Shakespeare to memory was my way out of a sour home when I was a lad. It allowed me to be there, and not there, if you take my meaning. And when I couldn't find my way onto the professional stage, as I'd hoped, I found another home with Mr. Fielding and his Bow Street Runners. I was all of sixteen years of age."

A silence fell between them, Nightingale gazing absently at an envelope that lay on the table before her.

"The war is all but over," said Field, "as I understand it."

She looked up sharply. "*It might have been over and done two years ago, before it ever started!*" she said with sudden heat. "The Russians offered to withdraw, but the great men, British and French, decided it wouldn't reflect well on them to turn round and go home after they'd spent so much money getting here! All these deaths, needless!"

Her cheeks had reddened, but Nightingale was looking gaunt to Field's eyes, her hair newly cropped short and the lines of her face more pronounced. He could imagine how many young men had come under her care, only to slip away with their last words in her ears. It occurred to him to wonder how many young men of wealth and birth had sought her hand in marriage in earlier years, had sought her love, before she devoted herself to God and good patient hygiene.

"I won't leave until the last British soldier sails for home," she said. "There's still much to do. For one thing, we'll need to return to Balaclava, Mother Bridgeman having decided to take her nurses and go."

"I see."

There was another silence. Nightingale seemed to be struggling with something.

"You say a person here passed himself off as John Hall," she said. "Well, the real John Hall most certainly passed himself off as a doctor. They've just given him a KCB for his efforts here. A knighthood!"

"I hadn't heard."

"There's blood on his hands, Mr. Field. *Knight of the Crimean Burial-grounds* would have been more appropriate. I am certain Dr. John Hall never strangled any women, but I do believe he attempts to throttle their voices. And mine. By his example, he paves the way for an unhinged person to do so as well, and *not* metaphorically. I have done everything in my power to avoid distraction from the work at hand. Including the distractions that might be engendered by, say, a murder investigation. Also, the distractions of fame. But now, to my dismay, I find that I'm famous."

Field cleared his throat. "As Shakespeare put it, 'Some have greatness thrust upon them.'"

Nightingale laughed again and reached across the table to squeeze Field's hand.

"Yes, Inspector. But that line was in a comedy and spoken by a fool."

He nodded ruefully. "True."

"Who did it?" She shrugged. "Our Great Enemy may wear many

faces, but ultimately the evil is the same. To return to Shakespeare, it's the nasty schoolboy who idly pulls the wings from flies, merely to see them suffer."

She stood.

"Thank you for all you've done or attempted to do for us. I hope someday to see you again in more congenial circumstances."

Field rose and bowed. When he was gone, Nightingale sat again and took a note from the envelope on her desk. It had arrived that morning.

There was the obscene stick figure she'd come to expect. And the scrawl.

You wont never make it home

INSPECTOR FIELD'S SECOND farewell interview was to have been with Nurse Jane Rolly in a quiet moment, just the two of them, but when he found her, she was on the ward assisting an older soldier using a bedpan. She had been on duty for some hours without a break. Her hair hung lank over her forehead, and her uniform was stained with blood and perspiration.

"I wonder, miss, if I might have a word in private," said Field.

Jane glanced at him incredulously. "Are you mad?"

"Sorry, Jane. Mrs. Rolly. It's just that I'm leaving now and won't be coming back."

To the soldier, Jane said, "You might be a little helpful, actually, sir, instead of making me stand here waiting! What's that you say, Mr. Field?"

"I was wondering, when you return to London with Miss Nightingale, whenever that may be, wondering, might I call on you sometime?"

"What for?"

Field had no ready answer for this.

"All finished, Mr. Thompson?" said Jane. "Good." She covered the bedpan with a cloth and turned from the bed. "So you're leaving us, is it, Mr. Field?"

"Yes. Directly."

"Travel well, sir," she said, moving past him. Then she hesitated and turned back. The look she suddenly gave Field pierced him to the quick. "Of course you may call on me, Mr. Field," she said. "I should be pleased."

"Oh, wonderful!" said the inspector. "I mean, it would be nice to see you again."

"I'd shake your hand, sir, only . . ." She indicated the bedpan.

"I do hope your return to London will be soon," said Field.

"Goodbye, then!"

And Jane was off, bearing her burden.

FIELD WALKED OUT of the Barrack Hospital into a pelting rain and hurried down to the carriage where Robert Robinson, wearing a slicker and rain hat, was waiting, holding the reins.

"Hallo, Robert!" cried Field, stowing his satchel beneath the seat. "Nice day, ain't it!" Field climbed up into the carriage, hunching his shoulders against the wet. He looked about expectantly. "Is not Mr. Kilvert here?"

"No, sir, it seems not. Sir, I've had good news, sir! Miss Nightingale is going to sponsor me back in England, she says, when this is all over! Or in Ireland, or wherever I end up."

"That's wonderful, son."

"*And* William, *and* Peter, *and* Ahmed, all four of us!"

"She's a remarkable woman, is Miss Nightingale," said Field.

Robinson was about to shake the reins and get the horses moving when the inspector stopped him.

"I was certain Kilvert planned to join us. Let's wait a minute longer, shall we?"

"Of course, sir. Oh, this came for you, sir, I almost forgot it." Robinson reached into his coat and emerged with a blue fold of thin paper that he handed to Field. The telegram was from the Marseille Sûreté.

Retired colleague recollects deranged Italian 6 years ago. Confessed mothers murder Rome 20 years earlier. Sewed mouth shut with rose said Italian. Marseille police turned him away. No clue where man is now. Hyacinth

Field stuffed the flimsy blue paper in a coat pocket.

A deranged Italian. Confessing his crimes. So where is he, the Mendicant? Where is Massimo Flammia?

Images of Field's room in the hospital came into his mind. *The wardrobe, the basin. The razor, the cameo.* The inspector pulled out his watch. His steamer would not wait for him.

"There he is, Mr. Field!" cried Robinson.

Field looked up to see Josiah Kilvert, mud-splattered, coming toward them across the grounds from behind the hospital at a run. He slipped, fell, and got up.

"Inspector!" shouted Kilvert. "You must come!"

The three of them, Kilvert, Field, and Robinson, struggled across the sodden acres of the British military cemetery, their feet sometimes sinking into the porous earth. In the distance, three soldiers materialized like ghostly statues, motionless in the downpour, heads down, standing in a circle, leaning on shovels. To one side of them lay a muslin shroud, the size and contour of a human, ready for burial.

As they drew nearer, other details of the scene came into focus. Were those human fingers sticking up from the muddy earth at the soldier's feet? Yes, the decaying fingers of two hands, arms outstretched, reaching upward, imploring. And a grotesque muddied face, one lens of a pair of spectacles intact, the other a dark hole, the bullet's entryway to the brain.

"Inspector," said Kilvert, "this is Dr. James Talbot."

Field stared at the corpse in silence for a moment. Finally he said, "Shoddy way to bury a man, even a suicide, just inches below the ground."

Robert Robinson abruptly put a hand over his mouth and turned away.

"Robert," said the inspector, "go back to the horses now, and put the carriage away. I'll not be needing it just yet."

"Yes, sir. Thank you, sir."

The young man hurried away and soon was lost to sight.

"I've seen many suicides, Josiah. If a pistol is involved, it's generally pointed at the side of the head or inserted into the mouth. It's hard to imagine pointing the gun from the front, directly at one's own eye. Even in such a dire strait, I would tend to flinch, wouldn't you?"

Field crouched beside the remains, the rain still falling on him and on the body. Fabric protruded from beneath one shoulder. He tugged at it.

A shroud? No, a bedsheet.

He glanced up at the windows of the hospital, directly above.

You could wrap him up in a sheet and tip him out the window. Then run down here, dig a little hole, and arrange the body in it. Save you carrying a bloody great weight down the stairs, wouldn't it.

Field covered his own mouth and nose with a handkerchief and bent closer. He scooped mud away from the torso and felt one arm and then the other. He stood, rubbing his hands with his handkerchief.

"Dr. Talbot is dissolving, Josiah, but I'm willing to wager both arms were broken, either before or immediately after death, possibly in a fall. Either way, it would be *most* unusual for a suicide."

"Indeed, sir."

Field glanced at Kilvert. "You're bloody cool. I've known veteran policemen in the Metropolitan who would have been sick all over themselves by now."

"Thank you, sir."

The inspector looked up again at the hospital's fourth floor. He raised one arm high, pointing at one window. With his other hand, he pointed down at the corpse, drawing a trajectory in his mind.

"Our man's up there, Josiah," said Field. "The Mendicant, Massimo, this was his work two and a half months ago. More recently I'm quite confident he's been coming and going secretly in the hospital and perhaps has taken up residence there, hiding under our noses. Let's go."

One of the soldiers spoke up. "What are *we* to do, sir?" He nodded toward the muslin-covered form. "We got this lot here to bury."

"Dig another hole, man! And put a tarp over this one."

THE PORTERS WATCHED in dismay as Field and Kilvert, shedding mud, strode at speed through the corridors of the hospital and then up the stairs.

First, Massimo crept down from his little room at the end of the corridor in the Dinkins Inn, Field was thinking, *and garroted the Mary Dumphries woman, God knows why.*

Dr. Hall, descending the stairs with another doctor, said, "I thought you were leaving!"

Field didn't answer, taking the steps two at a time now.

Talbot, lying in that bed with Mary Dumphries, either woke to what Massimo had done or watched him a-doing it. Later that night Massimo located Talbot back in his room here at the hospital and put a bullet in his brain to shut him up.

Soon they encountered Jane Rolly coming down.

"Inspector, haven't you left yet?"

"Jane, if you see the old Italian, Massimo, get away from him, fast, and then blow a whistle!" Field and Kilvert ran up one more flight and along the corridor to the room where the inspector had lodged.

The poor housemaid, Helena Swain, happened by and saw what she shouldn't have. Perhaps she saw Massimo dragging Dr. Talbot in his sheet to the nearby window sometime before dawn. Killer hadn't planned on her, had he. So, a fancy rose for Dumphries and whatever came to hand for Helena Swain. My God, he might have torn that cheap rose from whatever the poor woman was wearing.

To Kilvert, he said, "This was Dr. Talbot's room and where I've been staying these past two months. Massimo's been in and out of here, I'm sure of it."

Field tried the door but found it locked. He kicked once, twice, and on the third go the lock splintered and the door flew open.

No one seemed to be within. The key he'd left on the bedside table was there still. Someone else had locked the door with another key. Was there another way into the room?

Field moved along the walls, looking for hidden openings. He examined the window casement and then crouched down beside the bed.

"Odd," said Kilvert, standing at the wardrobe he'd just opened.

"What's that?" said Field, searching the floor beneath the bed for a trapdoor.

"This little cameo, sir. Pretty little picture, pretty young lady."

The inspector stood, brushing lint and dust from his trousers. "What's odd?"

"Looks like someone took a razor to it, sawing across the girl's mouth. *This* razor, quite possibly." He picked up Talbot's razor lying next to the portrait, its blade wide open.

Field took the cameo from Kilvert and stared at it. After a moment he said, "He did this just minutes ago. Massimo somehow watched me pack up and leave, and then he went back into action. We must get Miss Florence out of here. We must get all these women to a safe place until we find this man!"

40

"Where did you sing, Massimo?" she asked.

"Where did I not? At Milano, at Roma. At Venezia. La Fenice, you know it?"

"Indeed, I do know La Fenice."

The two of them sat facing each other in near darkness as the wind hurled fistfuls of rain against the windows. He had appeared in Nightingale's office before she was aware of it.

"Oh!" she'd gasped. It had taken her a moment to recognize him, standing motionless in the gloom, staring at her. "I so rarely use that door, I forget it exists."

This was not good. Suddenly she feared he was not *harmless old Massimo*. Her mind racing, she had invited him to sit. She'd offered him tea, but he only looked about nervously, unspeaking. If she could get him talking, perhaps he would not harm her. Perhaps. In desperation, then, she'd asked him about his career, and that had been the key. He had been *one of the greats*, he said, *for a time.*

"Die Staatsoper in Berlin. Lepeletier in Paris. I sing only once in London," he said. "Maybe you heard me?"

Nightingale hesitated.

"*No,*" said Massimo after a moment, "*certo che no.* I was very young then, and you? Very, very, very young. Perhaps unborn!" He smiled briefly. "It was *not* Covent Garden where they book me. The hall was inferior. *Non é importante.*" The smile was gone. "All long ago. Nothing left for me now but ashes, dust."

"Surely not."

He looked up sharply at her. She had not so much as a hairbrush nearby with which to defend herself. Perhaps her aunt would knock. Or someone, anyone.

"How did you come to be here, Massimo?" said Nightingale. "You know you should not be here uninvited."

"He told me to come, he bring me to your door."

"Who did?"

"I don't know why."

"Who?"

"He wants to be like me, John Hall, but I think he is the devil."

"*John Hall?*"

But Massimo was miles away.

"Mama said there would be so much, I would have so much. What she took from me would be as nothing, compared to the glory ahead. But what is glory to me? What good is glory?"

"Indeed," said Nightingale. "John Hall, you say?"

"I confess my crime to the priest, I confess to the police, they all laugh."

"What do you confess, Massimo?"

The haggard man looked at her. "You are sure?"

"If you wish to confess and repent, this is good. Our Savior says he will forgive us if we repent."

"For what I done? I don't know."

"Oh dear," whispered Nightingale.

"I confess, Mama! Hallo, Mama, I confess! Two others I choke, but to me they all are Mama when the anger come! *Tacete, Madre!*"

"'Be still'? Is that what you say?"

"*Sì.*"

"So it was you who killed these poor women here at Scutari? And tried to do the same to my nurse at Balaclava?"

"No!" he said with sudden violence.

"Please, Massimo . . ."

"Not me!"

Did he have a weapon? It was so dark in the room.

"When she cut me, Mama, she talk and talk and talk. She sew me up and still she talk. She say, 'Now tell Mama thank you for make you famous and rich.' Well, when I *was* rich, *was* famous, I came back for her. And still she talk! On and on. *Chiudi la bocca!*"

Nightingale saw there were tears running down his face.

"After I squeeze Mama with my scarf, I took her needle, her thread. Her housecoat! I give her money, I make her rich, but *this* she wears? *This* cheap robe? Ugly. All over red roses. I cut one rose and sewed it to close the mouth, but there wasn't no need, already she was quiet, *finalmente.*"

There was a silence, and then, from Nightingale, came a burst of laughter. She quickly clapped a hand to her mouth. "Sorry, sorry, I laugh when I'm nervous, and Massimo, I am. I am nervous."

"*He* laugh, too, John Hall." Massimo was trembling. "I thought he was kind man, to listen to me. Like he understand me, like he feel bad for Massimo. But no, he want Mama's roses, he want to be like me when the anger come."

This must not go on, she thought. *How can I distract him?*

Suddenly she had an idea.

"I wish I had heard you perform, Massimo. I don't have a program or bill from one of your performances, but perhaps you would let me have your signature anyway, as a souvenir?"

She saw a faint light flicker in his eyes. She rose carefully, went to the opposite side of her desk, and produced a blank sheet of paper. He stood and approached, and Nightingale dipped a quill in the well and held it out for him. When he took it from her—with his left hand, she noted—one of his fingers touched one of hers and he responded as if to an electrical shock. His eyes flew up to hers.

Oh dear.

"Please, sir," she said, gesturing toward the paper. "If you would be so kind."

He bent over the desk, and the quill scratched across the page.

Nightingale heard a quiet footstep just outside her door and looked to see if Massimo had noticed.

He stood upright and offered her the quill. "I make my confession," he said. "Now comes penance. Holy Mother say suicide is forbid."

She spoke loudly enough, she hoped, to be heard through the door. "Suicide *is* forbidden, actually, Massimo."

He looked to the nearby window.

"First Mama, then the others. My sin has wore me out, signora."

The door flew open and Field burst in, running straight at the Italian. Massimo shot an accusing glance at Nightingale, and then, with amazing speed for one his age, he dodged furniture to vanish into the darkness at the far end of the room and out the other door. Field pursued, but an ottoman felled him, hard. Kilvert ran in after, helped him to his feet.

"You stay with Miss Nightingale, Kilvert!" said Field, already running out the rear door and down the corridor.

Nightingale stood motionless, seemingly transfixed by the autograph on the paper that lay before her. It was the back-slanted writing of a left-handed person. Moreover, it was a left-handed person with a significant tremor.

FIELD SPRINTED TO the next corner and rounded it, bringing him into the corridor that led to Dr. Hall's rooms. He came to a sudden stop. At first Field couldn't take in what was before him. A vast sea of red, from one side of the corridor to the windows opposite. At its far end stood Massimo, glaring at Field.

Of course, it's Dr. Hall's big red carpet, being moved or replaced or cleaned.

The expanse of red wool had been bunched up to fit the confines of the corridor. It had ridges and valleys, and when Field started to cross it he stumbled, dropped to his knees and immediately scrambled to his feet again.

Hanif emerged from Dr. Hall's rooms.

"Stop, Mr. Field!" he cried. "Your shoes are all mud! Stop where you are!"

But the inspector continued to advance slowly along the undulated rug. And then, suddenly, just outside Dr. Hall's door, stood John Stanhope.

"What's all this?"

The Italian turned, saw Stanhope, and recoiled. He backed away from him onto the carpet and found himself caught between the two men. "What more do you devils want of me?" A flash of lightning momentarily lit the dark window nearest him. He turned back to Field. *"What?"*

"Steady on, old man." Field approached slowly, picking his way. "I just want you to answer some questions, that's all. I won't harm you."

Massimo stared at him for a moment. "You know who is the Father of Lies?"

"Can't say I do, but it ain't me."

"No?" The Mendicant looked back at Stanhope and then again at Field. "He is the devil. The devil!"

What happened in the next few seconds later seemed to Field the climax of a magician's act. Stanhope stepped forward onto the carpet, Massimo lurched away from him, and Field tripped again. He was down for only an instant, but when he stood, there was a vacancy. The sound of a great wind rose, and it suddenly went very cold. Stanhope was staring, but where was Massimo? It made no sense. Field realized the window was wide open, with rain blowing in and the lace curtains flapping furiously.

He gaped for a second, then made his way to the window and put his head out.

Far below, barely distinguishable in the downpour, lay the twisted, motionless human shape of the late Massimo Flammia.

IN THE DAYS that followed, Florence Nightingale was distraught. She finally took to her bed with a high fever. Thinking it might do her good, Inspector Field assured her that the threat to her women had passed from this world, but she seemed not to believe him.

"Massimo was left-handed!" she kept saying. "His hand shook! It can't have been him!"

"What do you mean, miss?"

But she would trail off, and her ramblings were put down to a fever-induced delirium.

In an exchange of telegrams, police in Rome confirmed the bizarre murder of Signora Flammia years earlier and shared their suspicions that her death likely was linked to the subsequent strangulation of at least one streetwalker. Convinced that the Beast of the Crimean had leapt from the hospital window, Field took his leave of Scutari for the second—and he assumed—final time.

41

JULY 1856

He had been back in England pursuing Dr. William Palmer for several months when he received a letter. It was addressed to Detective Field, and the return address was *Jane Rolly, Barrack Hospital, Scutari*. He opened it immediately.

My dear sir, I do wish you might return to us if at all convenient. Miss Nightingale has been took queer again these past weeks and I cannot explain it unless it is the Fever returning, which is possible, and you recall how ill she became when you were leaving us and that evil man jumping from the upper floor had us all so upset, but I worry it may be something else with Miss Nightingale, namely Fear. Your presence amongst us would be welcome I know by those of us in Miss's service, but I know you are a busy man.

Sincerely,

J. Rolly, nurse

When Field received this communication, he was in Staffordshire, working with insurance companies to make the connections between Dr. Palmer and numerous suspicious deaths in the region. London was 160 miles away; Scutari nearly 2,000 miles distant. The case, he felt, was nearly complete. He sent Jane Rolly a telegram.

Powerless at present to leave post. Please keep me informed. Electric telegraph is quicker. Yours to me was 2 weeks in transit. Charles Field

Field was certain that Dr. Palmer had poisoned his brother, his wife, possibly four of their children, and likely others, in order to collect insurance policies he'd taken out on their lives. But he had covered his tracks well, and, as a doctor, had interfered in autopsies to conceal his guilt. The most recent suspicious death, that of John Cook, a friend of Palmer's, was the final link that allowed Field *to put his man in a corner.*

He surprised Palmer at the doctor's local pub and made the arrest. The venue for the trial was changed from Staffordshire to London, and Field arranged to escort him, manacled, to Newgate. The doctor was convicted in short order by a jury of his peers. The Prince of Poisoners, as he became known in the press, actually congratulated the lead prosecutor on his work. Inspector Field was widely applauded within the Metropolitan Police and among the general public. He might have basked in his moment of triumph had he not been summoned not long after to the war secretary's private home.

"Inspector, my congratulations on the apprehension of the Palmer fellow," said Sir Sidney Herbert.

"Thank you, sir."

The secretary's appearance had changed in the months since he'd seen him last. His complexion was sallow and he appeared to be unwell.

In charge of this bloody war, I'm not surprised.

"I'm afraid I need to send you out once again to the Ottoman Empire, Field, but this time no one is to know about it, either before you leave or after you return."

"Sir?" said Field.

"As you may know, Miss Nightingale is soon due back in this country. I want you to superintend the arrangements and to ensure her safety and well-being on the journey."

"But, sir, how would I keep such a thing secret when the whole world is talking about her return?"

"You will be apprised of the details by my assistant before you go," said Sir Sidney. "There are powers at work here, Field. Kingdoms, principalities." He sighed. "It all may be a teapot tempest, but with Miss Nightingale we cannot take chances. As I said, my aide will give you what you need to know, and what you're allowed to know, before you go."

"And when is that to be?"

"Tonight, sir."

Field traveled round the clock until he arrived at Marseille, where Detective Hyacinth Manuel had everything in readiness for the passage to Constantinople.

IN GREAT BRITAIN the headlines proclaimed the imminent return of Miss Florence Nightingale to her native shores. Preparations were made for the public reception at which Nightingale would receive the thanks of a grateful nation. Statesmen wrote speeches. Choirs rehearsed hymns.

Her Majesty's government sent a three-masted man-o'-war, the HMS *Collingwood*, bristling with cannon, to convey the beloved nurse from Constantinople. Its bow was festooned in bunting, and Union Jacks fluttered from each mast. On the deck, officers of the Royal Navy stood at attention. A twenty-one-piece naval band, in full dress uniform, played one rousing tune after another as the ship was towed into the harbor.

Out of the corner of his eye, nineteen-year-old Eamon Doyle, a drummer with the Royal Marine Band on deck, watched the knot of uniformed officials board the *Collingwood* and take their places, awaiting the arrival of Nightingale and her entourage.

Those'll be the officers and doctors, thought Eamon.

The July day was hot, and everyone was glistening. Eamon fretted over his sweaty hands; it went without saying that his performance had to be perfect, and a slippery drumstick could be disastrous. Drops of perspiration fell from his brow to the drumhead.

This must be them now, he thought as a large group of uniformed women, two uniformed men, and two boys climbed the gangplank and boarded ship. One of the boys had only one leg and walked with a crutch. To Eamon's surprise, several of the nurses held small children, and to his further astonishment, a large dog trotted after them. The dog was followed by a stocky man with a stubble beard and shapeless hat. He was smoking a cigar that Eamon could smell from where he stood.

Which one of the women, I wonder, is Nightingale?

The conductor rapped his baton, and the band launched into "God Save the Queen."

Eamon watched as one of the newly boarded men, dressed in the garb of a Royal Navy ordinary seaman, and one of the nurses, a plump woman, middle-aged and ginger-haired, went forward to meet the row of dignitaries and doctors. They spoke to one of the doctors. He spoke to them.

With some agitation, thought Eamon.

That man summoned the ship's captain who joined them. The rumpled, cigar-smoking man inserted himself into the small group as well. They spoke at length. The band began "God Save the Queen" again from the beginning.

They look red in the face, but then it is *bloody hot.*

The band conductor's face was red as well. He glanced repeatedly over his shoulder at the officials. He raised his baton again and directed the band to start a third rendition of the anthem.

The sticks in Eamon's hands were fairly swimming.

JUST THREE SLIPS down the harbor, the French frigate was almost ready to sail, with several hired men hurriedly carrying final trunks and luggage up the gangplank. From the deck two men watched the late arrivals.

"This is all a great mistake, Mr. Field," said John Stanhope.

"What's that, sir?"

"All these changes at the very last minute? Without notifying anyone?"

"But you helped!" said Field.

"I implored Miss Nightingale not to do it, I implored *you*, sir."

"In fact," said Field, "you've been so very helpful, you've almost won my heart."

"Very gratifying, I'm sure. You actually expected someone to be lying in wait to attack her on a British warship?"

Field shrugged.

"Dr. Hall will be discovering this awful deception right about now," said Stanhope. "He is doubtless calling for *me* at this very minute. Whatever will I tell him?"

"Well, at Aylesworthy you lied or you died, isn't that what you once told me? By the way, your old school don't seem to recall you."

"What?"

"I checked into it. Your name rings no bells there. How can that be?"

Stanhope's face was now brick red.

"Not that it's any of your business," he said, "but I was obliged by the terms of my grandfather's will to take my mother's name upon my majority. In order to inherit, you see."

Field nodded.

"You're a cad, Field. A low-born cad, and always will be."

Stanhope strode to the gangplank, pushed his way through the men carrying trunks, and made his way off the frigate. Minutes later a trio of women climbed the same gangplank and boarded the *Némésis*. They were greeted by a uniformed French police officer.

"*Mesdames*," said Hyacinth, "*je vous souhaite la bienvenue à bord. Je m'appelle l'agent Hyacinth Manuel.*"

Florence Nightingale, in turn, expressed her gratitude to Agent Manuel and to the French nation. Hyacinth ushered them to the door leading to the staterooms below, but Nightingale hesitated at the door and looked back. Mai Smith and Jane Rolly did the same. Sailors were hauling up the gangplank. There were shouts from above and below. Shrill whistles sounded. The French ship's horn blew, and slowly the *Némésis* withdrew from her berth.

Field scanned the harbor.

There he is.

Stanhope had found a bench. He sat watching the departing frigate and chewing a thumbnail. Finally, he stood, raised one knee high, and then the other. He twisted his torso this way and that, this way and that, and then he dwindled to a blur in Field's sight.

What an odd fellow.

Through it all, as the city of Constantinople receded into the distance, from HMS *Collingwood* came tunes of God and glory.

42

Despite the excellence of the food and wine served in the captain's cabin, dinner aboard the *Némésis* that first night was uneasy. Everyone present knew there would be repercussions to the French having whisked the famous heroine out from under British noses.

"Many of the women we put upon the *Collingwood* were our own nurses, of course," said Nightingale to the captain of the French vessel, "and happy we were to start them on their way home in such style. The rest of them were the abandoned war widows whom we dressed as Scutari nurses. The poor women hardly had a scrap of clothing of their own, and their utter neglect by the army maddened me. I do hope no harm comes of it."

Inspector Field interjected. "We did also put the *Times* man, William Howard Russell, aboard the ship."

"That was Mr. Field's idea," said Jane Rolly, and Field's heart leapt within him.

"We thought," said the inspector, "the threat of a writer reporting on the treatment of British women and children, no matter their class, might encourage good behavior from all and excuse Miss Nightingale's absence. So we hope, anyway."

"Hear, hear!" cried Hyacinth, beaming. He already had consumed a good portion of the fine wines.

"Let us also praise Monsieur Hyacinth Manuel," said Mai, "who arranged with the highest ranks of his government to provide this gracious transport!"

When they had drunk his health, and that of the French nation, a silence fell over the table.

Nightingale raised her glass again and then set it down. In a low voice she said, "Perhaps we might remember also poor Signor Massimo Flammia, once *one of the greats* and now one of God's lost lambs."

Field, Mai Smith, and Jane Rolly exchanged concerned glances. It was not the first time Nightingale had mentioned the man's name with something like regret. Now Nightingale turned to the other women. "Mai? Jane?"

Mai Smith and Jane Rolly rose from the table. The men all stood and bade the ladies good night. Then the men took cigars and brandies on deck at the stern. Finally the others, all but Field, went below to their berths.

A half-moon appeared behind gathering clouds over the dark waters of the Aegean. The French sailors at their posts silently watched the inspector as he stood alone at the rail, beneath a lantern, leafing yet again through several papers Jane had passed him secretly before they embarked. She had found them in a wastepaper basket in Nightingale's office. They'd been torn in pieces, and Jane had glued them together.

The notes disgusted and alarmed him.

Why did Miss Nightingale not tell me, or anyone, about these? Why did she hide them?

He realized Nightingale had given him an answer during his leave-taking interview, months earlier. She feared they might cause a *distraction*. Nothing but *nothing* was to distract from her life's work.

It's the sort of conclusion you reach if you've got God talking to you, direct.

Field suspected that the spelling errors were deliberate, meant to suggest it was a less-educated person penning the threatening notes. It didn't occur to him to consider the handwriting itself—right-slanting and assured—or to recall what Nightingale had said when the fever was upon her.

Field put the notes in a breast pocket and descended to his bunk below. Without undressing, he climbed into the narrow bed and was asleep in moments. He dreamt of stick-women, defaced and defiled.

43

The journey back to England was uneventful. Nevertheless, for Field, it was painful. Jane Rolly was not hostile, but she gently spurned his attempts to court her. She seemed to retreat further from him the closer they came to home and finally rejected him altogether, it seemed, as they parted company in London on a platform of Euston Station.

You misunderstood me all along, Mr. Field. I summoned you to help Miss Nightingale, not me.

But I don't want to help you, Jane, I want to marry you!

Exactly.

Field winced to recall the conversation.

Go, Mr. Field, the train is waiting, Miss Nightingale is waiting. Take good care of her. She is tired and unwell and frightened still.

May I, when I return to London, call on you again?

Oh, Inspector, I don't know. I simply don't know.

She'd turned then and walked the length of the platform.

He found Nightingale in the compartment where he'd left her. She was staring out the window at the gray station and drizzly gray day. She barely glanced up when he entered and sat. This suited Field's mood as well. He'd sooner not talk just now, and anyhow, they'd already been traveling together for days.

So they journeyed north, Inspector Field accompanying the famous Florence Nightingale to her family home, traveling incognito because of her great fame and because at the end of her vast labors and despite the death of the man who, according to Field, had menaced her and the British women at Scutari, she remained fearful. She firmly declined to discuss any of it.

The key, Inspector Field, she said, as if she hadn't already said it a dozen times before, *lies in the two realms of sanitation and accountability. Those men whose negligence allowed so many to die were not held accountable for their omissions but were rewarded for them. And still, to this day, there is no thought given to clean linen, clean air, or well-maintained drains.*

The train's whistle shrieked, and the nurse flinched at the sound. In the hours to come, she would recoil each time their train, or another, would blow its horn. Field saw in Nightingale's flinch what he'd seen when he'd reached out a hand to Jane Rolly. The fear, and the response, were the same.

Once, after a great silence, as if she'd been reading his mind, she spoke up.

Don't give up on her, Charles. No one comes out of war unaltered.

Eventually, as they entered the midlands, the land grew hilly. Sheep raised their heads as the train passed.

"It's very green hereabouts," said Field, wishing he had better words to describe the beauty, the grandeur of the landscape.

"It's my favorite part of the world, sir. I shall live in London, in a place of my own, but this is where my heart dwells." She turned to him. "The town of Matlock is only four miles beyond my stop. I've booked a room for you there at the inn and booked your passage back to London tomorrow."

"Thank you, miss."

Finally, the conductor was calling out *Whatstandwell Station!* up and down the train, although he was fully aware that only Miss Smith would be leaving the train here and also aware of Miss Smith's true identity. Nightingale's trunks had been sent on earlier. Now she had only one valise, which Field lifted down for her.

"You're sure you don't want me to carry this to the house for you, miss?"

"Quite sure."

The inspector stepped down onto the platform and offered a hand to Nightingale, who stood framed in the open door, eyes closed, breathing deeply of the country air. She took his hand and descended. As she did so, Field saw that lines of anxiety, which had creased her face for so many miles, faded a bit. A warm smile appeared there.

"Thank you, Charles. And for all else, thank you." The stationmaster hurried toward them. "Here's Mr. MacAllister at a run," she said, "who can't be less than a hundred and twelve. He'll send my valise along to Lea Hurst for me."

"Miss Nightingale!" the old man cried, and then stopped and put his hands on his knees to catch his breath.

"Mr. MacAllister, you're looking fit, sir!"

The old man looked up and beamed.

"Well, then," said Nightingale, and she was off, striding down the grassy slope, observed by knots of sheep, Inspector Field, and Stationmaster MacAllister.

To Field's eye, the house was massive. A kitchen maid, stepping out into a courtyard to shake an apron, looked tiny by comparison. The young woman glanced up and saw the approaching figure. She looked again, stared, and then turned and ran into the house. Moments later, Florence was engulfed by the embraces of father, mother, sister, and soon the entire household staff, one after another. Field faintly heard the laughter and the cries of joy, and then he reboarded the train.

PART THREE

LONDON, 1854

The young man walked away from the Haymarket Theatre, turning up the collar of his overcoat and hunching his shoulders against the cold drizzle. His cheeks still burned from the words of the producer's assistant and the stifled laugh from someone in the dark audience house, perhaps the producer himself, as the aspiring actor stood alone in the onstage glare.

Unforgettable, the assistant had said when he finished his recitation. But not in a good way. He knew when he was being mocked. *That little routine you performed before your recitation, with the raised knees and so forth?* The actor replied that it was a practice of the great Edmund Kean, which he emulated. *Of course.* The assistant was reading from the résumé he'd given them. *It's not surprising you emulate the greats, given your lineage. Doesn't get more exalted than that, I must say!* There it was. The muffled guffaw.

A passing omnibus sent a spray of filthy water across his legs. Tears of rage came to his eyes as he glared after the 'bus.

John Stanhope Hall. To his parents, he was Jack. He would have liked his friends to call him John, but he had no friends. He would have described himself, whether it was true or not, as the younger son of Yorkshire gentry whose fortunes had diminished in recent years—again, had there been anyone to tell.

Growing up, the daughters of neighboring gentry were warned away from young Jack Hall; there was a cloud over his reputation. He made people "uncomfortable," young women especially. Lower-class girls were less shielded, and the repercussions for any misdemeanor he might commit with them were minimal. He often contrived, successfully, to lay blame on others. If a local boy was known to smoke cigars, there would be a half-smoked butt at the scene; if another wore a particular cap, a cap very like it would be found. The girls themselves hardly knew who had assaulted them: he always came from behind. There were rumors of restraints. Ropes and scarves.

Mothers glowered as he passed in the street, and on at least one occasion a father had accosted him, knocked him down, and booted him in full view of the village. Jack's own father suggested he'd only got what was coming to him.

Mr. and Mrs. Hall's unlooked-for demise was investigated by the coroner, yielding a verdict of "death by mischance" and put down to food poisoning. Jack's dissolute older brother inherited what little remained of the family fortune. Had Jack's late mother set up a small independent portion for her youngest, as he liked to tell himself? Or had he merely helped himself to the household cash in order to move to London? In any event, he found a bedsit for himself in Clapham, and there he studied his Shakespeare assiduously. In doing so, he invented a family history for himself preferable to the one he'd lived.

Shakespeare's son was dead. His daughter, Susanna, had married a man named Hall. The sixteenth-century Dr. John Hall and his wife had a daughter who died, thus ending the Shakespeare family line—so history states. But Susanna at one point had been accused of adultery. Her accuser failed to appear in court and the suit was dismissed, but in Jack's mind the adultery was real and produced a child. This forgotten boy, according to Jack, was his ancestor, thus linking him in a direct line to the immortal playwright. He even fancied, regarding himself in the mirror, that he *looked* like Shakespeare, with his pronounced brow.

Nevertheless, neither Jack nor John prospered as an actor. Again and again, he was not hired, despite his illustrious "ancestor." His claim was not a good calling card, but rather the opposite. And so he stood on this foul winter's day in 1854 outside the Royal Haymarket Theatre, staring with impotent rage at the disappearing omnibus that had soaked him as it passed. Then he saw, at a nearby news stall, his own name. He approached, fishing in his trousers for a coin.

The article had to do with this war being fought somewhere in the East. Up to now Jack had paid little attention to it, but here was the name John Hall, an army physician who had been recalled from duty in India to supervise the British military's hospitals in the Crimea. To the would-be actor, who inhabited a world largely of his own invention, it was immediately clear. This could not be coincidence. Here was another ancestor of Shakespeare's daughter. They even bore the same name! Jack and Dr. John Hall were kin, they must be!

But the report was not good. The article was critical of Dr. Hall, suggesting that he and others were failing the sick and wounded British soldier. Young Jack glanced up at the byline. *William Howard Russell.*

From then on, Jack paid close attention to the reports from the front. British casualties were mounting up. In article after article, the journalist from *The Times* claimed the troops were ill equipped and uncared for, and laid particular blame on the British hospital at Scutari and its head.

Lies. Slander. The world was treating the doctor with the same disrespect it dished out to him. And then, to the sound of trumpets, a passel of *ladies* had gone out to Scutari to correct Dr. Hall's many errors! Their presumptuous leader? A society female named Nightingale.

It was not to be borne. Suddenly a daring plan occurred to him.

He would go out to the Crimea himself, yes he would. He would find a way to be of service to his namesake, as a volunteer. He would not reveal himself as a Hall initially; he would be a patriotic volunteer named, like his late mother, Stanhope. Was this perhaps the role that history had in store for him? Yes. He would make these females turn tail and run! He would help restore the family reputation to what it once (or never) had been. He would play a role not at the Haymarket or the Adelphi but upon the world's stage!

Along the way, of course, Jack would find ways to amuse himself.

44

LONDON, 1867

It was the embroidered rose stuck in Susan Hythe-Cooper's mouth and the identical rose-shaped embroidery pattern in the pocket of the strangled nurse trainee, Alice Wheeler, that captured the public's attention. A writer for one of the afternoon papers dubbed the crimes the *roseate murders*, and that's how they soon became known universally. Theories explaining the symbolism of the image sprang up and multiplied overnight and spun off into ever wilder speculation in the days that followed. To no one, of course, did it occur that the rose's inspiration had been stolen from a cheap housecoat worn by the mother of a long-dead Italian—to no one except Florence Nightingale, who had heard it from the old Italian himself, minutes before he plummeted from a window in Turkey.

The fact that one of the victims was an MP's wife gave the murders added prominence. There was an initial feeling of sympathy for Mr.

Hythe-Cooper, the bereaved widower. For Alice Wheeler, who came from no family to speak of, there were less respectful questions in the press. Had she been in league with the murderer? Was it fit for young women to enter such a profession as nursing? (Florence Nightingale had become a revered icon in the public's mind, the gentle *lady with the lamp* of popular poetry, but her actual work and what she stood for had faded from general memory).

At the inquest, the Honorable William Hythe-Cooper was asked when he had last seen his late wife. *He'd spent the night at his club, so he'd seen her the day before or maybe two days before her death, he couldn't quite recall. They definitely had gone together to some reception or other that week.* And on the morning in question, where had the member for Reigate been? *He had gone home to collect his post.* Where was his home? *Hanover Gate.* Not far from Hanover Terrace, is it? the coroner suggested, with his bushy eyebrows elevated. What was the state of Mr. Hythe-Cooper's marriage, would he say? *Like any other, he supposed. Better than some, no worse than most.*

Jeremy Sims, MP, described how he came to discover the body of his friend. The nature of the friendship between Sims and the dead woman? *They met to discuss public policy.* There was laughter in the inquest room, and the coroner's gavel came into play. Could Mr. Sims account for the delay of several hours in his reporting of the discovery? *He'd been in shock.* The coroner raised his eyebrows again at this, and newspapers subsequently reveled in lurid speculation.

Mrs. Tupper, the charwoman, was called to testify. How long had she been employed at No. 8 Hanover Terrace? *Long enough to know.* What did she mean by that? *They come and they go, them folk, and best keep your head down.* What folk? the coroner wanted to know. *Them as should know better,* replied Mrs. Tupper. *We seem to find ourselves in a testimonial cul de sac,* said the coroner, provoking another round of laughter. He turned on the crowd. *You do understand that we are here looking into the violent death of a young woman?* Silence followed.

What prompted Mrs. Tupper to investigate Flat 4?

The woman pointed directly at the former chief detective inspector for the Metropolitan Police, Charles Field.

When he took the stand, the coroner wanted to know how he, too, had happened to come upon the body. Field replied, almost truthfully, that *he had a friend living at Hanover Terrace, but he wasn't in.* The name of this friend? *Mr. Wilkie Collins, sir.* The famous novelist? *The same.*

"You seem to cultivate novelists, Mr. Field," said the coroner.

"Not my fault, sir, with all respect." Another round of laughter from the crowd was again gaveled to silence. All this was detailed in the press. Nurse trainee Alice Wheeler's inquest was reported on, too, because of the seeming connection between the two deaths and the remarkable fact that Charles Field had been present at *that* murder scene as well. Detective Inspector Llewellyn explained, almost truthfully, that he'd invited his former colleague to join him there *because of, well, having happened upon Mr. Field and his son, Tom, on the way.*

When Matron Wardroper took the stand, she finished by stoutly maintaining, almost truthfully, that Alice had been the only one of all her girls to have flaunted the rules of the Nightingale School.

Sister Prudence Underwood had to be asked twice by the coroner to speak up. She was pale and tremulous but seemed determined not to cry, and she didn't. Yes, she had found the body in the gazebo by the pond. She'd looked there because it was where Alice sometimes met her beau. *Did the beau have a name?* Pru said she'd seen him twice but couldn't be certain of a name and didn't like to fling a name about when she wasn't sure. And so, Arthur Tuttle was not mentioned by anyone. *Do you think you would recognize the man if you saw him again?* Prudence nodded.

"Yes, sir, I'm certain I would."

These words, too, were printed in the papers.

45

J ack (Stanhope) Hall closed and folded the newspaper thoughtfully and put it to one side of his breakfast things. He had
followed the career of Charles Field closely in the years of his
own decline. Since the Crimean War, Jack had seen Field's rise in the
ranks of the Metropolitan Police and his marriage to the nurse Jane
Rolly. He took note when the couple adopted an orphan girl, and later,
making his frequent observations of Field's own home, he saw that a
male youth also seemed to have taken up residence. Jack had rejoiced
at Field's unexplained downfall from the Metropolitan, reduced to his
current occupation as a mere private detective. Now, though, Field was
again in the newspapers, provoking laughter in the coroner's court and
seemingly as popular with the people (and with novelists) as he ever was.

Twelve years earlier, Jack's final interview with the other John Hall,
the doctor, had not gone well, to say the least. Dr. John Hall had been

enraged that Nightingale had ruined the send-off that he'd hoped would shine a bright light on his own achievements. Instead, it was a debacle, a grotesque embarrassment. He was either forgotten or, worse, blamed for Nightingale's absence. And where had Stanhope been? Aiding and abetting this disgrace!

But, Stanhope protested, he had been busy trying to *prevent* the entire scheme! He'd done everything in his power!

Dr. Hall was unmoved.

Stanhope told him that it was he who had been behind trying to starve out the nurses the previous year and ordering up the wrong ship for Nightingale when she was ill. He had done his utmost to hinder *her* and help *him*!

It was as though Hall hadn't heard a word.

"When you failed to appear on the deck of the *Collingwood*, young man, I made inquiries," said the doctor, "via the electric telegraph. You were not, as you claimed, sent me by Dr. Graves of Harley Street. I asked him, you see, and had his reply within two hours. The letter with which you introduced yourself to me was bogus. Dr. Graves never heard of you. So who in bloody blazes is John Stanhope, anyway?"

"Your namesake, sir. John Stanhope Hall."

"*What?*" said the doctor.

"We share a common ancestor," said Stanhope. "The sixteenth-century Dr. John Hall? Husband of Susanna. Daughter of the poet-playwright, William Shakespeare."

The army doctor looked at him in astonishment.

"Good Lord. Not only are you a fraud and an impostor, you're also an unabashed lunatic."

Jack's face went red.

Dr. Hall continued. "You think we didn't know about your clandestine activities, Stanhope? All of us? We let you go about your dirty work, feeling no need to dirty our own hands with it. Did you actually kill, too? No, don't tell me, I don't want to know. You're a sick man, whoever you are. Get out!"

Jack had considered tightening Dr. Hall's cravat for him. It wouldn't be difficult, and it wouldn't take long. In the end, though, Jack simply left and made his way back to England, leaving the name John Stanhope behind him. The contacts he'd made in the medical world and in the army were now useless. His attempts to find employment as an actor named Jack Hall were no more successful than John Stanhope's had been. He grew a full beard and dyed his hair and beard black, hoping to create a new look for himself. He committed new audition material to memory. All to no avail. He finally was reduced to taking work in the West End as the dresser to a pompous fool named Tuttle, who assumed Jack had adopted this look, so like his own, in order to get the job.

The demon that had driven him in his youth seemed to sleep. He lived quietly on the south side of the river and walked over Waterloo Bridge each evening to one or another of the theaters, depending on where his employer was appearing, and at the end of the night, he walked home again. If life was less interesting now, it was at least safer. But then the reform movement arose and, with it, Jack Stanhope Hall's demon.

It doesn't take a genius to realize that expanding the vote for men will lead to allowing the filthy bints to vote as well. The women must be stopped, and the men who would have them rule over us.

Of equal importance to Jack was the intolerable Inspector Charles Field in the press, winning laughter and applause, his nemesis from all those years ago, the man who had mocked and humiliated him.

Jack folded his paper and stood. He moved his breakfast things to the nearby sideboard. Two steps away was a tiny desk on which rested his journal, bound in paperboard. He opened a drawer that held his few remaining embroidered roses. There would be no more unless he found another seamstress. *It's a pity Alice Wheeler went round to the theater and saw the real Arthur Tuttle.* The roses were a bother, but they had worked for him at Scutari, they had shifted suspicion to the Italian, and they'd instilled fear in the women's hearts. He had no Italian to shift blame to now, but he'd used them again all these years later to instill fear and to give Inspector Field uncomfortable memories.

And that brought Charles Field back to mind, front and center.

The cunt.

He needed to strike him where it would hurt the most. The items in the press about John Stanhope made it clear that Field now knew how he'd failed at Scutari, blaming the Italian for the crimes. Jack Hall would make him fail again, spectacularly, painfully.

He looked out the window. It overlooked a featureless brick wall. The gas ring to make his coffee and cook his egg was down the hall, and the privy was an outhouse behind the building. Until recently, this had been his world. But then the exceedingly strange Lord Seabury had taken notice. He had plucked him from the anti-suffrage meeting and brought him to his townhouse. Now three times Jack had returned. By invitation! The Duke had given him tours of his underground realm. Did the Duke fancy him? It didn't matter, Jack could handle himself. But that home of his, with its secrecy and the insane tunnels! It felt like Jack's life was starting all over again.

He opened his journal and with a thick lead pencil he wrote a single name on the day's page. *Jane.* He underscored it until the lead broke.

THE CHANCELLOR OF the exchequer had put down *The Times* and was writing a note at the breakfast table. Across from him, Mary Anne Disraeli used a slice of toast to push baked beans onto her fork. She looked up to see her husband sign and fold the note.

"Benjamin?" she said. "Is something the matter?"

He shook his head. "Not really, my dear. The day of the big demonstration in the park, you sent along a message to me. Do you remember?"

Mary Anne looked blank and then brightened. "Why yes, I do as a matter of fact!"

"How did it arrive?"

"The envelope? Mrs. Higgs brought it to me with the other post and said a messenger had delivered it. Is it important?"

He picked up the note he'd just written, pushed back his chair, and rose. "No, not at all. Must run, my dear."

She lifted her head for a kiss, and her husband affectionately obliged.

MEANWHILE, JOHN STUART Mill, the famed liberal philosopher and member of Parliament, was seated before a stack of manuscript pages, which he read aloud from while his stepdaughter Helen Taylor stood listening. Mill at age sixty looked much as he had at age thirty: bald with a knobby forehead, thin lips, and piercingly intelligent eyes. He glanced up often at Miss Taylor. She was tall, her figure erect, her hands pressed together, her fingertips just touching her lips, her eyes half-closed in concentration. Helen had been an actress.

Every now and then she interrupted with a question or a murmured affirmation. Each time, Mill paused in his reading and made a notation in the manuscript. He took Helen's opinions seriously, as he had valued her late mother's, when Harriet Taylor was his friend of twenty-one years and then his wife for seven. In John Stuart Mill's mind, Harriet Taylor had been a beacon, and theirs a labor of absolute equality, male and female. Now her daughter, Helen, occupied that position of coequal collaborator.

The work in which they were engaged currently was titled *The Subjection of Women*. They had been through numerous drafts, constantly revising and expanding it. Mill broke off his reading to turn a page. He stopped and looked up at Helen.

"What is this?" he said.

Helen Taylor opened her eyes and glanced down at the square of fabric lying on the page. "Oh, that. I use it to mark my place."

"Where did you get it?"

"I'm not sure. Oh, I know. I found it in the hall when I was gathering up the morning post earlier this week or last. I thought it pretty."

"It is, in its way." He reached for the newspaper at the end of the long worktable. "But let me read you out the account of an inquest held just yesterday."

As he read, Helen listened in growing dismay. When he finished, she pointed dramatically at the embroidered rose.

"He kills women, the person who put that thing through our letter slot," she said. "It's a communication from him to *us*!"

AND IN CHELSEA, a young physician appeared at the local constabulary, as he'd done every day for several days. As always, he was hoping for word of his vibrant young wife, an activist with the suffrage movement, who had gone missing. There was none.

46

"Jeremy Sims is sticking to his story," said Llewelyn to Field, the two of them sitting across from each other in Llewelyn's cramped office. "He swears that he met weekly with Susan Hythe-Cooper to discuss policy and nothing else, full stop. 'Which policy was this?' says I. Mrs. Sims all the while is watching her husband with a wicked-sharp eye. 'The subject was and is confidential,' says he. The man is petrified, that's obvious, but Charles, I'm telling you, he's scared of something or someone more fearsome than his wife, and that's saying something."

Field stood and moved to the one window, whose outside surface was so covered in soot it would be difficult to say what it faced.

"How'd he react when you thrust the embroidered rose in his face?" said Field.

"How did you know I surprised him with the rose?"

"You had good training. So, he went all white?"

"Like a bedsheet," said Llewellyn.

"Not surprising," said Field. "He'd last seen it in his dead mistress's mouth, hadn't he."

Suddenly the office door flew open. The veteran reporter for *The Times*, William Howard Russell, stood there, dressed all in black. He looked from Llewellyn to Field.

"They allow *you* in here, Charlie?" To Llewellyn, he said, "Shouldn't someone be summoning the police?"

"It's customary to knock, Mr. Russell," said Llewellyn. "Shall we adjourn to the Eagle and Child?"

Within minutes, Llewellyn had ushered the two men out of his office and into the public house across the road, knowing that neither one of them would be particularly welcome in Commissioner Richard Mayne's headquarters.

"I've been looking for you, Charlie," said Russell. "Little bird told me I'd find you corrupting the morals of this young man here."

Field raised his glass. "It's been a long time, old friend."

"Covered the Indian uprising, covered the Civil War in America, covered too damned much, frankly, instead of stopping at home. Charlie, my dear Mary is gone. Just up and died, and all I can think of is how many more memories I might have had if I'd only stopped at home."

"I'm very sorry to hear it."

"I'm a broken man, Charlie." He took a cigar from his breast pocket. "Oh, I know you've seen me when I was on the job in foreign lands and feeling my oats, but my heart was always with my dear Mary."

"You have my sincere condolences, Will."

"Thanks, old man." He searched for matches, hesitated, and then put the cigar back in his pocket. "She couldn't bear these things, but did I stop? Charlie, I wish I'd stopped." Russell brushed tears from his eyes. "Forgive me, Llewellyn."

"Nothing to forgive, Mr. Russell," said Llewellyn. "My sympathies, sir."

"So, Charlie, I've come to you about the past."

Field nodded. "You've read about the inquests, then, and the roses?"

Russell looked blank. "I've had my hands full this past week with the services and the burial and all, I haven't looked at a paper in days."

"Well, Willie, two young women in the past few days were garroted by someone whose signature seems to be an embroidered rose."

"Dear God," said the reporter. His eyes narrowed. "I decided years ago to overlook the fact that you once suspected *me* of those crimes back at Scutari. Don't tell me it's entered your unclean mind again!"

"Calm down." Field took a folded sheet of paper from a pocket. "Take a look at these names from our time in the Crimea and tell me what you know about them as they are today."

Field slid the list across to Russell, who cast his eyes down the page rapidly. Without seeming to think about it, he took the short cigar from his pocket again and lit it.

Massimo Flammia
John Stanhope
Dr. John Hall
William Howard Russell
Alexis Soyer
T. G. Taylor
Mary (Mother) Seacole
Nigel Cox
Benj. Disraeli

"These are not all *persons of interest*, surely?" said Russell.

"Of course not. They're simply people Llewellyn or I may want to interview."

The reporter took a steel pen from his pocket and, with a sharp glance at the inspector, used it to cross through his own name. Then he struck out Dr. John Hall's name as well.

"Dr. Hall took his place in the operating theater of the firmament a year or two ago," said Russell. "After Scutari he dedicated his life to writing a refutation of Florence Nightingale and all her works and all her ways, but he was waylaid by a stroke, and spent his remaining days touring Europe. I think it was in Pisa he finally laid down his Baedeker."

He hovered the pen over the rest of the list.

"John Stanhope," he said. "You thought he smelled bad, as I recall."

"I did," said the inspector. "I still do."

"Where is he?"

"Dunno, do I," said Field. "The War Office has no record of him, they say. At Somerset House I found records of a great number of John Stanhopes throughout the UK but none that fit my man's age and occupation."

"Which was what?" said Russell. "Toady?"

"Good point."

"He could have been a volunteer back then. There were a number of them out there. Women, mostly, trying to out-Nightingale Nightingale, but there were blokes, too. Ah, the French chef, *Alexis Soyer*. He left us, too, I believe perhaps ten years ago. An odd duck but *amiable*, as the French say. I once got quite completely foxed with him at my Scutari tavern of choice but not on the swill they were serving. He sneaked in his own bottle, and I'm telling you, it almost converted me to the French way of thinking. *T. G. Taylor*. Did a bunk, didn't he?"

"Yes," said Field, "after he'd been found with Mother Dinkins dead in a sack, a bit of cloth stitched to her lip."

"Seems to me I heard somewhere that the man joined a circus."

"A *circus*?" said Field, to which Russell only shrugged. He moved the pen down the list.

"They raised a fund for Mother Seacole, I believe, as her selfless work on behalf of the British soldier left her destitute. Dunno where she is these days." Russell pointed at a name low on the page. "Why'd you cross through Nigel Cox's name?"

"On account of the man committing suicide."

"He did not! Although there are some who think we'd be better off if he had done. No, Charlie, Mr. Nigel Cox is in the House of Commons."

"Never! That young idiot?"

"He's a fat, middle-aged idiot now, Charlie. Do you pay no attention to affairs of state?"

"I read his suicide note myself," said Field, "blaming the whole world for his troubles, especially the women in it."

"Sounds about right for Mr. Cox," said Russell. "I imagine when it came to pulling the trigger he lost his backbone—he shows no sign of having one today."

Llewellyn pointed at the last name on Field's list. *"Benjamin Disraeli?"*

"I had a note from him this morning," said Field. "He wants me to come see him tomorrow at the Palace of Westminster. The man's had a patch of floral embroidery sent him."

"Well, there's a coincidence." Russell pulled an envelope from a pocket and shoved it across to Field. "This is what moved me to seek you out, Charlie. Mr. Disraeli's not the only one to find such a treat in his letterbox. This is mine."

The square of fabric was inside, and a message.

For yor crimes against *man* you will be punished

"It's the Crimean Beastie all over again," said Russell, "or I'm much mistaken."

"The Crimean Beastie threw himself from the top floor of the hospital at Scutari," said Field. "It's someone imitating him who's at work today."

"If you insist, Charlie."

"I do." The inspector asked the barman for pen and paper. "Perhaps, Sam, you might have your people look out for a Mr. Theodore Gabriel Taylor? A Black man, possibly working in a circus."

"For God's sake, Charles, you are not my superior officer!"

Field looked up from the note he was writing and raised his eyebrows.
"But yes," said Llewellyn, "since you ask politely, I'll do that."

"Thanks kindly," said Field. "I'm now politely asking Disraeli if he might arrange a meeting between me and Mr. Nigel Cox, MP, since I'm making the trip anyway."

47

That same morning, Belinda Field responded to a knock at the family door by cautiously opening it a crack. She saw a tall, slender gentleman standing there, hat in hand. "Hallo?" he said.

After a moment Belinda said, "You look all right," and admitted the man, quickly shutting the door behind him. Belinda explained that her people were otherwise engaged.

"In that case, kindly give Mr. Field this note—" he started to say, taking an envelope from his coat, but Belinda was off and running.

"Mrs. Field is with Miss Nightingale who has had another attack of the Crimean Fever, poor dear, and who could blame her for taking to bed when one of her own students meets such a cruel end and the papers print such vile things about female nurses?"

"I do not blame her in the least," said the gentleman, John Stuart Mill, "but I'm sorry to hear that Miss Nightingale is ailing again."

"As for Sister Prudence, who found the poor dead girl, well, my people want Pru to move in here with us until such time as she's herself again. I met her myself and held her hand whilst Mrs. Field talked to her. She's having a hard time sleeping, she's *that* frightened."

"Quite understandable, the young woman's fear. As a matter of fact, I believe my own dear stepdaughter may have reason to share that fear, so it was actually Inspector Field I was hoping to see."

Belinda smiled and shook her head. "He's not really an inspector now, but it pleases him to call himself one, aren't men funny?"

"They are, indeed." He took a calling card from his pocket. "Do tell Inspector Field that Mr. Mill called, won't you, my dear? And give him this note?"

Mill handed her the envelope.

"I'm called Belinda Field, by the way," she said. "I'm to be a nurse myself."

"And I'm Mr. Mill."

"What do you do?"

Mill was taken aback for a moment. "Well, I write things, and think about things, and I'm in the House of Commons—is that what you mean? That sort of thing?"

Belinda nodded wisely. "Please let your stepdaughter know that my father and my brother, Tom, are looking to protect her, in a very real sense, even as we speak, Mr. Mill."

"I certainly will. Thank you."

"Be assured, they are both wonderful protectors. Mind you, I'm not saying 'all will be well,' because that's just something men say to women to keep them quiet."

Mill stared. "Extraordinary. I do hope my Helen will have a chance to meet you, Belinda. I think we both would be interested to hear your views."

"Oh, Mr. Mill, a girl's got to have *views*. Otherwise, where would she be?"

Just minutes later came another knock at the door. Once again, Belinda opened it cautiously and did an appraisal. The man's full black beard was off-putting somehow, but then he smiled warmly and said, "Belinda, I can stay only a moment. It *is* Belinda, isn't it?"

48

A dapper young man strode toward Inspector Field on the pavement outside the Houses of Parliament.

"Mr. Field?" he said.

"The same."

"I'm Monty, private secretary to the chancellor. He received your note and is happy to comply with your somewhat puzzling request."

"Sorry to puzzle the chancellor but grateful nonetheless."

"As a consequence, you'll meet with him here rather than at Number 11."

"I'm in your hands, Monty."

Carriages were pulling up and discharging passengers, tall-hatted gentlemen were coming and going, and there was a general hubbub of charged conversation. One striking figure emerging from the House of

Lords got Field's attention. His top hat was fitted with a black veil, completely hiding his face. He was followed by a man with a full black beard and dark swept-back hair. Field stared at the veiled man.

"That's our Invisible Peer, as he's known, sir," said the secretary. "Lord Seabury. Comes and goes unspeaking, unseen. Eccentric."

Field watched as a liveried footman opened the door of an oddly antiquated carriage. The veiled man climbed in, followed by the bearded one.

The private secretary coughed discreetly. "This way, Mr. Field."

Benjamin Disraeli at age sixty-two had a somewhat drooping, melancholic demeanor in repose, but as soon as the inspector was shown into his presence, he leapt up and his face became animated with wry humor.

"Mr. Field," he said, "it is an honor finally to meet the man about whom I've read all these years."

"Honor's all mine, sir."

"We encountered each other not long ago in the home of Miss Florence Nightingale, but at the time I didn't realize I was in the presence of *the* Inspector Field. Had I known, I would have genuflected or done something appropriate. That'll be all, Monty, thank you very much."

The secretary bowed and left the room, closing the door behind him.

Disraeli looked keenly at Field in silence for a moment, seeming to take the measure of the man. Field stood a little straighter.

"I generally prefer to read the novels I myself write," said Disraeli, "to those written by some other fella, but I make an exception when it comes to Mr. Dickens. Now that I look at you, you seem *like*, and *not* like, the famous inspector Bucket of *Bleak House*, at least as I imagined him."

"I've never seen the remotest resemblance, myself," said Field.

"Ha! Very good. Well, to business. Do sit!"

Field chose a chair and Disraeli made his way round the desk and picked up the envelope lying on it.

"At the beginning of May I had a rather nasty note sent me concerning my Hebrew heritage." Disraeli sat and waved the envelope like a pennant. "Now, this is not at all uncommon for me, I receive a number of such messages each year, some signed, most not. When I was a much younger politician, on the hustings, I had verbal brickbats hurled at me with great regularity. *Jew, Jew, Jew.* One had to take no notice. As my career rose, the vitriol didn't decrease, so I paid no particular attention to this most recent note, at least not until I read newspaper accounts of these roseate murders. You see, my written brickbats don't usually come accompanied by red sewing patterns."

He pushed the envelope across the desk, and Field took from it the square of fabric he'd come to expect. There was a note. *Do you think weel let a filthy Jew betray the nation?*

"Lines of concern just now creased your brow, Inspector Field," said Disraeli.

"Well, yes, my concern for the welfare of the women of this city is very great. But now, in the past two hours, I've seen threatening notes that were delivered to two *men*."

"Is the other recipient also a Jew?"

"No, sir. But your note and the other seem to suggest there's not only some deviancy at work here but something else as well. Something political, perhaps."

"To what did the other note pertain?"

"It promised punishment for 'crimes against *man*,' whatever that means."

The two men sat in silence for a moment.

"Sir," said Field, "I must tell you that similar crimes were committed twelve years ago at Scutari, Turkey, during Miss Nightingale's service in the Crimean War."

The chancellor nodded. "Very similar?"

"Very. In fact, the same handwrote notes like this back then, with similar spelling errors, deliberate errors to my way of thinking."

"One had heard rumors back then," said Disraeli. "Oh dear, is *she* quite safe? Miss Nightingale?"

"My wife is looking after her."

The chancellor leaned forward. "And you're confident *she* is safe, your wife?"

"No, sir, not entirely. May I take this note and the fabric to my colleagues at the Metropolitan Police, sir?"

"Certainly, Inspector."

Disraeli waited for a response, but Field seemed to be elsewhere.

"Mr. Field?"

The inspector was staring off, his face flushed.

"Got away with murder, all these years," said Field, "didn't I." He didn't seem to be speaking to the chancellor. "Not a peep from me, quiet as a mouse. But now I'm back in the game, and then some. Branching out, right? Here, there, everywhere. Striking fear, I am."

"Field?" said Disraeli.

The inspector looked at Disraeli, blinking, as though he'd never seen him before. He looked down at his fists and seemed surprised to find them clenched.

"Forgive me, sir," he said, looking up at the chancellor again. "Old habits. I try sometimes to get inside the skin of the man I'm looking for. Most times it don't work, but now and then I've had luck that way. Load of nonsense, most like, but out there, in the Crimea, I never could get a feel for him. Just now, though, I thought I caught a glimpse."

There was a gentle knock at the door.

"Come!" said Disraeli, and the private secretary put in his head.

"It's Mr. Cox, sir."

"Oh, yes." To Field, he said, "I cannot imagine why you'd voluntarily wish to spend a moment with Nigel Cox. He's one of my least favorite Tories."

Field stood and tugged at his sleeves. "He was in the Crimea twelve years ago with the rest of us, sir."

"Was he, now?" Disraeli stood as well.

"Oh, yes," said Field, stepping to one side of the room. "It was where he committed suicide."

Disraeli regarded the detective for a long moment. "More *like* Mr. Bucket than not, I believe," he said, finally. "Monty, show the man in, please."

49

The portly gentleman who entered was bald on top, with carefully coifed graying hair cascading in waves on the sides and a walrus-sized brown mustache in front. Field never would have recognized him. Nigel Cox was not quite forty years old but looked older and had a swaggering air that was only beginning to burgeon when he was a callow youth with a trim figure, endowed with abundant brown hair.

"I'm glad you sent for me, Chancellor," said Cox, waving a sheaf of papers as though he were shooing flies. "The numbers you have given us—members of your own party—are *intended* to deceive."

Disraeli smiled cordially. "Good afternoon to you, too, my dear Cox. Have you lunched?"

"Never mind lunch!"

"I only inquire," continued Disraeli, "because an old friend of yours stopped by and asked particularly after you. I thought you two might like to reunite over a chop, you see."

Inspector Field moved toward the center of the room. "Mr. Cox, sir, I don't know if you'll remember me, Charles Field of the Metropolitan."

Cox stared blankly. Field wondered if the man was as stupid as he looked or if he actually was cunning and thinking fast.

"'Course I do," said Cox, finally. "You were the police constable out there in Turkey. Lot of good you did." The MP narrowed his eyes shrewdly. "Good Lord, the roseate murders. They're linked to those ones back then, are they?"

Field said nothing.

"Well," continued Cox, "I hope you have better luck with the crimes today than you did then and will soon catch the man who dispatched the wife of my esteemed colleague and friend, Mr. Hythe-Cooper."

"As a matter of fact," said Field, "I'm shocked to see you so fit and . . . well, upright. Having read the note you left behind, you seem to have recovered nicely from your suicide."

Cox looked from Field to Disraeli and back again. "I see, I see. One snake entertains another."

"A bit harsh, old man," said Disraeli.

"Oh, the clever ones!" said Cox. "It's always been the same, from Eton to that wretched hospital at Scutari, to the present day—they all think they're above people like me, but where are they now, and where am I, I ask you!"

Disraeli smiled deprecatingly. "You're in the presence of the chancellor of the exchequer, old boy."

Cox looked at Disraeli and Field with pure hatred.

"For your information, Mr. Field," said Cox, "when I saw that note twelve years ago, tucked under a blotter on my desk, I knew I was looking at my death sentence. He'd invaded my rooms somehow and planted it there. So I footed it. Caught the next steamer out of that fetid hole and never looked back."

"You didn't write the note?"

"No more than James Talbot wrote his!"

"Who did write it, then?"

"Thick as fenceposts, all of you. Stanhope, of course! John Stanhope!"

"You knew this for a certainty?" said Field. "How?"

"Well, for a certainty? No. But publicly kowtowing to Nightingale while privately talking about despising her? And then, at the Dinkins Inn, he had a reputation for being rather rough on the girls. Anyway, wasn't that *your* job, Constable, to ferret out the wrongdoer?"

"In my job," said Field, "I'd wonder if it was Nigel Cox who wrote James Talbot's suicide note before putting a bullet in Talbot's brain and then, since that worked so well, wrote his own farewell. But that's just a lowly constable thinking his thoughts and remembering that it was Nigel Cox who was the last to see the sweet young woman named Rose before she was strangled."

Cox blanched. "No, that was Stanhope."

"For a certainty? Remember, you and Stanhope both were with me when I was summoned to view the body."

"Stanhope."

"And you neglected to tell me this? On the night?"

But Cox had nothing further to say, it seemed.

"In the meantime," said Field, "d'you happen to know where your old chum Stanhope is?"

He shook his head.

Field advanced on Cox until they were nearly toe to toe. "Detective Inspector Llewellyn will be calling on you in short order, eager to hear your memories of bygone days and to learn about your current activities, *Nigel*."

Cox turned to Disraeli. "*This* is the sort of person your Reform Act would empower with the vote. Welcome to the end of the world, Disraeli!"

MEANWHILE, HAVING ASTONISHED the world by appearing in the House of Lords in company with another human being, the Duke did the same at Boodles, the exclusive gentlemen's club. Once he and Jack Hall were seated at the Duke's usual corner table, Seabury removed his hat and veil, and an attendant took and set them on a small stand placed there hurriedly for the purpose. The attendant quickly withdrew.

"So, what'll it be, Jack?" said Seabury in his hoarse whisper. "D'you fancy a slice of roast fowl?"

"I'd rather the beef, sir," said Jack Hall, glancing about in wonder.

Seabury's gaunt, cadaverous face registered surprise. "Jack, I must ask you not to speak to me here, in case it might encourage others to do the same."

A waiter appeared, looking silently at the paneling above Seabury's head.

"Herbie," said the Duke, quietly, "I'll have the usual and a *full* bottle of the claret this time, in honor of my guest. He *says* he wants the *roast*." Seabury shrugged, as though to say there was no accounting for tastes.

Herbie bowed in the general direction of the Duke and left them.

"Herbie is wonderful," said Seabury. "I like a man you can count on."

But Jack's eyes were on a table across the room from theirs, where William Hythe-Cooper sat reading *The Times*. Jack froze, but moments later Hythe-Cooper folded his paper and left.

"Yes, my lord," said Jack. "I, too, like a man you can count on."

50

It was early morning, and Tom Ginty paused at the entrance to the stables at Great Scotland Yard, breathing deeply of the rich odor of horses. He heard the chatter of his mates as they mucked out the stalls, and the gentle whinny of their horses, having their morning feed. Tom found his row and walked down it toward Sallie's stall. As he did so, and as his mates noticed him, their voices fell silent, one at a time. They carried on feeding and grooming their mounts, but no one spoke to him, no one looked at him. Not one.

Sallie's stall was empty. Tom felt his world tilt.

"Where is she?" he said to the young man working in the next enclosure. He seemed not to hear. "Mick, where has Sallie got to?"

There was no answer. Tom turned about. There was Sergeant Butts walking toward him.

"Might be you have friends in high places, Ginty," said Butts, "but you got no friends here."

"Where's my horse?"

"*Your* horse? You never had no horse and never will. Your friends in high places can force you back onto the Metropolitan, maybe, but not in the Mounted, oh, no."

"Where is she?" said Tom.

Butts drew back a fist and knocked him flat. The room spun for a long moment. Tom put a hand to staunch the blood from his nose and lips and glared up at the man.

"*Sauce*, from the likes of you?" said Butts.

Tom struggled to his feet. "Where is she?"

"Just watch him, boys," said Butts to the stunned recruits. "Watch him run cryin' to his friends, watch him run to that Inspector Bucket, who only took him in outta pity for the tooth-bit creature."

Tom flinched. He feared pity more than almost anything.

"Where is she?"

"Go find Sergeant Cooper. He says he's got a very special beat for you to walk. For the select few, he says. Me? After disobeying a direct order, I only wish I'd 'a' shot you dead on the spot."

Tom stared at Butts for a long moment, then turned and walked toward the door, wiping the blood coming from his nose. One young recruit, fervently grooming his horse, said in a low voice as he passed, "Two of me brothers was in the crowd we didn't shoot at that day, Tom. Gotta thank you for it, but we'll be sacked if we have any truck with you."

Tom put his head under a pump in the yard and cleaned his face. He found Sergeant Cooper, from whom he received the uniform and helmet of a constable, a map, and a whistle. No one would be assigned to partner him, he would be on his own, patrolling the banks of the Thames, all dug up now for the new sewer works going in, from the City to Chelsea and back again. All day, every day. Sergeant Cooper grinned. Not good-naturedly.

Tom dressed himself in the costume of a constable, drab by comparison to his former glory. He found one consolation, however: the helmet hid more of his *tooth-bit* ear. Tom took a deep breath and started walking.

51

Belinda Field was aggrieved.

When Inspector Field returned home, he found John Stuart Mill's calling card and the note he'd left. At first he'd seemed grimly satisfied. To Jane, he said, "It's political up one side and deviant down the other, just like I suggested to Mr. Disraeli. It's not only women he's going after but prominent males as well. Up till now, we've had no male corpses, but who knows if there mightn't be one out there somewhere? He may have victims, male or female, we've yet to discover."

Belinda spoke up. "This was just what was so upsetting to Mr. Mill. He was very worried about his stepdaughter."

Field looked at her for a moment. "How do you know how Mr. Mill was?"

"He told me, didn't he."

Field and his wife looked at each other.

"Through the door, Belinda?" said Jane. "When he dropped off the note for Mr. Field?"

"Well, I didn't like to leave him standing on the step!"

"Good God!" said Field. *You had the man in?*"

"He was a perfect gentleman," said Belinda.

"Of course he was, but what if he hadn't been, Belinda!" Field was growing red in the face. "We've got a bloody maniac going about town murdering women, do you not understand that? *Oh, do step in, Mr. I-Never-Met-You-Before! Have a seat!*"

"I am seventeen years of age, but you treat me like a child!"

"Because you act like one!"

"All right," said Jane, "that's enough, both of you."

Inwardly Belinda trembled. Now she never could tell her parents about the other man she'd invited in, never mind he was an old friend of theirs from their time in the Crimean War. He was just passing by and saw his friend Mr. Mill leave. The man didn't seem to want anything, apart from knowing how everyone was and what they were doing, Mother and Mr. Field and Tom. *No,* he'd said, *you needn't tell them I was here. When I call again, I want it to be a surprise!*

Belinda felt a wriggle of doubt in her belly. She turned and climbed the stairs.

"Now Charles . . ." said Jane in a warning tone.

But Field shouted after his daughter. *"I just want you safe!"*

Later that night, Jane Field knocked at Belinda's door, opened it, and found the bedroom empty. Jane walked back to Tom's room and rapped. When he opened the door, Jane said, "Missed you at supper, Tom."

"We drilled until late."

"I thought as much. Have you seen Belinda?"

"No." Tom stood, suddenly alarmed. "Is something wrong?"

"Not at all, she's about somewhere, I imagine." She was about to go when she turned back. "Is that lip swollen?"

"Walked into a post, I did."

"Everything all right, Tom?"

He looked at the woman who had taken him in and treated him like her own son. Out of pity, was it? "Right as rain, Mrs. Field, thank you. Let me know if you need help finding her."

Jane hurried down the stairs and finally found Belinda sitting alone in the unlit back parlor, her chair beside the window.

"He's right," said Belinda.

"Who's right?"

"About me being a child."

Jane made her way across the dark room, found a chair near Belinda, and sat.

"I know he already regrets his words," said Jane.

"Because he told the truth? He shouldn't regret telling the truth. Funny it took so long for me to see it, come to that. I make mistakes all the time, one after another, I can't seem to help myself." The young woman looked up at her mother. "You told me I could be a Nightingale nurse, like you, but you don't really believe it, do you?"

"Of course I do."

The young woman looked out the darkened window again. "You have to say such things, you're my mother. Isn't that the same as men telling women 'all will be well' when really it won't be? Isn't that a way of keeping me quiet?"

Jane was silent.

"So I'm to stay here at home with the door shut and never admit anyone and never leave."

"At any other time, Belinda, what you did today, inviting Mr. Mill into this house and treating him with courtesy and grace? Why, that wouldn't be considered a mistake, it would have been the proper thing to do. It's just that these are not normal times. It's a gift you have, to be interested in people and wanting to talk with 'em. Not everyone's got that, you know."

Belinda continued to stare at the opaque window.

"A long time ago, Belinda, after I went out with Miss Nightingale to Scutari and then came back here to London, I was lost. All what I'd seen out there of the war never left my eyes, even when I slept. And that evil man out there, the one who spoke in my ear, who tried to stop my breath, he never left my thoughts. 'So, no—that's it,' I said, 'I'm finished, I'm not a nurse no more, I'm nothing.' Here I had this very good man proposing marriage to me, Mr. Charles Field . . ." Jane smiled and shook her head. "Again and again, night and day, the fool! But I knew I couldn't accept him, because I wasn't any good anymore, as a nurse, as a woman, as anything."

Belinda was staring now at her adoptive mother.

"I didn't know what to do with myself, so I walked the streets. I needed to find a position, and quick, to earn my bread, but I couldn't make out what that would be, so I just walked and walked and felt more like a ghost than a real person. And then I saw another ghost, comin' toward me along the street. Haunted look on his face, a lost look. 'Mr. Kilvert?' I said. 'Is that you?' Josiah Kilvert was out there in the Crimean, serving with us at the Scutari Hospital, and then he'd gone back to Wales.

"Well, the two of us had a cup of tea, but he didn't look at all well. 'How's your girl back in Kidwelly?' I said, like an idiot. And he said, 'She's somebody else's girl now, and I'm tryin' to work up nerve to ask Inspector Field for a position.' And then Belinda, I busted out cryin', and said, 'I think I'm tryin' to ask Mr. Field for a position, too.' And believe it or not, the two of us went together to Scotland Yard and found Mr. Field, and—well, I let Mr. Kilvert go first."

Belinda hazarded a tentative smile. "But you didn't nurse no more?"

"Oh, yes, when we were first married, I nursed at St. Bart's and then St. Thomas. And now, you see, I'm nursing Miss Nightingale. You'll make a fine, one, Belinda, just you wait."

A long moment passed. Then Belinda said, "I had my bad man, too. I still see him when I dream. I don't know how I'll ever get away from him."

"But you *are* away from him, Belinda. Well away. The man is dead."

"You're not just telling me 'all will be well'?"

Jane sighed. Finally, she said, "A very wise, very kind woman once saw the fear in my eyes, and she gave me this, to scare away the bad people, the bad thoughts."

Jane took a string from around her neck, at the end of which hung Mother Seacole's totem.

"I've seen it before," said Belinda, "and wondered how you could keep such a big thing round your neck."

"You get used to him. Now I want him to be yours."

She passed the carved wooden peg to her daughter, who looked at the totem, with his row of tiny sharp bright white teeth, and up again at her mother with a laugh.

"Well," she said, "he's a little scary *himself*!"

Jane laughed, too. "And a good thing he is, my dear! A good thing!"

The two women embraced. For a moment Belinda considered telling Jane about the other man she'd let in the house that day but then decided against it. It was too shaming, and she'd just begun to feel better.

"Thank you, Mum."

52

Like all great cities, London began small: a clearing in the dense forest bordering a great snaking river. Lesser rivers and streams flowed among the trees into the big one, all teeming with fish and sparkling clean water. Tribes came and went, until finally invaders from the south claimed the clearing and soon started to pave it over. The Romans called the riverside village Londinium. There they thrived, building shrines to their gods and expanding their rule far to the north. Finally, nearly four hundred years later, they were forced to abandon their holdings in the island by urgent circumstances closer to home.

Centuries passed, and still the waters sparkled and the fish leapt.

But as Londinium became London, the smaller rivers were shunted underground to make way for the city above. Cesspits were dug alongside them. The human population grew. Finally, by the mid-1800s, Londoners' waste, channeled directly into the Thames, had killed all the fish and made the river stink so horribly that members of Parliament had been moved to action. Joseph Bazalgette was appointed director of perhaps the largest civil engineering project since the Roman era. He came up with an audacious design and marshaled an army of workers to execute it. Together they would create vast embankments on each side of the river, through which would run his new sewer pipes. Now, in 1867, he was more than halfway through his massive project.

Today, one of his younger engineers had asked for an audience.

"You've encountered a problem, Ahmed?" said Bazalgette.

"Well, sir, I don't know that it's a problem, but it may become one. Right now, sir, it's more of a strangeness."

"Yes?"

Ahmed ran a hand through his hair. "My men feel we're not alone down there, sir," he said. "*I* feel we're not alone."

Bazalgette raised his eyebrows. "There are a great many of us working beneath the streets of London just now. Hundreds. You and your workers certainly are *not* alone."

The two men, Bazalgette nearly fifty years old, Ahmed Selim, only twenty-six, stood together above a table on which was spread a diagram: a map of the sewer pipes of medieval London. The ancient pipes led toward the river, along with the buried rivers that ran beneath the city, all of them heading to the huge tube designed by Bazalgette to intercept these old lines and redirect what they carried, the fresh water and the sewage. No one ever had constructed a sewer pipe this large. Its creator claimed it would channel all the city's waste downstream, even when rainfall was sparse, to pumping and treatment stations from which it would be released into the lower Thames estuary. When rain was plentiful, it would scour the tubes with ferocious speed. Bazalgette had calculated the size pipe needed for the entire population of London and then doubled it, to cries of *extravagance* from the politicians.

"I think of you as one of my more promising young men, sir," said Bazalgette. "I'm trying to remember where you schooled. You've obviously had fine training."

Ahmed looked from his boss to his boots. "Whatever I might know I learned in the kitchen, sir."

"What do you mean, son?"

He looked up. "My school was the Barrack Hospital kitchen out at Scutari, sir, and I was taught by Mr. Alexis Soyer and Mr. T. G. Taylor. They always said, if you can make your way round a kitchen, you can make your way round most anything."

Bazalgette looked at Ahmed in astonishment. "This was the famous French chef, Alexis Soyer?"

"And Mr. Taylor, sir," said the young man. "After the war I made my way to London with help from Miss Nightingale."

"Extraordinary. And this was the sum of your engineering training?"

The young man shrugged. "Running a big kitchen is a complicated affair. It's all a kind of engineering." He turned back to the map and put a finger on it. "Still, something's not right, right about here. When we're down there laying pipe or shoring up the old bricks, well sir, there are voices. My men hear 'em, and I hear 'em. It's like, when our shifts end at the close of day, someone else's begins. If there's somebody down there digging who shouldn't be, well, it poses a danger, don't it? To the workers, to all of us. May I have your permission to go down in the night, sir? To listen and look?"

"Of course not, it's not safe, you know that. What if it should rain? Even if you took another with you, it's dangerous enough down there when the city above is in daylight. At night the perils only increase." Bazalgette regarded the earnest young man. "Remember, Ahmed, the earth itself makes sounds beneath ground. It's a mysterious globe we tread upon. I hope you won't be too disappointed to realize it's just the cries and lamentations of a fatigued world you hear."

"Disappointed? No, sir, I'd be relieved if it's only a downhearted globe talking to me and not two other blokes."

53

Thanks to Detective Inspector Llewellyn, the morning papers all ran the same message: a person calling himself John Stanhope was being sought to assist the police with their inquiries regarding the roseate murders. Field read them with satisfaction as he ate an early breakfast. When Tom clattered down the stairs and headed for the street door, Field stood and shouted, "How's it all going at the stables, Tom?"

"It's going well, sir."

"Happy to hear it!" But Tom was out the door.

Another who read the morning papers was Jack Hall himself. Seeing the name in print made a part of him wish he'd not given up John Stanhope. It sounded so much better than Jack Hall. Still, it never would do now.

Jack picked egg yolk from an incisor with a fingernail, trying to think what his next move should be. He'd been astounded when the young woman at Inspector Field's house invited him in. It had been sheer impulse to knock, after watching the house and seeing J. S. Mill enter and leave. He'd been tempted to do the strange girl then and there and leave her as a surprise for Field and his wife, but there were others who actually posed imminent danger. There were the two MPs who had put him onto the source of the anonymous column in the *Evening Standard* and the other MP who had aided the writer. There was the nurse in training who claimed she'd recognize him if she saw him again. He opened the drawer in his desk. In it lay Dr. James Talbot's revolver, the one Jack had used years earlier to shoot the man dead. He put the gun on the desktop and tried to think things through.

MANY OTHERS READ the notices with interest. Among them were members of the theatrical community in the West End, for whom it jogged memories of a would-be actor. For others, veterans of the army hospital at Scutari, the name also rang bells. One of these was Lieutenant-Colonel Charles Henry Spencer-Churchill. He got in touch with a family friend, the novelist Wilkie Collins, who in turn arranged a meeting with Inspector Field. They gathered at a pub off Fleet Street in the early evening.

"I do remember you, sir," said Field. "You were one of the few friendly faces I saw at an otherwise hostile drink-up with the doctors." He nodded toward Wilkie Collins. "How do you come to know this fellow?"

Collins himself answered. "Spence belongs to one of the few families of quality who tolerate me."

"Whatever gave you the idea we tolerate you?"

Field answered. "He's got the imagination of a novelist."

"Ah, yes, that would explain it," said Spencer-Churchill.

"Here I am, trying to do a public service," said Collins, "and all I get for my pains is mockery."

"Surely you're used to it by now, old man," said Spencer-Churchill.

Collins removed his wire-rimmed spectacles and gave them a

polishing with a handkerchief. "Indeed, I am." Short, bald and bearded, kept two wives and had children by each woman in two separate households. He was in fact inured to mockery, both good-natured and the other kind.

"Inspector Field," said Collins, "what were you doing, bandying my name about in a coroner's court?"

"I was protecting the name of my client, Mr. Hythe-Cooper, whether he deserved it or not, in hopes he will one day pay me, and I'd hoped to protect the public reputation of his slain wife, who certainly deserved no less."

"Hythe-Cooper," said Spencer-Churchill with some distaste. "He was out there in the Crimea, we were acquainted."

"Was he?" said Field. "Oh, for God's sake! That fellow who was with you when we met, you called him Coop!"

"I did."

Spencer-Churchill laid a thin leather case on the bar.

"Well, sir, I opened the newspaper and there was the name John Stanhope staring at me, and your name, Inspector Field, and Hythe-Cooper's, and as I was reading about the inquests, certain memories came straggling back. Including a batch of photographs I obtained from a photographer fellow back then. I seemed to recall a picture he took of the head doctor out there, John Hall, and his aide, this Stanhope person. Here it is, sir."

Spencer-Churchill drew out a photograph and slid it across the bar toward Field. "It occurred to me that a man's appearance may change from one decade to the next to some extent, but there will be features that remain the same."

Field examined the photograph. There was Dr. Hall, standing beside a horse whose reins were held by the servant, Hanif. Standing a half step behind Hall was the man he'd known as John Stanhope, seeming to stare with something like devotion at the back of the doctor's neck. He was young and smooth-cheeked, with a broad brow and high hairline.

"He was always at one's elbow, if you know what I mean," said

Spencer-Churchill. "'If there's anything at all I can do for you, sir?' and
that sort of thing until you wanted to scream. I saw him and Dr. Talbot
heading into town more than once, and Hythe-Cooper. I didn't like to
think what they got up to at old Mother Dinkins place."

"And what did you imagine that might have been?"

Spencer-Churchill shook his head. "No idea, really. None of my business, but something about them felt *not right*, at least when it came to
women."

"May I keep the photograph, at least temporarily?" said Field.

"By all means."

The three men shook hands all round, but when Spencer-Churchill
and Wilkie Collins left, the inspector remained at the bar. He drew out
the photo from his pocket, and with it came a single folded sheet of
foolscap. He set the picture aside and examined the paper. It seemed to
contain the minutes of a meeting.

Where the devil did this come from? His mind raced. *Of course.*

He'd found it on the fifth of May, beneath the bed that held the lifeless body of Susan Hythe-Cooper. Parliamentary minutes. At the time
Field had pocketed the page, thinking he'd examine it later. And from
that moment to this, he hadn't thought of it once.

The pub was dimly lit. Field strained to read the print. A few lines
had been lightly underscored.

Mr. Mill. The reform put forward by my own party offers token
reform and would accomplish nothing. The reform currently argued
by Mr. Disraeli falls far short of justice, which I hope is the goal of
every soul in this chamber. Replace a single word in Mr. Disraeli's
proposal, however, change the word *man* to *person*, and then we will
have accomplished a great thing indeed.

It took Field a moment to work out what that would mean.
The vote! For women!
Wait a moment, he'd read this somewhere else, or words like it.

Again, May 5. Sitting on a bench in Regents Park, keeping an eye on No. 8 Hanover Terrace. The anonymous column in the *Evening Standard*, arguing that the vote should be granted not only to a greater number of men but to women as well. To do so would require only the change of a single word! So who was the anonymous writer?

Susan Hythe-Cooper's husband was an MP also. Perhaps she had got this page from her husband and brought it to share with Jeremy Sims so he could write the column? Or perhaps . . . Was she *returning* it to Sims? After she'd used it as the basis for an article *she* had written? Was Susan Hythe-Cooper the author of the weekly column in the *Evening Standard*?

"Barman," said Field. "Do you have a boy who would run a message to Scotland Yard for sixpence?"

"I do." The man called up the stairs. *"Fred?"*

"And a scrap of paper, please? And pen and ink?"

To Detective Inspector S. Llewellyn, wrote Field. *Sam, I have a feeling they* were *meeting to discuss public policy, Jeremy Sims and Susan Hythe-Cooper. I think it possible that Susan Hythe-Cooper wrote the Notes from Our Future column in the* Standard *and was murdered because of it.*

The boy took the fold of paper and the coin and went off at a run.

Miss Nightingale's words came back to the inspector.

The Reform Act is what brought Mr. Disraeli here today. And Mill and Carlyle and Gladstone. Everyone wants one to weigh in on this side or the other.

Field laid it out for himself in his mind.

Florence Nightingale was one of the most famous and loved women in the kingdom. Her siding for reform, or opposing it, would have tremendous influence. To someone for whom expanding the rights of women was to be stopped at all costs, what would a few female lives matter? And if that person was someone who could form bonds with women only by binding them, one who actually took pleasure from it, well, that person could pretend he was acting in a righteous cause. Somehow.

Field's eyes moved from the parliamentary minutes to the

smooth-skinned young man in the photo, standing just a step behind the doctor.

John Stanhope or whatever you're calling yourself these days, if you're here in this city, someone is going to recognize that big forehead of yours, someone is going to remember the name Stanhope, someone is going to know where and how you live. And then we'll get you.

54

It was early evening. Defying the direct instructions of his revered boss, Ahmed Selim chose a manhole not far from All Hallows by the Wall and climbed down. *Why?* he asked himself. He felt the same flutter in his belly now that he'd had as a youngster, about to do something of which Mr. Soyer or T.G. would certainly disapprove. He carried a bull's-eye lantern and had a pouch of biscuits and cheese in one pocket.

The Walbrook River had been paved over and buried again and again by successive generations for centuries, but in the past year it had been newly rebricked for the great sewer project. There were arched passages here and there, leading into the main branch from smaller, nameless tributaries. The waters of the Walbrook were thereby supplemented or, when necessary, could be diverted while the bricks of the main branch were maintained.

Ahmed was used to working down here with dozens of others and in a blaze of lantern light. It felt completely different to be alone in the eternal night of this underground world, armed only with a single lamp and a biscuit. He followed the brook in a southerly direction, down from London Wall toward Threadneedle Street. The water was flowing at ankle height, and the bricks beneath his boots were slippery.

He reckoned he was under the Bank of England itself now, or nearly there.

Think of all them gold bars, just above me head!

As he continued on, he saw ahead of him a dim thread of lamplight. It seemed to come from a small breach in the bricks on his left. Ahmed covered his bull's-eye lantern, approached warily, and peered in through the gap.

The gaunt face staring back at him froze his blood.

"My stupid workmen have broken through since we were last here," said the cadaver. "They shouldn't even have been in this room." Ahmed wondered if the man could be speaking to him, but then he clearly turned to someone else.

"Perhaps it was Mithras, trying to get out!" said the cadaver.

Another voice spoke. "Or the bull, more like."

The white-faced man laughed and withdrew, and for a moment Ahmed saw a confusing glitter of color before another face appeared in the slot where bricks were missing. Black beard, swept-back hair, red scarf. Prominent forehead.

Ahmed remained motionless.

"We'll need to have it mended as soon as possible." It was the hoarse, whispery voice of the cadaver. "One cannot be careless down here. It's a matter of life and death, really."

The man with the beard peered through the breach in the wall, looking this way and that, this way and that. *Surely*, thought Ahmed, *he can see me, he's looking me straight in the face.*

"Come along, Jack!" said the cadaver. His face withdrew and the lamplight within bobbed away.

Ahmed began to breathe again. Then he took a piece of chalk from a pocket and marked the wall opposite the breach, scoring the greasy surface again and again until his *X* became clearly visible. Only then did he realize that the waters had risen to calf height. What was that sound?

No. Surely not.

He listened. Yes, in the world above, it was raining. His heart began to pound. He pivoted slowly, toward the way he'd come. One step at a time. He mustn't rush, he mustn't fall. He mustn't let his lamp go out.

One step at a time, but the water was inching toward his knees.

Maybe go just a bit faster.

How far to the Bank of England? There was a ladder and a manhole above, just this side of it. Or was it the other side? It was a big building, almost the biggest in the world, he thought.

His feet went out suddenly from under him. He scrambled to his feet, upright, drenched, but his lamp was out.

He was lost in the utter dark.

The next time he fell, not long after, the Walbrook took him swiftly downstream toward the river.

55

The rain grew heavier as night came on. A passerby, hurrying to get out of the wet had stumbled over the body. It lay across the pavement before a modest townhouse in Watling Street that turned out to be the victim's own home. The man's stunned wife, after telling the police what little she knew, had been taken back inside by a solicitous neighbor. A small knot of constables now stood in the rain looking down on the corpse with Detective Inspector Sam Llewellyn, who had just pulled up in a carriage.

"The wife said he heard a noise, took an umbrella, and stepped out to see what it might be," said one of the constables. "Most likely it's just a very nasty street robbery. The wife said he always carried a coin purse in this pocket here, sir, and now it ain't there. Maybe the victim struck at the thief with his umbrella—you see how it's broke, sir—and that's how a pistol came into play. We wouldn't a' brought you out in the rain, but when we learned he was the MP involved with one of these murdered *roseate* women, well, we thought you'd want to know."

Jeremy Sims had been killed by a bullet through his left eye. His arms were splayed wide, the umbrella a few inches from his right hand, bent almost double. The rain washed the blood from his face. Llewellyn, looking down on the man, was aware of the note in his own pocket from Charles Field, suggesting Sims was innocent of illicit relations with the late Susan Hythe-Cooper.

"Cover him up, then, and wait for the coroner's men," said Llewellyn. "I'll go in and talk with the wife."

56

Jack Hall returned to his room in Clapham, drenched and exhausted and smarting from a blow to the head.

The son of a bitch nearly brought me down with his damned umbrella!

All this tearing about town, it wouldn't do. And it was scandalous, the sums he was paying out to the hackney cabmen of London, especially now that he was unemployed. He took the pistol from his coat, and the MP's coin purse, and laid them on the desk where they made a little puddle of rainwater. He opened the purse and counted out seven shillings, two sixpence, and a few pennies. A windfall, but how long would it last? He felt a mixture of exhilaration and terror. He'd shot a man, not in a far-off foreign land but in the center of London. A prominent man, a member of Parliament. There was no turning back now, there could be only forward motion.

But his life had grown too dangerous, he needed to make a change. Jack felt it likely the Duke would welcome him to his mansion and was confident, too, that he could manage any unwelcome advances that might ensue. He wouldn't need to take much; he didn't *have* much. His journal, certainly, would go with him. A change of clothing. His little sewing kit. The pistol, of course.

The pistol. So much less effort than my red silk garrotes! Less risk, too, of difficulty with the kicking and flailing one sometimes endures with strangulation!

His thoughts spun off into tangents, he really must sleep.

Had there been someone in the Duke's tunnel tonight? Before he'd gone out to find the MP? There had been a moment when he thought he'd seen a ghostly face in the darkness amid the sound of rushing water and the swirling sewer odors.

That's insane! There was no one there, of course there wasn't!

Jack Hall was done with thinking. He threw himself onto his bed, wet clothing and all, and slept like a dead man.

57

The notice from the Metropolitan Police the previous day seeking help with their inquiries had been of use, without doubt, but today's front-page illustration of the young Stanhope in Scutari reaped even greater rewards. The *Illustrated News* editor had been keen to publish it when William Howard Russell brought the photo to him, and doubly so when word came within the hour that Jeremy Sims, MP, had been murdered outside his own home. The story wrote itself.

Mr. Sims, the reader will remember, had been linked to the strangled Susan Hythe-Cooper. Now he, too, has suffered a violent death.

The illustrator was set to work immediately.

THIS WAS JOHN STANHOPE IN 1855.
WHO IS HE TODAY?

Detective Inspector Sam Llewellyn and his men were kept busy from the moment the paper hit the streets. They had to sift through reports that ranged from the dubious to those which might have merit (*I was a patient of Miss Nightingale's at the Scutari Hospital, and that man, Stanhope, held my best mate down whilst Dr. Hall sawed off his right leg, and dead he was, my mate, within the hour!*) Would the veteran know him to recognize him today? (*Dunno, that would depend, wouldn't it.*) There were several of these.

Inspector Field found Llewellyn that afternoon, not in his office but in a larger meeting room across the hall. Two of his officers sat at the far end of the table, writing reports based on notes taken during interviews throughout the day.

"Sam, was Jeremy Sims shot through his left eye?" Field asked without preamble.

"However did you know?" said Llewellyn. "It wasn't reported in the press."

"That's how the bastard got James Talbot a dozen years ago," said Field. "I had a suspicion he might be a creature of habit."

"Well, he must be, when it comes to red roses. We've a theatrical producer coming in now, if you'd like to listen in, Charles."

"I'm to keep mum, am I? As I'm no longer one of you lot?" The two constables watched Detective Llewellyn to see what he would say. Field held up a hand. "Don't mean to put you on the spot, Sam. I'll be quiet like the grave."

He moved to the end of the table with the other two and nodded to them as he sat.

"Right," said Llewellyn, consulting a list before him. "Show in Mr. Banbury, will you, Mr. Thompson?"

One of the constables rose and went to the door.

"Sir?" said Thompson. "Detective Inspector Llewellyn will see you now."

He held the door open and an older, elegantly dressed white-haired gentleman entered, taking in the room and the persons in it with a keen eye. Llewellyn rose.

"Mr. Banbury, sir," he said, "it's good of you to come."

"Not at all," said Banbury. "Happy to help."

"If you'll have a seat, we're eager to hear whatever it is you might have to tell us. Your full name, please, sir?"

"Francis Northcote Banbury. The third, if anyone's interested, which I assume you're not."

"You recognized the person pictured in the *Illustrated News*?"

"Oh, yes, no question," said Banbury. "I heard the man's audition years ago, and although he had no talent, his claim to have been a descendant of Shakespeare was entertaining enough that he stuck in one's memory. He even pointed out that bulging forehead of his as evidence of his ancestor, old Will."

"And his name was John Stanhope?" said Llewellyn.

"Indeed."

"When did this interview take place?"

"Mid-1850s, I'd say," said Banbury.

"Since then, have you encountered the man?"

"Never. He simply seemed to disappear, as far as I know."

"Well, we are grateful for your willingness to share what you know of this person, sir," said Llewellyn.

"Wait a mo'!" said Field. "On what did he base his genealogical claims, apart from his damned forehead? The Shakespeare line died out with his daughter, didn't it?"

Banbury smiled. "I saw you lurking down there, Mr. Field. We met years ago, when I was producing a benefit show for Mr. Charles Dickens. D'you remember? You provided . . . security, let's call it."

Llewellyn looked to the ceiling and shook his head. "Quiet like the grave, that's you, Charles."

Field looked hard at Banbury and then returned his smile. "Indeed I do remember, sir. We were successful: no rotten tomatoes were hurled at the stage, and the Queen was not inconvenienced."

The two men rose and joined each other for a warm handshake.

"Shall I order in sausage rolls, gentlemen?" said Llewellyn.

"Forgive us old men, Detective Llewellyn," said Banbury, "for indulging a fond remembrance. Back to the business at hand!" He resumed his seat. "Stanhope's claim was entirely bogus, of course, because *no*, there were no direct descendants of Shakespeare after his daughter and his son-in-law, Dr. John Hall, died without offspring."

Field's smile faded.

"I never knew the son-in-law's name," he said. "Good God."

"Studied at Cambridge in the late 1600s, I believe, and—lucky him— became the only physician in Stratford-upon-Avon. Convenient way to meet the Bard of Avon's daughter."

"Dr. John Hall," said Field, "just like the man in the picture, the man I knew at Scutari, the one Stanhope is staring at with devotion. I wonder . . ."

An angry voice rose from just outside the room. Llewellyn opened the door to reveal a man with swept-back black hair and a full black beard, brandishing a copy of the *Illustrated News* and shouting.

"I insist on seeing this Llewellyn fellow immediately!"

"He stands before you, sir," said Llewellyn.

"My dear Tuttle," said Banbury, "what *can* have got your cage so rattled?"

Arthur Tuttle, tragedian, lately playing a minor role in the West End comedy *Go to Putney*, registered shock and embarrassment to see the urbane producer in the room.

"Sorry, Banbury, I imagine we're all on edge these days." Tuttle saw Charles Field staring at him from the end of the table, and his confusion grew. He remembered him as the lunatic who'd stood him a drink after the show a few weeks earlier.

"Hallo, Mr. Tuttle!" said Field, waving gaily.

"We'd be most interested, sir," said Llewellyn, cutting Field off, "most interested in anything you might tell us."

The actor nodded and pointed to the paper he held.

"I employed this man for years," said Tuttle, "until only recently when he stopped showing up for work. I assumed his dyed hair and beard were affectations designed to flatter me. My God, to learn now that he's suspected of being the roseate monster? I put my life in his hands on a nightly basis, it's almost more than I can bear!"

"How exactly did you employ this man?"

"Why, Jack Hall was my *dresser*!"

In the presence of a *name*, the room grew suddenly very still.

"Jack Hall," repeated Llewellyn.

"Jack Hall," said Field.

"Jack Hall," said Banbury. "Yes, one saw him about, at this theater or that. Always gave the impression of following one with his eyes. But then, with what else would the fellow follow you? The hair and beard were dyed, obviously, but that's not uncommon in our profession. I never would have taken him for Stanhope, though, the smooth-skinned faux descendant of Shakespeare, but I see it now."

"We can slap a black beard and a wig on our illustration," said Field, "and show the world our suspect. John Stanhope Hall, now known as Jack."

"Mr. Tuttle, sir," said Llewellyn, "do you happen to know the home address of your former employee?"

"I do, as a matter of fact. It's 42 Dunwoody Road, Clapham. I never fail to send a card to each of my various people at Christmas." Llewellyn and his two men rose, as did Field. "I'm known for it, as a matter of fact, throughout the West End and throughout . . ."

Tuttle trailed off. The men were no longer in the room.

"Without so much as a *thank you*," he said.

The producer Banbury said, "Poor old Tuttle. No one appreciates you half so much as you do."

58

The men barely had room to turn around in the tiny bed-sit. The landlady at 42 Dunwoody Street hovered apprehensively on the landing, looking in at Flat 3.

"What's he done, then?" she said, but the policemen did not respond.

"Someone rather damp spent the night here on top of the blanket," said Llewellyn, feeling the rumpled bedclothes.

"He was out in last night's rain, wasn't he," said Field. "Top of the desk is wet, too."

"Wardrobe's empty," said Thompson.

"And the sideboard," said Constable Wilcox, "except for a half round of bread."

Llewellyn turned to the woman in the door. "You didn't notice Mr. Hall leaving this morning?"

"I did not. Normally he keeps regular hours, Mr. Hall does, and very quiet he is, going out to work in the West End round six most every evening and coming home God knows when, but well after I'm asleep, that's sure. Theater folk, you know. What's he done?"

Field was opening and closing drawers. "He's done a lot of writing here, the desk is heavily stained with ink." He leaned down and put his nose close to the desktop. He rose up again with a look of triumph. "Ink . . . and black powder. His gun was still wet with rain. He set it down here as soon as he returned and left it here while he slept."

"I do believe he's our man, all right," said Llewellyn.

"Something's nagging at me, Sam, and I can't make out what it is. The beard? The hair?" Llewellyn waited, but the inspector shook his head. "It's gone."

Llewellyn turned to the landlady. "Does Jack Hall have friends or family, ma'am, where he might have gone?" said Llewellyn. "Someone who might have taken him in if he was in difficulties?"

"Not a single one, Officer. In all the years Jack's let this room, I never saw him with one single friend!"

One of the constables, on his hands and knees beneath the bed, stood up, clutching a crumpled man's jacket, still wet. "He kicked it under the bed rather than take it. And look, Officer Llewellyn—you can just make out a spray of blood on this lapel."

"Blood!" cried the landlady with an air of satisfaction.

"Ma'am," said Field, "is there a cab stand nearby?"

"Oh, yes, sir, just round the corner."

The cabmen were eager to talk, the three of them speaking over each other to tell Field, Llewellyn, and anybody else who would listen, about their new customer.

He never used to hire a cab before, no, he walked always, wherever he went, mainly over the river and back. But these days? Yes, indeed! Not that they were complaining, they were glad of the custom, times being what they were. Still, something seemed not right. And in the past week or two, why, you'd think he was a right toff, the way he ordered us about.

"What about late last night?" said Llewellyn. "Or early this morning?"

The cabmen looked at each other blankly. None of them had seen him.

"Might 'a' left before our lot came on, might 'a' walked to another stand, or might 'a' walked on his own two feet wherever it was he was goin', which was his usual practice."

Field spoke up. "So, gents, were you taking Jack Hall all over town, or did he have his favorite destinations?"

"The City," said one.

The others nodded. Generally speaking, the City.

"Near the river," said a second.

"I picked him up once in Cheapside, I think," said another.

"Dropped him off somewhere in Threadneedle."

"Cloak Lane is where I once dropped him," said another, "but I don't recall just where."

What's he done, then? What's he done?

"We're hoping he might assist us in our inquiries," said Llewellyn.

The cabmen looked at each other knowingly.

"Generally speakin'," said one, "that means the beaks want to assist a bloke into a noose."

Llewellyn smiled. "If Jack Hall shows up here again, you will get in touch, won't you, gents?"

Aye. They touched their caps and nodded.

59

At the Duke's townhouse Thorne had opened the door to Jack Hall that morning, Thorne's hooded, rheumy eyes moving from Jack's rundown boots to his bulging traveling valise and up to a level just below Jack's eyes.

"Master has not yet risen, sir," he said.

"I understand, but I wish to wait for him," said Jack loftily. "Have the goodness to show me to the first-floor parlor, and let the Duke know that I await him at his earliest convenience."

It took Thorne a long moment to decide how he would respond to being ordered about by this interloper.

"Come this way, sir," he said, but made no move to take the luggage.

Jack hoisted the bag himself and made a mental note.

Thorne must go.

As the hours passed in the first floor parlor, Jack grew agitated.

How late do bloody dukes sleep, for God's sake?

He had shot dead an MP. He, Jack Hall. Jack Stanhope Hall. Thrilling. Terrifying. What if he were caught?

He found himself desperately hungry and rang for Thorne. Thorne did not come.

Thorne must go.

Back home they used to call me Jack-All, the shits.

Had anyone ever been kind? Ever?

"Good day, Jack," said the Duke.

Jack leapt to his feet. He hadn't heard a footfall, a door, nothing. He was momentarily speechless.

Seabury looked at Jack's luggage. "Traveling?"

"Actually, sir, I wondered if I might stop with you for a bit."

The Duke regarded the younger man for a moment. "Did you have a difficult night? You have a rumpled air."

Jack felt a surge of rage. "Yes, I had a difficult night. Yes, I have a rumpled air."

Mustn't give in to it, mustn't give in.

"Well," said Seabury, "if you're to stay here, you'll need a decent suit of clothing. I'll have Thorne lay out a couple of my old outfits in the yellow bedroom. There's a tub on that floor; I imagine you could do with a scrub."

There were no unwanted advances. The tub was filled with hot water by Thorne. The clothing fit him, as did the fine leather boots. The yellow bedroom was spacious, and a fire was lit to remove the damp from the bedclothes. Jack did not know why all these kindnesses should make him angry, but they did.

Dinner in the Duke's townhouse was muted.

"What are you appearing in now, Jack?" said Seabury.

Jack looked up at him. "I'm between engagements, sir."

"That would explain it. You see, Thorne here has been searching the papers and hasn't found a whisper of you in a theatrical way."

Jack shot a glance at Thorne, who remained impassive.

"I rarely open a newspaper these days," said the Duke. "The news is so awful, generally. Thorne gives me whatever information it is he seems to think I might need."

"There is an ebb and flow to my profession," said Jack. "A trickle today can become a flood tomorrow."

"Just so, just so. The actor's life. Thorne? A little more wine?"

The elderly butler refilled the Duke's glass, and Jack's, and withdrew again to the sideboard.

"Besides," continued Jack, warming to the subject, "it's all politics, and who's currently cozy with whom. The producers are either illiterate fools or insufferable snobs who wouldn't know real talent if it bit them!" He drank his wine in one go. "Thorne, more wine here, if it's not too much trouble!"

The servant moved silently to Jack's side, refilled his glass, and retired again to his station.

"Well, well," said the Duke. "All very enlightening. I must retire early, Jack, having slept very little last night. I never can sleep much when it rains. Rain brings out our ghosts, you see."

"Ghosts?"

"You open a door or a wardrobe and there one will be, just standing there, waiting. What are they waiting for? For you yourself to die and join them? Often you'll open your eyes to see one at the foot of your bed. Makes it difficult to fall asleep again." He turned to the butler again. "Thorne, which ones did we have last night?"

"It was quite a parade, my lord."

"The Drowned Boy shows up almost always," said Seabury, "and usually we see the Little Princess, and of course the former Duke, my papa."

"The Spanish Dancer put in an appearance, my lord," said Thorne.

"Oh, did she? Well, she gave *me* a miss, I'm happy to say!"

Jack looked from the butler to the Duke. Were they having him on? They seemed to be serious, but perhaps it was all a joke at his expense. He looked down at his partly eaten roast chicken and felt the bile rise in his throat. He looked up again to see the Duke grinning at him with his uneven, yellowed teeth.

"Are you quite all right, Jack?" said Seabury.

"Indeed I am, sir."

He saw that old Thorne was watching him, too. Did they already know what he'd done the night before? Did they know about the women?

"Give us some Shakespeare, won't you?" said the Duke. "I used to have whole passages stored right here in my head, but I don't imagine they're still in there."

Seabury attempted another yellow-toothed smile. Jack looked, and looked away.

"Wait!" said the Duke. "'If you can look into the seeds of time, and . . .' something . . . 'see which will grow and which will not, then speak to me . . .' and it goes on, but, alas, *I* do not."

Jack pushed back his chair and stood.

"Forgive me, my lord, I must excuse myself."

He stumbled to the door and glanced back as he opened it. The two old men, the Duke and his servant, were staring after him.

"So sorry," he said.

Jack climbed the stairs to the yellow room and threw himself onto the bed. There was no rain that night, and evidently the ghosts slept, but Jack did not. In the far reaches of the night, he emerged quietly from his bedroom. He moved down the hall and listened at a door. Cautiously he turned the knob and opened it. All was dark, not a glimmer of light. He listened. Silence. He eased the door shut and moved on to the next one along the passage.

This is madness, what am I doing?

When that door creaked open, it was very dark within, but a rectangle of dim light hung in midair on its other end and showed Jack where a window was. He made his way toward it slowly and then stepped on something that reared back and struck him sharply on his thigh.

Aaagh!

He slapped at it blindly and then, peering closely through the darkness, saw that his assailant was a large rocking horse. He was in the nursery.

Hard to believe there ever were children in this house. Wonder what became of 'em. Oh, of course! One of them is my host, Lord Seabury!

Jack turned and retreated, stepped on something with wooden wheels, which propelled his feet up into the air, and he fell hard onto his back. He struggled to his feet and got out of the room, slamming the door shut behind him.

"Looking for something, Jack?" said the Duke, standing just outside in his robe.

The pain in Jack's back was excruciating. He struggled to draw breath.

"It really won't do, you know," continued Seabury. "Thorne brought the day's newspaper to my attention, you see. You're wanted in a police investigation, it seems." He sighed. "I broke the rules for you, Jack, but I'm afraid you'll have to move along."

To Jack, the Duke's pale face seemed to levitate above the man's dressing gown.

"You may see ghosts, my lord," said Jack, "but I *make* them."

The Duke's final thought, as Jack quickly drew out the belt from the old man's robe, was that the bearded gardener who had befriended him as a child was nothing like this man.

60

Something was bothering Jane Field. But how or when to bring it up?

Florence Nightingale sat at her desk, inscribing the title page of a newly published book.

"You've been up and working for hours, miss," said Jane, draping a shawl about Nightingale's shoulders. Her recurrent bouts of Crimean Fever often involved chills.

"I'm sick to death of bed. Besides, I'm better today." She moved the book so Jane could see what she had written. "Do you think this will do? I've inscribed it to my mother."

The book was titled *Mortality of the British Army during the Russian War.*

Jane had to wonder if Florence's mother would be pleased. She knew that Mrs. Nightingale had been crushed when her daughter had turned down perfectly eligible suitors and insisted on going into nursing.

Mrs. Nightingale, read the inscription, *Accept, my dearest mother, these little (!) works from your ever-loving daughter, Florence Nightingale. 1867.*

"Oh, yes, miss," said Jane, "any mother would be proud."

"You haven't met *mine*, have you." Nightingale blotted the page and closed the book.

"Shouldn't it have your name on it, if you wrote it?"

Nightingale smiled. "My dear Jane, no one must know! The world must think a *committee* wrote it, or the men on the committee would be very put out."

"But why?" said Jane.

"Because women don't write such things."

"Well, that's not fair!"

"Of course it isn't, my dear. I believe I shall have a lie-down, after all."

As Jane helped her into bed, she said, "Miss? That nasty little rose you received at the beginning of May, how did you come by it, d'you remember?"

Nightingale's face clouded. "I don't know. Wasn't it found by a trainee at the school?"

"And someone from St. Thomas brought it along?"

"Or Mrs. Digby brought it up with the post, I don't know."

"It didn't come with a note, did it?" said Jane.

"I don't believe so, no."

Jane took a deep breath. "You know, Miss Nightingale, I found those awful notes you got back at Scutari, the ones you ripped up. I pieced 'em together and showed 'em to Mr. Field."

"I know you did, dear. Your husband told me, long ago."

Of course he did, thought Jane. *Wish he'd told me!*

"But there wasn't a note this time? One you might 'a' ripped up?"

"No, there wasn't. Now Jane, please—*enough*."

"I'm sorry, miss."

When Jane left her, she descended to the kitchen, where she found Mrs. Digby polishing silver.

"Afternoon, Mrs. Digby."

Digby nodded.

"Would you fancy a cup of tea?" said Jane.

Digby looked up at Jane. "No, Mrs. Field, I would not, thank you." She remained staring, a half-dozen forks in one hand and a silver-cleaning cloth in the other, while Jane smiled wanly. "Was there something you wanted, Mrs. Field?"

"Well, now you ask, yes, as a matter of fact. Do you remember the sewn blossom Miss Nightingale received some time ago?"

"Certainly. Odd thing to post."

"It came in an envelope, then? Brought by the postman?"

"I imagine so. I can't stand about talking all afternoon, I've work to do."

"Miss Nightingale said there was no note. Was the sender's name on the envelope, Mrs. Digby?"

"I don't believe so, but I can't be sure. Is that all, Mrs. Field?"

"Miss Nightingale told me it was found by a nurse in training at St. Thomas'."

"Then that's what happened."

"But then it didn't come by post, did it. And how did Miss Nightingale know how and where it was found? If there was no note, no accompanying letter? Unless someone told her."

Mrs. Digby's face flushed with displeasure. "How am I to know!"

"You see, it's never made sense to me how that little square of fabric got into this house and into Miss Nightingale's hands."

Digby looked down at the silverware and cloth she held, as if wondering how they came to be in her possession.

"Did someone give it to you, Mrs. Digby?" said Jane. "The rose? To give to Miss Nightingale?"

The woman's sigh ended in a shudder.

"He said he was an old friend. He said Nightingale would know what it meant. He said it would make her smile."

"Who did?"

"He was a regular at the anti-suffrage meetings, I saw him there week after week."

"You're anti-suffrage yourself?"

"I am a God-fearing woman, Mrs. Field, and know better than to put aside God's decrees."

Jane nodded. "What was this man's name? The one who gave you the rose?"

"He seemed decent enough, although a bit haughty. Big black beard. I never knew his name, but he knew mine, and knew where I worked, and for who. I should 'a' wondered at that, I see that now. But I passed the thing along to Miss Nightingale, and then I read in the papers about that woman's body bein' found with a rose, and, well, I'd 'a' like to 'a' died. I told him then, I didn't want no trouble, but he walked away so rude and went off with a man who wore a veil over his face. Top hat and a veil, imagine that!"

Digby looked at Jane.

"Now you'll tell Miss Nightingale and I'll lose my position."

"I don't believe I will, Mrs. Digby, but I believe *you* should."

Jane turned and left her standing there, and Digby called after her.

"I never meant no harm!"

61

B efore the brewery was established on Cloak Street in the late eighteenth century, the structure it occupied had undergone multiple transformations, stretching well back into London history. Long ago, before the Walbrook had been pushed beneath the streets of London, a dock had been erected at the far end of its cellars. Here merchandise had been loaded onto flatboats manned by rivermen who poled them along the stream the short distance to the Thames. The ancient warehouse was long gone, the stream buried, and the pier abandoned for so many ages that it was forgotten.

Ahmed Selim knew nothing of this. He did not know that the Walbrook had deposited him on this ancient pier. He did not actually believe that he was still alive. He lay there motionless and knew only complete darkness. For a day? A year?

But then, finally, a mysterious voice whispered strange words very close to what used to be his ears, and fingers moved down what once had been his body.

Une armée marche sur le ventre.

The fingers found a pouch of wet biscuits in a pocket, and the wet biscuits found his mouth.

Curious, ain't it, that the dead should feel such hunger.

62

J ane met her husband at the door the moment he returned
home. Belinda, who had been alone all day, came running
halfway down the stairs and stood above her parents, listening.

"Charles," Jane said, "Mrs. Digby was the one gave Miss Nightingale
her red rose."

"Oh, was she?"

"It wasn't found at St. Thomas," said Jane, "and it didn't come in the
post. Those were just stories Digby made up to hide the fact that it was
herself who put the hateful thing into Nightingale's hands."

"Well, where did Digby get it?"

"From a man at an anti-suffrage meeting. A man with a full black
beard who said he was an old friend of Miss Nightingale and said the
rose would make her smile."

Belinda sat suddenly on the stairs.

Field looked up at her. "You all right, then?" She nodded.

Field turned back to his wife. "Well, the man with the full black beard who wanted to make Nightingale smile is called Jack Hall. Back at Scutari you knew him as Mr. John Stanhope."

"Oh, my Lord!" said Jane.

"Where does this Jack Hall or whoever he is live?" said Belinda.

"Until very recently, my dear, Clapham. Having looked over his flat yesterday, we're pretty sure he's moved on from there in a hurry. We don't know where he's got to, but we do know he started traveling recently to and from the City."

"Mrs. Digby said the strangest thing, Charles," said Jane. "She said the man who gave her the rose had gone off with a man who wore a veil."

Field froze.

"It hung down from his hat, she said."

The inspector stared, and then his face lit up. "That's what's been nagging at me! *I've seen him!* With my own eyes I have seen the present-day Jack Hall, né John Stanhope, but paid him no mind because I was watching the man with the veil! They were coming out of the House of Lords together, Jack Hall and the other one, the veiled one, the day I met with Mr. Disraeli, and the veiled man was . . . the veiled man was Lord Somebody. *Lord Seabury,* that's who! Belinda, kiss Mrs. Field for me, will you? I'm off to see Mr. Llewellyn about a man in a hat!"

He threw open the door and stepped into the street, shouting for a cab. But Mr. Llewellyn was not to be found at Scotland Yard, having been summoned earlier to the district of Chelsea. And Belinda was not available to kiss Mrs. Field, having climbed the stairs silently before Jane noticed.

This is the worst, the very worst I ever did. Belinda stood before the mirror in her room, not liking what she saw. *I invited that man into this house and spoke with him. I gave him a biscuit! Nothing but a fool, that's me. What good am I? To anyone?*

She pulled out Mother Seacole's totem from around her neck and clutched it in hopes it might protect her against everything she was feeling.

63

An artist setting up his easel on the Chelsea riverside had found the body, bobbing in the shallows. It was snagged on something—a length of rope or rigging. The tides likely had taken the woman out into the river and put her back again multiple times. The artist sobbed as he went in search of a constable. The constable he found was Tom Ginty, on his solitary beat.

Tom followed the man the short distance down to the river's edge. The sight of the woman in the water stopped him for a moment, but then he waded into the murk, found a rope wrapped round an ankle, and, as gently as he could, drew her onto the verge. He knelt by the corpse. She had a partial wrapping of long, trailing weeds. Tom felt certain that she had been quite young, in her twenties, perhaps. He saw a wedding band on a distended finger. Bending close down beside it he read an inscription.

Tom stood. Since he had no partnering constable, he would have to summon help himself. The artist stood apart, staring at the corpse, his own face drained of blood.

"Sir," said Tom, "are you up to keepin' guard over this poor creature whilst I fetch others?"

The man nodded. Tom looked back at the still form on the shore. He took off his police tunic and was about to cover her with it when he noticed a thread trailing from the woman's lip back into the Thames. He pulled on it and brought in a flap of cloth bearing the faint outline of a blossom. It wasn't unusual to find bodies in the river or along its shores, but this signified something else altogether. He would go straight to Llewellyn. First, though, he would cover her up.

Give her what dignity I can.

"WHAT WERE YOU doing, walking the streets of Chelsea?" said Llewellyn.

"Sergeant Butts sent me, sir."

Llewellyn nodded. The two of them had relieved the artist of his vigil, inspected the body on the shore, and waited until the coroner's men arrived. Now they were riding in a police carriage, speeding to Chelsea Precinct Headquarters.

"Did Sergeant Butts also dress you in the uniform of a constable?" said Llewellyn.

Tom stared straight ahead. "Please don't tell Mr. Field I been demoted, sir."

"We'll discuss it later."

At the precinct house they were introduced to a physician who was well known to the Chelsea police. He'd been coming into their offices daily for several weeks, searching desperately for his missing wife. Now, while the coroner's men did their work, Llewellyn and Tom introduced themselves.

"You have word of her, Inspector?" said the young Dr. Cairn.

"I wonder, sir," said Llewellyn, "if you had a pet name for Mrs. Cairn, perhaps from a time before the two of you were married?"

The blood drained from Cairn's face.

"Oh, dear God, you're frightening me with the past tense."

Llewellyn didn't answer but held the man's gaze unflinchingly.

"Dr. Cairn?"

"Yes, damn it, yes!" said Cairn. "*Kitty*. Nothing original about it. There must be any number of 'em out there, women called Kitty, apart from my own."

Llewellyn glanced at Tom, who nodded.

"Sir," said the inspector, "I must ask if you had that name inscribed on your bride's wedding band?"

Cairn's knees buckled. Tom stepped forward and caught him before he went down and shifted him into a chair. It took time, but finally the doctor spoke. "It's all because of her suffrage work. I'm sure of it. I tried to tell your men this, but no one listened. She cast a vote last year before anyone noticed, as a protest, and when they did notice, they locked her up for a night. And very proud of it she was. As was I! But then, a year later, that column in the *Standard* told her story and, dear God, put her name in the paper. And then she vanished."

The man looked up at Llewellyn, tears streaming down his face. "May I see her, Inspector Llewellyn, my Kitty?"

"Soon, Doctor." Turning to Tom, Llewellyn said, "You may go, Officer Ginty, but go with the thanks of the Metropolitan for your work here today."

Tom nodded and left, but his mind reeled with what the dead woman's husband had just said.

They put her name in the paper and then she vanished.

Prudence Underwood, the nurse trainee at the Nightingale School, they'd put her name in the paper, too.

And then Pru vanishes? Ends up in the river?

No. Not if he could bloody well help it. But how could he get to her?

64

Charles Field left Scotland Yard having failed to unburden himself of the news he was bursting to share with Sam Llewellyn, that there was a connection between Jack Hall and a peer of the realm. He stood, momentarily at a loss, and then walked briskly to No. 11 Downing Street, where he told a porter that he wished to speak with Mr. Disraeli's secretary. When the porter hesitated, Field identified himself as a detective with the Metropolitan Police.

The chancellor's secretary greeted Field cordially but was confused by the inspector's request. "You wish to know the address of Lord Seabury's London residence?"

"I do, sir," said Field.

"Our Invisible Peer? Whatever for, if I might ask?"

Field summoned a smile that conveyed an air of amiable regret. "If

I could tell you, sir, I certainly would do. This is all along of my recent conversation with Mr. Disraeli, of course."

"Of course. I'll just see if I can find it for you."

"Quick as you can, please, and believe me, it's of great importance."

THE INSPECTOR STOOD before the Georgian townhouse in Cloak Lane and looked up at the four stories above him. The windows made him think of the eyes of the blind: they had not looked out, nor had anyone looked in, for the longest time. On his left was a tall, ornate black iron gate, beyond which was a cobbled courtyard and a building beyond that.

He tugged at the bellpull and waited. And waited.

Then he used the big brass knocker on the door, rehearsing what he'd say to the servant, if one ever responded. He was about to turn away when he heard a bolt thrown back. The door edged open. There before him was the tall hat with the black veil hanging down from the brim. It was the Duke himself.

"D'you mind not looking at me quite so directly?" A thin, hoarse, whispery voice.

Field glanced down and said, "My Lord. Sorry to disturb you. I need to speak with you about someone you may know, a Mr. Jack Hall."

The veiled figure did not move, did not speak.

"I should have introduced myself, forgive me. My name is Detective Inspector Charles Field, and I'm with the Metropolitan Police."

"Oh dear. The police. He's not a bad lad, Inspector, but I had to send him away." The words were so faint they barely penetrated the veil. "I thought he might be a friend, but he was not."

"Do you know where he might have gone, sir?"

The man behind the veil seemed to sigh.

"Where do any of them go?" he said. "You think you've found friendship, someone with whom you might see eye to eye, and then? Either they're off, or you must send them off. Good day, Mr. Field."

"My lord, a moment, please. Finding this man is of vital importance to your own safety, as well as that of the general public. We believe this Jack Hall may have been responsible for the violent death of a member of the House of Commons, as well as others—perhaps many others."

"Oh, dear God. Jack! Jack!" The hat and the veil trembled, and the man's voice dropped to a bare whisper. "I broke the rules for him, you see? And now look."

He turned back into the house and called hoarsely. "Thorne? Thorne!" The door swung shut.

MOMENTS LATER, FROM a window in the front parlor, Jack Hall watched Inspector Field walk away from the house.

"Brilliant," he murmured to himself, taking off the hat and veil. He moved into the dining room. "What did *you* think of my performance, Thorne? You liked it? Oh, I am glad."

The old butler seated at the dinner table seemed to be asleep, his head resting on the white tablecloth, with what looked like a map of Italy done in red extending halfway across the cloth.

Jack hadn't slept. It had been a laborious task the previous, eventful night, shaving off his big black beard using the cold, leftover bathwater. The cuts still stung. He was light-headed but felt he was entering a new state of existence (*like one of those worms that breaks out of its binding, opens bright-colored wings, and off it flies!*) He was powerful. He could do anything.

"Now, Thorne, with your permission," said Jack, "you're going to write a note of complaint to Commissioner Mayne of the Metropolitan Police. We've got a man impersonating an officer of the law. It won't do, you know. Where do you keep ink and paper? Speak up, man! You needn't worry about waking the Duke. Come! I'm having a late lunch at Boodles!"

65

C harles Field ordered a pint at the Eagle and Child, having sent a message to Sam Llewellyn asking him to meet him there at the end of his work day. Llewellyn arrived and headed directly for his former boss.

"Sam," said Field, "I've got news!"

Llewellyn looked about and then said in a low tone, "I've got news for you, sir. You're to stay out of this whole business from here on out. You're to keep well clear of it all, d'you hear me?"

"Sam?"

"It seems Commissioner Mayne had a note today from the head porter at the Central Lobby, Palace of Westminster, inquiring after the professional status of one Charles Field who claimed to be a policeman. *And* a note from Lord Seabury's man, a Mr. Thorne, suggesting that impostors posing as members of the Met might be discouraged from dropping in on the Duke in future!"

Field signaled the barman to draw a beer for Llewellyn.

"Listen, Sam—" he said.

"Sam, nothing! Oh, I've had a lovely afternoon."

"Sam," said Field, "I know where Jack Hall went, I found where he spent the night."

The barman placed the pint in front of Llewellyn, but he seemed not to notice. "And the dressing down from my boss came *after* another victim was found on the Chelsea riverside, a young woman with a red rose attached."

"Oh, dear God," said Field. "Newly dead?"

"No. Likely weeks dead. It was your Tom found her, actually, with the help of a riverside artist."

"My Tom?"

"I had to inform her husband, who is now in profoundest grief. Oh, yes, it's been a fine afternoon. Whenever you do something wrong, Charles, something horribly, grotesquely wrong, Commissioner Mayne blames *me* for it!"

"Go back a bit, Sam. What's all this about *my Tom*?"

"He spotted the red rose, hanging by a thread. It very easily might 'a' been lost, had it not been for Tom."

"But what was Tom doing on the Chelsea shore?" said Field.

Llewellyn glanced sidelong at the inspector. "I'm not sure. But this new victim shows us that our man has been operating for some time, and maybe he's got others out there we just haven't found yet."

Llewellyn seemed to see the pint of beer in front of him for the first time and took a long draft. Then he put down the glass abruptly.

"Wait, Charles. You found out *what*?" he said.

"When Jack Hall fled his bedsit in Clapham, he repaired to the home of the Fourth Duke of Seabury."

"Good Lord."

"Evidently the two of them are somehow linked in this anti-suffrage movement together. Anyway, the Duke told me he'd sent Jack packing, but he seems heartbroke about it."

"So where did our man go? Did the Duke know?"

"He says no, but evidently my brief conversation with him put the Duke's nose out of joint, so who knows if what he says can be trusted."

Llewellyn had another pull from his beer. "How am I going to get leave from Commissioner Mayne to talk to the Duke, now that you've put your beak in?"

"Had I not put my beak in, dear Sam, you'd still be scratching your head over where Jack Hall got to after he left Clapham."

"I know, I know," said Llewellyn.

"Do what I'd do. Don't get Mayne's bloody permission. Go ahead and do it and tell him after."

Llewellyn was suddenly shouting. "*Charles, grow up!* It's not a joke, it's not a game!"

Both men were shocked. Llewellyn had never spoken to his mentor quite like this. He lowered his voice. "I've a wife, Charles, I've a son. I've a position with the Met that I worked hard to get and that I don't want to lose."

Field nodded and looked away. "I understand, Sam." He lifted his glass, found it empty, and pushed it across the bar. "High-handed, that's me. As you well know. Always have been. Jane tried all these years to teach me better, but it seems some dogs can't learn."

A silence hung between them. Finally Llewellyn indicated Field's empty glass. "Another?"

"No, Sam, thanks. I've two questions for you before I go. Was the poor woman found today the one Susan Hythe-Cooper wrote about in her column, the woman who cast a vote?"

Llewellyn nodded in wonder. "Aye."

"Second," said Field. "Has Tom been sacked? Or demoted?"

"Demoted."

"Thought as much. I remember Sergeant Butts of the Mounted. A right pig he always was, we loathed each other. I imagine that gave him added pleasure, bringing Tom down."

"He didn't want you to know."

"Of course he didn't," he said. "That's why he's gone to such pains not to be seen by me in uniform each morning. Afraid of what I might say or what I might think of him. I wanted him to think of me like I was his father. How could he do that, when I'm so damned high-handed?"

"Charles . . ."

"I'll shove off now, Sam. I wish you all the luck in the world. For the sake of our women, and for all our sakes, God speed you with your investigation."

"Charles, stop a moment. How did you know about the woman we found today?"

"The Jack Hall I'm getting to know likes to punish, don't he. Lives for it. In his mind, the woman who trespassed on male territory by casting a vote needed punishing, and so did the woman who wrote her up. How, I wonder, did he know the identity of the writer? You might find out if Hythe-Cooper ever attended the anti-suffrage meetings, Sam. Perhaps he let slip what his wife was doing with Jeremy Sims. Perhaps he did so deliberately. In any event, Jack will go on punishing until you stop him, good and proper."

Field rose and left.

66

"I called them buffoons to their faces," said Nigel Cox in a low voice at his usual table in Boodles. "The great inspector Field *and* Disraeli. I told them we all guessed it was Stanhope back then, doing all the mischief in the Crimean."

"Was that wise, I wonder?" said Hythe-Cooper. "You're almost admitting complicity there."

"Complicity! *You* should talk! Tell me, did you *tell* Stanhope what your wife was writing for that paper and then hire Field to see what would ensue?"

Hythe-Cooper sighed and said, "Do shut up, Nigel."

"Still, I get the feeling they're closing in on him," said Cox, oblivious. "I doubt we'll see Jack Stanhope again, unless it's at the end of a noose."

"Putting a bullet in the brain of a member wasn't the brightest thing

Jack ever did," said Hythe-Cooper, "in his long, blundering career. Old Jack-All lives up to his name yet again."

"Are you making a night of it tonight?" said Cox.

"Oh, yes, it's the Spotted Horse for me," said Hythe-Cooper, naming one of Soho's bordellos, popular with Parliament men. "Join me?"

"Can't. Got a bloody charity function to attend." Cox drew a silver pick from a narrow case and used it to dislodge a bit of fish from between his teeth. "Oh, sod the charity, I'm with you!"

When the two men rose and left, a man in a veiled hat watched them go. Then he, too, made his way out of the club and found a hackney cab. Once seated, Jack Stanhope Hall took off the Duke's hat and set it on the seat beside him. He had plenty more at Cloak Lane, should he need them. He touched one of several cuts on his newly shaved face and winced.

THE BORDELLO WAS not much different from the many Jack had visited in his life, never mind this was one of a higher-class sort. Were the girls any different? For that matter, the men? Certainly not the men.

He watched *his* men drinking at the bar prior to going upstairs.

Hythe-Cooper always did need to soak it up before having a go, even when he was twelve years younger. Cox—well, Cox was most of the time foxed, anyway, wasn't he.

When they did climb the stairs, Jack ordered a drink for himself. He knew from experience at the Dinkins Inn at Scutari that he wouldn't have long to wait.

A HALF HOUR later, at the far end of a dark corridor lined with mostly closed doors, William Hythe-Cooper leaned against a banister at the top of a staircase, smoking a cigarette. Piano music rose from the floor below, and from the cubicles came other noises.

"Coop?"

Hythe-Cooper looked behind him, down the corridor. "Yes? Who's there?"

"How was she, Coop? You can tell me."

Hythe-Cooper squinted into the murk. "*Coop* is not my name, whoever you are."

A figure emerged from the dark, walking toward him along the passage.

"Sorry, old man, no offense intended."

To Hythe-Cooper, the man walking toward him seemed familiar, like someone he'd once known. There was that long red scarf draped round his shoulders . . .

"I'm at a loss here. Am I supposed to know you?"

"I've shaved since last we met." The men were now face-to-face.

Hythe-Cooper stared. "Good God. Jack."

"*Jack-All*, according to you."

Hythe-Cooper turned and started down the stairs. Jack looped the red scarf over his head and round Hythe-Cooper's neck, yanking the man backward. It was all Jack could do to hold on, with the kicking and thrashing, but he hooked the ends of the scarf over the banister and reminded himself that he was *a new creature now, and could do anything.*

The furious tattoo on the steps gradually subsided and then stopped. Jack tied the ends of the scarf to the newel and started down the stairs.

"Coop?" said a voice from behind him. He turned and saw Nigel Cox seeing him. Jack fumbled in his pocket for his pistol, but Cox started shouting.

"Help! Police!"

Jack turned and sped down the stairs, through the crowd of arriving customers and out into the night.

67

In the morning, when Jane Field was about to leave home, Belinda asked if she might go with her to Miss Nightingale's house. She could make herself useful, she knew she could. Jane looked at her daughter with compassion.

"You are going half-mad cooped up here, aren't you, my dear?"

"I am, actually."

"Today won't do, Miss Nightingale wants me to take her to St. Thomas to speak to the students, but tomorrow you'll come with me to her home and spend the day, and I have no doubt you'll be a great help."

Belinda nodded and left the kitchen without speaking.

Later Jane would tell herself, *All I had to do was say yes, of course, Belinda, of course you'll come with us today to St. Thomas! Of course you will!*

As the carriage transported them over the Thames to St. Thomas' temporary quarters, Jane cast an uneasy glance at Nightingale. She was well wrapped up in a coat and shawls and had the resolute set to her jaw that Jane had come to recognize. But to Jane's eye, the anxieties of the past weeks had taken a toll on the famous nurse.

"I hope this is wise," said Jane, "you going out like this."

"You know what it's like to be in fear of your life. We both do. And now, so do those girls of ours. They need us."

As the horses emerged from the woods and made the turn into the long circular drive at the temporary hospital, Nightingale added, "I'll want to speak first to the young woman who came upon the body of Alice Wheeler."

"Her name is Prudence Underwood, miss."

Prudence herself stood at the door of her room on the third floor, aghast. Tom, in his constable's uniform, stood just outside it, a large bouquet of blossoms in his arms.

"Whatever are you doing here?" she cried. "You can't be here! Men are not allowed on this floor!"

"I asked at the front desk where I would find you and the porter said up here. Sorry! These are for you."

"What am *I* to do with 'em?"

"They're from Bowers Flowers, Covent Garden."

"I don't care where they're from, if someone finds you here I'll be in such trouble! Oh, this is a nightmare!"

Evidently Tom's face expressed his own personal nightmare that moment, and Prudence saw it, because she softened her tone. "Very kind of you, Tom, I'm sure." She took the oversized bouquet from him and looked about frantically. "But you couldn't have come at a worse time—Miss Nightingale herself is coming to speak to us!" She turned and retreated with the flowers into her room, nudged a chamber pot with her foot from beneath her bed, and stuck the stems into it. Coming back out, she said, "We've got to get you out of here without anyone seeing!"

Tom looked into the room with some concern at the bouquet, which now splayed from the porcelain pot and across the floor. To Tom, they represented two weeks' wages, and a great deal more than wages, but Prudence took him by the arm and led him to the back staircase. She went first, which is why the man coming up the steps didn't initially see Tom.

Pru froze. There was something about him.

"Miss Underwood?" he said, smiling.

The man had no beard. Was it the shaving cuts, perhaps? The forehead? Suddenly she knew. "It's him," she whispered.

"I see it's true what they say in the papers," said Jack Hall, "that you'd recognize me anywhere!"

His smile vanished when Tom, in his constable's uniform, joined Pru, the two of them side by side, staring at him. Tom started down the staircase.

Jack turned and ran, and Tom propelled himself down after him. Jack stumbled at the bottom and fell but scrambled to his feet and sped out the door toward a waiting hackney cab. Tom emerged from the building after him, stooped to pick up a stone, and hurled it, hitting Jack square in the back.

Tom heard the man yelp and curse and saw him throw himself into the carriage, shouting at the cabbie to *drive!* The carriage started up, Tom running furiously after it as it moved along the long curving path. It picked up speed and disappeared into the woods.

Pru and Tom sat at the refectory table where they'd had their first awkward interview, the night Alice Wheeler was killed. Jane Field and Florence Nightingale sat across from them, with Mrs. Wardroper and the other nurse trainees at the next table. At any other time the young women would have been thrilled to be in Nightingale's presence. Now, though, they were simply frightened.

"He doesn't have a beard anymore," said Pru, "he's shaved it off. Badly."

"But it was the same man you thought of as Alice's beau?" said Jane. "You're sure of that, Pru?"

"Aye, I'm sure."

"Tom?" said Jane.

"I saw him, clear as clear, before he turned and run. Big forehead, black hair starts up here"—Tom put two fingers just above his own hairline—"and goes back from there."

"He was bold as brass when he thought it was just me alone," said Pru. "'Howdy do, Miss Underwood, I see you *do* recognize me.' Soon as he caught sight of Tom, though, he scarpered like anything."

She glanced gratefully at Tom, which was almost more than he could bear without coming quite completely apart. He stood.

"I've got to get back to my beat," he said.

"Your beat?" said Jane.

He blushed but looked at her steadily and said, "I'm not in the Mounted no more, Mrs. Field."

"And you never told us."

"No, ma'am."

"Did you think we would be any the less proud of you?"

"Sorry, I must be leaving."

Pru stood. "Tom?"

But Tom left the refectory without looking back.

Nightingale put a hand on Jane's shoulder and reached across the table to hold Pru's hand. "He's a fine young man, you two," she said. "I'd say you're both lucky."

Jane turned to her. "I have to tell you, Miss Nightingale, my husband thinks the man committing these crimes was at Scutari with us."

"Yes?"

"Yes. Calling himself John Stanhope."

"Oh, dear Lord. No."

"Yes, miss."

Nightingale was silent for a long moment. "Your husband told me not to trust him back then, and I didn't listen."

"He's consorting today with an aristocrat who wears a veil, he says, a Lord Somebody."

Nightingale looked up at her. "Seabury. My father knows him. Lives in a sad, old mansion in Cloak Lane and goes about like a ghost. Quite mad, of course."

She put her face in her hands. "Stanhope! I gave him free rein!"

Jane put her arms around the nurse and held her.

"It was him all the time?" said Nightingale. "Doing those unspeakable things, attacking those women? He attacked *you*, dear Jane, and I considered him my secret ally."

"He fooled us all, miss."

"He didn't fool Inspector Field," said Nightingale bitterly.

68

London was on edge.

The morning headlines proclaimed yet another roseate murder, this one committed weeks earlier. Young Dr. Cairn, the bereaved widower, pleaded in the press for anyone with knowledge of this crime to come forward. The *Evening Standard* finally identified the late Susan Hythe-Cooper as the author of its weekly pro-suffrage column, Notes from Our Future, and acknowledged that the late Kathryn (Kitty) Cairn, found in the Thames, was the woman mentioned in the last column Susan Hythe-Cooper wrote. The paper also identified the late Jeremy Sims, MP, as the go-between who delivered the column to the *Standard*.

Women stayed home. If they went out, they traveled in pairs or with an accompanying male. On the omnibuses passengers glanced at each other cautiously or not at all.

Jane was preparing breakfast when Charles Field came into the kitchen.

"Tom up?" he said.

"He left half an hour ago," said Jane.

"Of course he did. Did you two speak?"

"He was out the door before I could say a word."

She did not look at her husband and he did not look at her, each of them—had they known it—for the same reason.

"Tom seem all right to you, do you think, Charles?"

"Well, I hardly see him, do I."

Jane did glance at Field now, who sat at the table, seeming to stare at nothing. "How could Tom confide in me, when he feared I would condemn him? He was sent down from the Mounted Branch, Jane."

"I know that, Charles, he let it slip yesterday."

Field shook his head. "I wanted to be a good father, Jane."

"You are that, Mr. Field. You *are*, very. You and Tom, you're *men*, neither of you can help that."

"What on earth can you mean?"

"Go call up the stairs for Belinda, will you, Mr. Field? She's going to spend the day working with me at Miss Nightingale's."

Just then came a loud knocking at the front door. When Field did not move but simply stared up the kitchen stairs, Jane said, "Charles?"

"The door," he said.

"Yes, dear, the door!" Jane was dishing eggs from the pan to a plate. "I'm in the middle here!"

But still the inspector didn't move. "Have you ever heard of a peer of the realm answering his own door?" he said.

"What *are* you on about, Mr. Field?"

"It wasn't the Duke behind that veil. I wasn't talking to Lord Seabury, it was bloody Jack Hall talking to me!"

"I'm sorry, *what*?" said Jane.

But Field hurried up the steps, threw the bolt, and opened the door, revealing a young constable.

"Yes?" said Field.

"Sir, Inspector Llewellyn requests your presence at headquarters, sir."

"Excellent!" Field shouted down into the kitchen. "Jane, Llewellyn wants me."

"What, *now?*"

"Hope you and Belinda have a good day together, my dear!"

The inspector grabbed his hat and ran out.

Jane looked at the eggs and bacon in her pan and hoped Belinda was hungry. But when she failed to appear, Jane climbed the steps to her room and found a note lying on her pillow.

> Dear Mother and Father, I will find Lord Seeberry for you. I cannot
> be forever useless. Your loving dotter, Belinda.

Jane ran down the stairs to the street door, but of course by then Inspector Field was long gone.

69

Belinda did not consult *Burke's Peerage* to find where Lord Seabury might live, nor did she go to Somerset House or inquire at the Palace of Westminster. She simply made her way on foot to the City and asked one shopkeeper after another if they knew where the Duke of Seabury's townhouse was. She got only baffled or amused responses wherever she asked, but finally a butcher laughed and answered her.

"You mean the *chicken man*? He represents fully a quarter of my custom, bless 'im. I deliver hens by the crateful to that address weekly. Whatever do you want with the likes of him?"

"I have questions to ask of him," said Belinda gravely.

"Oh," said the butcher, "*questions*, is it? In that case, miss, you'll take the third turning to the right and then the second left. No. 2 Cloak Lane, but I doubt you'll get an audience with His Nibs."

But Belinda was already on her way. The hot summer afternoon had clouded over. The town was lit by an eerie greenish glow. As she walked, she thought about what she would do once she arrived at Seabury's townhouse.

Knock, I suppose. Ask if I mightn't speak with the Duke. Tell his lordship that he's consorting with a very bad man, if he doesn't know it already, and if he does know it, ask him why he would do such a thing.

A warm wind rose. As she made her way to Cloak Lane, Belinda clutched her shawl about her and looked at the sky with apprehension.

70

What Field found at the Yard was pandemonium. Outside, dozens of Metropolitan constables were being assembled and herded together in hastily formed units. Police carriages were coming and going at a furious pace, and within the building, grim-looking men sped upstairs and down. It was Sam Llewellyn who located his old friend trying to make his way through the hive-like activity in the lobby.

"Charles! Over here!"

Field elbowed his way through, and Llewellyn pulled him into a corner. "What in God's name is going on, Sam?"

"Another member of Parliament found murdered. It was bad enough round here when we found Jeremy Sims dead in the rain, but now Commissioner Mayne is locking down the town until further notice."

"Which MP?" said Field.

"Hythe-Cooper, you'll be interested to know, found at the Spotted Horse."

"Dear God, the bastard's thorough! But listen, Sam. It wasn't the Duke I was dealing with . . ."

Above the din in the police headquarters came a distinctive Irish voice.

"Llewellyn!" shouted Commissioner Mayne. "You there, Detective Llewellyn! And you—Field! What are *you* doing here?"

"Just leaving, sir," said Llewellyn.

"No, you're not," said Mayne. "You're coming with me to explain how it is you seem to work for *that* man instead of me." Mayne turned to an aide standing at his side. "Officer, arrest Mr. Charles Field on charges of trespass and impersonating an officer."

"Commissioner," shouted Field over the din in the lobby, "Detective Llewellyn just now ordered me out. He was escorting me to the door, sir!"

"Not fast enough," said Mayne. "Officer, apprehend him."

"That's not going to be possible, I'm sorry to say, sir," said Field, "as I've urgent business elsewhere." He pointed to his friend Llewellyn. "He *was* chucking me out, it's what he does every damned time I set foot in the place!"

Mayne's aide advanced through the crowd toward the inspector, but in an instant Field was moving with a group of constables who were leaving the building. The aide blew his whistle.

"There, that man!" cried the aide, pointing. "Just there!"

One of the constables in the scrum grabbed Field roughly by an arm, yanked him out and round the corner of the building. Field flung him off, cuffing him in the face, and the constable's helmet fell off.

"Tom?" said Field.

"Run."

Tom stooped and picked up his helmet.

"They'll have your hide for this, Tom."

"You overpowered me. Run."

The inspector nodded. "Tell Llewellyn, No. 2 Cloak Lane."

Tom pulled Field into an embrace, then pushed him away.

"Father—run!"

He ran.

71

No. 2 Cloak Lane. She felt a reluctance to approach. The house was unfriendly; the front door seemed to scowl. She climbed the two steps to the door. She considered the bellpull and the heavy brass knocker and chose the knocker. When she brought it down, the door swung slowly open on its own. This seemed not a good thing. She stepped cautiously over the threshold, shut the door behind her, and stood still in the silent house. A graceful staircase rose on her left. A long, narrow hall table on her right held a row of tall hats, each with a nest of black tulle beneath. There was an aroma of roast chicken, mixed with another smell—sweet but unpleasant.

She walked cautiously into the dining room. An old man slept at the near end of the long table. But as she approached she saw the dried blood on the cloth, she saw the crusted eye socket, she saw that he did not sleep. She did her best to tamp down her fear. Was this the Duke?

Her impulse was to leave. Now. But she couldn't, she had to summon the courage to go on.

I cannot be forever useless, the girl had written.

She listened again. All was still, except for the wind pressing against the shutters. She returned to the staircase and climbed to the first floor and then the second. The house seemed to be empty. On her way to the top floor, she stopped. Was it a footfall she heard?

Silence.

On the third floor she found the yellow room, the unmade bed and the cast-off men's clothing on the floor. There was something *unclean* about it, she thought. *Vile*, even. She was eager to shut the door on it.

Next was the children's playroom.

Toys were scattered here and there on the floor and positioned on shelves against the wall. There was a large rocking horse, its paint chipped and faded. In an almost life-sized toy bed lay a row of large dolls tucked under the covers, with just their heads showing above the blanket. One of them wore a black top hat fitted with a black veil.

Dear God.

She went to the bed, pulled back the covers, and stifled a cry. It was indeed human, dressed in nightclothes and robe. She lifted the veil to reveal a face with gray skin and bulging, lifeless eyes.

No, this was the Duke.

The jaw was fixed wide open, and a few jagged yellow teeth were visible beneath the square of cloth tacked to the upper lip: an embroidered rose.

"Jane."

She wheeled about.

"It's been too long," said Jack Hall, standing just inside the door. "It's you I've most wanted to see, you *do* know that, don't you?"

Without thinking, Jane reached for the amulet round her neck, but it was not there, she'd given it to Belinda.

"If you've come about the creature you call your daughter, she's dying to see you, I'm sure, but she's tied up at the moment."

"My husband is coming for you," Jane managed to say.

"Well, if I'd known the entire Field household was dropping by, I'd have had Thorne lay the table for you. D'you fancy roast hen?"

Jane's eyes went past Jack to the nursery door, but he followed her glance and shook his head. "No, *Missus Rolly*, no."

"The police know all about you. They know who you are and where you are. Take me to my daughter, and then run. You can still get away."

Jack laughed. "I'll have no need to run. My benefactor there"—he pointed to the body of the Duke—"has provided me with a more gracious means of egress. Any number of them, in fact."

"Take me to my daughter."

"Oh, she's a strange one, she is."

"She's not strange. You are."

Two strides took him within reach. He slapped her and she slapped him back, hard enough to make him stumble. He righted himself then, but now he did not laugh.

Three stories below them the bellpull at the front door sounded. And sounded again.

Jack produced a pistol from a pocket, grabbed Jane, and pulled her after him to the staircase, down one floor after another, and then down farther. He seemed surprised to find the floor there running with water.

72

Belinda, captive in the Mithras chamber in the old brewery cellar, did not hear the bell.

He's a very bad man, but I've dealt with worse. And that's just what I'll tell him when he comes back.

Belinda was seated on the little gilded throne. She had come to consciousness there, just as the bad man was leaving. She remembered the tickle she'd felt at her neck soon after she entered the big house, she remembered fighting him, twisting round to glimpse his face before she stopped remembering.

The bellpull fabric he'd used to choke her was tied firmly around her ankle at one end, and to an arm of the throne on the other. The seat itself was anchored to the floor. She wasn't shouting for help anymore; she already had shouted herself ragged. She wasn't pulling at the fabric that bound her. She couldn't undo the knots, and she had tugged until her hands were raw.

The beautiful and terrible statue held her interest. The young man in the funny hat did not look cruel, but he *was* stabbing the bull with a big knife. The fish leaping across the floor looked playful. The women's faces on the wall were mild, with little half smiles. From where Belinda was, she reached and managed to touch one of them but then pulled her hand quickly back from the sharp glass tile. A drop of blood swelled on her fingertip. She put the finger into her mouth and turned her attention back to the little hole in one of the walls, the brick one.

That's where the bad smells come from.

Through the breach came the sound of a rushing stream and, spilling down, a little water sluicing into her small prison. She looked up; the ceiling wasn't but a foot above her head, seated up on this gilded chair.

It crossed her mind that the bad man might *not* come back. As frightening as he was, that thought was even worse.

A brick fell from the hole in the wall and more water spurted in. Then two bricks fell and then three of them. Almost without thinking, Belinda reached for the totem that hung about her neck. She held the little man up, clutched in both hands, an amulet against this and all the evil she'd known in her young life, watching the water spill into the cubicle.

And then she discovered that the little man had a secret.

73

Inspector Field pulled the bell again.

A male voice behind him said, "Who are you, then?"

Field wheeled about and saw a sturdy young man on the pavement and a middle-aged woman in kitchen garb who stood just behind him.

"Who are *you*?" said Field.

The woman answered. "I'm Mrs. Took and this is Abel, one of our grooms. We all saw you standing out here and couldn't make you out."

"You all?"

"His lordship's staff, sir." She tilted her head in the direction of the gated courtyard, to a building abutting it. "That's our quarters just there, in the old winery. If you're here about the trouble, walk right in—that's what the young woman did."

"What young woman?" said Field. "What trouble?"

"No orders from Thorne in two days and chickens piling up in the kitchen!"

"I don't quite understand."

"I'm cook to this exalted household, Took the Cook, but I'm only allowed below stairs. Same with all of us. We come and go through a tunnel he put in from the winery to the kitchen below. Thorne comes down to give me and the others our instructions, the Duke insists on it. We send meals up in the dumbwaiter, and Thorne does all the rest. It's not right, all that work at his age?"

"You mentioned a young woman?"

The groom and the cook nodded in unison. "And the older one who come after."

"The young one said she'd come to warn the Duke," said the groom.

"And in she went!" said Took.

"*Who* was this?"

Mrs. Took looked at Abel. He shrugged.

"I asked her and she told me. What was it? Field! That's it, *Linda Field!*"

The inspector blanched. He pushed open the door and stepped in. The house was quiet except for the rising wind outside. Field moved to the parted dining room doors. At a glance he guessed the corpse seated at the table was the butler and guessed, correctly, where he'd find the entry wound. Field ran back to the hall and paused.

"Belinda!" His voice resounded through the silent house. "It's your father!"

He listened for the reply that didn't come. "Jane? Are you here, too?"

He continued along the ground-floor hall. The next door revealed a library. On a central table was a stack of newspapers. A copy of the *London Illustrated News* was on top, featuring a drawing of a massive tunnel through which strolled elegantly dressed gentlemen and ladies.

THAMES TUNNEL GRAND OPENING

That thing opened when I was a young man, thought Field. He noted the year of the paper: 1842.

The next paper in the stack was a yellowed copy of *The Times*.

THAMES ARCHWAY TUNNEL COLLAPSE

From 1809, this was! Clearly, someone here's got a bug for tunnels.
Field left the library and ran down the staircase to the kitchen floor. "Belinda!" he shouted again. "Jane? I've come for you!"

The huge kitchen was empty of humans, but at one end there was a cage occupied by two live chickens. Three roasted fowl lay beneath a cloth on the central table. The air was filled with their aroma. Field opened a door set in the wall, revealing a long passage.

A tunnel. The cook said the Duke had it put in. Had the Duke who doesn't wish to be seen, even by his own staff, put in other tunnels?

He climbed again to the ground level and continued up to the first floor where he found a parlor, a dressing room, and then what he guessed might be the Duke's bedroom. The windows were shuttered. The bed's curtains were parted, the cover was turned back and the linen mussed, as though a sleeper had just risen from it.

He sped up to the second floor and found another bedroom hung with dust covers, and, down the hall, another parlor.

On the third floor he found the yellow room, he found the soiled clothes on the floor. The embers in the grate were dead but not long dead.

He moved on to the next room. A nursery. From across the room, the corpse in the dolls' bed wearing the top hat seemed to glare at him, its mouth open in a silent scream of rage.

He sped down the staircase and returned to the dining room, quickly looking about.

"Tell me, old man," he said to the corpse at the head of the table. "You know where it is, I'm sure of it. His lordship's face wasn't the only thing he hid from the world, was it. There's a hidden realm here, and that's where the bastard's took my people."

He retraced his steps to the foyer and the front door and back again, searching for any anomaly, a knob, a seam in the woodwork, a flaw in the marble. He ran back to the library and tugged at the bellpull there, but that produced only a distant tinkle from the kitchen below. He felt the bookcases for false books. He flew down the steps to the kitchen again, looked about frantically.

Jane. Belinda.

He started out and then turned back, picked up a heavy meat hammer lying on the central table, and ran up to the dining room again. There were portraits of ancestors above the wainscotting, and Field examined their features and the frames that held them. He touched them, he pushed them, he shouted at them and cursed them and threatened them with the hammer. Then he found himself staring at the only painting in the room that wasn't a portrait.

A bunch of blossoms, ain't it. And one single little bird.

He ran to the end of the room, touched the robin, and the wall swung open.

74

Jack pulled Jane along, Jack in front with his pistol. The water coursed over the tops of their shoes as they walked.

"Where are we going?" said Jane.

"Anywhere I want. Calais? Ostend?"

"*What?*"

"There are any number of ways out of the Duke's house," said Jack.

"If Belinda comes to any harm, Mr. Stanhope, you'll beg for the hangman rather than face my husband."

"It is my fondest wish to face your husband again. I've waited years for it."

He slipped on the wet stones but caught himself and cursed under his breath.

"Something wrong, Mr. Stanhope?"

"It's *nothing*. It's called *rain*. And don't call me Stanhope, Stanhope is long gone." He went on muttering to himself. "Rain makes the ghosts come out, according to his lordship, oh, yes! Mocking me, they were." Jack quickened his pace and then slowed to a stop. The door to the Mithras cubicle stood open.

"No." His voice was hoarse.

He sloshed to the threshold, with Jane right behind him. The throne was empty. One end of the bellpull lay on the seat, the other still tied to one of the arms. Jack circled the gilded chair. Water came in at a steady clip through the gap in the brick wall.

"Where is she?" he said. *"Where is she!"*

"Too clever for you, wasn't she!"

He wheeled about, grabbed Jane, and flung her against the throne. He stepped out of the cubicle, slammed shut the door, and turned the key. Then he looked up to see someone walking through the water.

"You're a dead man, boyo," said Field, striding toward him, meat hammer in hand. "Open the door."

Jack fumbled in a pocket for his pistol.

"Open the door before I tenderize you."

Jack raised the pistol and fired. Field winced but kept coming.

"You like to shoot a man's eye out, don't you, you twisted shit. This hammer's going to find a home in your twisted brain."

Jack raised the gun again.

"Hallo!" A male voice sounded from the opposite direction, from the dark far reaches of the brewery cellar, and Jack wheeled about.

"She found me!" The voice echoed from the brick walls. Jack stared and the inspector stared as the apparition approached them. The emaciated figure was covered in muck and blood, with dark circles beneath his eyes. Even from a distance, he reeked.

"You're the Drowned Boy," said Jack in wonder.

"I am that," said Ahmed.

"The Duke told me about you, that you're a ghost."

"I expect I am. Mr. Stanhope, ain't it? I remember you from Scutari.

So you're dead, too, are you? And look, if it ain't Inspector Field! Fancy you here. It's me, Ahmed."

A figure joined him, another mud-spattered ghoul, her long black hair hanging in strings down her drenched, filthy, clinging dresses.

"*She* found me," said Ahmed again.

The second ghoul held a wooden figure before her and walked steadily toward Jack Hall.

"Belinda!" cried Field.

Ignoring him, she spoke only to Jack. "I want you to understand, sir, that I've known worse than you."

Jack hissed, "*You're my safe passage!*"

She raised the totem. "*I'm not your nothing!*"

Jack lunged for her, grabbing her round her neck and putting the pistol to her head. Field seized him by his hair and yanked him back, the gun exploding again with flame and echoing sound. Jack Hall's hair began to slip from Field's grasp, so he hoisted him up by his armpits. That's when Field saw that Jack had dropped the gun. His hands were at his throat, where a fountain of red had begun to pulse.

Field looked at his daughter. Belinda stood upright, with her hands at her sides. One hand held the bottom half of Mother Seacole's little man. As he lowered Jack to the floor, Field saw the top half of the totem, with the little man's row of shiny white teeth, twitching from Jack's throat. Field pulled it out, revealing the blade. He looked again at his daughter, and she raised her eyes to his. The man at their feet convulsed, his legs kicking, his eyes wide with terror, and then he was still. The water ran over his face, spreading out in a red fan from his head.

Field stepped over him to the cubicle, turned the key in the lock, and the door flew out with a cascade of water. Within, he found Jane lying unconscious in running water. He crouched and lifted her head.

"Jane!"

Suddenly Belinda was at his side. "Get her into your lap."

Field put his hand to Jane's wrist.

"Into your lap, Father!"

He knelt in the flowing water and raised Jane's head up. Belinda put a finger in Jane's mouth and cleared it. She put her own mouth to her mother's and blew in. Again. And again. She pressed down on her mother's chest, and lifted it up, and covered her mouth with hers again. And again.

Belinda leaned back. "Mum?"

Suddenly Jane shuddered and coughed up water. And then, with a gasp and a series of coughs, Jane Field came again to life.

"Listen!" cried Ahmed from the door of the cubicle. From somewhere not far off came a growing roar. "The tide is turning, we need to move along now!"

With Belinda's help, Field got to his feet and hoisted his wife up into his arms. And then the bricks of the wall along the Walbrook began to topple rapidly, and with them the neighboring walls of the cubicle. The gilt and green and blue tiles, the dolphins, and the mild-eyed, smiling women began to shoot out from the wall. A dolphin tile hit Field's cheek, and a bit of mermaid's smile lodged in his brow.

Putting their heads down, Field carried his wife out of the cubicle and Belinda followed.

"Just look at that!" cried Ahmed.

With the river side of the chamber gone and the Thames' tide turning, the waters that had poured into the cellars were now rushing out, and the lifeless body of Jack Stanhope Hall had wrapped itself round the base of the statue of Mithras and the bull. And then the floor beneath the shrine began to give way. The ancient statue tilted, teetered, and finally toppled back into the dark depths of the underground torrent, carrying Jack with it.

Those who lived stood staring for a moment.

"Right, then," said Field. "Let's go."

They made their way against the roiling waters, with the sounds of ruin behind them sounding in their ears. Finally they climbed the steps into the dining room of the 4th—and last—Duke of Seabury, just as a dozen members of the Metropolitan Police poured into the townhouse.

Sam Llewellyn and Tom Ginty stopped dead for a moment, taking in the macabre sight: the corpse sitting at the end of the table, and the four others, covered in filth, bruised, and bleeding, standing unsteadily before them.

"There is a tide in the affairs of men—" Field began.

Jane squeezed her husband's hand and said, "Not now, Charles."

"Quite right, my dear."

"We need to get them to hospital," said Tom, "all of them."

"Yes, of course," said Llewellyn. "Charles, what about Jack Hall?"

"He belongs to the ages, Sam, and the ages can bloody well have him."

There was a sudden rumbling thunder from below.

"I suggest we get out," said Tom.

Field nodded. "Right, then."

75

The newspapers proclaimed the death of the Roseate Murderer by drowning while in pursuit by the former chief detective inspector Charles Field.

With Sister Prudence and Tom Ginty watching over them at St. Thomas' Hospital, the Fields—Charles, Jane, and Belinda—soon recovered from their underground ordeals. It turned out that in addition to the Roman tiles embedded in Field's face, a bullet had grazed his cheek, but the wounds were quickly patched over. Ahmed Selim, however, took longer to mend. He'd lain in the utter dark of the subterranean pier for days; he was malnourished and disoriented. He was visited by Nightingale herself, who brought one of the marrow jellies she had created for the wounded soldiers in the Crimea. Ahmed recognized her smile, and the flavor of the tasty jelly. Bazalgette came briefly, scolded the young engineer for his foolishness, and promised him his job back as soon as he was fit. However, Ahmed most often was cared for by Belinda Field, whose lengthy lectures finally seemed to convince him that he was *not the least bit dead.*

Field was again a London hero, but he was mainly concerned for his beloved daughter.

"Never doubt it, Belinda," he said on a quiet occasion when they were alone. "You had no choice, and if you hadn't done it, I would have."

She didn't seem to understand what he was talking about. When he showed her the blade end of Mother Seacole's totem, she clapped with joy.

"I wondered what became of him!" she said, taking the other end from the string round her neck. She fitted the blade into the bottom. "Now he's all whole again!"

"Belinda?"

She looked up at him, beaming. "Yes?"

He did not get the sense that she was shamming. She honestly seemed not to remember what she'd done with Mother Seacole's little man. Whether she did or not, Field never spoke of it again, to Belinda, to Jane, or to anyone else.

Soon after, Benjamin Disraeli encountered Commissioner Mayne of the Metropolitan Police at the Athenaeum Club. Mayne was taking port in the after-dinner room, and Disraeli stopped by his chair.

"Good evening, Commissioner," said Disraeli.

Mayne smiled and nodded. "Evening, sir."

"Say, listen," said Disraeli, taking an adjacent seat, "I just this morning had breakfast with the former home secretary, and the current one, and the talk turned to the sixth of May demonstrations."

"Oh, yes?" said Mayne.

"We were remarking, sir, how pleased we were that we saved who knows how many British lives by granting them access to the park that day. So, thank you very much!" Disraeli seemed about to rise, but then a look of distress crossed his face. "Oh, sorry, no—that wasn't you who stopped the policemen firing on the populace, you were the one who ordered it. That was *the home secretary* preventing it and, of course, a young constable in the Mounted Branch who refused to do it."

"Very amusing, Disraeli," said Mayne.

"Young man named Ginty, I heard. Your man Butts demoted him, but we all thought you reinstating him to the Mounted Branch would be a worthy gesture." When Mayne seemed about to protest, Disraeli interrupted. "A gesture of atonement, sir. Whether or not our Reform Act passes, had the police mowed down members of the Reform League in the streets on your orders, it might have been seen as a blot on the Metropolitan and your fine reputation." Disraeli's tone hardened. "I have the backing of the prime minister on this."

"As commissioner of police for thirty-eight years, I've seen prime ministers come and go," said Mayne, "and I'll see your lot to the door as well."

"No doubt," said Disraeli, "no doubt. But after breakfast I had my regular audience with the Queen, who follows these matters closely and who asked me to explain the whole folderol. I didn't mention your name, of course—at least for now—but I told her that public meetings are the recognized and indispensable organs of a free constitution. The safety valves, as it were."

Disraeli stood, and so did Mayne, looking grim.

"Finally," said Disraeli, "given the headlines your former chief inspector is garnering for putting a dramatic end to the Roseate Murderer when you did not, you'd be a fool not to reinstate Charles Field to the Metropolitan as well. But then, the leopard is not known for its ability to change its spots, is it."

The two men never spoke again. Charles Field was *not* reinstated to the Met, but Tom once more became a member of the Mounted Branch. Tom and Pru Underwood, from those days on, kept company on a regular basis, while Belinda joined the other trainees as a student at the Nightingale School. She often went out walking with Ahmed Selim at the end of the day when his shift in the sewers, and hers at the hospital, ended. Jane Field's work for Miss Nightingale tapered off and eventually stopped, as Nightingale continued to keep herself removed from the world she sought to reform.

When the inspector was sufficiently recovered, he accepted an invitation from Charles Dickens to join him and Wilkie Collins for lunch at the Reform Club in celebration of Field's recent triumph. He met the two writers on the street outside the grand Italianate building, the writers making much of the sticking plasters on Field's face.

"Your badges of honor, sir," said Dickens.

A small crowd had gathered at the steps, not to see Inspector Field or Charles Dickens but to watch several constables and a workman attempting to remove two women who had chained themselves to one of the club's stone balustrades.

"What's all this?" said Field as they climbed the steps.

"I can't imagine why women would want to join a stuffy men's club," said Dickens, "can you?"

Field looked back at the women.

That might as well be my wife or my daughter, he thought, *or both. One day it likely* will *be them.*

The magnificent soaring lobby of marble and tile took Field's breath away. But as they ascended the grand staircase to the dining room above, Dickens said, "My apologies, gentlemen, but I am only able to escort you to your meal today. Unforeseen complications have arisen concerning my upcoming tour of the United States, one headache after another. I don't even wish to go, but the Americans simply shovel money at one, so how can one decline? Anyway, bon appétit, and congratulations, Charles."

He handed them over to the maître d'hôtel, and Dickens was off.

"The 'complication' is that young mistress of his," said Collins to Field under his breath. When they'd been shown to their table and seated, Collins said, "I'm amazed I've not been asked to leave, now that the great man is gone."

They were not asked to leave but enjoyed a leisurely meal and a good quantity of wine. Then the dessert arrived. Field stared. He took a bite of the colorful pudding, looked thoughtful for a moment, and put up his hand to summon the maître d'.

"Is something wrong, sir?"

"I wish to speak with the person who made this," said Field.

"But sir . . ."

"If you please."

The man went off to the kitchens.

"What in God's name are you doing, Charles?" said Collins. "Everything was going so well . . ."

Heads turned throughout the dining room when a tall Black man dressed in white and wearing a chef's hat made his way to the inspector's table. Field stood.

"I see you've mixed in red cherries with the black, but what's the secret liqueur?"

"If I told you, t'wouldn't be a secret, now would it, Inspector."

"True," said Field. "May I, T.G.?"

"Oh, yes, for God's sake," said T.G., and the two men shook hands.

"I heard you joined a circus."

"Well," said T.G., "I am joined *to* a circus, sir. Pablo Fanque's Fair. Only Black-run circus in the country. My love is a slack-rope walker, just imagine that."

Field glanced around at the other diners. "Sorry if I made you a spectacle."

"I'm used to being the only Black man in sight, sir. I was the only one at my dear Alexis' funeral, too." He turned to Wilkie Collins and made a little bow. "Mr. Collins, I enjoyed *No Name* no end. You've got a bit of *clafoutis* on your shirtfront, sir."

T.G. turned back to the inspector. "Been reading about you in the papers, Mr. Field, you and my friend Ahmed." He indicated the plasters on the inspector's face with a questioning look.

"Dolphins, T.G.," said Field, "and young women."

"You want to take care, Inspector."

"You, too, T.G."

"Now then," said the chef, "eat!"

AFTERWORD

━━━━

In the days that followed, the Duke of Seabury's townhouse was pulled down, deemed unsafe after the collapse of the neighboring brewery. He left no heirs, and the remainder of his estate went to the Crown.

On August 6, 1867, Parliament passed what became known as the Second Reform Act, giving the vote to a vastly increased number of British males, including workingmen. Ironically, the bill was put forward by the Conservative Party, longtime opponents of a broader enfranchisement. As authored and hastily revised by Disraeli, it went far beyond what Conservatives or Liberals or even Disraeli himself had imagined. The workingman showed his gratitude by voting out Disraeli and his party in the next elections.

Florence Nightingale had turned down John Stuart Mill's earnest plea that she endorse the vote for women, for fear it would cause a distraction from the work to which God had called her. She continued to claim fragile health as the reason for her self-imposed seclusion but remained active and influential behind the scenes and died with many honors at the age of ninety.

Women in Great Britain won the right to vote in 1928. In 1981, the Reform Club became the first of the traditional gentlemen's clubs to admit women on an equal basis. At the time of this writing, Boodle's is still strictly for men only.

During his time serving in Miss Nightingale's Scutari kitchens, Alexis Soyer observed the malnourished state of the soldiers coming off the battlefield and designed a camp stove for the troops. It remained in continuous use by the British army until 1982. Soyer's relationship with T. G. Taylor, who is described in Robert Robinson's diary as "a coloured gentleman," remains open to speculation, but it's believed that Soyer plucked him from the street without benefit of a formal introduction. They traveled across Europe together, dining in the finest restaurants and sharing hotel rooms. After Scutari, unfortunately, T.G. vanishes from record.

However, a Black circus performer and equestrian named William Darby changed his name to Pablo Fanque and came to own and manage his own circus. Famous in its day, Pablo Fanque's Fair all but disappeared from historical memory until John Lennon bought an old circus poster in an antiques shop, which advertised a performance "being for the benefit of Mr. Kite." The song Lennon wrote, using the advert's copy, became a classic in the Beatles' 1967 album, *Sgt. Pepper's Lonely Hearts Club Band*.

Joseph Bazalgette's massive innovative sewer system helped clean the Thames and the air above it in the nineteenth century and continued to serve the populace of London until the 1980s.

In 1954, archaeologists working at a building site in the City found the marble head of Mithras beneath Walbrook Street but not his body or the bull he was sacrificing to bring life and renewal back to earth. The head and other Mithraic artifacts from the Roman era can be seen today at the Museum of London.

No part of Jack Stanhope Hall was ever found.

ACKNOWLEDGMENTS

I want to thank my esteemed editor, Charles F. Adams, and Betsy Gleick, publisher and editorial director of Algonquin Books, for the meticulous care they gave this manuscript, and me. I'm grateful for linguistic and historical help from Angelo Smimmo, Leah Hausman, Julian Munby, and Angela Marvin and for story help all the way along from Leo Geter. I took massive liberties with the life of the extraordinary Florence Nightingale; for readers who desire her true story, I cannot recommend highly enough the engaging *Nightingales* by Gillian Gill. As always, I am indebted to my agent, Gail Hochman, for unfailing support. For those many fans of *The Darwin Affair* who urged me to write another Inspector Field novel, here you go.